The Christmas Eve Journey

Book 5

A Time Travel Romance Novel by

Elyse Douglas

COPYRIGHT

The Christmas Eve Journey
Copyright © 2021 by Elyse Douglas
All rights reserved.

This is a work of fiction. Names, characters, places and incidents are either the product of the author's imagination or are used fictitiously. Any resemblance to actual persons, living or dead, events, or locales is entirely coincidental. The copying, reproduction and distribution of this book via any means, without permission of the author, is illegal and punishable by law.

ISBN: 9798549276369

BROADBACK BOOKS USA

"A journey is a gesture inscribed in space; it vanishes even as it's made. You go from one place to another place, and on to somewhere else again, and already behind you there is no trace that you were ever there."

—Damon Galgut

"There are no coincidences, just destinations. You find only what you seek, and you seek what is somehow hidden in the deepest and darkest part of your heart. In the end, it seems you end up meeting the people you must meet."

—Ernesto Sabato

To our readers. Thank you for time traveling with us.

The Christmas Eve Letter - Book 1

The Christmas Eve Daughter - Book 2

The Christmas Eve Secret - Book 3

The Christmas Eve Promise - Book 4

The Christmas Eve Journey - Book 5

THE CHRISTMAS EVE JOURNEY

PART ONE

CHAPTER 1
New York City 1904

Twenty-seven-year-old Annabelle Palmer moved along the busy sidewalk toward Martin's Fine Jewelry Shop, just off West 39th Street. Horsecars, hansom cabs and drays trotted by, the city in full, bustling vigor as morning lengthened toward noon.

Annabelle was hourglass-figured, with a swan's neck and lush, chestnut hair piled high on top of her head in a softly swirled pompadour.

She had a coltish manner, an arrogant nose, and clear, focused hazel eyes. Her mind was calculating; her steps measured; her smile suggesting gentle contentment, but her expression could swiftly shift to flirty invitation or steely coldness as the situation warranted.

On that bright, early October day, she relished the challenge to come, and each shop window was a mirror for her to steal quick glances at her pretty features, all stubbornly and supremely confident.

She wore high heel ankle boots, a smart feather-trimmed hat, and a long, dark dress stitched in corselet fashion from the waist to below the breasts. Her blouse was a pale blue, the tailored jacket a royal blue.

Men noticed her with obvious pleasure, some touching the brim of their hats as they passed, and if most respectable women would refuse to acknowledge such brazen behavior, Annabelle rather fancied it.

Her outfit was one of her many disguises, and she had a talent for disguises, and she had a talent for the sleight of hand.

With a gloved hand, Annabelle opened the door to Martin's Fine Jewelry Shop, and the tiny bell above jingled a welcome.

It was a smart and tidy shop, warmly lighted with amber lamps, and scented with rose and vanilla. Annabelle held her smile, while coyly surveying the room and its usual pieces. Glass display cases held many delectable items, such as watches, silver flasks and gold cigarette cases. Violins and ukuleles were artfully exhibited on one wall and, displayed nearby, was a gilded framed photograph of the President of the United States, Theodore Roosevelt, looking back at Annabelle with stern, bold eyes and a strong determined jaw, as if to say to her, "Behave now, young lady."

Samuel Martin stood behind the counter near the cash register. He was a small man with large, suspicious eyes, a tightly trimmed mustache, and thin graying hair combed back from a broad forehead. Two other customers lingered over a glass case that contained gold watches, necklaces, and diamond tie pins.

Mr. Martin clasped his hands behind his back, straightened his spine and appraised the room with vigilant care. His eyes rested on Annabelle, and he went to work sizing her up.

She caught his watchful eyes and smiled at him pleasantly, then approached the man with light, feminine steps.

"Good morning, sir," she said in a caressing voice. "I trust you can help me. I have been searching the city for a bracelet. A very special bracelet. It is for my dear mother, who has fallen under the dreadful spell of some illness. The doctors cannot say, or perhaps they do not dare say, what that illness is, and I am so worried about her. My mother loves jewelry, and if I can find the right piece for her, I know she will improve, if not recover completely. Will you please show me what you have?"

Samuel's eyes softened on her. She was quite attractive, in her late twenties, well dressed in the latest fashion, and wearing a stunning diamond brooch. Her speech was refined, as were her manners. Mr. Martin concluded that the young woman was of good breeding and from a high social class.

He felt the itch for a sale—for that warm, exhilarating sensation after a profitable transaction. The gentle throb of his pulse made him feel alive and happy to be the successful merchant that he was.

"Madam, I have many such pieces I believe you will appreciate, and I trust you will find the perfect item, the right piece, that will be highly efficacious in restoring your dear mother to full health."

Samuel Martin moved toward a glass display case, tugged a keychain tethered to his vest, and removed a set of keys from his trouser pocket. He selected and inserted a key, turned it ever so gently, and lifted the glass case.

Annabelle's eyes expanded and glowed as she took in the dazzling display of shiny gems in white and yellow gold jewelry: rings, necklaces and bracelets dazzling with diamonds, emeralds and rubies.

"Oh, these are most lovely, each one more beautiful than the next," she said.

"As you can see, madam, there are many graceful and feminine pieces to choose from."

"Yes, you are so right, sir. They are truly a feast for the eyes… well, what I mean to say is, they are works of art, aren't they? I fear it will not be a simple choice. I may need some time to look, touch and decide."

Samuel nodded patiently. "Take all the time you need, madam. I am the proprietor, Samuel Martin. I will step away to assist my other customers, but should you need me at any time, simply lift a hand and I will attend to you promptly."

When Martin moved away toward a well-dressed man and woman, Annabelle's nimble eyes went to work, appraising the contents of the case. With agile and practiced skill, she reached for one bracelet after the other, moving them around at a dizzying pace, sliding them on and off her hands and wrists.

When Samuel glanced over curiously, Annabelle lifted a hand toward the light, pretending to be enthralled with a bracelet, turning her wrist this way and that, and then nodding her approval to Mr. Martin, who smiled with smooth satisfaction. When he turned back to his customers, Annabelle swiftly scooped up a platinum diamond brooch and dropped it into her hidden skirt pocket.

A moment later, Mr. Martin glanced over again, with pleased alertness. Annabelle was amused, without smiling. *This will be the best of challenges,* she thought. *Mr. Martin is a worthy adversary.*

When Samuel was distracted by a customer's question, Annabelle made her move. With expert skill, she slid a pricey ruby and diamond bracelet into her opposite hidden skirt pocket.

She kept her poise, staring into the case as if perplexed, as if she were struggling to decide. Although her heart thrummed, Annabelle didn't move, confident from vast experience that Mr. Martin would sense he was about to lose a sale and hurry over. Then she'd execute the second part of her plan.

Mr. Martin was soon standing by the case, his forehead pinched in concern. "Have you made your choice, madam?"

Annabelle gave a shy, quick little smile. "Well, I don't know. My mother is particular and I'm not quite seeing... well, how should I say it? I'm not seeing the perfect bracelet for her among these lovely pieces."

Samuel was a seasoned merchant. He sensed mischief. His eyes lowered on the case and then widened when he noticed a bracelet was missing. A glance at Annabelle's wrists revealed nothing.

Perspiration popped out on his forehead. "Madam, there is a bracelet missing."

"Is there?" Annabelle exclaimed innocently.

He blinked rapidly, searching with care. Then he lifted his eyes and focused on her with growing accusation. "Is the bracelet on your wrist?"

Annabelle lifted her arms to show that both wrists were bare. "No, sir. I replaced each one in the case from where I took them. Well, of course I did."

He rounded the case and stood next to her, his expression wary, his lips tight, jaw clenched. "Madam... I know the contents of the case, and I can assure you that a bracelet—a very expensive bracelet—is missing. It has rubies and diamonds."

Annabelle did not show offense. She matched his anxiety and concern. "Oh, my, sir. It must be here. It simply must. This is most worrisome. Most upsetting."

Mr. Martin straightened his back, his eyes hardening. "I will not be mocked, young lady. That bracelet was in this case when you walked in here, and I can assure you that I have not opened it for anyone else this morning."

Annabelle's eyes darted about, examining the area. She bent and searched underneath the case, appearing flustered. "It must be here, sir. It simply must."

In the distraction of the moment, Mr. Martin did not notice Annabelle's left hand slip inside her secret pocket, draw out the bracelet, and stealthily lay it on the floor. This sleight-of-hand trick had been relentlessly practiced and successfully executed many times before.

"Oh, my, Mr. Martin!" she exclaimed. "Here is your lovely bracelet. It is here, beneath the case."

Samuel Martin crouched, saw the bracelet, reached, and snapped it up as if he were snatching up dice after a winning toss.

Annabelle put a hand to her heart, her breath coming fast. "My word, Mr. Martin, you gave me quite the start. Thank God, we found it."

Mr. Martin was no fool, and he suspected a near theft from the woman, but his relief at finding the bracelet diverted him from returning to the case to examine it further.

His voice was calm, controlled, but firm. "Will you be purchasing anything, madam?"

Annabelle was all fluttery. "I am so distraught now, Mr. Martin. I will need some time to recover my wits before I decide. Perhaps I'll return later today or early tomorrow."

Mr. Martin's eyes were large and cold. "Then a good day to you, madam."

Annabelle smiled sweetly. "Thank you, sir, and a good day to you."

Outside, Annabelle turned and walked briskly east, across 39th Street, her chin up, her throat tight, her heart pounding. She didn't have much time. Mr. Martin would soon discover her ruse—that she'd returned the bracelet but kept the diamond brooch.

She removed her hat, then released the two pins that held her hair in place, letting her hair drop freely to her shoulders. After she'd slipped out of her jacket, tucking it under her arm, she felt a bit safer.

Annabelle glanced back over her shoulder, ducked into an alley, found a trash can and stuffed her hat and jacket inside it, under some coal cinders. There was a ladies' shop nearby, one she'd scouted two days ago.

Inside, she purchased a bottle-green pleated dress and a light winter coat, changing clothes in the fitting room. She placed the diamond brooch into a red velvet drawstring bag that she tied around her wrist and pushed under her long right sleeve.

Back outside on the street, she carried a box containing her old clothes. When she was sure she wasn't being followed, she walked three blocks and found another narrow, dank alley with garbage cans and two discarded wooden barrels. She darted in just as a black cat hunched his back, hissed at her, and then went skittering off into the dark depths. Annabelle recoiled, frowning. She'd always been a little superstitious, thanks to her frequently boozed-up mother, who had immigrated from northern England as a young woman and found work with a traveling circus, reading tarot cards and performing psychic readings.

"You don't mess with the cards, dearie. They's the only truth in this world that you're ever gonna find. That is, the cards, and a good glass of sweet gin. The cards don't lie and they don't steal, but they only tell the truth to those who know how to listen without ears, if you get my meaning."

Annabelle did not get her meaning, and she never would. And she would never play with tarot cards or with anything else that might offer a glimpse into her future.

Annabelle had just jammed the clothes box into a half-empty garbage can when her attention was suddenly drawn to an old, toppled-over lantern near a wooden barrel. She stood staring at it, gently captivated. The black caterwauling cat startled her, and she jerked toward the sound, spotting the cat a short distance away, eyeing her with pale moon eyes.

"Shut up and get away from me!" Annabelle shouted.

The cat flitted away, and Annabelle took three careful steps toward the lantern. It wasn't a particularly attractive lantern. The wire guards were bent and one of the panes of glass was missing, another cracked. But it seemed to call to her.

Annabelle leaned over, reached for the wire handle, inhaled a breath and lifted it. She was surprised by its weight. Why was it here, tossed into this grimy, damp alley?

Without another thought, she started to exit the alley with the lantern in her hand.

Just then, a policeman went striding across the entrance, glanced in and saw her. Surprised, he came to a complete stop and faced her fully.

She hesitated. Did he recognize her? Were the police looking for her? The sun fled the sky, sliding under a dark cloud.

"Now, what will you be doing in there, Missy?" the cop said, with an Irish accent.

Annabelle did a quick examination of his face and eyes. No, he didn't recognize her. She saw the blooming light of attraction.

Annabelle, ready for another performance, spoke to him in an English accent. "Well, hello there, officer. I'll be looking for me cat that has dashed off yet again. I've got me lantern here to help in the search, but I ain't found the rascal yet."

"Shall I help you, then?"

"No, thank ye, officer. I must be off now before me husband gets sore and comes a-looking for me. I'll find the cat later. I always do. He won't go far from the food, you know, just like me husband. And just like most men, I'll be bound."

At the mention of "me husband," the policeman's face fell a little in disappointment. "All right, then,

Missus," he said, touching his billystick to his felt helmet. "You be careful in this alleyway. There's a gang of ruffs who hang out here throwing the dice for a chance to strike it rich, and they've been known to have a good fight or two."

Annabelle smiled. "I've got me own game of chance, don't I, officer?"

"And what will that be, Missus?"

"Matrimony. You know what they say. Matrimony is the only game of chance the clergy favor."

He grinned. "Well, now, I'll not argue with that. But from the fine looks of you, I'd say your husband's a fortunate man."

"And I thank you for that, and I'll tell the man as soon as he returns from the pub."

"All right now, a good day to you."

When he was gone, Annabelle breathed out a sigh and crept out of the alley, back into weak sunlight. She waved down a hansom cab, climbed inside and told the driver to take her to Orchard Street.

As the cab trotted downtown, Annabelle set the lantern next to her and gazed at it.

"Well, old friend, what is your story? Now that I'd like to know."

CHAPTER 2

Annabelle Palmer's second-floor, one-bedroom furnished apartment was clean and spare, in the back hallway of an eight-story tenement building. It was a lower middle-class building; an immigrant building and a family building, and that suited her just fine.

She could have lived in one of the finer hotels in the city or taken rooms in a brownstone in a more fashionable and well-to-do neighborhood. She certainly had the money. But she didn't want to draw attention to herself, and she was nomadic, never living in one place for very long, in case the coppers got on to her.

Annabelle had not left her apartment for five days, the time she usually sequestered after a successful heist. It was necessary to stay out of sight and be patient, to let some of the heat of the theft cool down. Time allowed the cops to grow weary and bored with the search, and they'd lose their edge. Some would be pulled from the case, and placed on a larger theft, a kidnapping or a murder.

Five days always seemed to do the trick.

The day after her heist, Annabelle had found an article on page eight of the *New York World*, one of the two newspapers she had delivered to her door every day. The headline read,

BRAZEN DAYLIGHT ROBBERY BY FEMALE!

Martin's Fine Jewelry Shop, off West 39th Street, was the unfortunate target of a jewelry theft yesterday morning. Police are looking for a young, attractive woman, well dressed and well spoken. The police believe she has struck before, noting the style and character of the theft.

Detective Amos Hackett stated that the woman poses as various personalities, both young and old, adapting her costumes and makeup accordingly. He added, "She disguises herself so successfully that making a positive identification of the young woman is a time-consuming, arduous task. But we'll catch her. Make no mistake about that. Thieves are never as smart or as lucky as they think they are."

It was reported that the woman took money and jewelry worth over five thousand dollars before making her daring escape.

It was further reported that Mr. Martin, the proprietor, subsequently showed signs of mental stress so severe that he was taken to the Highland Asylum on 62nd and Third Avenue for rest and treatment.

Annabelle had frowned at the article and then tossed the paper away. Of course, she hadn't taken money, only the diamond brooch. And she had serious doubts about Mr. Martin having a mental breakdown and being sent to an asylum. He wasn't the type. There had been strength and cold calculation in his eyes. And, anyway, he would have been insured. The merchants on 39th Street were all insured.

The papers never got the story right, and they often sensationalized things or made them up to increase sales.

So, five days had passed, and Annabelle had occupied her time sleeping, eating and reading two novels, one, a rags-to-riches story by Ruby Faraday, and the other, an adventure story by Sherman Jackson, a pseudonym for the female writer Rose Duckworth. Jackson's novels were always wild stories, and the one Annabelle had just read was about a woman who'd finally had enough of her husband's drunkenness and beatings, so she scraped up enough money to book passage on a clipper ship to San Francisco. She'd nearly been killed as the ship had sailed around Cape Horn in a horrifying storm.

Annabelle loved the book, and it had given her an idea. Like Detective Hackett had said, *"Thieves are never as smart or as lucky as they think they are."*

Maybe it was time for a change of location. She'd been lucky in New York—smart and lucky—but how long would her streak last? Luck always ran out, no matter how careful and skilled you were. Isn't that what had happened to Farley Carp, her ex-boyfriend gambler?

On Monday night, six days after the heist, Annabelle ventured outside for the first time, wearing a frumpy, drab gray dress, a frayed thin coat and a white shawl covering her head and shoulders.

To add age, she used a make-up technique she'd learned from an actress in the circus she and her mother had travelled with when she was a preteen.

First, she applied light foundation over her entire face and then blended in a dark foundation where she wanted to create creases. Next, she applied light and dark foundation to highlight the creases and wrinkles, and then she dusted translucent powder over her entire face to lock the makeup in place. Finally, she added even more powder; making her skin appear rough and old.

Fog spilled out of the sky and rolled through the city as Annabelle wandered the streets, stopping in a dim café for dinner. Sitting alone at a back table, she ate boiled beef, cabbage and a potato. It wasn't bad, and it reminded her of her father, her loser of a father. He'd loved boiled beef and cabbage.

At a table close by were two uniformed cops eating beef steaks, beans and potatoes. They mumbled complaints about the weather, their jobs and their wives.

Annabelle smiled inwardly and thought, *Hello coppers. Guess who's sitting so close to you she could spit on you? And she would love to spit on you. I'm Annabelle Palmer from Brooklyn. I'm Agatha Parks from Pittsburg. I'm Prudence Riley from Dublin. I've made more money in my brief life than you'll ever see in your long ones, that is, if some petty scoundrel doesn't shoot you while you're walking your beat.*

Annabelle drained the last of her coffee and eased back confidently in her chair. A life on the run had not always been an easy one—yet for Annabelle, the rush of criminality was a considerable incentive. She loved the challenge. She loved the excitement and the thrill of walking away with a piece of jewelry that was worth more than those two coppers would make in twenty years.

Annabelle didn't see herself as a thief, a criminal, but as someone outsmarting a world that wanted to keep her, and all women, down. A world that forced women into low-paying jobs; forced them to be clerks or secretaries or seamstresses working twelve- to fourteen-hour days. An even worse fate was to be the wife of a man who controlled her, beat her, and abused her.

Annabelle was not currently involved with a man, nor would she ever let herself be at the mercy of a man again. Once was enough. She'd learned her lesson, and it had been a hard and brutal one.

Back outside, a misty rain dampened the cobblestone streets and fog shrouded the streetlamps, making the world appear eerie and out of focus. She hated to admit it, but a night like this made her lonely, and it made her a little mean, although she didn't know why.

She rambled for a time, while carriages clopped by, a dog barked in the distance, and a baby cried from an upper window. Finally, Annabelle found herself near Shanty's Saloon. Why she stopped and why she even considered going in was beyond her. She knew Farley Carp hung out in there. He was a no-good bum of a gambler, but he was handsome, and he was funny, and he was a magnificent lover.

She filled her lungs with cool night air, pushed the door open and stepped inside, hoping he wouldn't be there, and hoping he would.

It was a cheerless place, filled with dim light and shadows. No one gave her a second look, a haggard old woman in shabby clothes.

Annabelle allowed her eyes to adjust to the dusty light and peer through the clouds of cigar and cigarette smoke. Conversation was loud, the language rough, and the characters rougher. Some were old seaman, some were dock workers and others, like Farley, were no-good, cheating card sharks, or worse.

The tables were round, wooden and rickety. The chairs rocked and leaned. The bar was stuffed with smelly men and brassy women, all clutching mugs of beer, their faces shiny, eyes bleary, laughter harsh.

Annabelle spotted him. Farley was easy to spot. He stood at the corner of the bar, his back straight, his face half-in and half-out of light from an overhead hanging lamp. His raven black hair gleamed, his black suit fit to perfection, and his black boots gave him height, almost six feet. He was chatting up a cheap-looking buxom blonde, whose lips were painted; whose cheeks were painted; whose eyes held lust.

Annabelle grinned and started over. When she was but three feet from Farley, she paused. He gave her a dismissive glance and returned his seducing attention back to the blonde.

Annabelle stayed planted, staring at him. He swung another glance at her, looked her up and down with obvious displeasure, and angled his body away from her.

In a cockney accent, Annabelle said, "Giz a butcher's at than then, will you?"

Farley sighed and looked at her. When he spoke, it was in a slow, Southern drawl "What did you say, madam?"

"Get out of it. You be hearing what I'm sayin' to you, you do. Do I got to translate? Well, all right then. I said, let me have a look at you then."

Farley summoned the last of his patience. "Look, madam. With the kind respect I can summon for this unhappy occasion, I am not giving you any money, so you'd best be on your way now like a good old lady, and don't you further disturb me and my fine lady here."

At that moment, a heavy, round faced black man pounded the table and shot up, his face wadded up in anger, his chest broad, his forearms thick. When he spoke, his voice was a rich, booming bass baritone, his eyes glassy from drink. The room fell into startled silence as all eyes shifted to him.

He lifted his arms to the heavens as if looking for angels. "I will not submit, nor will I bow to any white man's God, as it concerns the repugnant incidents of brutal slavery. Do you hear me?! No, I will not! May my God forbid it!"

"Ah, shut up and sit down, Lucas," said one of his drunken sea mates seated at the table. He seized the orator's arm and pulled him back down into his chair and handed him a mug of ale. "Let's drink to the fickle winds, and to the swelling seas, and to all the girls we ain't kissed."

Lucas tipped back his mug and chugged it down in four swallows, his Adam's apple working.

Seeing that the outburst and the entertainment were over, the room quickly resumed its riotous drinking and noisy conversation.

Annabelle moved her face close to Farley's, to see if he'd recognize her. "Your fine lady is not the right crumpet for you, mate," she said. "And every bloke at the bar sees it. I be the one you're looking for and make no mistake about it."

Farley pushed away from the bar, throwing his fists to his hips. "Now look, madam, I'm only going to ask you once more, as a gentleman of the old South, to kindly walk away and leave me and my good lady here in peace."

Annabelle was enjoying herself immensely, but now she was ready to spring her surprise. She winked at him and lowered her voice. "So, how's the scar on your right arse a-doin', dearie?"

Farley stiffened. His eyes widened, and he canted his head. "What did you say?"

"You got the lick-of-the-knife in a card game gone wrong, didn't you, Mr. Carp? I knows the truth of it because a little birdie told me so."

Farley's face went blank with disbelief. He peered into her eyes, searching the depths of them.

Annabelle grinned flirtatiously, and moved even closer, half-hooding her eyes. She dropped the accent. "Hello, Farley Carp, you no-good swamp rat from Louisiana."

His face opened in stunned recognition. When he opened his mouth to speak, she put a hand over it.

"Yes, Farley. It's me," she said with a sultry wink. "Let's go. I want to touch that scar of yours again."

CHAPTER 3

The next morning in early light, Annabelle lay in her bed next to Farley, listening to his rhythmic snore and the rain striking the windows. She laced her hands behind her head and stared up at the ceiling, feeling a gnawing unease and a low-level ennui. A change was coming. She could feel it, just as some people can sense a coming storm or a change of luck.

Careful not to awaken Farley, Annabelle slid out of bed, naked, shouldered into a warm robe and walked into comfortable slippers. In the snug kitchen, she reached for her Hanson Goodrich stove-top percolator, poured water into the pot and put a generous amount of coarsely ground coffee in the top chamber.

By the time the coffee was squirting up into the glass dome, Annabelle had dressed in a long skirt and white blouse, twisting her hair up into a pile on her head and pinning it. She'd placed her two-shot derringer in her skirt pocket, a habit she'd picked up after her first marriage.

When she poured a cup of the steaming coffee into a cup, Farley stirred, wiped his eyes and sat up.

"Does that fresh-made coffee not have the scent of heavenly winds, my dear and lovely Annabelle? Its fine aroma awakened me from a poker game dream, where I had a royal flush. But it's worth it, just to see your beautiful face on this incomparable morning."

Annabelle sat at her kitchen table, enjoying the look of his tousled hair and bare, hairy chest. "Do all southerners have your rakish charm, or is that particular to you?"

Farley leaned back against the headboard. "Did I ever tell you that my old pappy traveled to and fro, down the great Mississippi, from Cincinnati to New Orleans?"

"No, you didn't."

"Well, he was Rake Senior, Miss Palmer. I gained my entire education from him. He was a charmer of the first water, a card shark, and a scoundrel through and through. It was said, and I have no reason to doubt it, that he was shot by one angry woman, stabbed by another, clubbed over the head by yet another, and finally sent to the great world beyond by a jealous husband who'd also been cheated at cards. He shoved my Daddy off the Mary Queen Riverboat and, alas, because he could not swim, he sank to the bottom."

Annabelle gave him a meager grin. "And your mother? What about her? Is she alive?"

"Oh, yes. Very alive. She is a lovely woman, born and raised on a plantation... a rather dilapidated plantation these days. I'm afraid it has progressively fallen into a tarnished ruin since the Civil War."

"And I bet she's charming?"

"She is a lady of the highest order, who is so fond of rice griddle cakes."

"And what is a rice griddle cake?"

Farley scratched his head. "Well, let me see now. If memory serves, and my mother's instruction is still fresh, you boil rice in milk until it's quite hot, then you stir in a little wheat or rice flour. You let it cool, then add two eggs and a pinch of salt. Then you make small, thin cakes and fry them on the griddle."

"You must make me some, one of these days. And is your momma still living on that plantation?"

"Oh, yes, ma'am. She's a lady who will still shoot a Yankee on sight, if he should lose his way and wander across her now meager and unfortunate patch of fallow land."

"And do you send her money?"

"When I have it."

"How has your luck been of late?"

"Some old boy from Savannah said it best: 'The only sure thing about luck is that it will change.' I've been waiting for bad luck to vacate my premises for months now and go find some other poor sucker to take up with. But it seems the bad luck bully enjoys my company more than I enjoy his. He simply refuses to leave."

They sat in silence for a moment, while Annabelle blew the steam from her coffee and sipped at it.

Farley gave her a long look. "I've been reading about you in the papers."

She studied him, sipping, blowing ripples across the surface of the coffee. "I can trust you, can't I, Farley Carp?"

He grinned, showing his lovely white teeth. "I fear, Annabelle, that this humble servant from the South could use a loan. Just a small loan to help me keep up the pretense of success and the genteel style of living that my card-playing, riverboat gambler daddy brought me up to enjoy. Anyway, the way I see it, based on all those newspapers stories about the lady jewel thief, you must be as rich as Andrew Carnegie himself by now."

Annabelle's eyes darkened on him. "Didn't I give you a loan the last time we met? Let's see, when was that?"

"Two months ago, give or take. And yes, you were kind enough to offer me funds. You know, Annabelle, the truth is, you always were my best luck charm."

"And were you lucky with the last loan, from two months ago?"

"At first, yes. Then..." He lifted a hand and let it drop. "I ran upon a lady friend whom I felt it was my duty to entertain. She was rich, or so I thought. Turned out, she thought I was rich. The joke was on us. She took it badly, and very nearly cut my throat in the night."

Annabelle's eyes were critical. "Have you ever made an honest woman of any woman, Farley?"

He gave her a wistful smile. "Two times, if you can believe it."

"I believe it. What happened those two times? You've never told me the sordid details."

"I guess I liked them when I married them, but not much after. But you, Annabelle... well, you would be different. As the poet said, 'It's the fire in your eyes, and the flash of your smile. The swing of your waist and the joy in your feet.' And what about that keen, intelligent head of yours and those swift, sure hands that never miss, even when you reach for me?"

She gave him a freezing glance. "And you have the gift of gab, don't you, Farley? The gift of words that can heat up a woman with that southern tongue of yours, so she's all fluttering eyes and melting butter. Then you snap a finger or two and carry her off to your bed."

He smiled, pleased by the compliment. "We would make a beautiful and successful couple, Annabelle. You know we would, and we don't do so badly in the bed chamber either, do we?"

She eyed him closely, purposefully letting the silence draw out until Farley grew uneasy.

"What's that face mean, Annabelle? I can't read it."

"It means, I'll give you another loan, but it will be the last. The very last, understand?"

Farley didn't respond. He'd heard the tangible bitterness in her voice. He sat up a little taller, combing his hair with a hand. "Don't you want to have a family, Annabelle? A family with me? Isn't that what all women want in the end?"

A sudden burst of anger pushed her to her feet, and her face flushed scarlet. "Is that what you think all women want, Farley? Are you so stupid after marrying and abandoning two women that you don't see the truth? Is your handsome face stuck on a supremely empty head?"

Farley's face twisted in offense. "What did I say? What's the matter with you?"

Annabelle folded her arms tightly across her chest, her eyes filled with fire. "A woman wants everything a man wants, Farley, and more. Much more. She feels more, knows more, is smarter, and she can work harder than any man, and she can endure pain, much more pain and suffering than any man. I don't need a man. I can have whatever I want, and I don't need a man to get what I want. I can buy it, or I can take it. And, no, I will *not* marry you. I married once, and after he beat me and was finished with me, my baby was dead, and I was barely alive. I will never have a family. He saw to that after the last beating. Now get out of here and away from me. The very sight of you makes me sick, with all your bad-luck weakness and sugary, southern words. I want you out, now. And I never want to see you again."

The room swelled with tension. Farley gave her a stiff nod and a sour smile. "All right, Annabelle, if that's what you want. But remember this, I'm not the one who approached you last night. You approached me. It was you who took me to your bed."

She scowled at him. "And I got what I wanted, didn't I?" she said forcefully.

Farley threw back the sheet and swung his legs to the floor, keeping his naked back to her. He dressed in anger, mumbling curses under his breath.

Annabelle hadn't moved from her spot near the kitchen table, and she hadn't lowered her crossed arms.

When Farley stood facing her, dressed in his black suit made from the finest cloth, his lace silk shirt of the latest fashion, and his tie fixed into an artful bow, she decided against giving him the loan.

"I've changed my mind," she said coldly. "I will not loan you any money."

When he burned past her, she stepped back, ready to reach for the derringer and shoot him if he swung at her. Men loved to hit women, but if he did, he'd be dead before he could leave the room.

But Farley didn't swing at her. At the door, he turned, skewering her with a stare. "You shouldn't throw friends away, Annabelle. You might need them someday. I'd wager you don't have many. I'd also wager that you have many enemies, and you just made another one. Good luck, dearie. Someday your luck will run out too. It happens to us all, and it happens when we least expect it."

After he was gone and the room fell into a pulsing silence, Annabelle relaxed her arms at her sides and looked down at her trembling hands. "That was stupid," she said aloud. "Why did you lose your temper like that? Why do you always lose your temper at men?"

She removed butter and cheese from the icebox and sliced a piece of bread. After refilling her coffee cup and taking a drink, she cursed herself. Now she'd have to move. Farley's threat was real. He was the cold, vengeful type if you crossed him; if you insulted him; if you bruised his precious self-esteem.

Her head filled with noisy questions. Last night, why had she lost her discipline and entered that saloon? Why had she brought him home? Why hadn't she controlled her sexy itch? It had been the mistake of an amateur, letting loneliness and the naughty craving for a roll in the sack get the better of her.

After breakfast, Annabelle dressed and began to pack. It didn't take long. She pulled her trunk and suitcase from the front closet and went to work. Because of her nomadic life, she was an expert packer;

an expert at knowing what to keep and what to toss. She should have tossed Farley a long time ago.

As she worked, she speculated as to where she'd go. Uptown, perhaps, to the West Side. There were plenty of mid-sized hotels to choose from. There was the Cliff Haven, just off Broadway at 62nd Street, and the Broadmoor, south of the newly built Ansonia Hotel on 73rd and 74th Streets. She'd heard that the famous tenor Enrico Caruso lived at the Ansonia. She'd love to move there, but she wouldn't. It was too public. She'd try the Cliff Haven.

When the trunk was fastened and locked and the suitcase stored by the front door, Annabelle swept the room once more to ensure she hadn't forgotten anything. And then she saw the lantern tucked away in a corner.

Why had she taken it in the first place? She knew why. She was a hopeless sentimentalist, that's why. She'd seen the thing lying on its side, beaten and broken, tossed away in that dirty alley and forgotten. Isn't that what had happened to her after her husband had beaten her and tossed her out?

What was she going to do with the thing? She couldn't just leave it.

CHAPTER 4

Annabelle carried the lantern into the bathroom and began cleaning it, patiently washing the grime from the tarnished green/brown patina. With straining fingers and a grimace, she bent the wire guards back into place and, as best she could, she polished the anchor design on each side of the roof, one anchor painted a faded red, the other a faded blue. Finally, she checked the wick. It was frayed, black and old, but she was certain it would light.

Back at the kitchen table, she set the lantern down and searched the drawers for matches. In a matchbox she found five remaining matches. Standing by the lantern, she struck the match against the box striker and watched the flame burst to life.

With care, she guided the flame through the broken glass door and touched the wick. It refused the light. When the match fizzled, Annabelle struck another, determined.

When the wick crackled, smoked, then flared, Annabelle brightened, stepping back, smiling with satisfaction. "There you are. And you thought you were finished."

The rich, buttery flame swelled and expanded, filling the room with a warm, serene light. Annabelle was drawn to it, captivated by it. She grew light-headed, disoriented, astounded to see blue, glittering sparks of light falling from the ceiling like snow. Lost in a childlike wonder, she watched the dazzling spectacle as the lights encircled her, increasing in density, the cool flecks bathing her, tingling her face like snowflakes.

In sudden terror, she felt the floor begin to give way; saw the walls dissolve; saw her hands become translucent. She could see right through them! She tried to scream out, but it got caught in her throat. There was a whirring sound, like a motor just above her head and, all about her, the world was melting away, like fresh paint washed away in a rainstorm.

With a desperate, nearly disembodied hand, she grabbed for the handle and, with all her strength, she inhaled a breath and blew on the flame. It danced, bent, wavered, but kept burning. She heaved in another breath, filling her lungs. With her heart jumping in her chest, she puffed her cheeks and blew a jet of frantic air toward the flame. It fluttered, struggled, then died, blue smoke rising, curling up toward the ceiling.

Shivering and stunned, Annabelle staggered, sucked in another breath and then backed into the nearest chair and dropped, her chest heaving, her eyes wild, searching the air.

As she stared at the lantern, an unnamed terror beat through her veins. It was a live thing, an indefinable piece of magic; a kind of magic wand. She'd had such a toy wand when she was a little girl, traveling with her mother in the circus.

Having lost all sense of time, Annabelle finally managed to push to her feet and stand on wobbly legs. She moved away from the table and the lantern, afraid it might seize her and drag her off into some underworld.

"What are you?" she said aloud, in a frightened, scraping voice. "What kind of hellish thing are you?"

The lantern sat, quiet and innocent, the last of the wispy smoke drifting away into thin air, like a vaporizing ghost. She paced the room, working to steady her breath, throwing cautious glances toward the lantern, seeking answers, seeking reasons, seeking to make sense of what had just happened.

She stopped, waited, then haltingly approached the thing. With a swallow of fear, she studied it, tilting her head left and right, looking for a clue as to what made the thing work.

Her voice was low; it quavered as she spoke to it. "Are you evil? Are you good? Where did you come from?"

She half-expected it to answer her. But it didn't answer. It was still.

Annabelle felt cold sweat on her face and back. She'd seen and experienced many things, but she had never, not ever, seen or experienced anything like this. She recalled the black cat that had crossed her path in the alley, just before she'd spotted the lantern. Bad luck? Was this the beginning of her bad luck? Had Farley cursed her?

Her eyes darted toward the door and the waiting trunk and suitcase. She needed to leave. If Farley was going to betray her, he'd do it right away. He wouldn't wait. Why should he? She should have given him the money.

"Is my luck running out?" she said to the four walls.

She pivoted back to the lantern. "I'm leaving you, you devil. I'm leaving you for the next poor sucker that comes along. You're not taking my luck from me. You're not sending me to hell."

Just then, she heard a fist hammering on her door, and she swung toward the sound, frightened.

"Annabelle Palmer!" a gruff male voice yelled. "This is the police."

There was another thunder of fists. "We know you're in there. Let us in! There's no way out. There are men at the back of the building, and more waiting just outside your window. Let us in before we break the door down!"

Annabelle felt the heat of panic. That no-good bastard *had* turned her in.

More fists thudded into the door. They'd put their shoulders to it soon enough, and she'd be caught. Who knows how much time she'd get? The coppers would fake evidence, that was for sure. No doubt she'd be tossed into the notorious Tombs, a prison all women wanted to avoid. It was known to be dreary, punishing and suffocating. The fifty cells were under the supervision of a chief matron who was known to be brutal.

Annabelle had a two-shot derringer. Maybe it was time to use it. One shot to the head would finish her, and that would be that. But could she do it? Her mother had always said that suicide was the chicken's way out. The coward's way out.

"Don't you ever be a coward, Annabelle," she'd often said. "Take your licks as they come and fight back."

The threatening voices grew louder. "All right Annabelle Palmer, we're coming in, and there will be hell to pay!"

Annabelle rushed to the door and slid the chain lock through the latch. Next, she turned back to the lantern, her pulse thudding in her ears. Without another thought, she moved to the table, grabbed the box of matches, reached for a match, and aggressively struck it against the box. The match burst to life.

She glanced at the door and heard the heavy thump of a shoulder. With a grim face and spooked eyes, she lowered the lighted match and touched the wick.

It seized the flaring match and exploded to life, its light trembling, expanding. Annabelle stood stiffly, completely at the light's mercy, as the swirling blue and golden glow bathed her and encircled her, finally sweeping her up into it.

In a cry of fear and horror, the world shattered, and she was flung away like an arrow shot from a bow, flying through boiling blue clouds, hearing the tingling of windchimes all about her.

She was either going to hell or to her death, and she was as helpless as a newborn child to do anything about it.

CHAPTER 5
New York City 2021

"THIS REALLY FREAKS me out," Eve said.

"What?" Patrick asked.

Eve and Patrick Gantly sat at the dining room table in their newly renovated, three-bedroom brownstone, eating a breakfast of scrambled eggs, bagels and coffee. Eve was scrolling through her cell phone and Patrick was reading the newspaper, a habit from the nineteenth century that he'd never been able to break. He wanted the hard copy. He wanted to feel it and smell it; he wanted to fold it and walk down the street with it under his arm. After all, he was truly "old school."

"Listen to this from CNN," Eve said. "'Archeologists in China have discovered two perfectly preserved fossils of a new, 125-million-year-old dinosaur species. Scientists believe that they were trapped by a volcanic eruption while resting at the bottom of their burrows.' Okay, what's a burrow?"

"A hole?" Patrick said.

Eve quickly looked it up. "Here it is. A burrow is 'a hole or tunnel dug by a small animal, especially a rabbit, as a dwelling.' Okay, so even if dinosaurs were not small animals, somebody decided to call their homes burrows, and these dinosaurs were discovered 125-million years after they were buried by a big mound of lava and stones. Wow. It's hard to get my mind around that. And here's another one. This is wild. Archeologists have also recently discovered a dinosaur 'mummy' so well-preserved that it even has its skin and guts. It's also about a hundred and twenty million years old."

Patrick looked up from over the top of his newspaper. "That's a long time ago. It puts our time travel adventures into a whole new light, doesn't it?"

"No way would I ever, ever, want to go back that far. Never," Eve said, absently lowering her hand and stroking the ears of their two-year-old dog, Colin, as he gazed up at her, begging for a snack.

"How long have human beings been around now?" Eve asked. "Maybe two hundred thousand years?"

"That sounds about right."

"And listen to this," Eve said, reading on. "Scientists say that dinosaurs lived on the Earth for about 165 million years."

Patrick lowered the paper, pondering. "We will never last that long."

"What do you mean, we?"

"Human beings. The human species."

Eve set her phone aside. "Are you going to give me a profound and learned psychological explanation, now that you've finished your degree in Forensic Psychology?"

He nodded, wisely. "Yes, I am, just so I can show off all my newfound knowledge to impress you, and thus gather points for later on, if you get my meaning?"

Eve sat up erect, grinning. "Oh, I get, Patrick. I get, and maybe you'll get… if, and I stress IF, I'm impressed by what you're about to say. So, I'm all ears and eyes, and nose and mouth, and speaking of mouth, you didn't kiss me this morning."

"Yes, I did kiss you, just after you fed Colleen. Obviously, my kisses don't carry the same memorable power they once did, if you don't even remember."

Eve glanced up at the ceiling, contemplating. She nodded, then lowered her eyes. "Okay, yes. Now I remember. Yes, you did kiss me. But let me tell you why I had a momentary slip of memory."

Patrick scratched his cheek. "Oh, Lord, may the saints be with me now."

Eve's voice was light with humor. "Mr. Gantly, you left the bed at four o'clock this morning and slept the rest of the night in the second bedroom."

Patrick held up a hand. "Guilty. Yes, I did, madam. But then I joined you at around six and, as I recall, we had a bit of a romp."

"Let's not change the subject. Did you leave because I was snoring?"

"Eve, it's all right. All of us snore a bit, don't we?"

"Well, my handsome, former detective, may I point out that you snore like a lumber jack, but I have never left our bed to sleep elsewhere."

"Because, until we moved into this three-bedroom brownstone, we didn't have a bed to sleep elsewhere. That old couch was a lumpy trap and, anyway, Colin would wander over and lick my face every time I rolled onto my right side."

Eve winced. "Was I snoring that much?"

"Let me put it this way, at one point, I was dreaming I was being chased through a dark forest by a big, growling, black bear."

Eve made a face. "That's terrible. Women aren't supposed to snore; not loud, anyway. I'm not supposed to sound like a big, growling, black bear."

"I believe you snore the most when you take a sleeping pill," Patrick said.

Eve reached for her blue coffee mug, took a sip of the lukewarm coffee, and then turned pensive. "I couldn't sleep."

"I know."

"How many times in the last year have we been through this, Patrick? How many times have we talked about this since last Christmas?"

Patrick put down the newspaper and folded his hands. "I said we should do it, Eve. So why not finally, once and for all, make the decision and just let the lantern go?"

"Because I always come back to the same thing. Is it the right and ethical thing to do?"

"Eve, once we donate the lantern to some antique dealer, then it will literally be out of our hands. Whoever purchases it, and what they choose to do with it, will be their choice, not ours. How they use its power will be up to them."

"But Patrick, if the lantern hurls them off into the past, they won't have any way to get back to the present. They won't even know any other lantern exists in the past. They won't know what happened to them and they'll be trapped wherever they are. I mean, who knows where that lantern will take them?"

Patrick leaned back. "Nikola Tesla was not a stupid man, Eve. Most likely, whoever lights that lantern will either not time travel at all or, if they do, they'll wind up back at his laboratory in 1884, like you and Joni did. So, he'll give them another lantern so they can go back home."

"He didn't give *us* another lantern, Patrick. Remember?"

"Yes, but that was different."

"How?"

Patrick shrugged. "I don't know. Okay, so maybe you're right."

Eve took another sip of coffee and then held the mug out. "Would you do me a big favor and refill this, please? I'm feeling lazy."

Patrick got up, went for the coffee pot, and poured their mugs full.

Eve sighed. "I must be driving you crazy. I just can't make up my mind. And part of me is scared to death that if we donate the thing, time will be reset again, and you and Colleen will disappear."

Patrick returned to his chair. "That's not going to happen. We're not going to destroy it; we're just going to off-load it onto someone else. Eve, your father suspects something. He knows something strange has been going on, and he knows it has something to do with me. Even your mother suspects something. You've seen the way they look at me. A few months ago, your perceptive father said there was something about me that seemed all wrong, as if I didn't belong. Remember?"

Eve shook her head. "He's always been suspicious."

"The point is, Eve, it's time we got rid of that lantern. It feels right. We've no need for it and we don't want it."

Eve stayed silent.

"Eve, you said it. Neither of us wants Colleen to grow up and find the thing. We would never want her to use it. And we can't will it to anyone, so we might as well get rid of it now. Here it is the first Sunday in October and we agreed to give it away last Spring. I think we should remove it from the safe and donate it to the first antique dealer we can find. Then it's over, once and for all time—yes, this time, we'll be free of it."

Eve dropped her head in a slight nod.

Patrick continued. "And if you want to write a note explaining the lantern's power to the person who takes the thing, and stuff it inside, then do it."

Eve lifted her eyes to him. "It's those thoughts that live in my mind between night and day. And it's all the memories, and all the smells and faces that rise up from the past."

Patrick smiled, gently. "When it's done, you won't be nervous and upset, you won't have to take sleeping pills, and you won't snore and force me to sneak off to another bed."

Eve laughed a little. "So that's what it all comes down to? My snoring and your abandoning me in the middle of the night?"

"Well, as my old Da used to say, 'There's nothing sweeter in life than a wife's warm caress, and nothing worse than her own, growling snore.'"

"Your Da didn't say that. You did!"

In playful anger, she snatched up a piece of her bagel and flung it at him. He threw up a hand to protect his face, but it struck him on the side of his head and fell, bouncing on the floor.

They heard Colleen crying out from the dining room, so Eve got up and went to her. When she returned to the kitchen, cradling her, Patrick was loading the dishwasher.

"Say, 'good morning' to Daddy, baby girl."

Patrick glanced over. "Hello, little lass."

Colleen reached her arms out to him and said, "Daddy."

Eve handed her over.

"So how are you this morning, little lady?" Patrick asked, kissing her cheek.

Colleen, now nearly two years old, had a pretty, round face, with curly blonde hair and glorious blue eyes.

"You're getting heavy, Colleen."

Colleen reached for her father's nose and squeezed it. "Mine."

"No, little one. That nose is mine," he said, touching her nose. "That's *your* nose."

Colleen shook her head and again pulled on his nose. "Mine."

Eve laughed. "She likes your big nose, Patrick."

"Big, is it? No one has ever said my nose was big."

"Well, your daughter certainly thinks so. Why don't you two go play, and I'll finish cleaning up the kitchen. Play the Lotto Game with her or the online Coloring Game."

"She'll never stop," Patrick said. "She threw a fit the last time I tried to pull her from it."

Patrick set Colleen down and took her hand. "Let's get out of here, Colleen, before your Mom puts us to work."

As they started for the living room, Eve said, "Hey, what were you going to say about the human species? You were going to give me a psychological explanation."

While Colleen pointed ahead, making an impatient whine, Patrick turned back to Eve. "I was going to say that humans have two primary drives: survival and procreation. Both have made modern man very left brain, logical. In our modern times, the right brain, the intuitive brain, has been largely unused, labeled vague, dreamy and devoid of facts. We live primarily in our left brains, the rational, fact-driven and practical side."

Colleen looked up at her father and fussed. "Daddy... Games..."

"All right, Colleen. One moment." To Eve, he said, "We, as an evolving species, must learn to connect our left and right brains more effectively so that we are complete human beings. Technologically, we modern humans are quite advanced. But emotionally and intuitively, we're still about Colleen's age, and we have a long way to go."

Eve stared at him in amazement. "I can't believe it. Is this the man I first met and fell in love with back in 1885? Is this the practical, worldly Detective Sergeant Patrick Gantly, who used to work in one of the grittiest police precincts in old New York?"

He grinned and shrugged. "Well, my dear Eve, see what time travel and a twenty-first century education will do to you?"

A shadow crossed her face. "Patrick, let's do it. Let's donate the lantern and be done with it."

Patrick nodded. "How about next weekend? Saturday? Find an antique store upstate, or in Pennsylvania or New Jersey, and let's go."

CHAPTER 6

"THEY SAY KINGSTON is historic and that it attracts young, creative types," Eve said, reading from her phone. "At least that's what this article says."

The day was bright and sunny. A cool, crisp wind was stirring the trees, which blazed yellow, golden orange and red. Patrick was behind the wheel of their silver Nissan Armada, with Eve in the passenger seat and Colleen in her car seat in back.

"It looks nice enough," he said, glancing about. "And this is called the North Hudson Valley?" he asked as they entered the town.

"Yes... And listen to this. It was the first capital of the State of New York. It has live music, street festivals, lots of restaurants and a farmer's market every Saturday. It says it's charmingly small, has a growing art and foodie scene, and has lots of art galleries. *The New York Times* named Kingston one of the top ten best artist communities in the United States."

"I'm impressed, not that I know much about art."

"That's why I chose this town," Eve said. "I think it will be the perfect place to donate the lantern. These people will appreciate it."

"And you said it has many antique shops?" Patrick asked.

"Yes. Shops, flea markets and a warehouse filled with vintage lighting, farmhouse sinks and hardware. But, like I told you yesterday, first I want to visit an old café that has a lot of antiques. It's called The Bus Stop Café."

"How far is it?"

"Just up the road on 310 Wall Street. We can have lunch there and look around."

PATRICK HELD COLLEEN'S HAND and followed Eve along the sidewalk and up the two stairs into the busy café. They'd left the lantern in the car's trunk until they were sure this would be the right home for it.

Inside the half-antique store/half-organic café, there was a trendy clientele, some sitting at wooden tables and chairs, some standing near a glass display case studying the day's desserts and muffins, others placing orders at one of two counters that stood at right angles to each other. Shelves of antiques lined the walls from front to back.

Eve paused and looked around, viewing lamps, clocks, a red wagon from the 1940s, a 1960s turquoise radio, a 1950s-style toaster, a lovely rose-colored Victorian lamp, two hanging vintage Coca-Cola signs, and a pewter hot water bottle from the 1860s.

"Well, this is different," she said to Patrick.

"It has a kind of Brooklyn, New York feel about it," he answered.

Patrick found an empty table near the back of the room while Eve went for paper menus and a booster chair for Colleen. After Colleen was settled, Eve and Patrick sat, studying the items.

Colleen slapped the tabletop with both hands, pointing out the window. "Doggie. I see a doggie."

Eve turned. "Yes, it's a black doggie. A black Labrador doggie, bigger than Colin."

"I want that doggie," Colleen said.

Patrick said, "Colleen, my love, you can't take home every doggie you see."

She looked at her father and twisted up her face. "I want that doggie."

Eve distracted her, holding up the menu. "Hey, Colleen, they have chocolate chip cookies. Do you want one?"

Colleen lit up, nodded, and grinned, clapping her hands. "Cookie. I want a cookie."

"Okay, we'll get one for you."

Eve looked at Patrick with a slight frown. "It's all vegetarian. Are you okay with that?"

He frowned. "I was hoping for some mutton chops," he said, with a playful wink.

"Get out of here," Eve said. "You with your mutton chops. Seriously, do you see anything here you like?"

"Since I didn't have much breakfast, I think I'll have the huevos rancheros. Sounds good: eggs with tortillas, black beans, cheese, ranchero sauce, pickled jalapeños, pepita salsa, avocado and greens."

"Won't that give you heartburn?"

"Probably, but it's the only thing that appeals to me."

"I wish I had your cast iron stomach. If I ate that, I'd have gas for days," Eve said. "And I'd be swallowing Mylanta like it was water. I'm going for the scrambled eggs with goat cheese and kale. And it comes with salad and gluten-free toast."

"I'll never understand the gluten-free thing," Patrick said. "I think it's just one of those trends that people get swept up into."

"With some people, yes, but I have patients who feel much better not eating it. Of course, Dr. Wallister thinks most people aren't really gluten-sensitive and they're just wasting their money, because gluten-free products are so expensive."

"Good for Dr. Wallister. In the old days, people just ate what was in front of them, and they were glad to get it."

"Lord help us," Eve said. "When you start in with the 'old days,' I know it's time to order."

Patrick looked about. "I guess we order at the counter and then they deliver to the table. I'll go place the order. Do you want some coffee?"

"Oh, yes. I'm desperate."

By the time the food arrived, Colleen had colored most of the farm animals on her placemat and Eve had nearly finished her mug of coffee. Eve managed to feed Colleen some of her scrambled eggs in between bites of the warm chocolate chip cookie.

"That is one good cookie," Eve said. "You should try it, Patrick. I may get another one or two to take home. How are your eggs?"

Patrick took a sip of water. "Hot."

"I told you."

"But good."

"Did you eat spicy food in the nineteenth century?"

"They didn't have this kind of food back then, as you know. But what I do miss is the smoked pork and chicken. There was a little restaurant close to the police precinct, called Tidewater Trading Post, that had a lovely, smoked pork with beans. That food tasted better than anything I can get today."

Eve rolled her eyes.

"I know, Eve. I know you've heard me say it time and again, but you were there. You know."

"Okay, yes, some of the food was good, but most of it was awful, and mostly inedible."

"You just had to know the right places."

Eve forked another piece of her scrambled eggs and guided it toward Colleen, who shook her head and pointed. "Cookie."

Eve shrugged. "Well, she ate a little."

"She likes meat," Patrick said. "I don't think she's going to be a vegetarian."

When they'd finished eating, Patrick wiped his mouth with a paper napkin. "So, what do you think? Does this place seem right to you?"

Eve cleaned Colleen's hands with a damp napkin. "Yes, I think so. What do you think?"

"It's as good as any. The crowd has thinned out. Maybe this is a good time to find the manager."

Eve nodded. "I'm nervous."

"Once it's done, you'll feel better. In a few days, it will all seem like a dream."

Eve took a quick breath. "Okay, here I go. Be back in a minute."

At the counter, Eve asked to speak to the manager. Minutes later, a young woman of about thirty-five appeared at the counter. Her auburn hair was long, tied back in a ponytail; her mouth was small; her face pretty. She looked at Eve with pleased alertness.

"Can I help you? I'm Stephanie Gray, the manager."

"I'm Eve Gantly," Eve said, in a small voice, surprised by her seesawing emotions. Could she really give the lantern up? She swallowed. "I have an antique... I have an old lantern that I think might fit in with this place. Are you the person I should be speaking to?"

"Yes... But we don't buy antiques anymore. We have so many, as you can see. They're mostly just for show, although last week a woman bought an antique metal lampshade that someone had left with us on consignment. Did you want to leave the lantern on consignment?"

"No. I'm not interested in selling it. I just want it to have a good home, and I think this is the place."

Stephanie looked confused. "Oh. Well, do you have it with you?"

"It's out in the car."

"Okay, then bring it in and let me see it."

Eve turned and started for the front door, waving at Patrick. Shortly, she returned with the lantern, and Stephanie came from around the counter to examine it. Eve noticed Stephanie's impulsive pleasure as she reached for it.

Eve handed it over, and Stephanie held it with both hands.

"Oh, wow. It's heavy. Really nice and unique. Where did you get it?"

"From an old friend."

Stephanie's eyes traveled up and down the lantern. "I love it... Just love it."

"It's a one-of-a-kind antique," Eve said, almost rolling her eyes at the stupidity of her statement.

Stephanie couldn't pull her eyes from it. "There's no way I'll put this on the shelf. Somebody would grab it right away. I want it for myself, and I'll pay you for it. It's so charming. How much?"

Eve jerked a startled glance to Patrick, who questioned her with his eyes. Colleen was squirming and fussing, wanting to go.

A breath caught in Eve's throat. "Stephanie..."

Stephanie gave her a few seconds of evaluation. "I can see it in your eyes, Eve. You don't really want to let it go, do you?"

Eve sought the right words. "There's no charge. It doesn't light. I mean, it doesn't have a wick, and you can see the burner and the fuel tank cap are damaged. But you can put an LED candle inside."

Stephanie lowered the lantern. "Well, that's no problem. I can get it repaired. But let me pay you something for it."

"I'm not going to sell it to you. If you want it, it's yours."

Stephanie stared, trying to understand. "Well, all right, if that's what you want."

Eve fixed her with a firm gaze. "Enjoy the lantern, Stephanie. And, if I were you, I wouldn't get it repaired. It's perfectly charming just as it is."

Stephanie said, "At least let me comp your lunch. It's the least I can do."

"If you want to, thank you."

As Eve, Colleen and Patrick left the café and started for the car, Stephanie stood in the picture window, cradling the lantern, watching them.

After they had driven out of town, Patrick turned to Eve. "How do you feel?"

"Like I just did something bad. Something wrong."

CHAPTER 7

On Sunday, December 5, Eve and Patrick were seated at the kitchen table, finishing brunch. Colleen was in her room, taking a late morning nap, and Colin was asleep in his Scottish doggie bed in the living room, having had his morning walk and breakfast.

Patrick snapped out *The New York Times*, while Eve chewed the last of her bagel and scrolled through her phone, searching for news.

A minute later, she stopped chewing and sat bolt upright, her eyebrows shooting up. "Oh my God!"

Patrick lowered the paper. "What?"

"I can't believe it."

"Can't believe what?"

Eve nosed closer to her phone. "Listen to this article: *Woman found rambling along Orchard Street, retro dressed in nineteenth century style clothes. An unidentified man said, 'She looked totally freaked out. She kept asking, where am I? What year is this?'*"

Patrick set the newspaper aside. "Isn't the Tenement Museum down there?"

"Yeah, I think so. Let me look."

Eve swiftly *Googled* it. "Okay, here it is. It's at 103 Orchard Street."

"So maybe she works for the museum. What else does the article say about the woman?"

"Let's see... The unidentified man said, 'She looked like an actress from an old, turn-of-the-century play or movie, and when I told her where she was and what year it was, she sat down on the stoop of a building and started cursing.'"

Eve looked up. "Then he called the police."

"And?"

"I don't know. Doesn't say."

"Keep looking," Patrick said anxiously. "Do a search or something and see if you can find out what happened to her. And when did this happen?"

Eve lowered her eyes on her phone. "Um... Saturday morning. Yesterday."

Eve searched, scrolled and blinked. "There's got to be more."

"Who published the article?" Patrick asked.

"Don't know. Didn't look. Hang on, I'm searching... Here's more, from a website called *Neighborhood Shout Out*. It says the mumbling woman was approached by two cops who asked her if she needed help. She said, 'Where am I?' They told her. She looked very upset and confused."

"Where did they take her, Eve?"

"Hold on... I'm looking. Whoa! She threatened the police with a derringer, and they wrestled, cuffed, and arrested her. It says she didn't fire the gun."

Patrick stood up, engrossed in his thoughts. "All right, then. What precinct?"

Eve's fingers worked fast. "Doesn't say. I'll find it in a sec. Hang on."

Patrick leaned back against the kitchen counter, his mind working. "I'd say, at least from what we know so far, chances are we have a time traveler. But how? From where, and what was the device?"

"A Tesla lantern, I bet," Eve said.

"We don't know anything for sure, so I'm not going to jump to conclusions."

"It sure sounds like it... Okay, it's the 7th Precinct. Do you remember it?"

Patrick pushed away from the counter and paced. He squeezed his eyes shut, straining to remember. "Of course, I remember it, even though it was so long ago. Lifetimes ago. The tenements down there were built between 1830 and 1880, before city code required buildings to have windows, airshafts, and a minimum number of bathrooms for each tenant. I should know, my family lived in one for a time. Many of the buildings had what they called cold-water flats. They had no hot water, no electricity, and only a gas stove for heat."

"You never told me that."

"It's not something one wants to recall, Eve. But... the Lower East Side had its own charm if you could block out the bad stuff. There were immigrants everywhere, Jews, Irish, and Italians. Everyone worked hard and pulled their way out of poverty in sweatshops. Ground-floor shops lined the streets. I used to go roaming about them with my lads. There were hatmakers, matzo factories, winemakers, delis and push carts everywhere. By the time I joined the police, some of those people did well enough to move to Brooklyn, Queens, the Bronx, and even the suburbs."

"So, do you think this woman came from there?"

"I don't know. Let's not get ahead of ourselves. The woman may not be from that time at all. Maybe she's a little crazy or something and didn't time travel. We just don't know."

"But if she came from that time, it would have to be after 1884. Tesla didn't create the lanterns until 1884, so there couldn't be a lantern before that time. And the man who first saw her said she was dressed in turn-of-the-century clothes."

"He was probably guessing," Patrick said.

Eve put her phone down. "So… Are you thinking what I'm thinking?"

"Do you want to go see her?"

"Yes, visit her. Talk to her. Try to help her."

Patrick returned to his chair and massaged his forehead. "Now, wait a minute, Eve. Let's think about this and not jump the gun."

"We can at least go talk to her. If this woman did time travel, then I know how she feels. You know how she feels. It's a nightmare."

Patrick sighed. "Eve, as I said, she may be just an unfortunate woman who has taken leave of her senses. She may need medical help. We're speculating that she time traveled."

"So, let's go find out. We'll know for certain after we ask a few questions, right?"

Patrick turned his eyes up. "Do we really want to do this? We just got rid of that lantern back in October. We're finally free of the entire time travel business. I, for one, am not eager to get back into it, in any shape or form."

Eve pushed her chair back, pondering. "Patrick, I want to help her if I can."

"And how will you accomplish that? By telling her we have time traveled, too? I don't think it will help. And what if she falls apart and tells the police about us? That we have time traveled too."

"We don't have to tell her everything. We can use discretion."

"And will you invite her to stay with us if she has, in fact, time traveled and has nowhere else to go? As if I don't know the answer to that question."

"If it comes to that, yes."

"Without knowing who she is and what her character is?"

"We'll know all that when we talk to her. You can talk to her. You were the detective. You'll know."

Patrick didn't release her eyes. "I don't like it, Eve. And there's something else I don't like."

Eve spread her hands. "And that would be?"

"It would be something I haven't shared with you."

"Okay... Why? So, share it."

Patrick rose again. "Let's go into the living room and sit by the fire. We can clean up later."

Eve's eyes were direct and intense. "I don't like it when you keep things from me, Patrick."

"I was going to tell you... at the right time."

"Okay, well, this is the right time."

He pointed toward the living room.

Eve pushed up and followed Patrick into the living room, a much larger room than the one in their old apartment on West 107th Street. Eve sat on the sofa that faced the fireplace and Patrick sat in one of the two chairs to the right of her, resting his legs on an ottoman. The room was a comfortable mix of mid-century pieces with antique rugs and a brown marble working fireplace.

"I'm all ears," Eve said.

Patrick tried to appear at ease, but he was nervous. "Back in October, we donated our lantern to The Bus Stop Café. That was the lantern from Tesla in 1884; the lantern you retrieved from Abagail Tannin in 1884, right?"

"Yes."

"The same lantern that Joni willed us, and we received in the mail."

"Yes."

"Bear with me. This is complicated," Patrick said. "I used that lantern to time travel to 1925. Now, that lantern has been donated to Stephanie Gray. But… now stay with me here. Joni willed the 1925 lantern, the one I used to return here in 2020, to Lavinia."

"I'm with you so far," Eve said, wondering where he was going with the conversation.

Patrick scratched his head. "All right, then. I read in the paper a few days ago that Morris Kennan Vanderbilt passed away."

Eve didn't stir. "Okay… And?"

"He was sixty-six years old, and he was the grandson of Lavinia Vanderbilt, and the son of Alexander Vanderbilt, who was Lavinia's only son."

Eve tilted her head, thinking. "Go on."

"I think you know where I'm going with this, Eve. I'm thinking about *that* lantern. Lavinia's lantern. Remember Joni's letter to us last Christmas Eve? She wrote, 'So where is the lantern? No idea. Perhaps Lavinia will use it someday? Perhaps her descendants. Who knows?'"

"Patrick, we don't know where Joni's lantern is. Someone in the Vanderbilt family probably has it. We'll never know."

"I don't like coincidences, Eve."

"What coincidence? I'm not getting it."

Patrick lowered his feet and sat up. "A woman appears who may have time traveled at the same time Lavinia's grandson dies. We just got rid of our lantern. So why is my head clear but my thoughts are jumbled? Something doesn't feel right. I feel Tesla's mischief behind all this."

"Come on, Patrick. Nikola Tesla is dead. He wasn't a god, all-powerful and all-knowing. He created those lanterns as toys, as an experiment. He didn't entirely know how they'd perform or what would happen to a person if they lit the lantern."

"I still don't like coincidences, Eve. It's the former detective in me. My nose tells me something is off."

Eve's gaze wandered while her mind pondered his words. "All right, let me understand this—what do I call it? A once-upon-a-time story? Okay, number one, our lantern is gone; Stephanie has it. Good luck, Stephanie. Two, most likely the Vanderbilts have Joni's lantern; that's the second lantern you used to time travel back from 1925 to 2020. Morris Vanderbilt has just passed away... but we've heard nothing about a Vanderbilt lantern. Third, we just read about a woman who may have time traveled sometime after 1884. Conclusion: you think there's a connection?"

Patrick made a pyramid of his fingers, brought them to his lips and looked at Eve from over the top of them. "I don't know. Maybe."

When Colleen cried out from her room, Eve turned toward the sound. "Colleen's awake. She'll be hungry." Eve stood up. "I still want to talk to the woman, Patrick. I still want to help her if I can. Will you go with me?"

Patrick kept his steady eyes on her. "Of course, I will. But… We have to be careful, Eve. Very careful."

CHAPTER 8

Inside the Uber SUV traveling downtown, Eve turned to Patrick. "What's the normal procedure when someone gets arrested?"

"In my time, the woman would probably have been beaten up for pulling her derringer on the police. Then she'd have been tossed into the Tombs. You remember the Tombs, that dreadful women's prison downtown?"

"Yes, I remember it well. I almost ended up there in 1885."

"Anyway, back then, she would have been left in her jail cell for days, or even weeks, before she was brought before a judge. Sorry to say it, but she might have died of an inmate attack or some disease before her arraignment."

"Okay, and what about now, in 2021? What do you think has happened to our mystery woman?"

Patrick glanced out the window, watching snow flurries dance by. It was Monday afternoon. Eve had taken the afternoon off, and Patrick had yet to start his new job working for a mental health facility, The Hensel Forensic Psychiatric Center.

Colleen was with the babysitter, Pauline Clark, a twenty-five-year-old single mother and a painter/programmer, who worked from home. Her daughter, Melody, was three years old, and she and Colleen got along well. Pauline often sat them at a table with crayons, coloring books, and Play-Doh, and they happily played while she programmed or painted.

Patrick turned back to Eve. "The procedures for arrest are about the same now as they were in the 1880s. Our mystery woman was handcuffed, and no doubt escorted to a squad car. At the precinct, she was booked. She was searched, maybe strip-searched by a female officer. They'd take anything that could be used as a weapon. Her derringer, of course, would be bagged as evidence. If the derringer is an antique, that will raise suspicion."

"Not a good thing?" Eve asked.

"No. Anyway, an officer wrote down her name, her address, her employer, and so on. They'd want to verify her."

Eve pursed her lips, worried. "If she did time travel, that could be a problem."

"Yes, a big problem, especially if she's disoriented and scared."

"Okay, go on. This is fascinating. I've never been arrested."

Patrick continued. "She was fingerprinted, using a computer system, not that I have ever used one. Gone are the days of using ink. Nowadays, a scanner reads the prints, makes a digital picture of them and sends them straight into Albany's computer. If she is a time traveler, she will have a nonexistent criminal history."

"And so...?" Eve asked.

Patrick shrugged. "It will add to the cops' suspicions and to her mystery, and cops don't like those kinds of mysteries. They like to solve things, limit paperwork and move on. The mystery would be increased when she's allowed to use the phone, to call a lawyer, family member or a friend, who can call a lawyer. One is entitled to make up to three calls at the precinct. If the woman doesn't have a cell phone, well, the cops will know something is all wrong, because everyone has a cell phone. And, if she has come from the past, it goes without saying that she won't have anyone to call. The cops will hate that. They'll interview her—debrief her. I would hope she'd know enough to remain silent."

"When would they put her in jail?" Eve asked.

"First, she'd be placed in the precinct holding cell, probably alone."

"Why not with others?"

"She's too mysterious. There are way too many red flags being tossed."

"What then?"

"By law, the arraignment process is not supposed to take more than twenty-four hours, but it could take longer. I'd bet that the time between arrest and arraignment is much less than in my time."

"Would she have been read her rights?"

"Why the question?"

"I just want to know. Weren't you taught that at John Jay College of Criminal Justice?"

"Yes, my dear Eve, I was. It was on June 13, 1966, that the U.S. Supreme Court handed down its decision in *Miranda v. Arizona*, establishing the principle that all criminal suspects must be advised of their rights before interrogation."

"I'm impressed," Eve said with a cheeky grin. "You actually stayed awake in class."

He grinned back, leaned over, and gave her a peck on the lips. "Aren't you the smart, sassy lass today, Mrs. Evelyn Aleta Gantly?"

She touched his lips with a finger and batted her eyes flirtatiously. "And I love it when you call me by my full name. It makes me want to sit on your lap and have you arrest me."

He raised an eyebrow and smiled fetchingly. "We can do all that later, Mrs. Gantly, when no one is looking at us in the rearview mirror, and when a taxi camera isn't rolling."

Eve glanced out the window, her mood shifting. "I would imagine that pulling a gun on a police officer is a serious offense?"

"And you would be right. The woman would be charged with aggravated assault, a crime of the third degree. I'm fairly certain that it's an offense in which the charged person cannot be bailed. But that depends on the judge. If she's convicted, it carries a punishment of from one to five years in prison."

"Not a good thing… I wonder if our lady has been before a judge yet?"

"I don't know. They will have assigned her a court-appointed attorney, but it could be a while before there's any sort of hearing or trial. After the arraignment, she'll most likely be moved to a jail."

"Whoever she is, time traveler or not, she must be terrified."

"Or she's a career criminal who knows how to play the system. There are plenty of those around, in all times and places."

"My intuition, and that article, tells me that she's scared and lost," Eve said.

Eve looked at Patrick for approval.

He resettled his shoulders. "I believe I know the answer to this question, but I'll ask, anyway. Are you considering putting up bail for the woman?"

Eve glanced away. "Maybe… We'll see."

"I was afraid of that."

Eve faced him. "Patrick, if the woman's in distress, don't you want to help her?"

"I'm not sure. Didn't we have a similar conversation back in 1884, with regard to Miss Abagail Tannin, the same woman who told you where the time travel lantern was? At that time, you said, and I quote, 'Yes, I want to save the world. Why not?'"

Eve lifted her chin in defense. "And you said, and I quote, 'I do not believe it is idealistic, Miss Kennedy. As my old Da used to say, 'No one ever becomes poor in heart who gives freely to the sick and to the needy.'"

He stared into Eve's eyes, and they were marvelous. "Well, my dear Eve, since you've used my own words against me, and I have no further defense, I pray to the saints above that we find that this woman has been released from jail, and she is well on her way to her own blessed home. Otherwise, I think we'll both go on a journey to madness."

Eve smiled lovingly and winked. "Mr. Gantly, as my old college roommate, who was mad and crazy, used to say, 'Love the people you can be crazy with.'"

Patrick looked at her doubtfully. "We'll soon find out, won't we?"

"Look at it this way. When I was in distress in 1914, Irene Wilkes Casterbury helped me. In 1925, Sarah Finn helped you, and let's not forget that Nikola Tesla helped Joni and me in 1884."

"And he should have helped you. He's the one who gagged and hogged-tied us, figuratively of course, with his cursed time travel lanterns."

"But you get my point, Patrick. We're giving back. We're paying it forward."

"And I hope we don't regret it. Anyway, we need to be careful when we talk to anyone in that precinct. They won't trust anybody so, at least, initially, let me do the talking."

"You don't trust me?"

"It's not about trust. We first have to learn if this woman is a common criminal, or if the cops think they're being played for fools. They'll be suspicious of anyone who walks in there, especially if we're not related. If she's a criminal, they'll suspect we're ones too. If she doesn't have any ID, or if her ID states she's from the nineteenth century, well that presents another whole series of issues, doesn't it?"

Eve nodded. "Well... you're the psychologist. I'll leave it to you."

ENTERING THE FIVE-STORY 7TH PRECINCT, Patrick noticed the contemporary two-story lobby that provided a modern interface between the police and the public. He was also aware of the state-of-the-art security systems, something unimagined in the hard and gritty precincts of 1880s New York.

Patrick and Eve stopped at the Sergeant's desk and Patrick explained that they had come to speak to the woman who'd been arrested on Orchard Street.

As Patrick had expected, the Sergeant looked him over carefully, and then took his time studying Eve. "Are you relatives?"

"No, sir, we're not," Patrick said.

"Friends?"

"No…"

The officer leaned back in his chair. His name badge said he was Sergeant Nunez. He was a pleasant-looking man, with a muscular build, lively brown eyes and a soft voice, but, naturally, he was suspicious.

"What exactly is your relationship to the woman, then? Do you know her name?"

Patrick tried not to look as foolish as he felt. "Sergeant Nunez, I'm going to be honest with you. We don't know her. We read about her online."

Patrick continued, deciding to be direct. "It's not that my wife, Eve, and I are do-gooders exactly, but we thought perhaps we could help the woman in some way. Eve is a nurse and I'm a psychologist. Is there anyone we can speak to about her? The arresting officer or a detective in charge of the case?"

Eve gave Patrick a side-eye glance, impressed.

Sergeant Nunez hesitated. "I need to see some ID."

After they were provided, Officer Nunez entered the pertinent information into his computer. He picked up a desk phone and dialed a number.

Eve and Patrick were told they'd have to wait while a security check was conducted. They moved toward a row of plastic chairs and sat, watching the flow of police officers with their squawking radios, some glancing at their cell phones, some taking a hunched perpetrator toward a far door to be booked.

"Do you miss being a policeman?" Eve asked.

"Frankly, no. It's a hard, thankless job that eats away at you day and night. It clings to you like your own skin. You try to do the good and right thing and it turns out wrong. You try to help someone, and they turn on you. You try for a conviction and the courts often go against you. Most cops are good, but you have to deal with the bad ones, and sometimes you even have to work with them. No. These men and ladies have one of the hardest jobs in the city and, when they do save a life, or help a lost soul, or save a home, few will ever know it. I found it a private job, and a lonely one."

A medium-built man, wearing a dark gray suit and dark blue tie, entered the lobby from a side door and walked toward Sergeant Nunez. His suit was tailored smoothly, a perfect fit; his short, black hair, cut with care. He had a square jaw and a somber, weary expression that seemed to say, "Give me a break, already."

When the Sergeant pointed to Eve and Patrick, the man started toward them.

Eve and Patrick were on their feet as he drew up, his dark, skeptical eyes appraising them.

"I'm Detective Frank McAllen. Are you Patrick and Eve Gantly?"

"Yes, Detective," Patrick said, formally.

"Tell me why you're here," Detective McAllen said, directly.

In a straightforward explanation, Patrick used the same words he'd used with Sergeant Nunez, not deviating, not embellishing.

Detective McAllen took time to evaluate the couple, and Patrick imagined what he was thinking. Something like, "I don't have any leads. Nothing. A complete zero. Why have these people come? They say they're not family or friends. What do they want? What's in it for them?"

Detective McAllen pocketed his hands. "We can talk in a private room in back. Follow me."

CHAPTER 9

It was a small, square conference room, with one curtained window, a round mahogany table and five chairs. There were hanging color photos of uniformed policemen and women standing with smiling folks from various neighborhood events: an outside bar-b-que, an indoor Christmas party, and a schoolyard on a bright summer day, with teenagers and cops shooting hoops.

Eve and Patrick sat next to each other while Detective McAllen closed the door and stepped to a side table where small plastic bottles of water sat on a wooden tray.

He turned. "Water?"

They both said, "Yes."

Detective McAllen handed off the bottles and then sat opposite the couple, keeping his eyes on them.

"Mr. Gantly, you're a psychologist? Is that right?"

"Yes, a forensic psychologist."

Patrick saw the Detective's mouth twitch slightly.

"And you're a nurse, Mrs. Gantly?"

"A nurse practitioner."

"Sergeant Nunez told me you don't know the name of the woman you came to see. You read an article about her arrest online. You know nothing about her, where she came from or why she's here. Is that correct?"

"Yes," Patrick said.

The Detective twisted off the bottle cap, took a drink, swallowed, then took another. Eve swallowed some of hers. Patrick held his bottled water in his hand, unopened.

Detective McAllen squinted as if he were trying to peer into the couple's minds. "Why do you want to see the woman we have in custody? What do you want?"

Eve spoke up. "To help her, if we can."

"Why? You don't know her. She's a nobody to you."

Eve kept her voice soft. "Detective McAllen, nobodies often need the most help."

McAllen turned his gaze to Patrick. "Where do you work, Mr. Gantly?"

"I'll be starting a job at Hensel Forensic Psychiatric Center next Monday."

"Correct me if I'm wrong, Mr. Gantly, but your job is sometimes referred to as a Criminal Profiler, isn't that right?"

"Yes."

"And you work with law enforcement agencies to develop a profile of criminals, based on common psychological traits. Am I right?"

"That's a part of the job, yes."

"And you study the behavior of criminals and address everything from psychological theories to legal issues. Am I correct?"

"Yes, but I'll be involved in sex offense treatment, cognitive rehabilitation, trauma, and substance abuse programs. Also, group and family therapy, crisis intervention and consultation to other agencies."

Detective McAllen tipped back the bottle and took a long drink. After he'd licked his lips and set the bottle down, his expression had changed from suspicion to the dawn of understanding. "Okay, so now I think it's getting clear to me. You want to study this woman. Maybe you're writing a book or something? Maybe you want to publish a paper? Am I on the right track?"

Patrick was grateful for the suggestion. He should have thought of it. Cops are always looking for motives.

Eve kept her steady eyes on Patrick as she read his thoughts.

"You might say that, Detective," Patrick said, again not embellishing. "From what Eve and I have read, it sounds like an unusual case."

McAllen relaxed a little. "What is your degree in again, Mr. Gantly?"

"Criminal justice and forensic psychology."

Detective McAllen drained the last of the bottled water and put the bottle aside. "She's scheduled to have a full psychiatric evaluation tomorrow. So far, she has only given her first name. Annabelle. She had no purse and no identification. The derringer, which I'm sure you read about, has been evaluated."

"That was fast," Patrick said.

"Only because it was an oddity. It fascinated Ballistics. I know the guys. They did me a favor."

"What was their conclusion?" Patrick asked.

"It's an antique, a nineteenth century Remington Double Derringer, made sometime between 1888 and 1908. It measures 4 7/8 inches with two superposed three-inch barrels. Somewhat unusual for these times. It's in very good shape; has a blue finish, and the action's very strong. It was the only item found on her."

"And she pulled the derringer on the two officers who approached her?" Patrick asked.

"Yes. She threatened to shoot them if they came any closer. They'd been assigned to a Traffic Safety Team and were nearby distributing bike safety info."

"What happened when they approached Annabelle?"

"As I said, she pointed her pistol at them. Officer Lupe is a female. She gently talked Annabelle into relaxing and giving up the pistol. It took about ten minutes."

"The article we read said that cops wrestled with her," Patrick said.

"Not true. Annabelle threatened to shoot, but she didn't. As I said, she gave up the pistol without a fight."

"Was Annabelle scared?" Eve asked.

"The police report stated that Annabelle was frightened, disoriented and asking where she was, and what the date and the year were. Of course, both officers believed she'd been taking drugs, although they reported her eyes were clear."

"Have you received a toxicology report?" Patrick asked.

"Again, they did me a favor, rushing it through. I got the report just before I came to meet you. She was clean. No drugs in her system."

"Fingerprints?"

Before McAllen glanced away, Patrick saw the frustration in his eyes. "No match. No criminal record."

Patrick felt Eve's eyes on him, but he didn't look at her. "How was she dressed?" Patrick asked. "In the article, an unidentified man said she was retro dressed in nineteenth century-style clothes."

Detective McAllen folded his hands on the table. "A female officer strip-searched Annabelle. She was wearing a black tailored long skirt, a white blouse and a burgundy tailored coat, with black leather, high laced women's boots. She also wore a corset. I believe the correct name for it, according to our computer research, is an S-shaped corset. We evaluated her clothes, the labels, the style."

Eve's interest sharpened, and she leaned her head closer to the detective.

He continued, his voice clear and deep. "The label on the skirt and jacket said Lord & Taylor. On that same label, printed in small letters, it said Ladies' Mile, Broadway and 20th Street. You might know that Lord & Taylor closed its Fifth Avenue flagship store at the start of 2019. Amazon recently bought it. It will be its New York City headquarters, and the company reportedly paid more than two-thousand dollars per square foot for the property. My point is, the Lord & Taylor retail store where Annabelle supposedly purchased her clothes has not been on Broadway and 20th Street since 1915, when they moved uptown to

38th Street and 5th Avenue, the building now owned by Amazon."

Patrick's face was impassive as he screwed off the bottle cap and sipped at the water. He looked at Eve. She was absorbed and worried.

McAllen let out a little sigh. "So, what do we have here? A woman who likes to carry an antique pistol and wear old clothes that appear brand new, but she does not have a cell phone or any ID. I'd say she's gone to a lot of trouble to make herself stand out and get free publicity. Is that it?"

Patrick replaced the plastic cap and screwed it on tightly, distracted. "I suppose you did a social media search for the name Annabelle?"

"Yes. No match. We're working on a facial recognition match. Nothing so far."

"Has anyone, a friend or family member, called or come to visit Annabelle?" Eve asked.

Detective McAllen scratched the end of his nose. "No. No one, and she hasn't *called* anyone, and her name is probably not even Annabelle. Like I said, she has no cell phone. Nothing, just that derringer. She's also not talking to anyone, including me. She refuses."

"Is she still wearing her street clothes?" Eve asked.

McAllen nodded. "For now... Yes."

"Can we see her?" Patrick asked. "Talk to her?"

McAllen saw Eve was deep in thought, and that intrigued him. He didn't entirely believe the Gantlys' story, but he couldn't come up with a good alternative motive.

McAllen said, "I'm sure, Mr. Gantly, you know that persons in holding cells cannot have visitors. They can take calls."

"Can we post bail?" Eve asked.

Patrick wished Eve hadn't brought it up. At least not yet.

McAllen shook his head, his eyes shifting from Patrick to Eve. "She's been charged with aggravated assault, and she can only be bailed if the judge approves it."

Eve nodded. "I see."

"I can arrange a phone call, if she agrees to it," McAllen said. "Maybe she'll talk to you. Maybe you'll learn something. We're not getting anything from her."

"When does she see the judge?" Eve asked, not knowing the correct terminology.

"Tomorrow morning."

"Does she have an attorney?" Patrick asked.

"Yes… I know her. Her name's Amy Metzger. In her early thirties. Nice enough. Smart. Dedicated. Maybe too much dedication, but I'll let that go. Annabelle hasn't spoken to her either."

"Does Ms. Metzger have any theories?" Eve asked.

"None that she's shared with me. She's frustrated that Annabelle won't talk."

There was a brief silence before McAllen said, "Do you want me to ask Annabelle if she'll talk to you?"

Patrick faced Eve. She nodded.

McAllen rose. "All right. I'll go ask. It might take a few minutes. Bathrooms are down the hall to your left."

Before he left the room, Eve said, "Detective McAllen, when you speak to Annabelle, please tell her that I said this: lanterns aren't all the same."

Patrick shot her a severe glance.

McAllen hesitated, pondering. "What was that? Lanterns aren't all the same?"

Eve lowered her chin. "Yes…"

"I don't understand," McAllen said, looking to Patrick, who shook his head as if he didn't understand either.

When he moved his questioning gaze back to Eve, she smiled enigmatically, but said nothing.

When McAllen was gone, Eve's restless eyes met Patrick's. "So now we know, don't we?"

Patrick held her gaze. "We don't know anything for certain, so let's be on our guard until we know what this is all about, and who this Annabelle is."

CHAPTER 10

Detective McAllen returned to the conference room fifteen minutes later, more curious and suspicious than when he left. After he closed the door behind him, he stared soberly at the Gantlys, letting the silence draw out.

Patrick knew the bit about the lantern would puzzle and provoke McAllen, but he'd learned long ago that Eve was her own woman, and if she could be stubborn and rash, she was also a great problem solver and a smooth talker.

McAllen finally spoke. "Annabelle has agreed to talk to you... that is to you, Mrs. Gantly, and only to you. She agreed after I repeated your words that lanterns aren't all the same. She turned pale and started trembling, and she wouldn't look at me."

He returned to his chair and sat. "Mrs. Gantly, suppose you tell me what this whole lantern thing is about. I have the feeling I'm being left out of the party... and I like parties."

Patrick turned to his wife, wondering what in the world she'd come up with. Would she lie? Tell the truth?

Eve spoke nonchalantly. "It was just a little something to pique her curiosity. That's all. Obviously, it worked."

The detective exhaled impatiently. "And you will excuse me if I don't believe you."

Eve paused, hoping the atmosphere would defrost a little. "Believe what you must, Detective McAllen. The result is the same whether you believe or don't believe. Annabelle will talk to me."

Patrick felt an anxious tension building in his gut.

McAllen's eyes hardened as he looked at her with doubt. He pointed to the phone. "You can use that phone."

McAllen gave her the number, and Eve dialed it. After three short rings, Eve heard a soft, uncertain voice on the other end.

"Annabelle?" Eve asked, sitting up, her mind searching for questions, questions for Annabelle that wouldn't further raise McAllen's blood pressure.

"Yes... Is this Eve?"

"Yes."

There was a pause.

Eve said, "Annabelle, are you all right?"

"Yes... I'm fine. Confused. So very confused."

Eve felt the burning eyes of McAllen on her. Patrick's jaw tightened.

"I understand."

"No, you don't."

"Yes, I do, Annabelle."

After a pause, Annabelle said, "The detective said you were going to tell me something about lanterns…"

"Yes," Eve said, keeping her words simple and her eyes down and away from Detective McAllen.

"Why did you mention that?" Annabelle asked.

"Why did you agree to talk to me?"

Annabelle's voice was loud with desperation. "Because I'm scared. Where am I? What's happened to me? Do you know about the lantern? Is that why you told the detective to tell me about it?"

"Yes…"

"How… What? I don't understand anything. I don't know where I am or how I got here. I lighted that lantern and… What happened?"

Eve measured her words, softening her voice. "I understand what you're saying, Annabelle."

"Understand what? I don't understand anything other than I'm losing my mind. I'm trapped in a nightmare or, I don't know, I've fallen ill or I'm having hallucinations or… I don't know what. But I certainly don't understand."

"Annabelle… I'll help you."

"Can you get me out of this jail? Out of this place?"

"Not right away. Try to relax. After you see the judge, I'll post your bail and then you can leave."

"What do I do in the meantime? I have a woman lawyer… can you believe that? And the way these people talk and dress is so strange and odd. Someone told me the year is 2021… I saw these large auto machines everywhere. I saw things flying overhead… big flying machines that roared like some prehistoric animal. I tell you, I'm going out of my mind. I'm at the end of my rope. I'm afraid they're going to send me off to some sanitorium."

"Annabelle, listen to me. Try to relax and just listen to me."

Eve raised her eyes to see McAllen glaring at her. Patrick gave her a little nod of encouragement.

"Annabelle... I can't go into details, but you're going to be fine. I will help you."

Eve sought words of explanation; words that McAllen wouldn't be able to interpret, and words that would help Annabelle understand what had happened to her.

Frustrated, Eve cupped her hand over the receiver and spoke to McAllen. "Detective McAllen, could you please step outside so I can speak freely?"

He shook his head. "No."

Eve's shoulders sagged as she dropped her hand from the receiver and turned away from McAllen. "Annabelle, listen to me. I'm going to write you a personal letter. After you read it, I hope you'll have a better understanding. Okay?"

"Yes, Eve. Thank you. I need any help I can get. I don't know what to say to these people."

"For now, Annabelle, silence."

That irritated McAllen, and he shot up. "All right, that's it. Hang up the phone."

"Bye for now, Annabelle."

"Thank you, Eve. Thank you very much."

After Eve hung up the phone, McAllen seemed to tower over her. His narrowed eyes carried a warning. "All right, I've been patient enough. Are you both going to tell me what the hell is going on here? What kind of scam is this?"

Patrick stood up, straightening to his full six-feet three-inch height, three inches taller than McAllen.

"It is not a scam, Detective McAllen. As we told you when we arrived, we are merely trying to help a woman who is in distress. Eve is a nurse and I am a psychologist. It's that simple."

McAllen was seething, knowing full well that Patrick was lying. "All right, we're finished here," he said bluntly. "I will get to the bottom of this, whatever it is. If this is some kind of scam or publicity stunt, I'll make sure you all end up in jail."

Patrick stood firm, his color rising. He'd never taken lightly to being threatened. "Detective McAllen, you disappoint me. Threats are the cheap talk of a man who has neither the perspective nor the wisdom to be patient and try to see a thing from a new point of view. But then, I understand you a lot better than you think I do."

McAllen jerked his glance away, his breathing heavy.

"May I write that letter to Annabelle?" Eve asked.

"Do as you like," McAllen said, gruffly.

And then he left the room.

IN A CAB TRAVELING UPTOWN, Eve looped her arm into Patrick's and tugged him in close to her. "Well, that was stressful. I had to mention the lantern, or Annabelle would have never talked to me. And I knew that if she wouldn't talk with me, she hadn't time traveled, or, at least, she hadn't used the lantern to time travel."

Patrick lifted an eyebrow. "You shook me up so much back there that I need a pint of Gat."

"Now, that's a new one. What's Gat?"

"Gat's another name for Guinness. Anyway, I felt a little sorry for Detective McAllen. I know how he feels."

"We couldn't tell him the truth, that I used a Nikola Tesla lantern and time traveled to 1885 and met you. And I couldn't have said, Oh, and by the way, Detective McAllen, my husband, Mr. Gantly, was a detective sergeant in the New York Police Department way back in the 1880s. That's why we know about the lantern that surely flung Annabelle into the future from some unknown past."

Patrick faced his window. The light snow had turned to rain, and everything appeared gray and slightly out of focus. "What did you write in your letter to Annabelle?"

"I told her to say that she was confused and couldn't remember anything that had happened to her."

"Good advice. Otherwise, they might send her off to a psych hospital."

"How much do you think her bail will be?"

"I'd guess her attorney, Ms. Metzger, will plead that confusion and fear were motivations for Annabelle drawing and pointing the derringer. No doubt she'll tell the judge that Annabelle hasn't any prior arrests, and that she was only trying to protect herself. Then she'll say that they're waiting for the psychological evaluation. So, as you people in this time would say, if we cut to the chase, I'd guess the judge will grant bail, and that it will range from between two and five thousand dollars."

"That's a rather broad range, isn't it?"

Patrick looked at her and shrugged. "It's the best I can do. I'm not a policeman in this time, Eve, and they've recently changed the bail laws."

Eve eased back in her seat. "So, we'll know tomorrow whether we can keep Annabelle out of jail until her hearing, or whatever."

Patrick patted her hand. "I suppose you're going to bring her home?"

"Where else can she go? I know that feeling of being utterly and completely alone in another place and time. You've experienced it, too."

"But we know nothing about her," Patrick said, struggling to keep exasperation from his voice.

"We know she dresses well, and that she speaks well. My best guess, based on the description of her clothes, is that she comes from the late 1800s or the turn of the century, from say, 1900 to 1910."

Patrick shut his eyes and let out a breath. "I wonder how she got hold of a lantern."

"I've been wondering the same thing."

"What will we do with her?"

"I have no idea," Eve said.

"Shouldn't we form some kind of plan?"

"Yes, we should. Of course, we should."

Eve leaned her head against Patrick's shoulder. "If we had a lantern, maybe we could send her back to where she came from."

"If is a big word, my love. And she may not want to go back."

"From the sound of her voice, I think she'd go back in a heartbeat."

"That was then. Once she adapts to this time, she might think differently."

Eve turned her head and looked up at him. "Like you, you mean?"

Patrick opened his eyes and gave her a side-ways glance. "I'm not getting into this argument again."

"We don't have to argue. But if you weren't married to me, would you use the lantern to travel back to your own time?"

"We have this same conversation about once a month, Eve, and every time I say the same thing."

Eve sat up. "Oh, no, no, no, Mr. Patrick Gantly. You have said, 'Yes, I would go,' and 'No, I wouldn't,' and 'Who knows,' and, 'Why even discuss it, because it's never going to happen.' So, what is it?"

Patrick closed his eyes again and held up a hand to placate her. "Eve... after all this time, you still have to test me, don't you?"

"You're evading the question."

"I'm going to do what you told Annabelle to do. I'm going to remain silent, except to say, we have to stop at the market to buy milk, eggs and a pumpkin pie."

Eve settled back onto his shoulder. When she spoke, her voice held mild anxiety. "Will we ever be able to forget about those lanterns and live a normal life?"

"My love, how can we live a normal life, when our life has never been normal? Let's not forget that I come from the nineteenth century, and we have a daughter who was born in 1884."

Eve noticed the gray-haired cab driver's startled eyes were gawking at them through his rearview mirror. She grinned at him.

CHAPTER 11

Two days later, it snowed three inches. The sidewalk Christmas tree stands were busy, Christmas carols were playing in all the drugstores and gift shops, and there was a festive holiday mood in the crisp, cold air.

Eve and Patrick Gantly waited for Annabelle inside the 7th Precinct station lobby, having been told that they would release her on Wednesday morning at 11 a.m.

Annabelle's attorney, Amy Metzger, had pleaded Annabelle's case just as Patrick had said she would: Yes, Annabelle had drawn the derringer and she had pointed it at the two police officers, but only because she was frightened and disoriented. Because she lacked any records, Annabelle obviously had no prior arrest convictions.

Annabelle's psychological evaluation had been conducted, but the report had not yet been forwarded to the Court because of a backlog. The judge had granted Annabelle bail at $2,500, with a hearing date of Wednesday, February 2, 2022.

While Eve and Patrick stood waiting for Annabelle, Patrick shoved his anxious hands into his overcoat pockets and Eve blinked about, her face creased with anxiety.

When a far door opened, a middle-aged, uniformed policewoman emerged, escorting an attractive woman, who appeared to be in her late twenties. The woman glanced about, fearfully, as if she were about to be attacked. She was pale, showing signs of strain and fatigue, and her lustrous, chestnut hair was twisted up and pinned in an old-fashioned way, suggestive of the early twentieth century.

The last time Eve and Annabelle had spoken on the phone, Eve had taken down Annabelle's sizes. After ordering several outfits on the internet, Eve had sent Annabelle underwear, a pair of thick leggings, a cowl neck cream-colored sweater, and a stylish winter jacket.

Carrying a plastic bag with her old clothes inside, Annabelle seemed to float toward Eve and Patrick, looking frail, melancholy and very ill-at-ease.

Eve saw fear in her eyes, and Eve could almost smell the fear. She'd experienced what Annabelle had just been through—time travel—and she knew it in the very marrow of her bones. During her first time travel experience to 1885, Eve had learned about the size of her courage, and it was a lot smaller than she'd believed. Watching Annabelle approach, Eve was sure that this woman had discovered the same thing, and from all appearances, it had been a brutal lesson.

Patrick noted that Annabelle's eyes held watchful intelligence; she was poised, and she glanced at him with sudden interest. Whether that interest held attraction or curiosity, he wasn't sure.

The female cop left Annabelle at the Sergeant's desk, and Eve and Patrick moved toward her, Eve with a smile, Patrick with wary eyes.

Eve extended her hand. "Hello, Annabelle. I'm Eve Gantly and this is my husband, Patrick."

Annabelle took Eve's hand. "How do you do. I can't thank you enough for having me released from this place. You're an angel of mercy."

Annabelle slowly batted her eyes and took Patrick in. "Mr. Gantly... a fine pleasure to meet you."

"You can call me Patrick."

Her smile was weak. "As you say, Patrick."

"Have you eaten?" Eve said. "Shall we find a restaurant?"

"Thank you, but no. I ate some earlier. I'm afraid my stomach hasn't been quite right since... Well, since I arrived here."

"Shall we go then?" Patrick said.

Annabelle directed her gaze toward the front door and hesitated, anxiety rising in her eyes, tightening her face. "I'm afraid I'm not myself. There are so many machines around, aren't there? So many strange things and oddities. What will I find out there? I seem to be living in a confused, cloudy atmosphere, as in a dream."

"We're going outside to get into a taxi. You've already seen the automobiles. We call them cars."

Annabelle nodded. "Yes, I could look out my window and see them, and other wonders... the tall structures... buildings. They are so very tall, aren't they? Reaching so high, stabbing at the sky and blocking light. And so much glass, flashing in the sun. And those cars seem to be everywhere... moving about so briskly. I suppose there are no horses... wagons?"

"No, Annabelle. Here, take my hand," Eve said, reaching for hers. "We'll leave together. Just take it slow and easy."

"I'll take your bag," Patrick said, reaching for it.

In the Uber traveling uptown, Patrick sat up front with the driver, with Eve and Annabelle in the back. No one spoke as the car moved through clots of traffic, meandering around trucks, bicycles, motorized scooters and daring pedestrians crossing against the light.

Annabelle stared forlornly, her searching eyes taking everything in. She shrank back, enthralled and scared, like a child riding through a circus funhouse.

Once they were inside the apartment, Colin met them, excited, sneezing, and sniffing.

"His name is Colin," Patrick said.

Annabelle patted his head, and she began to relax. "He's young… still a puppy, I think."

"He just turned two years old."

Standing stiffly, Annabelle slowly took in the living room, the oak-plank floors, the quaint bay windows, the large screen TV, brown marble fireplace and furniture.

While Patrick hung the coats in the hall closet, Eve took Annabelle on a tour of the apartment.

The bedrooms were spacious, airy and comfortable and, in the kitchen, Annabelle stared, mute, at the stainless-steel appliances and the quartz countertops. She pointed at the in-home washer/dryer and Eve told her what they were.

"And where is this?" Annabelle asked. "I was so dizzy in that car. What part of town are we in?"

"It's West 105th Street. We moved in two months ago. We used to live on 107th Street, just two blocks over, but when our daughter, Colleen, started growing up, we decided we needed more space, so we moved here. It's been recently remodeled."

Annabelle turned to Eve. "Daughter?"

"Yes, she's with the babysitter. Colleen is two years old. You'll meet her. She's a little beauty."

When she finally spoke, Annabelle's voice was soft, controlled and weary. "I feel strange... a little faint. I think I need to sleep."

"I understand," Eve said.

Annabelle gazed at Eve sightlessly. "I have so many questions... So many things I don't understand."

"Get some sleep and, when you're feeling better, we'll talk. I'll answer all the questions I can. I have a few of my own to ask."

Annabelle nodded. "I really can't thank you and your husband enough."

"I'm glad you're with us."

Eve led her down the short hallway to the second bedroom. Inside, Eve turned back the blue comforter and pulled the curtains. "All right, sleep as long as you like. We'll be around when you wake up."

When Eve was about to close the door, Annabelle said, "Eve... can people travel through time? I mean, in this time, is it something people can easily do?"

Eve stepped back into the room. "No, Annabelle."

"But you know about the lantern. I lighted that lantern and... I went tumbling and falling into clouds, and stars, and nothingness."

"You need to sleep now, Annabelle. We'll talk later, after you've rested."

THAT NIGHT, WHILE Eve and Patrick ate dinner, Annabelle was still in her room.

"Should I go check on her?" Eve asked.

"Let her sleep. I remember sleeping for an entire day and most of a night the first time I time traveled," Patrick said, scooping up some peas.

"I'm eager to know who she is," Eve said.

"And what she left behind," Patrick added.

"I wonder if she has any family?"

"And maybe some little ones."

Eve took a sip of her white wine. "Patrick, I've been thinking. Should we go back to Kingston and get the lantern?"

Patrick stopped chewing. "I'd say, no. What's gone is gone. I don't want to court yet another possible lantern disaster."

"But what if Annabelle wants to go back?"

"Eve..."

Patrick set his fork down and leaned back. "Eve... You know there are no guarantees with that damned lantern. It could send her willy-nilly anywhere, as it did me when it sent me back to 1925. It's a cheeky, playful and unpredictable thing. Sometimes it seems a demon of a thing."

"I know, Patrick, but what if she wants to chance it?"

Patrick shook his head. "God in heaven, Eve. We decided. The lantern is gone, and I say, let it stay gone. Annabelle will have to adjust to this time and make the best of it. It will take a while, but she'll come around, just as I have done. She's been given a new life, a new start. How many people get that in this world?"

Eve nodded. "It's an ironic thought, isn't it? We get rid of the lantern and then Annabelle appears. What does that mean?"

"I don't know, and I don't want to know. As I said days ago, I don't like coincidences. Right now, I'm enjoying this baked chicken and potatoes, and I refuse to bend my mind around the mysteries of a universe that wants to snatch us by the collar, bully us and toss us back into the unknown."

Eve laughed.

"What's so funny?" Patrick asked, giving her an inquisitive squint.

"You still sound like Detective Sargent Patrick Gantly from 1885. 'Snatch us by the collar? And bully us?'"

"Yes, well, why shouldn't I sound like him? That's where I come from, and I snatched many a scoundrel by the collar and tossed him into jail."

Eve glanced at her phone, then rose. "I just got a text from Pauline. They're home. I'll go pick Colleen up. Pauline said she and Melody had fun at the puppet show."

Patrick grabbed his napkin and wiped his mouth. "No, let me go. If Annabelle wakes up, it will be awkward."

Eve nodded. "Of course. You're right."

Patrick forked the last of the chicken when the doorbell rang.

"Who's that?" Eve said, glancing toward the living room.

Patrick shrugged.

"I'll go," Eve said.

At her front door intercom, Eve asked who it was.

"UPS. Package."

There was something about the man's voice that disturbed her, and she was struck by a déjà vu moment.

Time became a weight that couldn't be moved, nor could she move.

When she buzzed the UPS man in, she felt something odd, mystical and deeply disturbing gathering inside her chest, like storm clouds rolling across the sky.

CHAPTER 12

Patrick and a tail-wagging Colin were waiting by the door when Eve returned, carrying the package into the living room. She moved slowly toward them, looking bewildered, wrinkling her forehead.

After Patrick had closed the door behind her, and Colin had wandered off to lie on the hearth near the meek fire, Eve stood motionless, staring solemnly at the wrapped rectangular box, as if it held the ashes of the dead.

Patrick murmured in an undertone. "Well, now, what have we got here? As if I don't bloody well know. You didn't give our address to that café manager in Kingston, New York, did you?"

"Stephanie Gray? No. The package isn't from her."

"Don't tell me… It's from the Vanderbilts," he said, flatly. "From Morris Kennan Vanderbilt, I'd wager?"

Eve examined the label. "It's from The Vanderbilt Estate, c/o Kenyon, Hudson and, Harwood, LLP."

Patrick sighed through his nose. "Well, that's that then. There's no mystery here. We know what's inside. You might as well open it."

Eve moved to the couch and sat down, placing the package in her lap. She sat there listlessly, unable to move.

"Do you want me to open it?" Patrick asked.

Eve glanced at him and spoke faintly. "Why, Patrick?" she said, with a dazed expression.

"I don't know why, but let's open the thing and see what we're up against."

In a frown of acceptance, Eve went to work removing the brown wrapping paper. Patrick handed her his pocketknife, and she cut through the tape and opened the cardboard box flaps. After removing the plastic bubble wrap, she set the box on the floor between her legs, reached inside and felt for what she knew would be there: the wire handle.

Holding her breath, Eve deliberately lifted the lantern from the box and rested it on her lap. Neither spoke as they gaped at it. All the old, chaotic emotions and all the old adventures and memories came flooding in.

It was Joni's lantern, the same lantern that had brought Patrick back from 1925. It was twelve inches high, made of iron, with a tarnished green/brown patina. There were four glass windowpanes, wire guards and an anchor design on each side of the roof, one anchor painted a faded red, the other a faded blue.

Patrick looked at the lantern with discontent, not allowing his mind to search for explanations. What would be the use? There was no rhyme or reason to it. No practical answer. This was a Tesla lantern, pure and simple. There was no making sense of how or why it had ended up in their possession so soon after they'd unloaded the other one, and just after Annabelle had arrived from another time and was now lying asleep in the second bedroom.

Patrick looked at Eve and he saw something fleeting pass across her face, like the shadow of a cloud moving across the surface of a pond.

"What is it, Eve?"

"It's like a bad dream. I'm sure you're thinking all the same thoughts I'm thinking."

"I'm thinking I'd like to drop the thing in the nearest sewer and let the rats have a go at it."

Eve leaned over and peered into the box. "There's a letter."

She removed and handed it to him. "It's from the lawyers. You read it. I don't have the stomach for it."

Patrick accepted the letter-sized envelope and stepped closer to the mantel, where a low fire gleamed. With plenty of light to read from a lamp nearby, Patrick slipped a finger under the flap and opened it. He drew out the letter, shook it twice and read.

"Dear Mr. and Mrs. Gantly:

Our law firm represented the interests of the late Morris Kennan Vanderbilt. I am informing you of his recent death, and of the subsequent execution of his last will and testament as it concerns you specifically.

Within said will, it was Mr. Vanderbilt's wish that you, Mr. and Mrs. Patrick Gantly, take possession of the enclosed antique lantern.

In a personal and private note to this attorney, Mr. Vanderbilt stated that said lantern had been untouched and placed in a private safe for many years. He further stated that it was his grandmother's fervent wish that the lantern be willed to Mr. and Mrs. Gantly in the event of his death.

If you have any questions or concerns with regard to this matter, please do not hesitate to contact me personally at the provided numbers, and at the appropriate hours listed herein.

Sincerely,
Richard A. Harwood
Kenyon, Hudson and Harwood, LLP"

Patrick folded the letter and replaced it in the envelope. "It seems that Mr. Morris Vanderbilt never lighted the thing. I wonder if he knew the power of it."

"I doubt it," Eve said. "I can't imagine Lavinia ever mentioned it either to her son, Alexander, or to his grandson, Morris. I wonder why?"

"Whatever the reason, the joke's on us."

"Yeah... but it's no joke. You know what just struck me? There are now three lanterns that we know about. This one, the one we gave to Stephanie Gray, and the one Annabelle used to time travel here."

Patrick shook his head. "I can't think any more about it. I need to pick up Colleen. If I were you, I'd take that thing to the bedroom closet and put it back into the safe where we kept the other one."

After Patrick had retrieved his coat from the closet and was about to open the front door to leave, Eve said, "Patrick... Why do you think Annabelle was sent into the future instead of the past?"

"For the love of God, I have no idea. Who knows where or from what year she came?"

"What are we going to do, Patrick?"

Patrick stared down at the floor. "Not a clue. My best thought is that we help Annabelle adjust, find her the means to support herself and then send her on her way, with a good luck and a prayer. What else can we do?"

Neither moved. Their minds were churning and overloaded.

"Patrick, should we tell her we have the lantern?"

"No," he said firmly. "Definitely not. First, we have to know who she is, where she came from, and why the devil she's here."

Eve set the lantern on the couch and folded her hands into her lap. "You'd better go. Colleen will start fussing."

Patrick lingered, stroking his lean jaw. "I had a thought a minute ago… We have time traveled and changed the world, in small ways, perhaps, but changed it, nonetheless. Now Annabelle will change it, let's hope in a small way. But then, what about Stephanie Gray? If she lights the lantern we gave her and is hurled off to some distant past, she will change the world as well."

Eve looked at him and tried not to let her fear show. "Yes… so, what are you saying?"

"Perhaps Tesla designed it that way. Perhaps he wanted to play God, and he designed those time travel lanterns as evolutionary devices—to change the world randomly in new and unexpected ways; to change what would have been the normal trajectory of the world's natural evolution through linear time, to a more scattered and arbitrary approach."

Eve breathed out a jet of air. "Wow, Patrick. I'm not even sure I understand that. It's not something that would have entered my practical head."

"Nor mine a few short years ago. Before I met you, my dear Eve, I was just a humble New York City detective living in 1885, thinking life existed in a somewhat predictable and comfortable square box. I never thought much about the past or the future. Now…" He lifted his hands. "I'm never quite sure what world I'm living in, nor why those blasted lanterns keep showing up on our doorstep, along with a time traveler from who knows where."

Eve stood up and went to him, stepping into his waiting arms. She pressed her head into his chest. "As long as we're together, Patrick, we'll be fine. Whatever happens, we have to make sure we and Colleen are safe and together."

"Have no worries about that, my love. I'll see to that, no matter what those bloody fates throw at us."

After Patrick had left, Eve picked up the lantern and started for the bedroom safe.

As she passed the second bedroom, she wasn't aware that the door was slightly ajar, and that Annabelle had been awake for some time, listening in. She hadn't been able to hear everything that Eve and Patrick had said, but she'd heard enough to terrify her. And she'd heard enough to know that Eve and Patrick had a time travel lantern.

She returned to her bed and lay there, staring into the darkness, hearing sirens pass in the distance; hearing the rasping sound of one of those gigantic airborne machines fly over.

Her fear was so great that she was sick with it. Every muscle was tense; every nerve on alert. She was certain that she'd gone completely mad, and she didn't know what to do about it. So, she lay dead still, cold, trembling and sweating.

CHAPTER 13

Annabelle didn't leave her room until she was sure Eve and Patrick had gone to bed. Then she crept out and wandered about, getting her bearings. She sat for a time in one of the living room chairs, found the lamp switch to her right and discovered the light was set to dim. That suited her. She leaned a hand over the side of the chair and gently stroked Colin's ears, a pleasure he loved and never grew tired of.

"You're a calm one to be so young, aren't you?"

Colin's eyes were slitted open, delighting in Annabelle's soft, caressing hand.

"And you're a doggie living in this strange and future world."

She lowered her lips to his head and kissed him there, and his eyes closed in contentment. Annabelle sat back with a little sigh, relieved to be out of that smelly, stuffy jail cell.

"Do you believe in pixies and fairies, Colin? In ghosts and things unseen? Do you believe in bad luck?

I do… It was that black cat in the alley that changed my luck. That little rascal with the golden eyes brought me the worst of luck, Colin. My mother used to say, they're genies in disguise. And now I believe it, for surely there was a genie in that lantern with its dancing, mesmerizing flame."

Annabelle stroked Colin's long ears, lost in memory. "After I saw that cat, I saw the lantern, Colin. Then I took the lantern. That's when my luck left me. And then stupidly, I went looking for that no-good, black-heart-of-a-man, Farley."

Annabelle jumped when she saw a tall shadow standing in the doorway to the living room. She brought a startled hand to her heart when Patrick entered, dressed in a blue and white flannel shirt and jeans. He wore socks, no shoes. He was tall, and he was broad, and he was so very pleasant to look at.

Yes, he was handsome, so handsome that Annabelle felt her temperature rise and her heart flutter, as they had the first time her tired and blurry eyes had first set their gaze on him in the police precinct. Now, alone in the night, the sight of him warmed her, interested her, and awakened her.

"I'm sorry if I frightened you, Annabelle," Patrick said, in a deep, rich baritone.

She wore a white terrycloth robe and the scotch plaid pajamas Eve had lent her. Self-conscious, Annabelle jerked her other hand from Colin's ears and sat up, finger-combing her tangled hair.

"I hope I didn't wake you," she said, in a breathy voice, a practiced voice that both disarmed and charmed.

"No, I couldn't sleep. May I join you?"

"Yes... Please do."

Patrick sat on the couch and Colin pushed up, gave himself a good shake, ambled over to Patrick and curled up at his feet. "I see you and Colin have become acquainted."

"Yes, what a good doggie he is."

Patrick reached and stroked his head. "He's a gentle animal, and a loving one to most, except for the squirrels and a German shepherd he often confronts during his walks in Riverside Park. They're arch enemies, and I'm afraid the German Shepherd is bigger than Colin and a bit more vicious."

"But you protect him, I'm sure, Mr. Gantly. You have the size and, I dare say, the manly strength to protect and care for the ones you love."

"... And so I do."

Annabelle swiftly changed the subject. "You have a honey of a place here. It has a cozy warmth to it, and it feels like a real home."

"Thank you. We're comfortable here. Are you feeling better after your sleep?"

"Yes, much better. Thank you. I'm still completely disoriented, but I suppose that is to be expected after my ordeal. And what an ordeal it was. I'm still feeling dizzy with it all. I feel like I'm living on the edge of a nightmare where every little thing seems foreign and strange to me. I keep asking myself if I'm somehow lost in an elaborate kaleidoscope and, instead of seeing beads, gems, seashells and colored lights, I see a brand-new world made of things I could have never imagined."

"It will take some time to acclimate yourself," Patrick said, knowing the truth of it in his gut. In some ways, he was still adjusting.

"Time is the proper word, isn't it?" Annabelle said, with a little shake of her head. "Who could ever believe in such things as leaping through time? Yes, it will take time for me to comprehend it all, if I ever do."

Patrick quietly, politely studied her. "Time would be the right word, yes."

"I'm afraid I surely look a mess," Annabelle added, again running her fingers through her hair, working to smooth it out. "My hair is so thick... well, it tangles easily in the night, because I can be a restless sleeper, and I must fuss with it with great patience in the morning. But I have been told by gentlemen that my hair is one of my most attractive qualities."

Patrick smiled, aware of her coy flirtation. He noted that Annabelle had a cool, seductive quality about her, as well as observant eyes that missed nothing. He'd noticed her watchfulness from the first moment she'd stepped into the precinct lobby, looking scared and mystified. This told him it was a genuine quality of her personality, surely refined over time, but natural, nonetheless.

Ever the detective, and now a psychologist, Patrick began evaluating Annabelle, making himself a part of the action and yet above it, as if he were witnessing the scene. This had become a genuine quality of *his* personality that had been developed during his time on the New York police force working as a detective in the 1880s.

Patrick played close attention to the selection of Annabelle's words; the elegant movement of her feminine hand and the tilt of her head as she posed, calculating his response to her.

"How long have you and your wife been married?" Annabelle asked.

"About four years."

"I am looking forward to meeting Colleen. I believe you said she's two years old?"

"Yes, a little over two."

"Well, Mr. Gantly, it seems you are a lucky man."

"Please call me Patrick, Annabelle. Society is not so formal in this time."

She allowed her twinkling eyes to linger on him. "It's yet another aspect of this time I must get used to."

"If it's not too forward, Annabelle, what is your last name and what year did you come from?"

Annabelle held his eyes, feeling her attraction for him expand. "It seems absurd now… but before I awakened in that little park off Orchard Street, it was October 1904. My last name is Palmer."

Patrick's concentration sharpened, but he didn't speak. She waited for him to say something and, when he didn't, Annabelle said, "It seems like you and your wife know about these time traveling things. And you have what I think is an Irish accent, although it's not so prevalent."

"Yes, my accent has faded somewhat from what it was."

Patrick decided not to tell her he'd time traveled from 1885. It was more information than she needed.

"Are you from Ireland?" Annabelle asked.

"No, I was born here in New York. My parents were Irish."

Annabelle gave him a hint of a smile. "You must know that I have so many questions."

"As do we."

"Your wife, Eve, wrote in her letter that you both know about these lanterns, and that they have some fairy or gypsy magic."

"It's not from fairies or gypsies that the magic comes, Annabelle, but the lanterns do have great power. Have you heard of the scientist Nikola Tesla?"

Annabelle turned the name around in her head. "The name is somewhat familiar. It seems I recall reading something in the newspapers about a man who might have been the man Tesla. He was building a tower with the financial help of J. P. Morgan, but I don't recall any details."

"Yes, that's correct. It was to be a tower that would help Tesla achieve wireless transmission—that is, transmission of energy without the use of electrical wires. The phones we use now are wireless telephones, and that's thanks to Tesla. Anyway, Nikola Tesla created time travel lanterns as experimental toys. When one is lighted, it sends the people who are near it off on a time travel journey, if they are susceptible. I know that sounds like the stuff of fables and fairies, but… well, you have experienced it, so you have your own truth." Patrick spread his hands. "And here you are."

Annabelle lowered her gaze. "So people in this time have lanterns that enable them to travel freely through time?"

"No… And this is difficult to explain. As far as we know, only a few of these lanterns were created. Eve and I know of only two… Well, three now, since a lantern sent you here from 1904. Annabelle, where did you find the lantern?"

Annabelle paused, taking on an introspective innocence, something Patrick was skeptical of. She was not the shy, retiring type. That he was sure of. He waited, sensing her vital, sharp mind was at work, concocting a story. But why? Why was she hesitating?

Although Annabelle's thoughts were still hazy and scrambled, years of living and working with peculiar people in a traveling circus, and years of surviving off her wits and honed skills on the streets of New York, had made her careful and calculating. Her self-preservation instinct was still very much alive. She must make the best impression she could with Patrick and Eve. After all, her very life might depend on it.

"I purchased the lantern at a shop," Annabelle said, lying. "It was a fine, reputable shop, and the lantern was not inexpensive."

"Did the person who sold it to you tell you anything about it?"

"No... There was no explanation whatsoever."

"What attracted you to it?"

"I thought it was handsome to look at, I suppose. I didn't need it but purchased it on a whim."

Patrick looked straight at her. "Are you married, Annabelle?"

Annabelle didn't have a ready answer, and she should have. Normally, she'd have created an entire back story, with names, places and dates. But she still wasn't herself, was she?

Hesitating would suggest lying. She had to speak up, improvise and hope for the best. "Yes... I'm married to a fine man."

"Do you have children?"

"Just one. Her name is Eliza."

"How old is the little girl?"

"She is… I mean, she was a little over three, not much older than Colleen."

"You must be in great distress," Patrick said, feeling compassion for her.

Annabelle had lied to gain sympathy, and from Patrick's softening expression, she saw it had worked. Now, she needed to keep him off-balance, to gain and maintain an advantage.

"It is a genuine feeling and my frank impression, Patrick, that you do not beat your wife, do you?"

Patrick thought it a strange question. "No, I don't."

"And it's easy to see that you and your wife are in love. That kind of love is rare in any time, I'd presume."

"Perhaps. Yes. Tell me about your husband and little girl."

Annabelle's mind was sluggish and too unreliable to continue creating stories. She knew that once a lie was told, she'd have to remember it in every detail.

Annabelle put a hand to a yawn. "Pardon me, Patrick, fatigue seems to be taking me again. May we continue our talk tomorrow?"

"Of course, Annabelle. We have plenty of time."

Patrick rose, Annabelle followed.

"Thank you again, Patrick, for all you and your wife have done for me. May I ask, what type of work do you do?"

"My official title is forensic psychologist. You may not know what that is."

Annabelle groped for words, not wanting to appear ignorant. "I seem to have heard the word, psycho..." she stopped, unsure how it was pronounced.

Patrick spoke up, seeing she was struggling. "Simply put, psychology is the scientific study of the mind and behavior."

Annabelle nodded in slow comprehension. "That doesn't sound so simple. What was that other word you used?"

"Forensic. Forensic psychology is a branch of psychology which relates to the law."

Annabelle stiffened, keeping her face under tight control. "The law?"

"Yes. Forensic psychologists are often called to investigate crime and criminals, and to testify in court."

Annabelle forced a little smile, although inside she felt a chill, a dread. Of all the places to end up, how was it that she had ended up in this place and with this couple, and with this man who was connected to the law?

"How fascinating," she said casually.

Annabelle needed time to think. Again, she yawned. "Please excuse me. I must get more sleep. It has been so very pleasant speaking with you, Patrick."

She walked around him and down the short hallway to her bedroom, closing the door softly.

When Patrick slipped into bed, careful not to awaken Eve, he rested his head deeply into his pillow.

"So, what did she say?" Eve said softly, turning toward him.

"I thought you were asleep."

"I'm not. I'm wide awake. Talk to me."

Patrick released a little sigh. "She's from 1904."

"I don't know much about that time. She's quite pretty, isn't she?"

"Yes, quite an attractive woman."

"What else?"

"I can't quite put my finger on it, but there's a practiced shrewdness about her. For a woman of her time, she is not demure or retiring, and I feel as though that is what she is trying to project."

"Is that a bad thing?" Eve asked. "Not to be demure or retiring?"

"No, not in and of itself, but she strikes me as a bit duplicitous. I sense an ambitious, bright, and self-possessed lady, traits of a more modern woman. And let's not forget that two-shot derringer she pointed at the cops."

"So, what are you saying, Patrick?"

Patrick wrapped an arm around Eve's shoulders and pulled her close. "Oh, I don't know, my love. Maybe nothing… but I don't entirely trust her."

"Did you check on Colleen?"

"Yes, just before I came in. She's sleeping soundly."

CHAPTER 14

Annabelle knew her strengths, and she also knew her weaknesses. She knew the emotional battleground of her inner world, and she also knew how to survive the brutality of the outer world. She was a successful survivor in 1904, and she'd developed her skills largely on her own. But here, now, in this strange time and place of 2021, what could she do? How could she survive? How could she turn bad luck into success and profit?

She switched on the bedside lamp and sat on the edge of the double bed, her bare feet on the tan carpet, and stared at a large black-and-white photo hanging on the wall, depicting a flock of pigeons flying above the New York City skyline. It appeared to be an old skyline, a familiar one to her, probably from the early twentieth century.

Was she trapped? Yes, for the time being, she was. She had no money and nowhere to go. And, if that wasn't bad enough, she was supposed to return to court in February and possibly face jail time. She had to devise an escape plan before then.

She'd once been tossed into a jail, caught for stealing when she was eighteen. It had been a devastating and brutal experience. After months of filthy quarters, beatings, and barely edible food, she'd nearly died. She *would* have died if her father had not rescued her. It was the one and only time in her life that he'd been there for her and actually helped her. Having just won a big pile of money in a back-alley card game, he'd used most of it to pay off corrupt and greedy officials to get her released. Well, God love him for that.

Afterwards, he'd given her some valuable advice. "Now listen to your old dad, Annabelle. You better get your stealing skills sharpened up or you'll spend your time walking the night streets for money or dying in some rat-infested jail." He'd smiled and patted her arm. "And dearie, I know you'll pay your old man back someday when you're flush, won't you? I'll be looking for it and needing it, whenever you have it."

Annabelle stood up, walked to the wall and studied a 5" by 7" framed color photo of Patrick that sat on a chest of drawers. He was sitting on a park bench reading a newspaper, glancing up into the camera, obviously surprised by the photographer, probably his wife, Eve. It was his eyes that held Annabelle's attention; one of his qualities that she found attractive and revealed a great deal about him. He was a man of tenderness, and yet also a man of fierce emotions. If provoked, those emotions would surely pump out manly strength and aggression. The tenderness aspect intrigued her; the evident aggression excited her.

Annabelle looked at herself in a round wall mirror which hung over the chest of drawers. She wet her lips and studied her face. Men had always found her attractive, a fact she'd realized at a young age. More than once, she'd paid the price for being alluring, but after her devastating marriage, she'd learned how to control it, how to finesse and focus it, how to use it at the right time and in the right place. She had a talent for getting what she wanted from men, and she'd used it many times.

She wondered, with a mounting pleasure, if she could use her practiced skills to entice Patrick to fall in love with her or, at least, to get him into bed—any bed in any convenient location that would serve the heated, erotic moment. She thought so. While she imagined it, she played with her hair, sweeping it seductively to one side, imagining herself staring into Patrick's eyes.

Men were so easy to seduce, such weak, lusty creatures. If she approached them at the right time and place, they inevitably fell under her spell and readily did whatever she commanded. All it took was a sultry gaze, the soft brush of a fingertip, or the spicy word delivered at the perfect time.

She turned and walked back to the bed, her thoughts of Patrick expanding into delicious fantasy. If she seduced Patrick, the solutions to her other problems would inevitably fall into place—or at least she'd have some fun.

Annabelle turned off the light and lay down in the luxurious double bed, drawing the quilt up to her chin, burying her head deep into the softest, most comfortable pillow she'd ever felt. And then, just as daylight dawned, she drifted off into rapturous sleep.

Annabelle awoke a little after 9 a.m., and she wandered sleepily into the kitchen, where Eve was stirring a pot of oatmeal. Annabelle looked her over from head to toe, noting her fitted jeans, white turtleneck sweater, and red and blue sneakers. Annabelle was especially taken by the tight jeans, and she wanted a pair.

Eve glanced over. "Good morning, Annabelle. Feeling better?"

Annabelle nodded, crossing her arms across her chest. "Yes, much better, thank you."

"Would you like some coffee?"

"That would be wonderful," Annabelle said, inspecting the kitchen. "I wouldn't know where to start or end in this kitchen. I couldn't even imagine it."

Eve set the spoon aside, reached for the coffee pot, poured coffee into a red mug and handed it to Annabelle. "Milk or sugar?"

Annabelle shook her head. "I like it black... full strength, especially this morning."

"Do you still feel you're dreaming?" Eve asked.

Annabelle allowed her nose to hover over the coffee. "Smells heavenly. Dreaming? Well, it was nightmarish, if I'm honest. Now I feel as though I'm lost in a peculiar wonderland; maybe I've fallen down a rabbit hole, like Alice. Do you know that story?"

"Yes," Eve said. "Everything seems logical, but it's all just a fantasy."

Annabelle nodded in recognition. "Yes, that's it. My being here seems like an elaborate fantasy, and yet it's so real. The worst part is that I don't understand why I'm here, or why it has happened."

"Perhaps there isn't a reason, Annabelle. Maybe it's all part of an experiment by the fates or some mad scientist. By the way, do you like oatmeal? It's a good day for it. It's only thirty-four degrees out there, and we may get a little snow."

"Oatmeal... Yes. Thank you."

"I also have whole wheat bread, apples, bananas and lots of peanut butter. I love peanut butter and apples."

Annabelle smiled her appreciation. "Thank you. Should I change into morning clothes? My dress?"

"No, no. We're very informal in this time. Stay in your bathrobe and jammies."

Annabelle sipped the coffee while Eve dipped a spoon into the oatmeal and tasted it.

"You're a nurse, aren't you?"

"Yes."

"When do you work?"

"Usually Mondays through Fridays, but I took yesterday and today off. I'll go back on Monday."

Annabelle looked around. "Are your husband and daughter about?"

"Patrick took Colleen and Colin to the park. She loves to swing, and Colin loves to bark at the squirrels. They should be back soon."

Annabelle leaned against the counter. "I spoke with Patrick last night. Perhaps he told you."

"Yes, he did."

"He mentioned a scientist, Tesla, I believe?"

"Yes, Nikola Tesla."

"Patrick said it was he who invented... or created the time lanterns."

Eve turned to face Annabelle. "Yes. He somehow infused the lantern's light with the ability to send a person backward and forward through time. To anyone who hasn't experienced it, of course, that sounds like an impossible fantasy."

Annabelle groped for words. "When did this man, Tesla, die?"

"In 1943."

Annabelle calculated dates and years. "Then, how... I mean..." She stopped, seeing Eve nodding the answer.

"Did I meet him? Did I know him? Yes, Annabelle, I met him in 1884."

There was a wooden stool tucked under the counter. Feeling dizzy, Annabelle slid it free and sat, deep in thought. "My head is much clearer this morning, but I'm still lost in a kind of fog."

Eve switched off the gas burner under the pot of oatmeal. "And you will be for some time."

"So that's why you came to the jail... That's why you wrote me about the lantern. You have traveled through time using a lantern."

"Yes."

Eve reached for the coffeepot and poured herself a mug. After sampling it, she took a carton of milk from the fridge, tipped a little into her coffee, replaced the milk and shut the refrigerator door.

"Okay, the oatmeal's ready, but let's wait for the others."

She snatched her cell phone and held it up. "You've learned about cell phones, right?"

"Yes... at the police station. A woman police officer showed it to me, how it takes photographs and makes calls and sends messages. The color must have drained from my face. She asked me if I was going to faint. You see, I've never seen a Negro woman in a man's police uniform, so you can imagine how I felt. I was overwhelmed by her appearance and the cell phone. She hurried to get me some water because I nearly fainted."

Eve looked at the phone. "Yes, this thing is a kind of miracle. In a 1926 interview in one of the popular magazines of that time, Tesla basically described the modern-day smartphone, a communication device so simple we could carry it in our 'vest pocket,' as he put it."

Annabelle let that sink in. "In 1926?"

"Yes, around that same time, Tesla also predicted a lot of what has already occurred. He said women would rise to powerful positions, and now the Vice President of the United States is a woman, and she is, as we say today, a woman of color. Tesla went on to say that the fight for women's equality would end in a new social order, with the female as superior."

Annabelle's eyes glazed over and she lowered her head. "I can't seem to take it all in."

"I know how you feel. I time traveled to the past, but you have traveled to the future. Which is the more shocking, I don't know."

After a few moments of silence, Eve said, "Patrick texted we should go ahead and have our breakfast. He'll be back in about fifteen minutes."

Annabelle lifted her head. "You returned… From the past, I mean. How did you return from 1884?"

"It's a long story… but basically I found a time travel lantern there."

Annabelle flashed on Eve's and Patrick's conversation from the previous evening. They'd received a lantern from a deceased man, and it was somewhere in the apartment. Would Eve and Patrick let her use it to return to her own time? Right now, she certainly didn't want to stay in 2021. Her way of surviving in 1904 would never work here. People here were being watched all the time. How did common thieves like herself survive?

Eve spooned out oatmeal and they carried the breakfast food to the dining room table. After they'd each taken a few bites, Annabelle looked at Eve with soft, innocent eyes. "Eve," she said, "do you possess a time lantern that would allow me to return to my own time? To my dear husband and beautiful child?"

Eve searched Annabelle's face. Annabelle's was a simple, predictable question, and yet Eve suddenly felt suspicious. Why? Was it because Patrick had said he didn't entirely trust her? Or was it a sixth sense she'd developed over the years, working as a nurse with people from all social classes and economic backgrounds?

She decided not to answer the question.

"Annabelle, what is your husband's profession?"

Annabelle didn't hesitate. Just that morning, she had created a story for her life in 1904. "Haberdasher… that is, he sells men's clothing at the Siegel-Cooper Department Store. Do you know of it?"

"No, I don't."

"Were you a housewife?" Eve asked.

"Oh, yes. I stayed home and took care of our daughter. I'm sure your husband told you about her. Little Eliza. She's the apple of her father's eye. Such a little beauty."

"You must miss them terribly," Eve said.

Annabelle gave her a slow, sad smile. "Oh, yes... So very much."

Just then, the apartment door opened, and Eve heard Colleen cry out with excitement.

"We're home, Mommy!"

Colin came romping into the dining room, barking his greeting, nudging Eve with his cold, wet nose, and then sneezing.

"Calm down, Colin," Eve said. "Take it easy... Easy, puppy boy."

Eve looked at Annabelle. "Now, you'll get to meet Colleen."

Annabelle brightened. "How delightful."

Eve and Annabelle rose as Patrick entered, still tugging off Colleen's coat. She peeled off her white hat, held it in her pudgy hands, and then stopped on the edge of the dining room, staring up shyly at Annabelle.

"Good morning, Colleen," Annabelle said, with a friendly smile.

Eve said, "Colleen, meet our guest. This is Annabelle."

Colleen avoided Annabelle's eyes, twisting back and forth.

"Say hello to Annabelle, Colleen," Patrick said. "Come on, little lass, you can do it."

Colleen spoke in a small, timid voice. "Hello..."

Annabelle's expression changed from anticipation to instant attraction, her face opening, her mouth softening, her eyes shining. "Oh, my... What a little darling. What a perfect darling she is."

Eve and Patrick watched as Annabelle's eyes misted over and then leaked tears. They exchanged sympathetic glances, each thinking Colleen must remind her of her own daughter, Eliza.

Annabelle felt a sudden stabbing in her heart as the past returned in a flash of violent fists, slaps and shouts. She felt the stinging pain, the metallic taste of blood from a split lip, the hard punch to her stomach. She saw herself fall to her knees, the breath beaten from her. She'd tried to protect her baby, the baby she was carrying, but the blows from her husband had rained down on her. He kicked and cursed her. She had tried to protect the baby that was trapped in her body, but the baby had died, and she'd miscarried.

Hot tears flowed down her cheeks and, without a word, Annabelle turned away and fled the room. Why had she taken that damned lantern from the alley? Why had her bad luck flung her here to see this beautiful child, to be reminded of her own lost baby? Why? Just so she could suffer?

"Annabelle? Are you all right?" Eve called after her, concerned.

Eve and Patrick stood in stunned silence as they heard her bedroom door close.

Eve looked at Patrick, sadness clouding her face. "We have a lantern, Patrick. We should let her use it to go home."

Patrick watched as Eve knelt down and wrapped her arms around a confused Colleen, holding her close.

"It's all right, Colleen. Annabelle isn't feeling so well. She went to rest."

Annabelle's behavior had caught Patrick off guard. He thought for a moment before responding. "I think we should wait a few days before we mention the lantern. Annabelle's emotions are too volatile right now." He rubbed his forehead and turned toward Annabelle's bedroom. He knew in his gut that something was amiss. There was more to Annabelle than she was telling.

CHAPTER 15

It took hours of isolation in her room for Annabelle to pull herself together and regain her composure. Finally, Annabelle the Survivor returned, and she contemplated the best way to use her moment of weakness to her advantage. She knew the benefit of playing on people's emotions and sympathy; that had been a large part of her success.

She paced the room, walking back and forth beside the bed, from the window to the wall. It wasn't that her unexpected emotion and the sudden tears at seeing Colleen hadn't been real. No, they'd been very real. The encounter had caught her off guard, punching her in the gut like a fist. Her reaction had been fierce and genuine; nothing faked. There had been no acting when burning tears sprang from her eyes.

Now, she was puzzled by the event. Why had she lost her self-control? The time travel experience must have shaken her to her core, making her unsteady and vulnerable. She hated feeling vulnerable. She hated recalling those painful memories of losing her child because of that brute of a husband.

The encounter had been so unexpected, her reaction so fierce. Seeing Colleen's pudgy, round face, adorable curly blonde hair and startling blue eyes had shaken loose the protective walls around her heart. Before she knew what was happening, they'd crumbled in an earthquake of emotion. She'd wanted to cry out in a terrible desperation. She'd wanted to pull Colleen to her breasts and never let her go.

In that moment, Colleen had seemed like a shining, angelic mirage, alive with the promise of everything innocent, true and good, all the qualities Annabelle had never possessed—all the qualities she'd hoped her own child would possess; qualities that would help save Annabelle from herself and her dark past, from the demons that often came to haunt her in the dead of night, robbing her of sleep.

She stared out the window, unaware of a stooped old man walking his dog or a young woman struggling to button her coat as she rushed down the sidewalk. No, Annabelle was deep in thought, visualizing potential scenes which played in her imagination. A plot was taking shape. If she seduced Patrick, then he might return to the past with her. He would be a good one to have on her side in 1904.

Annabelle's eyes lit up. Maybe she could even persuade him to take Colleen.

ANNABELLE EMERGED from her room in late afternoon, wearing grey leggings and a black shirt Eve had bought her, along with her own high laced leather boots. She hadn't pinned up her hair, leaving it long and gleaming, resting on her shoulders, the way most men liked it. As she'd brushed it, she'd recalled what her mother used to say of the lion tamer in the circus, "He's as fine a man as God ever built for the enjoyment of a lusty woman."

Annabelle loved a challenge, and Patrick Gantly would be a great challenge. Despite his calm, self-controlled demeanor, she believed he was as wild and free as the wind, and as naturally passionate as any beast who roamed the jungles and dark forests. She'd remind him of that passion; she'd unleash it in her arms.

Annabelle found Eve, Patrick and Colleen in the living room, decorating a large Christmas tree. Christmas carols filled the air with glorious music that came from a small, standalone speaker. Colin was curled in his doggie bed near the glass-enclosed fireplace, and the room was filled with the scent of the fresh Douglas fir.

It was a scene Annabelle had never been a part of. She'd never known the comfortable charm and simple pleasure of decorating a Christmas tree with a family she loved. Perhaps she'd seen such images in magazine ads during the Christmas season; perhaps she'd passed a home and glanced through a window to see a family together, celebrating, but she'd never been in that room, never been a part of any family. She'd always been an outsider, a vagabond, a loner. The one Christmas she was married, her husband was out with his friends getting drunk. She'd been sick, cold, and alone.

For only an instant, as Eve and Patrick turned to her with welcoming smiles, she felt it. A black hole in her heart. A burning jealousy. At that moment, she hated them, their sweet smiles, their cute dog, their beautiful daughter. In that moment, she wanted them to hurt as much as she had hurt. She wanted them to feel abandoned and alone and cold.

But she forced herself to hide it, swallowing it away with a pasted-on smile and friendly, sparkling eyes.

"Feeling better?" Eve asked.

Colleen pointed at Annabelle and then up at the tree, her eyes aglow. "See? Christmas tree. Daddy got it."

Annabelle's face brightened. "Yes, and it's so beautiful, isn't it, Colleen?"

"It's bigger than Daddy," Colleen said, her arms reaching over her head.

Annabelle was demur, smiling and apologetic, pleading forgiveness for her abrupt and rude behavior that morning. Predictably, Eve and Patrick were understanding and compassionate, and they asked her to join in, and she did, placing ornaments on the tree.

Later, Annabelle snuggled up with Colleen on the couch and watched, amazed and a little intimidated, while Colleen adroitly played a game on her notebook computer. Before and during dinner, Annabelle glanced shyly at Patrick several times, but he avoided eye contact with her. Annabelle concluded he was probably uncomfortable with the lusty feelings she provoked. She'd have to be patient and choose the right moment.

THE NEXT DAY, SATURDAY, Eve took Annabelle on a stroll through the neighborhood, browsing local shops and the outside farmer's market, finally walking along the carriage path in Riverside Park. Eve noticed that Annabelle was uneasy and quiet.

When Eve asked if she was all right, she nodded, but said nothing.

That night, while they ate pizza and drank wine in the living room, Eve streamed *The Sound of Music* on their wide screen TV. She and Patrick studied Annabelle's startled reaction as the movie began. Sitting on the sofa with a blank, entranced expression, Annabelle didn't move a muscle, watching intensely while the images played across the screen.

At one point, Eve reached for the remote and paused the movie, turning to gauge Annabelle's reaction. "What do you think, Annabelle?"

Annabelle blinked rapidly, struggling to find her voice. "It's so real, isn't it? So clear and so real. I feel as though I could reach out and touch them. And the music is so marvelous. Such lovely melodies."

"It's not my favorite movie," Patrick said. "It's a bit cloying, I think. But Colleen loves it, don't you, Colleen?" he asked, raking a strand of hair from her forehead.

Colleen nodded enthusiastically. "I like the bikes, and the kids singing," she said.

"Are there many such… movies?" Annabelle asked.

"Yes, I'd guess there are hundreds of thousands of them, including foreign films," Eve said.

Annabelle stared, feeling a strange confusion of emotions. "It's hard to believe these things. They're wondrous and unsettling. I feel as though I keep blundering through doorways into one secret room after another, and nothing looks familiar."

She looked to Patrick for comfort, but his eyes were on his wine glass as he lifted it for a sip.

That night, Annabelle slept fitfully. Her dreams were filled with strange encounters with angry, threatening people; with autos speeding toward her; with snarling flying machines overhead that had wolf-like faces and glowing eyes like red moons.

Deep into the night, she finally awoke in a cold sweat and sat up, her breath coming fast, her heart pounding. Her senses were scrambled; her emotions hot with fear and dread as images passed through her mind.

This world was crowded with chaotic machines and people who scurried around like ants; it seemed dangerous and filled with hazards. There was no privacy. There were cameras and TVs and cell phones; little windows that people watched and stared at; hypnotized by movement, sound, and news. Everyone seemed to observe everyone else, in a frightening dance of salacious curiosity and paranoia.

If she didn't succeed seducing Patrick, then she'd have to get the lantern in some other way. The past could be rough and haphazard for sure, but at least she knew it; knew how to live in it and knew how to survive in it. The everyday rhythms were slower, the people more private, the sounds less grating and intrusive. And the simple fact was, she could live well in 1904, and there was a lot of money waiting for her, if she could only return.

Eve had never answered her question about whether she could use their lantern. Why not? Did Eve and Patrick want her to stay here, like a prisoner? Did they have a plan to use her in some way?

Her eyes darted around the room. They didn't seem like evil people, but you could never be sure. She inhaled deeply, trying to still her pounding heart. She had to find that lantern and light it, and soon.

CHAPTER 16

On Sunday evening, Eve and Patrick were anxious about leaving Annabelle alone the next day. Eve was returning to work and Patrick was starting a new job.

"I'll be fine alone," Annabelle said. "I'm still feeling fatigued and shaky, so I'll just take frequent naps and read one of the many books you have on that bookshelf in the living room. Don't have a worry about me."

"I'll call to check up on you," Eve said. "And there are plenty of things to eat in the refrigerator. Are you comfortable using the microwave?"

Annabelle shook her head. "I'm afraid that machine is too daunting for me right now. Perhaps in a few days."

"You have my cell phone number," Eve said. "If you need anything or have questions about anything, call me from the landline in the kitchen."

"Yes, Eve, thank you. I will."

Annabelle felt the itch to ask them about the lantern, but she didn't. She would wait a few more days and then bring it up in casual conversation.

On Monday, December 13, Eve and Patrick left for work, with Eve dropping Colleen at Pauline's on her way.

Annabelle stayed in bed until after they'd gone, then she got up, showered, dressed and made coffee, following the instructions Eve had written down. Colin stayed with her for a time, then he retreated to his bed, flopped down and went to sleep.

After a breakfast of coffee, toast and cheese, Annabelle roamed the apartment, exploring the drawers and closets, finding the safe where she supposed the lantern was hidden. She opened Eve's jewelry box, but she restrained herself. There might be hidden cameras somewhere. She looked up to the ceiling, suddenly anxious that there were cameras in the room. She saw nothing to make her suspicious, but still, she didn't want to take a chance.

At noon, Eve called, as promised, and Annabelle reassured her. "I took Colin out for a short walk to the park," she said. "He's such a nice doggie. He doesn't pull on his leash the way other dogs do. He stays close like a perfect gentleman."

"Patrick trained him well," Eve said.

WHEN EVE AND PATRICK RETURNED that night, they instinctively examined the apartment, as if aware that Annabelle had snooped around. If she had, she'd left nothing changed except the placement of some of Colin's toys. Still, Patrick was uncomfortable, sensing that she'd been in their room. His detective eyes studied the clothes and shoes near the safe. He opened their bureau drawers but found nothing disturbed.

"I think we need to come up with a plan for Annabelle," Patrick said quietly after he and Eve had gone to bed. "We should find her a hotel room or a furnished room somewhere. I don't like her being alone here day after day."

"Patrick," Eve said, "not yet. She still seems shell-shocked. She's hardly spoken since she met Colleen and fell apart. She's not in any shape to be out on her own or to time travel yet."

Patrick didn't respond. In his opinion, Annabelle did not have the ways of a mother with a child.

"I think we should talk to her this weekend," he said decisively. "Give her the option to stay in 2021 with our help, or to take her chances with the lantern."

Eve turned to him in the dark. "Okay, but I want to be sure she's physically stronger before she time travels again. And we need to prepare her. Give her some jewelry to hock in case she ends up in a different time. Explain everything that might happen to her."

"We should start the process soon," Patrick said.

"Why such a sudden change?"

"Call it my old-world professional instinct, Eve. I've known her kind before."

BY THURSDAY, ANNABELLE was growing restless and irritable. She was tired of reading and sitting around all day waiting for something to happen, tired of being cooped up in the apartment, dependent upon someone else to meet her needs. She was pacing back and forth between the kitchen and the living room, feeling a growing impatience. She glanced at the digital clock on the microwave. It was 4:06 p.m. She'd have to sit around for another two hours before Eve and Patrick returned for the big event of the day: some tasteless store-bought dinner. How she longed for a Delmonico steak and a good glass of wine in a bustling, familiar restaurant.

And Patrick was not responding to her flirtations, each time rebuffing her, avoiding her eyes or ignoring her comments. Was he suspicious of her? So far, she'd been able to hold her pleasant smile and friendly demeanor toward Eve, but her patience was wearing thin. She was a person of action, and taking Colin for walks, sweeping the kitchen floor and stacking dishes into the dishwasher was not her idea of action. It was time for her to gain access to that lantern and get back to 1904.

She had just plopped down on the couch, staring at the walls, when she heard the front door open. She managed to grab a novel before Patrick walked in. Her face lit with a luminous smile, and she quickly rearranged her mood.

"Hello, Annabelle," Patrick said, as he closed the door and rubbed his hands together. "It's cold out there."

Annabelle lifted her chin. "And did you have a pleasant day, Patrick?"

Patrick removed his blue ski cap and began unbuttoning his coat. "I'm not sure I'd call it pleasant... perhaps interesting is a better word."

"Oh? And in what way was it interesting?"

Colin met Patrick and swam his legs. "Hello, there, Colin boy," he said, patting his flank. "Have you been a good boy?"

"Yes, Colin has been the best of doggies. We went for two walks today and he was as good as can be."

After Patrick stored his coat and hat in the closet, he moved into the living room. "Now, I believe you asked why my day was interesting?"

"Yes…" Annabelle said, her eyes becoming soft and dreamy. Men had often responded to that look. "I would love to hear all about it."

Patrick ran a hand through his thick, black hair and eased down in a chair near her. He noticed that her glowing face was expectant, her warm eyes resting on him with pleasure. Instinctively, he sat back and took a more formal tone.

"Since I'm still new at my job, I'm working this week with another, more experienced employee, to learn the ropes. This morning I did an assessment session for a court report. They asked me to evaluate the intellectual functioning, suggestibility, and personality of a woman who is awaiting trial for a violent offense."

Intrigued, Annabelle sat up. "And what was her violent offense?"

"She stabbed her husband to death with a kitchen knife."

Annabelle's eyebrows lifted, her interest growing. "Oh, my. Did you speak to her?"

"I did. My mentor and I traveled by train to Medford Hills Correctional Facility for Women in upstate, New York, and we met with the woman. She was soft-spoken, calm, and cooperative. I spent about two-and-a-half hours with her."

Annabelle remained alert. "And what did you learn about her?"

Patrick breathed in and exhaled. "She's in her late thirties, from a poor family; was abused as a young woman and abused by her husband. She's angry and frightened, and she feels guilty… not for killing her husband, but for not being there for her daughter, who's been forced to live with her grandmother because of her mother's incarceration."

"It's sad, isn't it?" Annabelle said, lowering her eyes.

"Yes, it is."

"Are you going to like this kind of work?"

"If I can help those who need it, yes. If not, I'll do something else. Now, enough about all this depressing business. How are you? How are you feeling?"

Annabelle blinked slowly. "I notice the most unusual things about this time, Patrick."

"For instance?"

"Teeth. People in this time have such straight and white teeth. And I do believe that, generally speaking, people are more attractive in this time. They seem healthier."

"The health care system is good for most, but not all."

Annabelle put a purr in her tone. "Your teeth are quite attractive, Patrick."

He nodded, watching her closely. "Thank you. I had to have a bit of work done when I first arrived…" He stopped, recalling that Annabelle knew nothing about his past, and he didn't want her to.

"Arrived from where?"

"Oh, from the backwoods, let us say."

Annabelle softened her voice. "I feel so vulnerable, Patrick. So lost, without my husband and child."

"I'm sure you do."

"My husband is... I guess I can say, is... or should I say, *was*, since I suppose he's been dead for so many years in this time. Oh, it's all so confusing. My husband was a fine man; and thinking about him being gone from this world makes me dispirited and confused. You see, I miss him so, and I miss my little Eliza. I'm sure you know that a woman needs a man... well, for many things, because a woman is only mortal after all, isn't she? With mortal needs and desires? I have been lonely for him, often in the dark of night. I feel so lonely then, and cold."

Annabelle glanced away, feigning embarrassment. "I suppose I shouldn't be saying these very personal things."

Patrick eased back in the chair, and when he spoke, it was the voice of an official, a bureaucrat seeking formal questions for a government report. "Annabelle, in the last few days, have you been thinking about what you want to do?"

Annabelle masked her frustration that Patrick wasn't warming to her. She answered his directness in kind. "I want to go back to my own time. Do you have one of those lanterns that will send me back home?"

He was quiet for a moment, assessing the mood of the room. "There is something about the time lanterns you should know, Annabelle. They're not dependable."

Annabelle noted he didn't deny having a lantern. "What do you mean?"

"As mad and foolish as this sounds, the lanterns are unpredictable. You might not be sent back to the time you left. The lantern might deliver you somewhere earlier than 1904, or later. There's no guarantee. I suppose that's the way Tesla wanted it… or maybe it's just the way it turned out."

Annabelle fixed him with a cool, challenging stare. "You have time traveled, haven't you, Patrick? I feel it… I sense you're not of this time any more than I am. It's the way you speak and move. I see it in your eyes and manner. Am I right? Have you, too, come from another time?"

Patrick considered her question, and he didn't answer.

She kept her eyes on him, allowing the hint of a flirtatious smile to form on her lips, inviting him in with her lovely, warm eyes. "Your silence gives you away, Patrick."

"And you seem a worldly, bold housewife for 1904, Annabelle. And I suspect few housewives in 1904 carried two-shot .41 caliber derringers."

His words startled her, but she swiftly recovered, laughing in a rich and lusty contralto. "Oh, Patrick, you are so suspicious. It doesn't become you. I did not want to carry the derringer. It was my husband's idea. He gave it to me for the protection of myself and little Eliza. There had been several robberies committed in our immediate neighborhood and he feared for our safety while he worked those long hours at the haberdashery."

Patrick heard the practiced tone and inflection of an actress, not the authentic voice of an average housewife.

She continued. "And, yes, I can shoot. My husband taught me. And I can be an aggressive woman when I must; when it comes to the protection of my little Eliza. Surely, you can understand that?"

Patrick regarded her carefully.

Annabelle saw she was losing him. "Well... Men and women alike have called me much worse than worldly and bold, Patrick. Yes, I can be bold because bold marches. Bold gets things done. Bold doesn't waste time, and boldness cuts through to the truth of any matter, don't you think so?"

Patrick canted his head. "It depends on what the truth is, Annabelle. Tell me, what is your truth?"

Annabelle shifted a little. Was he flirting with her, or was he questioning her like a copper? Annabelle raised her eyebrows and studied his face. She couldn't be sure, but she sensed he might be flirting, and she wasn't one to resist the thrill and electric heat of flirtation. Yes, her boldness attracted him. She was sure of that now.

"My truth?"

"Yes... the truth."

Being alone with Patrick was exciting and fun. She loved the animal attraction she was feeling for him.

"Truth can shift and change. For instance, right now I feel many things about you, Patrick... things that perhaps I wish I didn't feel, or I shouldn't feel. But it is a kind of truth. And a woman feels as a woman feels, isn't that the way of it? I mean, specifically, isn't that nature's way? So, what's the use of hiding and pretending?" Annabelle concluded in a caressing, low voice.

Patrick wasn't surprised by Annabelle's flirtation, but her sudden change of personality did surprise him, from innocent to provocateur. From the first, he'd sensed a strong woman, a calculating woman, and a fiercely ambitious one.

"What do you want, Annabelle?"

She laughed again. "Stop it, Patrick. You'll make me blush. I can see it in your eyes. I saw it the first time we met. You find me attractive. All right, so why not admit it? I find you wildly attractive, as well, and I don't mind saying it."

Patrick's gaze went flat, and his mouth tightened.

Annabelle smiled with a twinkle of satisfaction. "Look at it this way. I'm at your mercy, Patrick. I have nowhere to go and no one to take care of me. You might say, I'm helpless."

"Helpless? No, Annabelle, I doubt very much if you have ever been helpless."

Patrick's chilly tone made her uneasy, and she held her chin at a proud angle. "I see you disapprove of me because I am honest and forward, because I'm a lost and lonely woman who needs some kindness and warmth."

Patrick set his jaw. "My father used to say, 'Your feet will bring you where your heart is.' Where is your heart, Annabelle Palmer, and who are you, truly? Are you really married? Do you truly have a daughter named Eliza?"

Annabelle saw his eyes change, narrowing on her in stern suspicion. To her astonishment, Patrick's expression revealed no attraction to her whatsoever; there was no carnal interest flaming in them. How could she have misread him? Was he really so principled, true and faithful to his precious wife? She'd never met a man who was.

Annabelle shifted her position, suddenly uneasy. She didn't like being spurned and rejected, and she wasn't used to it, and she had no skills for managing it. Once she'd made it apparent to a man what she wanted, she'd never been rejected. Not even by that self-righteous minister, Paul Hanley, who ran a church in Chelsea. He'd resisted her advances at first, but she'd seen the lust in his eyes; she'd seen him burning for her. One touch did it. One look and one touch of her finger on his trembling hand, and he'd reached for her. It had been delicious.

So, who was this Patrick Gantly, looking at her with a frosty stare? How dare he refuse her?

Her anger wanted to rise, but she quickly stifled it. If she didn't recover at once, she'd be trapped in this doll house apartment with no money and nowhere to go.

Her survival instinct now in charge, Annabelle easily returned to her girlish expression and innocent smile. "You must think me an awful thing, Patrick. In all honesty, I can only say that I am frightened, lost and, yes, I'm lonely. Forgive me if I've been too brazen. But you must believe me: I do have a husband who is good to me, and yes, my little Eliza waits for me in 1904, and I am pining for her, like any good mother would. I will never, ever believe that she is dead."

Patrick's face sharpened and the skin around his eyes tightened. Yes, here was the dangerous, volatile and manipulative personality he'd sensed all along. In his new and expert opinion, Annabelle had an antisocial personality disorder; she was willing to do or say anything to get what she wanted.

Patrick met her pleasant face with one of his own. "I understand, Annabelle, and I don't judge anyone. If I did, I'd have to judge myself, and that's not a pretty prospect."

Annabelle was initially encouraged by his words, but then quickly realized he was just playing a game. Patrick was a formidable enemy, and she had no further wish to challenge him.

"Patrick, you asked me what I want. As I said before, I want to go home."

"And are you willing to light the lantern and time travel to wherever it takes you?"

She nodded. "Yes… I am. I'm not comfortable here. It's not my time."

Patrick nodded in agreement. "I understand. Then I'll talk it over with Eve. We want to help prepare you for what you might encounter."

"Then you *do* have a time travel lantern?" Though she knew the answer, she wanted him to say it.

"Yes…"

The silence lengthened as they stared at each other, each thinking, each calculating, each suspicious of the other.

When Eve and Colleen came in, Colin jumped up and rushed to the door, and Patrick and Annabelle both stood, awkward and tense. Annabelle said hello to Eve and Colleen, and then she excused herself and went to her room.

Now that she knew Patrick was willing to let her use the lantern, she could come up with her own plan. There was something she wanted to take with her to 1904 and, earlier that day, she'd found exactly what she needed to accomplish her objective.

CHAPTER 17

"YOU'VE BEEN quiet all night, Patrick," Eve said. "And you didn't talk much at dinner. Annabelle was quiet, too."

"I guess I didn't have much to say."

"Is there anything you want to tell me?"

They were lying in bed with the lights out. Eve was on her back, with her hands laced behind her head, looking up, and Patrick lay on his right side, facing her.

"Yes... There is something I want to ask you. Why do you always re-stack the dishwasher after I stack it?"

"I don't always."

"Most of the time."

"Patrick... how do I say this diplomatically?"

"You're not diplomatic, Eve. Just say it."

"Okay, I think you are dishwasher-challenged."

"Enlighten me."

"It must be a nineteenth century thing. I don't think you ever quite got the hang of stacking a dishwasher. You crisscross things; the plates, the cutting board, the bowls and the pans."

"My dear Eve, when you're not around, I seem to do just fine. Magically, the dishes manage to get clean, and I put them away, and you never know the difference. Did it ever occur to you that you are controlling?"

"Yes, I know I am, and I drive myself crazy over it, but that's beside the point. You often place the smaller plates in front of the bowls. Those bowls never get fully clean. Case in point. Tonight, when I went to stack my coffee mug on the top rack, I saw that two of the bread plates were blocking the soup bowls. That's why I moved things around. That's why I was explaining my technique to Annabelle, so she'd learn the right way."

There was a long silence.

"Are you mad at me, Patrick? Am I too controlling? I'm sorry if I embarrassed you in front of Annabelle."

"Eve... We should give her the lantern and let her go."

Eve turned on her side to face Patrick. "That was abrupt."

"That's what I've been thinking. That's why I've been so quiet."

"Yeah... I figured something like that. Did something happen today when you two were alone... before I got home?"

"Don't get your jealousy up."

"Oh, it's up, Patrick. It's way up. I've noticed the way she's been looking at you. She's making it obvious. Why?"

"I don't think Annabelle is who she says she is. I suspected her from the beginning. Respectable housewives in 1904, or wherever she comes from, don't carry two-shot derringers on them. She's hiding things. I feel it, and I know it, and she knows I know it."

Eve drew close and placed a hand on his chest. "Okay... So, I assume you told her that the lantern isn't dependable?"

"Yes."

"And that she could end up in any time or place after 1884?"

"Yes."

"And you told her we have such a lantern?"

"Yes."

"And did she come on to you?"

"That was a quick change of subject."

"Did she?" Eve persisted.

"Yes."

Eve jerked her hand away. "I knew it. There is something about her I don't trust and don't like."

Eve lifted up on an elbow. "What did you do? How did she come on to you?"

"It doesn't matter. It's all about control with her, Eve. She likes to provoke and gain control."

"Is that your psychological analysis?" Eve said brusquely.

"Don't be sarcastic. And throw the jealousy away. I have no interest in the woman, and you know it. I would have seen straight through her act in 1885, without modern psychology. I saw her kind many times back in those days. They were desperate and polished on the outside, and hard as nails on the inside. I had a girl like that take a shot at me once. The bullet grazed my arm, and she got away from me and I never found her. Anyway, there's little doubt that Annabelle hasn't had it easy, not that she'll ever tell either one of us the truth of it."

Eve eased back down. "Fine, let's give her the lantern and tell her to go. I have to tell you that she really pisses me off. We were so nice to her. We posted the bail, got her released from jail, and brought her to our home. And then, behind my back, and at times even in front of my face, she flirts with you."

Eve huffed out a sigh. "Dammit! I should have listened to you, Patrick. You were right. I should have been more cautious."

"And I'm also right about the dishwasher," Patrick said, going for a joke to lighten the mood.

Eve playfully punched him in the arm. "Shut up," she said, with a little laugh.

They lay in the quiet, feeling stress creep into the room like another person, like Annabelle.

"Okay, that's it," Eve said. "Let's go to Central Park tomorrow, light the lantern, and send her on her way. The sooner the better. I don't want her here. I don't trust her. Who knows what she might do?"

"I think she'll jump at the chance to go. She doesn't like it here. She feels scared and out of her element."

"Why am I so naïve and stupid sometimes, Patrick?"

"Don't reproach yourself because you have a good and generous heart."

"Well, the next time I want to do something good and generous, stop me, please, and then let's think about it for a week or so. Promise?"

"Like I could stop you. Anyway, let's hope there's no next time."

Eve sat up, wide awake. "Do you know what, Patrick? I have a better idea. Give her the damned lantern and send her on her way, and we stay out of it. Let's not even go with her. Whatever happens to the lantern, happens. That's it. As long as we have a lantern, this kind of crazy stuff is going to keep happening."

"Let's think about this, Eve. Are you sure you want Annabelle to take the lantern and leave it on some bench in Central Park for somebody else to take?"

"Yes. I'm sick and tired of the thing. Let them deal with it. Let them have their life disrupted and kicked and batted around for a change."

"Okay, okay, take it easy."

Patrick lowered his voice to a near whisper. "We've had this same conversation so many times. We both keep cursing the lantern, Eve, as if it were some evil thing, forgetting that it was one of Tesla's lanterns that brought us together and saved Colleen's life. A lantern helped to play Cupid and bring Joni and Darius together. So, we must balance the bad with the good. In and of itself the lantern is neither bad nor good. It has a function and, when the thing is lit, it performs that function."

Eve sighed audibly. "Okay, yes, it brought us together, and that is a great thing. And Colleen is a gift. The greatest gift."

After a brief silence, Eve slid down and lowered her head into the pillow. "I'll never be able to fall asleep now, knowing who and what Annabelle is, and that she's sleeping in the next room."

"Relax, my love. She can't do anything or go anywhere until we give her the lantern."

Eve snuggled in close to him. "Patrick... I want us to have a normal life and a normal marriage. I want to bake Christmas cookies and try that eggnog recipe again, the one we made last year. I want to go play in the snow with Colleen, and I want us to have a baby and move on with our lives."

"So we will. You can bake Christmas cookies tomorrow night and I can eat them. And you can also make that Irish stew you've been promising me since October."

"Oh, right. I forgot."

"Well, I didn't forget. My mouth's watering just thinking about it."

"Okay, I'll make it tomorrow night. By then, our guest will be long gone."

Again, the silence grew between them as they tried to stop their racing minds.

Eve's voice was small. "So why haven't I gotten pregnant, Patrick? It was so easy the first time, before... we destroyed that lantern."

"Let's not fall into that pit, Eve. It's not worth it."

"Sometimes I get all mixed up about the last five years. How is it that we remember your daughter, Maggie, and that we time traveled back to 1914 and saved her from being killed by Big Jim, and yet, because we destroyed one of those lanterns, everything got reset and it never happened? During this time, Maggie never existed. I just find it so... I don't know, impossible. Is she living in some other Earth world? Are we? Are there duplicates of us?"

Patrick stared into the darkness. "It's pointless to think of these things, Eve. We'll never know how those Tesla lanterns work or how the universe works. It's all a mystery. The important thing is, we're together and we have Colleen, and you'll have another baby, a boy or a girl. It doesn't matter to me. It will all happen when it's supposed to happen, but let's not bring up the past. It comes to nothing. It's all water under the Brooklyn Bridge."

In the quiet, they heard the steam hiss of the radiator, and heard a passenger jet fly over on its final approach to LaGuardia Airport.

"Consider our time travel adventures this way, Eve. It stretched our minds and lit our imaginations, unlike anything else ever could have. We've had experiences that most people could never even conceive of, let alone believe or understand."

"It's just that those lanterns keep intruding into our lives," Eve said.

"Yes, well, let's hope this is the last of it. Once Annabelle is gone, let's hope and pray we'll close the book on Tesla's lanterns for all time."

Patrick sat up and reached for Eve's chin, gently turning it toward him. He leaned over and tenderly kissed her. "We're here, my love. Right here. Now. This, as the wise ones say, is the present moment and the only one we have, or ever will have. Let's make the most of it."

Eve kissed him deeply, passionately. When he drew back, she felt his soft breath on her face. "Patrick… I love you so much. I want to have a baby for you. For us."

"And we will. Right now, let's try to sleep so we'll have all our wits about us tomorrow. I have a feeling we're going to need them."

Patrick moved on top of her and kissed her again. Keeping her eager lips close to his, Eve whispered, "Make love to me. I need to feel you… all of you."

CHAPTER 18

Eve was up before daylight, gently leaving the bed while Patrick slept. Wearing her pink flannel pajamas, she slipped into her fuzzy slippers and reached for a blue terry robe, belting it as she left the room. In Colleen's room, she hovered, watching her beautiful girl sleep so peacefully on her side, making little muttering sounds.

In the hallway, Eve lingered outside Annabelle's closed door, feeling a sense of darkness and dread. She wished the woman were already gone.

Eve was at the kitchen counter, sipping coffee and checking social media on her cell phone, enjoying the early peace of morning, when Annabelle appeared. She was fully dressed in her 1904 clothes, with her hair piled on top of her head and pinned, a few loose strands falling artfully on both sides. Her expression was pleasant, her makeup light, her eyes clear, as if she'd been awake for hours.

"Good morning," Annabelle said, lightly.

Eve managed a strained smile. "Good morning. Did you sleep well?"

"Excellently well, yes, but I awoke early. Anxious, I suppose. Anxious and filled with a combination of fear and exhilaration."

Eve didn't respond, although she knew what Annabelle was referring to.

Annabelle twisted her hands, then let them fall to her sides. "Do you mind if I just come out and ask you directly?"

"I guess you're referring to the lantern?" Eve asked.

"Yes... The lantern. Has Patrick talked to you about it?"

"So, you haven't changed your mind about using it, despite the risks?"

"I must go. I can't stay here. It's not my time and I'm not comfortable here."

Eve didn't meet her gaze, not wanting her to see the anger in her eyes. Eve felt betrayed by the woman, and she was having difficulty suppressing it. But what good would it do now? She was leaving, and that would be the end of it. Good riddance.

Annabelle spoke up to fill the silence. "Eve, you and Patrick have been so very good and generous to me. I wish there were some way I could pay you back for all your kindnesses."

Eve looked at her, offering an indulgent smile. There was no denying it. Annabelle was an attractive woman, with soft feminine features, a slim, elegant figure, and all the right curves that men are attracted to, in any time or place.

Of course, Eve had noticed these traits before, but after her pillow talk with Patrick the night before,

Annabelle's unpredictable charm and previously concealed, menacing traits now seemed revealed. They seemed a threat, and they were false in the early morning light. Annabelle was a conniving woman, a treacherous woman, not to be trusted, despite her pleasing expression and easy, casual banter.

Eve was itching to know the truth about her—who she really was in 1904—what kind of work she did, and if she was truly married and had a daughter.

"Eve... You never did tell me about your own time travel experience... and Patrick's. You never said how you traveled to the 1880s, and how you returned. You never said how you first found the lantern."

Eve set her phone aside, reached for her cup and took sips of the coffee, composing the words she wanted to share. "I found the first lantern in an antique shop a few years ago. To make a long story short, I lit it and I awoke in 1885. Like you, I was completely confused, scared and homesick. I met Patrick there."

Annabelle's eyes opened wider in recognition. "I thought so... There's something about him. He doesn't seem like a man from this time."

Eve let that comment go, not wanting to expand the conversation.

Annabelle's curiosity was engaged by a distant possibility. "So, the lantern returned you home, to this time?"

Again, Eve wanted to keep it simple. "Basically, yes."

"So, if that is true, when I light the lantern, it should take me back to 1904. Isn't that correct?"

"Theoretically, yes."

Annabelle eased down on a stool and turned her face toward the kitchen window, deep in thought. Snow flurries drifted by, and there was a moan of wind.

When she turned to face Eve, her expression had changed. Eve tried to read it, but she couldn't. When Annabelle smiled, it seemed manufactured, and there was a thin edge of anxiety in her voice.

"I want to light the lantern and go," Annabelle said quickly, her mind made up. "The sooner the better."

There was something in Annabelle's expression that troubled Eve. She sensed that Annabelle swam in several emotional currents, calculating, evading and scheming.

"Is it possible for me to use it this morning... now?" Annabelle asked.

Eve felt a surge of relief. "Yes, Annabelle. It is. Don't you want to have some breakfast first? Some coffee?"

"I'm too nervous. I'd rather go... the sooner the better."

Eve gave her a frank appraisal. "What will you do if you return to your own time and find the lantern you originally lighted, sitting there, waiting for you?"

Annabelle didn't wait. "I don't know..."

"Was your husband standing nearby when you lighted it? Was your daughter close?"

Annabelle looked away, hiding her eyes.

"No, Eve. It was just me."

Resigned and anxious to have her out of the apartment, Eve left her stool, went to the bedroom, and pressed a gentle hand on Patrick's chest to awaken him.

"What happened?" he asked, eyes opening.

"Annabelle wants to go."

"Now?"

"Yes. Why not?"

"What time is it?"

"A little before eight."

"Are you going with her?"

"I don't know... I'm still thinking about it."

"Should I go?"

"No."

Patrick sat up. "Why, no?"

"Because I don't trust her. Not. At. All. Who knows what she might do? No, I don't want you anywhere near her."

Patrick ran a hand over his jaw, feeling the rough stubble of beard. "I don't think she should go alone."

"Whatever. I'm going to get dressed, open the safe, and get the lantern. By then, I'll have made up my mind."

While Eve pulled on jeans, slipped into a blouse and pulled a heavy sweater over her head, Patrick swung out of bed, wearing only his shorts, and watched her.

He shook his head, yawning. "Just another dizzy, unpredictable day in the Gantly household."

Eve started for the closet. "Tell me about it."

Patrick left the bed, went to his closet, reached for his black terry housecoat, and shouldered into it.

When Eve emerged from the closet holding the lantern, they both heard Colleen cry out.

"She's awake," Eve said.

"I'll go," Patrick said, starting for the bedroom door.

"Wait. Let's go together."

As they stepped outside into the hallway, they saw Annabelle grasping Colleen's hand, holding her close. With the other hand, she was pointing a gun at them.

Patrick cursed. It was the pistol he kept in case of a break-in, a Colt police .32 revolver he'd purchased only a year before. Ironically, it had been manufactured in 1904.

Annabelle stared at them, and her eyes were as cold as glass. "Give me the lantern, Eve."

Eve couldn't pull her stunned attention from Colleen, from her sleepy, confused eyes. She was wearing her little red ski cap and dressed in a warm, blue onesie.

"Hi, Mommy. I'm sleepy."

Eve stared at Annabelle, and terror drained her face of color. "Annabelle, what is this? I said you can have the lantern. Let go of Colleen."

Annabelle slowly shook her head. "I'm taking Colleen with me."

Patrick stiffened, ready to attack.

Eve felt her blood turn to ice.

CHAPTER 19

"PUT THE LANTERN down and step back," Annabelle demanded.

Patrick's voice deepened with a threatening edge. "What is the matter with you? This is madness, Annabelle. Let go of Colleen. Now."

Annabelle pointed the revolver at his chest and bore into him with her eyes. "Or you'll do what?"

"I'll break your neck with my own hands."

She barked out a harsh laugh. "You're not a fool, Patrick. You'll be dead before you reach me, and you know it. I learned how to shoot a revolver like this when I was twelve years old, from an expert, a woman who used to work in a traveling circus with my mother. She fires guns at spinning human targets, and she never misses. Believe me, Patrick, it won't be worth it. After you're dead, I'll light the lantern and vanish. So don't be stupid."

Patrick swiftly calculated space and distance. She was right. He was too far away. She'd made sure of that, and she wouldn't miss from where she stood. And then there was Eve. Would she shoot her too? Yes, no doubt.

Eve's heart kicked painfully in her chest as she fought back a furious panic. "Annabelle, please let Colleen go. Please don't do this," Eve said, the words choking in her throat.

Annabelle's eyes narrowed and hardened. "You can have another child, Eve. I cannot. I am barren. I was beaten and then left for dead by my husband. I lost my child then and I'll never have another. But I will tell you this, with a sincere promise. Colleen will never want for anything. I'll make sure she gets all that she will ever want or need. I will raise her to be a princess, and a lady. That, I will promise you, and if you believe nothing else about me, and there's nothing else about me to believe, you can believe that. Now, set the lantern down and both of you step back into the bedroom. Do it now. I'm not going to take any chances."

Colleen tried to wrench free from Annabelle's grasp, but Annabelle held her firm and close. The little girl winced in pain, fear glowing in her wide eyes.

"Ouch, that hurts. Mommy... My hand hurts," she called, reaching out for Eve with her other hand.

Eve fought to keep her trembling voice under control. "It's all right, Colleen. Everything is all right."

"Put the lantern down. Now!" Annabelle snapped. "And then step back into your bedroom."

Eve automatically flinched, then shot Patrick a glance. He nodded for her to do so, and Eve reluctantly obeyed, stooping and setting the lantern on the floor.

"She's not your child, Annabelle," Patrick said, sharply. "Have you no moral compass? No sense of how wrong this is? How are you going to take care of Colleen?"

"No, Patrick, I don't have any sense of right and wrong. I can't afford to, and I don't have the time to give you my long, sad story."

She glanced down at Colleen with gentleness, but the gun never wavered in her hand, and her sure gaze shot back to Eve and Patrick in a heartbeat. "It's okay, darling Colleen. I'm not going to hurt you. Not one beautiful hair on your head."

The air felt wild and volatile, and Eve's wounded heart was beating madly. She wanted Patrick to charge Annabelle and seize the gun one second, and the next, she was petrified he'd do just that, and she'd kill him.

Annabelle looked at them coldly, imperiously. "I'm the best jewel thief 1904 has ever seen. I have enough money back there to live like a queen for the rest of my life. You can believe me when I promise that Colleen will never want for anything. Now, I'm finished. Step back into the room and don't try anything foolish or, so help me, I will kill you both and leave this time before anyone knows it."

Patrick would have attacked if Eve hadn't been standing next to him, but he couldn't chance Eve being killed as well. He was certain he could have stopped Annabelle before he died, but he was also certain Annabelle was more street smart than Eve, and she would shoot her.

Thoughts boiled in his head, but for now, he was out of options.

"At least let me go to Central Park with you," Eve pleaded.

"No, Eve. I'm not going to Central Park. I did some research on your computer machine and I learned that Riverside Park is much as it was in 1904; the same open spaces. I will light the lantern with the matches I found in your kitchen drawer and leave from there. Now, I'm finished talking," she said, thrusting the gun at them. "Get into the bedroom and close the door."

Both hesitated.

"Do it, now!" Annabelle said, her voice raw and deep.

Patrick took Eve's hand and they backed away. Just as Eve was about to enter the bedroom, she stopped, closing her eyes and shaking her head. "I can't do it, Annabelle. You'll have to shoot me. I can't let you take Colleen. It will kill me."

Annabelle stood firm, revolver poised. The shape of her mouth turned ugly. "Eve, believe me when I tell you I will shoot you. I have killed before, and I am an expert shot. I won't miss."

Eve's eyes opened, rage building. She wanted to kill her. Strangle her. Beat her.

"By the way," Annabelle said, "sweet doggie Colin is locked in my room. He's fine."

Patrick glanced at Eve, seeing the expression of someone who had just discovered a violence she had no idea was inside her. He grabbed Eve by the shoulders and nudged her toward the room, but she fought him.

"Let's go into the room, Eve. Come on."

Eve shook her head, violently struggling to twist free. "No! No!"

Patrick wrapped his arms tightly around her and forced her inside the room, then kicked the door shut.

Eve screamed. "No, Patrick! NO!"

Patrick vice-gripped her, pinning her arms as she squirmed and fought against him.

"Eve... Wait. Calm down. Stop it. Just stop it and listen to me. I'll go after her. As soon as she's gone, I'll go and get Colleen. I will. Relax now. We don't have much time."

Eve trembled violently, her face creased with agony, her eyes filled with chaos. She pulled back, staring at him through blurry eyes. "How?"

He whispered. "As soon as she leaves the apartment, I'll go. I'll get Colleen back. Don't panic."

Just then, they heard Colleen cry out and the front door close.

Patrick released Eve, tore off his robe, moved to his closet and snatched for clothes, climbing into jeans, pulling on a sweater and shoving his feet into shoes.

Eve felt her stomach clench. "Patrick, be careful... Who knows what she'll do if she sees you."

His eyes were hostile and moving, like two dark clouds whipped about by high winds. "I'll get Colleen, and if I have to kill that woman to do it, I will."

He left the room with Eve fast behind. "Patrick..."

"I have to go, Eve," Patrick said, yanking open the closet door, grabbing for his leather jacket and gloves.

"Let me go with you," Eve said.

"No! You stay put. I can't take a chance on you being shot by that crazy woman. Just stay here. I'll be back as soon as I can."

When Patrick was gone, Eve stood frozen to the spot, and the hysteria in her grew. Should she call the police? She didn't know. Should she grab her coat and run after Patrick? She didn't know. She had completely lost the balance of her mind.

PATRICK BURST OUTSIDE, bounded down the stairs to the sidewalk and shot glances up and down the street, but there was no sign of Annabelle and Colleen. For speed, Annabelle had surely carried Colleen in her arms and run for the park.

Patrick spotted footsteps in the snow, tracking west toward the park, and he hurried off through falling snow, his strides lengthening. There were already two inches on the ground and a dusting on the tops of cars and bare tree limbs. The wind was strong and gusting stronger. That was good. Annabelle would have difficulty lighting the lantern in a pushing wind.

Patrick's eyes were sharp and his mind alert. He consciously shoved away negative thoughts. He needed all his mental and physical strength; all his experience and courage, if he was going to find Annabelle and save Colleen.

He crossed Riverside Drive and stepped onto the wide, sidewalk-like carriage path of Riverside Park at 105th street, sweeping his gaze in both directions. The park was a tableau of winter colors. Dogs sniffed and barked, their owners huddled in early morning conversation, some glancing at their cell phones.

There was no sign of Annabelle. Conflicted as to which direction to go, Patrick strained his eyes, peering through the haze of falling snow, feeling the throb of his heart and the beat of his pulse. He decided to go south. White vapor puffed from his mouth as he panted down the carriage path, boldness and urgency driving him on.

Would Annabelle stay on the carriage path and use one of the park benches for her launch back in time, or would she go down into the park via the 103rd Street staircase, opting for more privacy? Patrick would have to gamble she didn't go north to the stairs at 108th Street, which also led down to the lower part of the park.

Patrick moved along the whitened path to the stairs, grabbed the iron railing for support and started down the three flights, his eyes peeled, every muscle taut, his purpose deadly clear.

He paused at the bottom of the stairs and stood as still as a statue, listening, surveying the area. To his left, four people were having a snowball fight. Down below to his right was a dog playground, dogs frolicking, yapping, wrestling. To his right was another path. He spotted footprints. Fresh footprints! One pair of footprints. He knew there were park benches placed along that path.

Patrick was breathing hard, and the condensed breath rose around his face as he pushed on, a silent prayer of hope whispering from his lips.

A bundled-up kid of nine or ten came galloping toward him, spreading his arms like wings.

Patrick called to him as he approached and pointed. "Hey, there! Did you see a woman and a little girl back there?"

The kid stopped about two feet away and dropped his arms. He cocked a suspicious eye at Patrick. "Yeah, maybe."

"Did you or didn't you!?" Patrick shot back. "Tell me!"

Suddenly intimidated by the big man with a face filled with fury, the kid stepped back. "Yeah, I did. Is that your wife and kid?"

Patrick charged ahead in an explosion of energy, not answering the boy, who watched Patrick dart away.

In a cloud of speed, Patrick ran, skidding ahead, spotting a dark coat and red cap about thirty yards away, standing near a bench in the blowing snow. He'd found them, but he knew that if Annabelle saw him, she would fire the gun. He didn't care. Even if she hit him, his forward motion and his size would drop her. Then he'd strangle her.

He had already formed his dark plan. After he strangled her, he'd light the lantern and send her dead body back in time, into oblivion. That's what she deserved.

Patrick gained on them. But something was wrong. He suddenly felt the terrible air of disaster. An explosion of light flashed out and jetted up into the sky, the light catching Annabelle's astonished face as she held Colleen tightly in her arms. They began to dissolve into a thousand tiny blue fragments.

Patrick let out a cry like a wild, wounded animal, charging ahead toward Annabelle's vanishing image. He leapt at her and reached out his arms to tackle her, but all he embraced was the cold, snowy air. He crashed to the hard white surface and skidded, the breath bursting from his lungs in an agony of pain and defeat.

He lay there for a time, shivering, his eyes filling with tears of defeat, shock and rage. When he heard a female voice standing over him, he didn't move. He couldn't.

It was Eve, standing dead still, tears streaming, staring into the white snowy world. "Patrick…" she said in a small, anguished voice. "Patrick… We've lost her. We've lost our Colleen."

CHAPTER 20

Eve and Patrick lived the next several days mechanically, eating little, sleeping little. Patrick's mood was knife-edged, bordering on crazy. How could he have been so stupid as to leave a revolver in the bottom drawer of his nightstand? He should have known that anyone who arrived from 1904 with a derringer, especially Annabelle, would look for a pistol to take back with her. Annabelle must have taken it on Thursday before he returned home. Why hadn't he checked that night? He'd let his guard down. He'd grown complacent, and he'd paid a heavy price for his negligence.

At first, Patrick was ready to light the lantern and be off, but Eve had calmed and restrained his galloping anger and emotions. More than once, tears had flowed down her clenched jaw. She locked herself in the bathroom and wept. Both were suffering from gale force winds of emotion.

Eve choked down rage, often feeling panic rise hot in her chest and face. But they had to keep their heads.

They had to think and plan and be patient, despite the horror of what had happened. They had to prepare for the journey, examining every detail.

They knew what they had to do, having done it all before, several times, so they set about preparing for yet another time travel journey, there never being any question about it. Both were sick at heart, but resolved and resolute to search for Colleen no matter the consequences, or how long it might take.

They would light the Tesla lantern and travel into the past, to wherever the whim of the thing took them, to wherever that time and place might be. Once again, fate would bend and test their spirits and their relationship.

Their battered souls had spent days suffering through the crucible of losing Colleen. When Patrick and Eve had returned home with the lantern and closed the door behind them, Eve had bent over, surrendering to the pain, feeling herself sink into a black abyss. It took her days to recover enough to leave her bed. She'd cursed herself repeatedly for inviting the woman in; blamed herself and begged Patrick and God for forgiveness.

Patrick did not blame Eve. He tried to comfort her, but his own suffering and guilt for leaving the gun accessible had blunted him. The weight of his sympathy toward Eve was great, but losing Colleen was almost more than he could bear.

After straining days of recovery, they began pouring their energies into planning for every possible contingency that they might face when they lighted the lantern and time traveled.

Eve's face was clenched around tightly shut eyes as she listened to Patrick run through their checklist time and time again, hoping to ensure they wouldn't forget anything. The list included jewelry they'd hock for fast cash, antibiotics, pain medication, a suitcase filled with a variety of clothes, mostly black, a revolver and a knife for protection, and two black-and-white printed photos of Annabelle, taken from Eve's cell phone.

They had wanted to leave as soon as possible, but it was Eve who suggested they give themselves enough time to plan and steady their volatile emotions.

"When do you want to go, Eve?" Patrick had asked. "I say let's go tonight. Now. Let's not wait. We've finished our preparations and we're ready. I can't take much more of this waiting."

They sat slumped on the couch, near the roaring fire, Colin curled in his bed, watching them with sad, liquid eyes that caught the firelight. He'd sensed something was wrong, and he'd been moping around for days, shuffling in and out of Colleen's room, looking for her.

"I think we should wait two more days and leave on Christmas Eve," Eve said.

Patrick looked at her. "Why?"

"Call me sentimental. Call it symbolic. Call it whatever you want, but isn't Christmas Eve the most special, mystical and magical night of the year? We're going to need all the help we can get. And I'll be praying."

Patrick stared at her, digesting her words. He got up and took a few strides to the window, pulled back the curtains and gazed out. "All right. If you want to… I guess it won't matter that much. That damned lantern will drop us where it wants to drop us, no matter what day or time we leave."

Eve stared into the fire. "Pauline said she'd look after the apartment and take Colin. She loves animals."

Patrick didn't turn. "That's good of her."

Eve kept talking to fill the sad silence. "She had a dog until about a year ago, when she had to put him down."

"Did you say that Pauline thinks we're going to visit relatives for Christmas?" Patrick asked.

"Yes."

Patrick turned to face Eve. "Doesn't she have a cat?"

"Two... Both black. Both the sweetest cats I've ever known."

"I hope Colin doesn't try to eat them."

"He won't. He's gentle."

"With us he's gentle. I don't know about cats. Anyway, it's a kind and generous thing for her to do."

Patrick sighed out his tension. "Have you made up your mind about the lantern?"

Eve nodded. "Yes... I say we light it, and then leave it right where it is. We won't ask anyone to come with us and keep it for us, for when we return. I'm finished with the thing."

"Are you sure?"

"Yes. I want it finished... finished, once we find Colleen."

Patrick heard the words, *if we find Colleen* in his head, because there was no guarantee they'd ever find her. But he didn't allow himself to say them.

Eve folded her arms. "So, we light the lantern and vanish. Then, once we're gone, whoever finds the lantern on that park bench… finds it. They'll have their own experience with it, like Stephanie Gray will… assuming no one else in Kingston has taken it from her shop."

Eve lifted her head and looked at him. "What do you think?"

His deep blue eyes latched onto hers, and he jerked a firm nod. "Yes. I want no more of this… this unholy business."

Eve stared into the fire that burned with a fierce glow, and her eyes strayed toward the Tesla lantern that sat on the hearth, to the left of the glass-enclosed fire screen. It appeared so ordinary; so harmless. It was just an old lantern from another time. But it was anything but ordinary or harmless.

"Just one more journey…" Eve said. "Let's hope the lantern takes us on one more journey."

"Yes, and that it places us in the right time and place so we can find Annabelle and Colleen."

"When we find Annabelle, what will you do?"

The angry words burst from him, too filled with rage to be contained. "I'll find the woman and, when I do, God forgive me, but I'll break her neck with my bare hands."

Eve looked at him soberly, blinking.

Patrick moved toward the chair and sat, leaning forward, folding his hands. "What she has done is unforgiveable. Not only to take our little child but also to risk Colleen's life by time traveling with that devil of a lantern."

He rose again. "God in heaven, who knows where they ended up. They might already be dead for all we know, the lantern having dropped them in the middle of the Atlantic Ocean or up on some craggy, snowy peak, where there is no escape and no earthly way to call for help."

Eve straightened. "Patrick, stop torturing yourself and me. The lantern always returned us to where we left from, so there's no reason to believe that it didn't return Annabelle back to her own place and time from where she left."

He flicked a glance at her. "No, Eve. You and Joni landed in Tesla's laboratory once, remember?"

"But we were safe… In the same city, and on land. We can't drive ourselves crazy, Patrick. We have to hold on to hope. We have to."

Patrick moved back to the windows and stood there, head down.

The knot inside Eve tightened, and she pushed down the cry that wanted to rise from her chest. "We have to have hope… We have to have faith that we will find Colleen."

Gradually, Patrick softened. He went to her, sat down next to her on the sofa, and wrapped a comforting arm about her shoulders, drawing her in close. He leaned over and kissed her hair, then laid his head against hers. "You're right, my love. I've been gripped with a kind of madness that burns through me like a grassfire, and I'm having difficulty controlling it. Once we're on our way—once we're moving and taking action—I'll be all right."

"Maybe we'll get lucky," Eve said. "Maybe we'll travel back just a few weeks or days into the past, before I read about Annabelle online."

She felt a pang of remorse, so she tried for a joke. "If that happened, we'd be younger. That would be good, wouldn't it?"

Patrick's smile was empty. "As my old Da used to say, 'No wise man ever wished to be younger.'"

"So, let's pray for a miracle, Patrick. We might get lucky. It could happen."

"It could also happen that we travel back before 1904, to the 1880s again; before Annabelle was born, or when she's a baby. Then what will we do?"

Eve's thoughts stalled. "I don't know."

THAT NIGHT OVER DINNER, neither said much. "I guess I'll wear that long black skirt and white blouse with the long, full sleeves," Eve said. "That will fit into most any time, except maybe the 1960s," she said, with a wry smile.

"A black suit and tie for me," Patrick said. "And a bowler, just in case. I'll even bring my old pipe, the one I never smoke anymore."

Eve found a gentle smile. "I like you in that bowler. It reminds me of… well, let me see, what does it remind me of? The good old days, literally."

"We've seen many of them, haven't we?" Patrick said, staring down dully at his slice of baked chicken. "Too many of them."

Eve took a sip of white wine. "Patrick, I've been thinking that, with any luck, we might end up seeing Joni again. I'd love to see her. Not this way, of course, and under these circumstances, but if we have to go, I hope she and I can meet."

Patrick lifted his eyes. "Eve…. I've been thinking that… well, if we do end up in the early 1900s, maybe we should stay there. Maybe we shouldn't take a chance and try to come back to the twenty-first century."

Eve was gently startled. She set down the wine glass and thought about it. "Do you think so?"

"Maybe... Just maybe. Let's at least think about it. Time traveling is always a gamble... and we'll have Colleen. Do we want to risk her life yet again when we light that lantern and hope to return?"

Eve felt the burden of his words. "I don't know. I've never thought about it. It would be so weird. We'd know the history that was to come. We'd know what's going to happen: the stock market crash of 1929, the two world wars, the depression... I don't know."

"Joni lived through it, and she made a life for herself and she seemed happy."

Eve sat still, her mind working. "We have two days till Christmas Eve. Let's see what happens when we light the lantern."

In the long, worrisome silence, Colin strolled in, looking for his dinner, and Patrick got up and reached into the cabinet for a can. After he'd opened it, spooned most of the dog food into Colin's yellow bowl, and placed the bowl on the floor, Patrick turned, looking at Eve with warm, loving eyes.

"Whatever we decide, Eve, we'll be together. Together, we'll manage whatever the fates throw at us."

Eve straightened her spine, as if to muster courage, but her expression was sad. "We have to find Colleen, Patrick. We just have to."

CHAPTER 21

As the sun was setting on Christmas Eve, delicate snowflakes drifted in a soft wind. Eve and Patrick left their brownstone and started off toward Riverside Park. Patrick carried an old suitcase, without roller wheels, filled with changes of clothes and toiletries. Eve carried the lantern in a department store plastic shopping bag, a retro canvas purse swung over her shoulder.

They wore long, dark overcoats, Patrick sporting a bowler hat, and Eve wearing a bonnet in dark brown velvet, with a curly green feather accent on top. It had a chin strap, and it was lined in silk. She'd found it on *eBay*, circa 1900, where she'd also purchased her long black skirt and white period blouse.

As they entered the park, they heard church bells chiming, echoing in the distance; the sound of gleeful children playing and dogs barking. There was celebration in the air; the festive spirit of Christmas was all around them. Both fought trepidation and despair. They'd had so many plans for Christmas: dinner with friends; a taxi to midtown to see the Rockefeller Christmas tree; and a stroll past the decorated department store windows on Fifth Avenue.

As they descended the staircase down into the park, they strolled the same path Annabelle had taken days before. While snowflakes flitted in the amber glow of lamplights, Patrick glanced over.

"Why didn't you leave from Riverside Park the first time you traveled, after you found the lantern?"

"Because I kept hearing the name Central Park repeat in my head; the fragment of a song about the benches in Central Park. I didn't really give it any more thought. It seemed fated, so I went with it. And when I awoke in 1885, the first person I met was Alfred Harringshaw."

Patrick nodded. "And now? Does this feel fated? Riverside Park?"

Eve shrugged and looked away. "I don't feel much of anything except I wish I'd never read that article about Annabelle Palmer, and I wish I'd never set eyes on her."

"Stop blaming yourself, Eve. Your motives were good and true."

"And reckless."

"No, Annabelle is reckless, and selfish, and twisted, not you."

As the path unraveled in a light gleam of snow, with trees on either side, they descended a slight hill and saw the bench ahead, partially lit by a park lamp.

"That's the bench," Patrick said.

When they arrived at the bench, they stopped and appraised the area. There was a hushed magic about the night. The chilly air was in slight movement; the snowflakes shifting and heavy in the entrancing evergreen trees.

"It's a pretty spot," Eve said.

"It is that," Patrick agreed. "I wonder if Annabelle chose it for a reason or just by chance," he said, placing the suitcase on the park bench.

Eve took in a deep, meditative breath and let it out slowly. "Oh, God, I can't believe we have to do this again. I wanted to look to the future… I always want to hope and plan for the future, and we always seem to wind up in the past."

Patrick stared out into the night and anchored his belief—that this time travel journey would put them exactly where they'd need to be to find Colleen and bring her home.

They felt the minutes slipping away, pushing them to the moment when they'd light the lantern and vanish into another time.

"It feels as though we're playing roulette," Patrick said. "We're about to toss a ball into the spinning wheel and God only knows where we'll end up."

Despite the cold, there was a thin sheen of sweat on his forehead, and he worked to wipe the nerves and anxiety from his face.

"Let's go, Patrick. Let's light the lantern and go."

Patrick looked about, warily. He felt as if the wind, the trees and the sky were watching them, anticipating the moment they'd disappear into another time, and into another world.

Using his gloved hand, Patrick brushed the snow from the bench and Eve sat down, ready to go. Patrick eased down next to her with the suitcase on his right. He watched as she removed the lantern from the shopping bag and placed it between them. Resigned now, she opened her purse and removed a box of kitchen matches.

Eve looked at him, determined. "Ready?"

His eyes widened a little. "Yes. Let's go find Colleen."

Eve opened the lantern door, the wick visible. She fumbled with the first match, irritated when the wind puffed it out. She reached for another, her hand trembling.

"Do you want me to light it?" Patrick asked.

"No... I'll do it. Just stay close to me. We don't want to get separated like we did in 1914."

Eve slid the matchbox open, drew out a second match, and struck it along the side of the box. The match flared. She swiftly cupped her free hand around the flickering flame to protect it, then carefully guided it in toward the open door to the wick.

A sharp wind blew a gust of snow, but the lighted match caught the wick, and it jumped to life, a golden-growing flame, dancing. Eve shut the lantern door, and she and Patrick stared in tense wonder while the light flickered, then rocketed up twenty feet into the air, into a blue/golden cone of pure, dazzling light.

Eve seized Patrick's hand, squeezing it. Their shoulders touched, and Eve held her breath. The wind gasped and circled, but the jet of flame never wavered as it swelled out into the night. Eve's thoughts flew back to the last time she'd time traveled, and she recalled the sensations of falling, of sailing, of losing all sense of time and place.

Patrick shut his eyes for a moment, fixing Colleen's pudgy face in his inner mind and holding it there. "Take me to her," he whispered.

Fear and apprehension washed over them; the fear of something going wrong; the fear of being killed or being flung off into nothingness; the fear of losing all awareness of life and losing consciousness forever.

There was a loud rush in their ears, sounding like a freight train approaching. The sound charged, passed, roared, then went thundering away into the park.

Then... dead silence. Hurting silence. Waiting silence. Eyes blurry. Hearts pounding. They stiffened and braced for what was to come.

The world seemed to shift on its axis, and gravity tugged them down into the center of a spiraling blue whirlpool of light, and they exploded into shards of quivering golden light. They were flung away like snowflakes into a fierce, north wind, helpless and reaching.

The sound of wind chimes. The sound of bells clanging. The sound of drumming heartbeats. The sound of panting breath. Silence, ringing, pulsing, breathing.

The shadows were black without shading. In hurling movement, Eve and Patrick sailed over land and sea. The meadows and forests were flooded with moonlight, and they saw the secret movement of prowling night animals and dark, winging birds. They saw the winking lights of great cities flash by in a heartbeat.

Flying across the oceans, they saw the water reflect the cool, white light of the full moon. Charging waves went crashing against towering cliffs, the noise like thunder, the spray misting their faces.

The moon went fleeing across the sky in a never-ending, dizzying spiral, throwing quivering shadows across the spinning world. Eve shouted out her emotion, half terror, half frantic laughter, feeling her hand locked in Patrick's, holding tight, his body a dark flying specter beside her.

When motion eased its speed, and the wind died away like the sigh of a breeze, Eve and Patrick thought the journey had ended; prayed that it was over.

When Patrick saw a mass of white, bubbling clouds galloping toward them, an ache knifed through his chest. Eve reflectively lifted a hand to cover her face as the towering, charging clouds rushed in and engulfed them, tossing them about like birds in a thrashing storm. Eve was ripped from Patrick's grasp, lost in the swirling fog.

Patrick shouted, and yelled, and groped for Eve's body, which he could no longer see. His breath burst hoarsely out of this throat as he called for her, as he tumbled and dropped.

From somewhere in his mind, he saw a .44 caliber Colt loom out of the fog, the black hole of the barrel pointed at him. And then a face emerged. The pinched, angry face of a woman. He recognized her. It was Annabelle. She was going to shoot him in the chest.

He saw the gun was cocked; the hammer was back. He saw the deadly intent on her face, and he stared into her eyes, which inspected him impersonally.

There was an explosion. He flinched, expecting the impact of the bullet. But Annabelle dissolved, and vanished into the clouds.

And then there was the cry of wind, and a smattering of snow. The hand of a pushing wind flung him through the clouds, and he saw the white Earth rushing up to meet him at an incredible speed. He was certain he would never survive the impact.

PART TWO

CHAPTER 22

Eve crashed through the outer branches of snow-heavy evergreen trees, dropping into a snowbank on a hillside. Though the snow cushioned the impact, the fall exploded the air from her lungs, and she lay unconscious for a time, in eight inches of snow, her breathing labored. Her hat had been blown away and her shoulder-length blonde hair lay in damp strands across her face.

A tremor of life force stirred her, and her eyes strained open. It was night. She was shivering, her eyes searching, ears listening. It was night, and snow continued to fall, swirling, gliding, landing cold on her face. The floating, delicate flakes held her attention for a time as she lay on her back, staring up, hearing the faint sigh of the wind as it wheezed through the evergreen trees that stood near her, glazed in snow.

Was she all right? She moved a finger, a hand, and then the other hand. Her feet moved, though she felt pain shoot through her left leg. Was it broken? No, she could move it, but it hurt like crazy. Gently, she lifted on elbows and looked around. Her arms were fine. Some pain in her left shoulder. She must have landed on her left side.

Eve's next thought was of Patrick. Where was he? What had happened to him? And then she recalled being ripped from his grasp, and she cursed. It had been the worst and most violent time travel journey she'd ever taken. There had been no soft landing, as there had always been in past journeys. The entire experience had been chaotic and frightening. Falling from the sky as she had, she was lucky to be alive.

But where was Patrick? Her throat tightened; her heart drummed; she fought panic. She'd have to get up and look for him. Was he close by, or had he ended up in a completely different time and place?

Where was she? What time had she dropped into? With a gasping effort, Eve sat up, feeling a pinch of pain in her lower back. She felt the cold seep into her bones, and she struggled to clear her mind and prioritize her next steps. First, she had to get up and out of the snowy night, or she'd freeze to death.

Eve labored to stand, first in a kneeling position, and then carefully pushing herself up with her hands. After three attempts, she was on her feet, but her limbs were weak, her head pounding and fuzzy.

Her face was clenched around pain-glazed eyes as she shivered, desperately scanning the area, searching for Patrick and the suitcase. She saw neither, only a blanket of snow lying fresh and deep all around her. Snow was gusting, forming soft mounds at the base of trees, glistening in the crooks of trees, lying like vanilla icing on the limbs.

She saw a standing lamppost—one single lamppost about twenty yards away, shedding its golden light upon the glittering snow, snowflakes flashing across the lamp.

Eve slapped herself for warmth and took another worried glance around, listening to the wind whistling and blowing across untouched drifts. Realizing she was alone, she trudged off, favoring her left foot, moving toward the lamppost, hopeful it was near a path, or led to one.

As she tramped ahead, the lamplight became a kind of beacon, and the whitened field was crossed by the long, eerie shadows of tall trees.

Eve was right. The lamppost stood vigil near a narrow path, identified by a pair of recent footprints, formed about two inches of snow ago. Heartened, she looked left and then right. Because of the open spaces, the abundance of trees, and the pathway, Eve surmised that she was in a park. Was it Riverside Park? She didn't recognize the site. If so, what year was it?

A bench was near, and so Eve slowly made her way to it, needing to get off her sore leg. With her gloved hand, she raked away a mound of snow, clearing a space big enough to sit, and she did so with a deep, weary sigh. Once again, she was alone, completely alone in some other time and place, and she had no idea where she was—or where Patrick was.

They had drawn up contingency plans for everything they could think of based on past experience. They'd decided that since Joni had remained behind in 1884, and would live until at least 1943, she would be their main contact. Her house would be their safe house. If anything went wrong, if anything separated them during the time travel journey, they'd visit the home of Mr. and Mrs. Darius Foster, and hopefully find the other waiting there.

That was on Eve's mind when she managed to get to her feet, turn and shamble off down the path. Limping on her left foot, she slipped in the snow and went down hard, striking the ground on her left side, feeling the pain shoot through her like fire. She lay there, suffering from the fall and the cold, unable to move.

Finally, with her teeth chattering, she struggled to a sitting position, wincing through the pain. From the corner of her eye, she saw the shadow of someone approaching and then enter the lamppost arc of light.

With pain in her eyes, Eve glanced up, seeing a medium-built man staring back at her with flat, suspicious eyes. Eve saw a scar that went from the corner of his mouth to his ear. *Not a good sign*, she thought.

The man was criminal in appearance, with a black, bushy mustache, hunched shoulders, a sharp gaunt face, clifflike brows, a small chin and a sharp nose. But on closer examination, Eve noticed that his long coat was not frayed, his gloves were without holes and the bowler hat, pulled down to his ears and frosted with snow, did not appear tattered.

He paused, bringing two fingers to the hat brim in a polite greeting. "Madam, my name is Antoni Bankowski. Have you distress? Is there injury about you?"

He spoke in an accent Eve didn't recognize. Ignoring the pain, Eve struggled to stand, and as she did so, the man started toward her, reaching out a helpful hand. "May I help?"

Eve couldn't pretend she didn't need the help. She nodded. "Yes... Please."

He took her cold, gloved hand and helped her stand.

"Thank you, sir," Eve said, studying his eyes. They didn't look threatening. There was kindness in them.

Antoni stood awkwardly, glancing about as if trying to understand where she had come from and why she was alone.

"Do you wait here for someone?"

The cold was invasive, knifing through her, and she couldn't stop her teeth from chattering. "No... I'm afraid I'm lost."

"I assist?" he asked.

Eve was desperate. She'd have to take a chance with the man. Her eyes came to his. "Perhaps you could help me... As I said, I don't quite know where I am."

"This place is Riverside Park... I assist you home if that be proper for you."

He briefly removed his hat and replaced it. "Will that be nice for you?"

Eve had to know what year it was so she could contact Joni. "Yes... Yes... that would be very kind of you."

He reached out both hands. "I take an arm, if you please?"

Eve nodded, and because of the time travel and the bitter cold, she could feel the strength draining out of her. She smiled meekly and offered him her arm.

"Have you the hurts, Madam?"

"I'm afraid so. My left leg and foot are injured. I may have to hobble a little."

He nodded shyly, and Eve lost all her fear of him. He had a sincere wish to help.

"I'll guide you then," he said, holding her arm with a steady gentleness, and they began their slow journey up the path.

"Where does this path lead?" Eve asked.

"Riverside Avenue and 103rd Street. We go slow to there."

"Riverside Avenue?" Eve asked, and then she recalled that the name Riverside Avenue had been changed to Riverside Drive sometime in the early 1900s.

Feeling a growing urgency, Eve decided to ask the man what month and year it was. "Sir, I hope you won't think it strange if I ask, but what are the month and the year?"

Antoni glanced at her in surprise, and then swung his gaze back to the snowy path. "The injury, it has disturb you... or, how you say, hurt your head?"

Eve seized on that. "Yes, sir. I'm not quite myself, I think. I fell back there. So, if you will be kind enough to tell me the month and year."

The Christmas Eve Journey

Eve saw him swallow.

"It is November 11... Saturday, November 11, 1905."

Eve stopped short, turning to face him, stunned, forgetting the pain. "It's 1905?"

He nodded. "Yes, madam... that is the year it is."

Eve stared, absorbing the information. It was 1905, not 1904. If Annabelle and Colleen time traveled back to 1904, then nearly a year had already passed. But then, Eve had no way of knowing what year Annabelle had returned to.

Antoni cleared his throat. "Madam, your home is close by, yes?"

Eve pulled her racing mind back to the present. "Actually, I plan to stay with a friend, downtown."

They crept on, and Eve's low, dragging energy, burning pain, and swelling in her ankle continued to sap her strength. She had to stop several times to catch her breath. It was growing obvious that she might faint if she didn't find some place warm to rest.

Antoni felt her slump, heard the heaviness in her breathing.

"Weather is bad tonight. You're hurt. My place is not far."

Eve was not going home with this man, that was certain.

"My wife, Grazyna, and my two girls are waiting. There will be food for you and hot coffee. I think maybe you come and rest there."

Eve stopped again, lowering her head, her energy nearly spent. What choice did she have? She'd never make it to Joni's. Did they have telephones in 1905? She didn't know.

Breathing hard, her feet like ice, her face stinging from the wind, she turned to him and smiled her gratefulness, touched by his fundamental compassion. "Okay… All right. Thank you."

Eve willed herself on, her chest straining for breath, and she wondered where Patrick was, and she wondered where Colleen was, and she prayed for help and guidance.

She fought tears. She fought despair, and she fought emotion. She had, once again, lost her beautiful family, and she didn't know what she was going to do. How would she ever forgive herself for what she'd done?

CHAPTER 23

Patrick awoke in the morning and sat up with a start. One window, covered by a ragged curtain, let in weak, gray light.

But what morning was it? He glanced about, his anxious, slitted eyes searching the surrounding space. The room was small and dingy, with the smell of booze, body odor, and poverty all about it.

As with the other men, Patrick was lying on a canvas, stretched between two horizontal beams, creating a kind of hammock bed. Three men were still asleep, looking like sacks covered by shabby blankets. One snored in ragged gasps, as if he were close to his last breath, one made frightened, whimpering sounds, and the other was so still that Patrick wondered if he was dead.

Patrick's bruised mind and sore body also awoke, punishing him with confusion, fragments of random memory, and discomfort. What day was it? What year was it? Where the hell was he?

He flung off the smelly, thin gray blanket and felt the cold seep into him. With stiff effort, he swung his legs from the hammock bed, anchoring his stocking feet on the warped wooden floor. He saw his boots. Why had he not put them in his bed? Why hadn't someone stolen them? Obviously, he hadn't been thinking clearly the night before—and he'd been lucky.

He tugged the boots on and pushed up on shaky legs. A name slid into his mind. Polly Jencks. Yes, this was her flophouse. No food served, and the bathroom was shared, such that it was.

He'd slept in his clothes, including his overcoat, and they were rumpled. They also didn't smell so good. Running a hand across his jawline, he felt his rough, one day-old beard. There was no mirror handy, and he was grateful. He no doubt looked dangerous and villainous, to quote Sergeant Dockery, who had worked in Patrick's old Fifteenth Precinct in the 1880s. Why had he remembered Dockery so easily, when he couldn't recall where he'd come from two days before, or why he was living in 1905?

Hunger pushed him out the bedroom door into a narrow, carpetless hallway, and then left, down to the bathroom.

Polly Jencks waited for him at the front door to the dismal place. She was a short, dumpy woman, looking like a mourner in her long black dress, with a black shawl draped over her narrow shoulders. She was in her 60s, with crinkly white hair, a round, wrinkled, sullen face, and the threatening disposition of a barroom bouncer.

"You comin' back tonight?" she asked curtly.

"No."

"You ain't gonna find a better place for seven cents."

Patrick stood near her, seeing the ice in her gray eyes and smelling her foul breath. She had an accent, maybe part British and part something else.

"I'd do better to sleep in a doghouse. Why don't you clean the place? It's filthy, and it stinks."

"You weren't complainin' none last night when you came stumblin' in here wantin' any kind of room, because you'd been kissin' the neck of a bottle of Irish whiskey."

"I wasn't drunk," Patrick said defensively. "I was lost."

She cocked a big, dark eye at him. "Says you, and nobody else. Just 'cause you be a big chappie with a good and handsome face that the girlies go lifting their skirts for, don't mean you can tells folks what they should do, and not do. So, get the hell away from my place then. If it ain't good enough for you, then I'll say goodbye to bad baggage."

Without another word, Patrick yanked open the door and descended the two stairs to the sidewalk.

Polly poked her head out the door, scowling. "And don't go sending any of your mates to me, hear? I'll toss them out into the street, I will."

Patrick kept walking and didn't look back. The morning air was cold and brisk, and he wished he hadn't lost his hat. He'd have to find a shop and buy another. It wouldn't do for him to walk around town, lost, confused, and without a hat. Everyone wore a hat in this time.

He walked aimlessly for a while, willing his mind to clear, but it didn't clear, and he wrestled with anger and frustration.

He entered the Arch Cafe at Washington Square South and Thompson Streets and sat at a table near a window, where he could watch the carriage and foot traffic; where he could watch the beat cops and gaze into the faces that passed by.

He ordered coffee, sliced ham and a porridge made from baked wheat, oatmeal and cornmeal. Across the street he saw a sign perched on a brownstone roof advertising **Krakauer Pianos**. He noticed a sign in a bank window that read **4% 20-year Mortgage Bonds**. Next to that was a real estate company with a sign swinging on outside hinges near the front door: **NEW SEMI-DETACHED BRICK HOUSES**.

Patrick read them with interest, hoping they would jar his memory loose; a word, a phrase, or an advertisement that would offer a clue as to where he'd come from.

He gazed out the window, searching the faces that passed, men in dark coats and bowlers, women dressed in long skirts and fitted winter coats, their hats broad and elegant. Nothing and no one looked familiar. He was lost in a nightmare.

He knew his name: Patrick Gantly. And he remembered much of his past, who his parents were and where they'd come from. He recalled that he'd been married, Emma being her name, and with sadness, he remembered that she'd perished in childbirth. That was in 1884, if his jittery, jumping mind was correct. But had their baby also died? For the life of him, he couldn't recall. For the life of him, he didn't know what in the dickens had happened to him.

As he ate his breakfast, he reran the last two days. It had all started when he seemed to fall from the sky, hearing a whistle in the air like that of an approaching artillery shell. He hit the ground hard, knocking the breath from him. Then a bright streak of light flashed before his eyes, and the world had exploded into millions of pieces. He'd blanked out.

When he'd awakened, he was somewhere in Riverside Park, in a pile of snow, shivering and chilled to the bone. His head throbbed from the fall, a feeling of being knocked silly, as if he'd taken a hard punch to the face. He was gazing dull-mindedly into the distant horizon as the sun set, and a cold, white moon rose. He'd forced himself up, dazed and hurting, struggling for direction. He'd half-walked, half-stumbled out of Riverside Park, trudged on in a stupor, finally finding himself on Broadway.

He had no identification, no money, and his memory was battered. In his inside coat pocket, he found a black-and-white photo of a woman, but he had no idea who she was.

In his trouser pocket he found two gold bands wrapped in cotton. Out of instinct, and weak from hunger and the cold, he'd found a jeweler nearby and sold both rings for a fair price. Incredibly, he did not ask the jeweler the date. He was that loopy.

So, he had money, and he could survive, but he needed lodgings. Sleep would heal his sore head and body. Rest would erase the amnesia.

It was at the hotel where he'd booked a room for a week that he'd received the stunning blow that had jolted him. As he'd signed the register, he saw the signatures of other guests, including the date: 1905!

After he'd awakened in Riverside Park, his last pulse of memory had been of him leaving Sean O'Casey's Saloon in 1884. There were other memories, but they were fractured, like pieces of a jigsaw puzzle scattered across the floor of his mind.

In his hotel room, Patrick had fallen asleep as soon as his head hit the pillow and he didn't awaken until the next afternoon. After cleaning up, he'd set off to Sean O'Casey's. When he arrived at where it was supposed to be, it was gone, replaced by a furniture store whose specialty was roll-top desks.

He'd been too shaken to visit the precinct where he'd been a detective sergeant. He was feeling too many emotions and crashing thoughts. He began to wonder whether he had gone insane.

He'd wandered off, lost in a fog of confusion and fear, frantically working to paste his thoughts and impressions back together. It was as if part of his mind was working fine, but another part had been closed off, a shut door, padlocked, preventing any memory from escaping.

As he'd struggled to recall his life, New York City all around him was in full motion, with hectic crowds, sleek carriages, and trotting hansoms and drays. Being distracted, Patrick had nearly been struck by an oncoming, crowded, clanging streetcar. He'd darted away as it rumbled by and found himself standing in a pile of unshoveled snow.

On the sidewalk, he'd stamped his feet and moved on, glancing up to see bundled children waving and grinning down at him from high terraces, joyful that a good blanket of snow had come in November, filling the streets and parks, coating the trees and buildings.

The garment district was loud and rushing, the newsboys hawking the dailies and the weeklies; the shops bustling with shoppers. It was the same town Patrick remembered, and yet it was not. The air had a new odor to it, merged with the familiar smells in the blowing wind. It was the smell of oil. To his surprise, Patrick saw an occasional automobile, a small, square thing, shaking and rattling up the street, spewing white smoke from its rear exhaust. The autos provoked comments from the passing crowds, and heads turned, and some of those heads shook in disapproval, others in wonder.

Patrick had inhaled a deep breath and tried not to shiver. What world was he in? And why?

Later that evening, on his first full day, Patrick had left the cold, biting wind and ducked into McNally's Pub, sitting alone at the long, busy bar. He'd considered visiting Colin and Megan O'Brien, his good neighbors in 1884, but he'd thought better of it when he realized how much time had passed. And then he'd had a shaky memory. Well, everything was shaky, wasn't it?

After downing two beers, Patrick had grown faint and lethargic. He'd left the pub, dizzy and ambling, wandering in a light snowfall. He knew he'd never make it back to his hotel, and that's when he'd blundered into Polly Jenck's flophouse, where he'd spent a restless night.

Patrick was pulled from his thoughts when the waiter presented the check, and he ventured a look at the man. *You never know*, he thought. *He might remember me.*

Patrick screwed up his courage. "Do you know me, sir? Have I been in here before?"

The white-haired, round-bellied man in a white shirt and black apron was brisk and businesslike. "No, sir. I have never seen you."

Patrick paid the check and left, taking to the street in a slight hesitation. It was time to take a chance and go visit Megan and Colin O'Brien. Of course, they may have long moved. After all, the last time he could remember seeing them was in 1884.

Patrick noticed a haberdashery across the street. After dodging busy traffic and another clanging streetcar, he went inside to purchase a bowler. His head was cold, and he needed a pair of gloves.

Inside the shop, as he was trying on the black leather gloves, something in his mind shifted. An old memory flashed, and he distinctly heard a woman's voice say, "Gloves are cheap, Patrick. You can buy them from a street vendor for five dollars. You should buy six pairs and keep them in various winter pockets. Even better, I'll buy two pairs and keep them in my pockets."

He knew the voice, but he couldn't put a face with it. When a smooth salesman drifted by, Patrick didn't notice him.

"Can I be of service, sir?" the salesman asked.

Patrick didn't hear him. Another memory had been shaken loose, and he heard his own voice in his head say, "I fell in love with you when we were across the street from Zarcone's Tea & Coffee House, and when you boldly walked up to me and said, 'Have you been following me?'"

CHAPTER 24

"I'M HAPPY YOU are feeling better, Evelyn," Antoni said.

Antoni and Eve sat at a square table in the humble kitchen, sipping tea from rose-colored teacups. Grazyna, Antoni's wife, stood at a cast-iron stove, stirring a pot of stew.

"Yes, much better," Eve said.

Behind them, in the parlor, the Bankowskis' two daughters played a game of *Jacks* while singing *Pop Goes the Wiesel*.

"Me and my Grazyna are from the same town in Poland," Antoni said, turning to his wife. "Isn't it so, Grazyna?"

Grazyna nodded shyly. "Yes... that is so. The very same town."

Grazyna was a petite, thin, soft-spoken woman with brown hair, styled in a simple pompadour.

Antoni continued, his lively eyes glowing with pride. "It is called Tomaszow-Mazowiecki. It is not such a big place, but it is a nice place, Evelyn. A good place to be from. But me and Grazyna came to America for things that are better. Isn't that right, Grazyna?"

Again, she smiled and nodded. "Does the tea warm you, Evelyn?"

Eve smiled. "Yes, Mrs. Bankowski. I'm feeling so much better. I don't know what I would have done if your husband hadn't come by."

"It was a rush job," Antoni said. "The lady said she must have her dress for a party this evening, so I work three days on her dress. I was returning from delivery when I saw you, Evelyn. A ladies' tailor's job is not so easy."

Grazyna glanced at him with mild consternation. "You stop that complaining, Antoni. The Lord above loves a grateful heart and takes away things from those who complain."

Antoni's eyes grew large with innocence as he spread his hands. "Grazyna, that was not a complaint I made. It was to show how God put me in the right place to find Evelyn in her distress. That is all I said."

Eve smiled inwardly, aware that Grazyna was not taken in by her husband's inventive justification.

The Bankowskis' apartment contained four rooms, a snug kitchen, a small master bedroom, a back bedroom for 4-year-old Hanna and 6-year-old Zofia, and a parlor where Antoni worked.

When Eve had first entered the second-floor walk-up, Antoni had helped her inside and over to the burgundy sofa, which sat near the quaint fireplace. Grazyna had left the kitchen with a puzzled look on her face, wiping her hands on her apron, her nervous eyes glued to her husband. She waited for an explanation as to who this strange woman was, and why he'd brought her into their apartment.

Eve hadn't had the strength to speak. She'd unbuttoned her coat, revealing her skirt and blouse, knowing it wasn't 1905 fashion, but she was too exhausted to care. She'd shut her eyes, lolled her head back and let the welcome heat from the fire relax and revive her.

Antoni had explained his adventure to his wife in Polish, his hands and face animated, his voice rising just over a whisper. When Grazyna had nodded toward Eve, speaking to her husband in a firm tone, Antoni had concluded his story in English.

Gradually, the room had seeped back into Eve's senses, and she'd opened her eyes. Blonde Hanna and dark-haired Zofia sat in wooden chairs near the fireplace, staring at Eve with shy interest, Hanna's feet swinging, Zofia playing with the ends of her curly hair.

Eve had smiled at them. "Hello... I'm Eve."

They'd blinked and returned a "Hello" when they were instructed to do so by their father.

Eve's eyes had searched the room, noticing rolls of fabric, a sewing machine on a table near the front windows, several sizes of scissors, and neatly stacked spools of thread. Next to the table were muslin-covered, wire figures of women's shapes—one a size 14, the other a size 20—that represented the fuller, non-diet-obsessed bodies of that time.

"I am a ladies' tailor," Antoni had said proudly.

Eve had also noticed two oval, black-and-white framed photos hanging on the wall, and she surmised they were the stern faces of Antoni's and Grazyna's parents.

While Eve had sat on the sofa recovering, Grazyna and Antoni had treated her like a queen, offering her a warm embroidered blanket and a basin of tepid water to soak her sore foot. A half hour later, she'd joined Antoni at the kitchen table, where Grazyna had promptly poured the tea.

Eve studied the room. "Do you have a telephone?"

"I'm sorry to say, no, Evelyn," Antoni said, frowning, "But there is a new pay-station in the grocery store down the block. There is also an older one in the drug store, but it is further. The new one is so easy to use," he said, his eyes bright with excitement.

Antoni mimed his explanation. "When you drop in your coins, the coins make different sounds. That lets the operator know what each coin is. Quarters make a gong noise, a dime is two little chimes, and a nickel is one chime."

Grazyna looked at her husband with mild disapproval. "Antoni, you don't need to go on so about these things. I am sure that Evelyn knows about such telephones."

But Antoni's enthusiasm couldn't be diminished. "But it is new, Grazyna... not like the old phone. You should go and try it."

"Of course, you want to call your family, Evelyn," Grazyna said.

"Yes... I have a friend I was going to visit when I fell in the snow and Antoni came to my rescue. I need to call her."

"I can take you to the grocery," Antoni said.

"Let her eat first, Antoni. She must be hungry. The stew is almost ready."

Eve *was* famished, as she always was after she'd time traveled. But if she could have, she would have passed on dinner to call Joni and find out if Patrick was there. She was burning to know, fighting to contain her eager restlessness.

If Patrick had gone to Joni's, and Eve prayed he had, he'd be worried sick.

After dinner, in a light snowfall, Antoni accompanied Eve along the snowy sidewalks to Flagler's Grocery Store, a block away. Her left ankle throbbed, and it was slightly swollen, but she didn't let it stop her. When she could find some privacy, she'd loosen her dress and remove her money belt, which contained a bracelet and a diamond ring, pain medication, antibiotics and twenty-first century ID and credit cards, for when they were ready to return to 2021, assuming they did return.

Patrick had declined wearing a money belt, pocketing two gold bands to be hocked, and slipping one of Annabelle's black-and-white photographs into his coat pocket. Eve had taken the other. She wished he hadn't been so superstitious when she'd suggested they both wear a money belt, in case they were separated.

"Call me daft, Eve, but if we both wear a money belt, we're guaranteed to get separated. If *you*, and only you, wear one, we'll be fine."

"That makes no sense, Patrick. It's not like you to be so superstitious."

"Eve, in the last few years, events have happened that have made me superstitious; that have made me question reality, luck, caprice and synchronicity. So, *you* wear the money belt, and when you light that lantern, we will hold hands firmly. All will be well."

Inside the narrow grocery store with close isles and tall shelves, Antoni led Eve to the wall-mounted, hand-crank, wooden box phone.

Eve had dreaded the moment when she'd have to ask to borrow the coins to make the call, but when she did, Antoni was delighted, and dug into his pockets, producing a nickel that he dropped into her hand.

He pointed to a wooden barrel filled with pickles. "I will give you your private time. I'll be over there when you have finished."

Eve had used similar telephones in 1914, although this one was smaller, and the hand crank was heavy and sturdy. She dialed the operator and waited. When she heard the pinched, muffled female voice, Eve asked her to dial the number for Darius Compton Foster.

A moment later, the operator instructed her to deposit the nickel and Eve did, hearing the single chime as the nickel slid down the inner slot.

While she waited, hearing the dull ring on the other end of the phone, Eve tapped her foot and scratched her head.

A deep voice on the other end said, "The Foster residence, Banks speaking."

Eve cleared her throat, pushing down excitement. "Banks, my name is Evelyn Gantly. I'm a friend of Joan Foster's. May I speak to her, please?"

There was a slight pause.

"Can you speak up, please? I could not hear your last name."

"Gantly. Evelyn Gantly. May I speak to Mrs. Foster? It's very important."

"One moment, madam. I will see if she is available."

Eve felt impatience and worry. She prayed Joni was there. Prayed Patrick was there.

And then Eve heard a sharp female voice say, "Who is this?"

Eve grinned. "Joni... It's me. Eve."

Silence.

Eve put her lips closer to the receiver. "Believe it. Joni, it *is* me. It's Eve Gantly. I'm here, in 1905. Can I come and see you? Is Patrick there?"

She heard a whoosh on the other end. "Did you say this is Eve? Eve Sharland?"

"Yes, Joni! I'm here. And I've lost Patrick. Is he there with you?"

"H-o-l-y shit! Are you friggin' kidding me?"

Eve felt a crashing relief, and she laughed out stress. Yep, that was Joni all right!

CHAPTER 25

Following Eve's telephone call with Joni, she and Antoni rushed back to the apartment. Eve thanked Grazyna for her kindness and said her goodbyes to the girls. Then she and Antoni returned to the lobby of the building, where Eve was to wait for Joni's carriage.

Overexcited and exhausted, Eve paced and worried about Patrick, conflicted as to what she should do and how to develop a plan of action. They had planned together, sure that as long as they stayed close, neither would end up in another time or place.

How would she find Colleen without Patrick's experience and expertise and, if she did manage to find her, should she then light Joni's lantern and return to the future without him, or wait?

Eve still felt a little bit out-of-body, a floaty sensation of not quite being totally present. After time traveling, it always took her a couple of days to adjust, and she didn't have a couple of days. She had to act. But how?

All the time Eve had been pacing and thinking, Antoni had been bantering about his tailor business and how smart and pretty his daughters were.

Eve listened, preoccupied, and readily agreed that Hanna and Zofia were bright and attractive.

"You're a very lucky man, Antoni, to have a lovely wife and two pretty daughters."

"Yes, Evelyn, I am a blessed man. A man who should be more thankful for my life and my little family. I must pray more, just as Grazyna scolds me to do. Speaking of family, Evelyn, I also make the silk shirts—a dozen at a time for some customers. When you find your husband, you come by to see me, and I'll make him a silk shirt. The best of silk shirts, I make."

"He would love that, Antoni," Eve said distracted, glancing out the window and down on the street. "Thank you."

"And I'll make him a suit, too. I have the best fabric. It has a faint stripe and is soft wool, 120 wool—the best wool you can buy. And I'll make the jacket single-breasted, with handmade buttonholes of course, and there will be a seamless lining, and a label reading Antoni Bankowski sewn on the inside right pocket."

"I don't think Patrick has ever had a suit of that quality, Antoni. I'll buy it and give it to him for Christmas."

Antoni's expression expanded with fervor and possibility, his hands cutting gestures in the air. "And then, I'll make you the most fine and prettiest dress you ever did see."

When Eve spotted Joni's black lacquered carriage approach, she let out a gleeful scream and burst out the door, with Antoni trailing behind, his eyes lighting up on the impressive carriage as it came drifting into view. It arrived amid swirling snow flurries in a gust of wind and, in Antoni's eyes, it was an object of romance.

Its glowing brass lamps, erect coachman in top hat and royal blue livery, and two white horses with ceremonial plumes were a rare sight in such a lower middle-class neighborhood. From the windows, Grazyna and the two girls stared out in wonder as Joni's carriage pulled up to the curb and halted, white vapor puffing from the horses' nostrils.

Eve gave Antoni a peck on the cheek, thanked him again, and hurried toward the carriage to meet Joni as the coachmen climbed down and opened the carriage door. Joni emerged and, when she saw Eve, she let out a girlish scream, and before the coachman could help her, she leaped down to the street, all smiles and emotion, her big, lavish hat and elegant cashmere coat revealing a rich, high society woman.

Joni's face and arms opened wide. "EVE!"

They fell into each other's arms, and rocked and laughed and wept, while Antoni and the coachman looked on with quiet interest.

Eve pulled back, holding Joni at arm's length. "Look at you, girl. You're as sexy as ever in that hat and gown. You haven't aged more than a month."

Joni twisted up her lips and blurted out a laugh. "A month? Don't bullshit a bullshitter, Eve. I'm fatter, older, and not a bit wiser. *You're* the one who hasn't aged a day, because you haven't aged at all. It's been over twenty years and I've given birth to two kids. And you're still, what, thirty-something?"

Eve gazed lovingly at Joni, her eyes filling with happy tears. "I'm so glad to see you again, Joni. I've missed you so much."

"You've missed *me?* I've been dreaming about this day for over twenty years. I gave up thinking you'd ever come back."

They hugged again, eyes shut, blissful tears streaming.

INSIDE THE CARRIAGE, they were all hand-holding and rapid conversation, Joni falling back into her twenty-first century slang and informal posture. They caught up on Joni's two kids, on Darius' thriving medical career, and Joni's various charitable organizations.

"I don't mean this the way it's going to sound, Eve, but I've kind of had it with all the charitable meetings and dinners and schmoosing with the Astors, the Vanderbilts and the Harringshaws. I'd give a kidney to get back into dancing, singing and acting again."

"Have you told Darius?"

"Hell, no. He'd have a heart attack if I even mentioned it. After all, he's the personal doctor of Charles T. Guggenheim, who made his fortune in such interesting ways as mining and smelting. Not that I know what the hell smelting is and could give a big rat's ass. But I pretend to when Darius brings it up. I smile, and I say, very sweetly, and very sarcastically, 'Smelting? How *utterly* fascinating.' Then he gets mad at me and leaves the room. But I'm not always so bad, Eve. Sometimes, I'm a good wife, and I put up with his bullshit, and I don't say a word. Well, welcome to marriage, right?"

"But you love your kids."

Joni melted a little, and her eyes went soft. "Oh, Eve, I love them with every cell of my body. Wait until you meet them. William's a bit like Darius, a little aloof and proper, but he's a good boy. Very smart with the numbers and business. Lavinia is a beauty, Eve. At fourteen years old she's all dreamy, elegant, smart and lovely. In just a few years, some rich man is going to sweep her off her feet and take her away from us. I'll love that day, and I'll hate that day. No way is any man going to be good enough for her."

Eve nearly divulged the fact that Lavinia would indeed marry Benedict Vanderbilt, one of the wealthiest men in the country, if not the world, but she decided not to. At least not yet.

It wasn't until they were about to arrive at the Fosters' Gramercy Park brownstone that Joni turned serious. "Eve, I've been doing all the talking, like always, because I'm so excited, but I'm dying to know why you're here. I want to know it all. Everything… but first, I have to tell you that Darius is, to put it mildly, freaking out that you're here."

"I was afraid of that," Eve said.

"We got into this big, friggin' argument just before I left and I stormed out, so I don't know what we're going to find when we get there. Sorry about that, but he is so scared to death of that lantern. He has wanted me to get rid of that thing ever since you and Patrick left in 1884."

"I know, Joni."

"How do you know?"

"It's a long story."

"I have time."

"… I'll tell you. But not now."

"Okay, so what's happened to Patrick? It's not one of those lantern reset things again, is it? He's not back in 1884 again, is he?"

Eve frowned. "No. I mean, I don't know where he is. We left at the same time. We were holding hands; we stayed close. We knew what to expect, but the travel was so rough this time. We were kicked around and tossed all over the place. Then we got separated, and I lost him. I fell from the sky like a rock and landed in Riverside Park in a pile of snow with the wind knocked out of me, and my left foot and leg hurting like crazy."

"But you're all right?"

"Yeah, I'm fine. My foot will be okay in a few days after I've taken some *Advil* I brought along. My leg is bruised, but nothing's broken, thank God."

"Do you think Patrick landed in another time?"

Eve's face darkened. "I just don't know. Like I said on the phone, we'd planned it all out. Every detail. If anything happened, we were going to meet at your house. So, if he hasn't contacted you or shown up, who knows where he is… and I don't want to think about it."

Joni patted Eve's hand. "Well, don't worry about it, Eve. You know Patrick. He's a survivor and he'll find a way. He loves you and he'll always find a way to track you down."

Joni adjusted herself in the soft leather seat. "We're almost at the house. Tell me why you're here. It's got to be a real doozy if you and Patrick lighted that lantern again."

Eve sighed. "It's awful, Joni. It's just the worst thing."

And then Eve gave her a detailed account of what had happened. When Eve had finished, the parked carriage had been in the driveway for over ten minutes, with the coachman patiently waiting outside.

Joni's expression went from shock to anger to compassion. She took Eve into her arms and held her close. "Oh... God, I hurt for you, Eve. I'm so angry and so sad. How could anyone do that? How is it possible?"

Eve rested her head on Joni's shoulder. "Annabelle's a cold one, Joni. I saw it in her eyes. I can't imagine Colleen being raised by her. It drives me crazy to even think about it. And if this Annabelle woman returned to 1904, which is where she came from, then Colleen is nearly a year older."

"Patrick must have been out of his mind," Joni said.

"He was. He didn't sleep or eat for days. He said that when he finds the woman, he's going to break her neck... and that's not so good, either."

Joni leaned in close to Eve. "And, knowing the Patrick of old as I know him—the 1884 Patrick—he *will* kill her."

"It's a nightmare, Joni. All of it... The lantern, the time travel; losing Patrick and Colleen. I'm so lost, and so scared, and so sick and tired of that lantern. I'm going to find Tesla and, I swear, I'm going to slap him silly."

"How did this crazy woman find a Tesla lantern?"

"She said she bought it in a shop. She didn't say what kind of shop."

"Do you think she got it from Tesla?"

"I have no idea."

Joni straightened up. "Well... we'll find Colleen. I'll help you all I can and in any way I can. Meanwhile, let's go inside and warm up and let the coachman get out of the cold. Then describe this Annabelle in detail. Who knows, maybe I've seen her or know her."

Eve took Joni's hand and squeezed it. "Even better. I have a photo of her."

"Perfect," Joni said.

"At least the lantern brought me back to you, Joni. It's not all bad."

They sat in each other's arms, feeling the cold seep into them.

"So maybe you should stay here this time, Eve. If you can't find Patrick and Colleen, maybe this time, you should stay, and build a new life here."

CHAPTER 26

After a good night's sleep in his hotel bed, Patrick had breakfast at a local café and then found a men's clothing store close by. It was his second full day in 1905, and he was still suffering from partial amnesia.

He bought two suits of clothes, two bowler hats, a stylish overcoat, ties, shirts, underwear and socks, and paid a tailor extra to hem his pants while he waited.

By early afternoon, he was fully dressed in a new suit and tie, full-length winter coat, stiff pair of new boots and a new bowler. He left his hotel and went striding past Madison Square Park, heading downtown, throwing caution to the wind, having decided to visit Megan and Colin. He hoped they were still living at the same place as they were in 1884, but what were the chances?

He had to contact someone he remembered. He had to see a familiar face and discuss the past; discuss what had happened to him. Maybe then he could fill in the missing gaps in his memory.

Patrick crossed Fifth Avenue. A thick layer of snow still covered the curbs and the streets. A large sleigh, piled high with luggage, slid past Patrick with ringing bells and the snapping of a whip. Patrick darted back from it, but he took a spray of snow onto the side of his coat from the sleigh's backwash. Cursing the driver, Patrick slapped off the snow and continued on, under a gray, moody sky, facing a chilly wind.

When he turned onto his old street, West 22nd Street, between Seventh and Eighth Avenues, he fought back apprehension. This was where he and Emma had lived for nearly two years. He remembered that much. He remembered her death, and it darkened his already black mood. There were more memories circling around in his head, but he couldn't grab them and put them into any logical sequence.

A hansom trotted by; a dog wandered, sniffing the ground for scraps; and on the other side of the street, a coal wagon stood, waiting to make a delivery to a house nearby.

Patrick pressed on with his hands deep in his pockets. He didn't look up, but he was aware when he passed his old house.

He glanced up nervously at the short flight of cement stairs that led to Colin's and Megan's porch. Inside had been their four-room apartment. He hesitated, then slowly mounted the stairs, a lump so large in his throat that he couldn't swallow it away. How would Megan react when she saw that he'd not aged in twenty-one years?

On the porch, Patrick paused at the front door, seeing a square window covered with a white lace curtain.

He lifted the brass knocker and let it fall. The noise seemed loud in his ears, and the wait was excruciating. When no one appeared, he rapped lightly on the door.

A moment later, the door opened a few inches and a young woman peered out. "Yes? What do you want?"

Patrick removed his hat and tried to smile, but he was afraid it was more of a smirk. "Excuse me for bothering you, but do Colin and Megan O'Brien live here?"

There was another pause before the door opened fully, revealing a young woman in her late teens or early twenties, with astonishing green eyes and red hair styled in lovely waves and falling tresses. She was freckled and striking in her youth and vitality.

She looked Patrick over, carefully. "Who are you?"

"My name is Patrick Gantly. I used to know Colin and Megan. I was in town and dropped by, hoping to see them. Do they still live here?"

"It must have been a long time ago," the young woman said. "I've never seen you and I know all their friends and relatives."

Patrick nodded, twisting the brim of his hat in his hands. "Yes, it was... a long time ago. May I see them? Are they about?"

She considered him. "My father's dead. My mother's in the kitchen."

"Colin? Dead?"

"Yes."

Patrick lowered his head, giving it a little shake. "I'm sorry to hear it. My condolences. He was a good man."

The young woman stepped back, her face impassive. "It's cold today. Come in. I'll tell my mother you're here."

Patrick entered lightly, and the door closed behind him.

"I'm Kathleen, Colin's and Megan's daughter."

Patrick removed his gloves and extended his hand. "It's a pleasure to meet you, Kathleen."

She took his hand limply, and he felt the softness of it. She averted her eyes. "Have a seat in the parlor, and I'll let mother know you're here."

Patrick unbuttoned his coat and moved to the nearest chair, but he didn't sit. He stood appraising the silent, comfortable room, with a glowing fire and functional furniture from the last century. Displayed on the mantel was a black-and-white photograph of a man Patrick recognized as Colin, although it was the photo of an older, more serious man than Patrick recalled.

It stirred his memories, and his emotions churned like dark, swirling pools of water; buried memories swimming below those waters; and for the life of him, Patrick couldn't reach down, grab those memories and yank them to the surface.

Megan entered the parlor quietly, like a shadow. Patrick had half-expected to see a young woman like Kathleen, a thin, attractive redhead with green eyes and kindly manner, but the Megan before him was nearly unrecognizable. This older Megan had a heavy figure, a tired, sad face, and lusterless eyes. She stared blankly, looking beyond him as if focusing on something else.

"Hello, Megan. It's Patrick Gantly."

Kathleen stood to the right of her mother, her body taut and erect, like a protector.

Megan blinked away clouds and focused on him. Her voice was whispery, as if she hadn't used it in a while. "Patrick Gantly? Is it really you?"

"Yes, Megan. It's been a long time."

Her eyes widened on him. "Patrick?" she said, her confused eyes exploring him.

"Yes… It's me."

"Young… But you are so young, you're like the strapping lad you were all those years ago."

Patrick tried for a grin. "I guess I've been strong and able to keep the bad leprechauns away."

She kept her eyes on him and gestured toward the chair. "Sit down, Patrick."

She turned to her daughter. "Kathleen, bring tea… some cookies. Those cookies you made yesterday. Yes, bring those."

Kathleen waited, concerned about her mother's state, and wary of Patrick and his motives.

"Go, Kathleen," Megan said. "Stop your hovering about me. I'm as good as the day I was born, and maybe a bit better. Go now and let me have a talk with Patrick Gantly."

Before leaving, Kathleen assisted her mother to the sofa and eased her down. After Kathleen was gone, Patrick removed his coat and placed it on the broad arm of the chair. He sat down, keeping his hat in his lap, noticing that Megan had not aged well. Her pale skin sagged, her shoulders had rounded, and she had tired, watery eyes. She looked older than her years, and that saddened Patrick. She had been a playful, intelligent woman, filled with life and enthusiasm.

Megan's eyes again traveled across Patrick's face, as if she were seeking a clue to his youth. "It has been so many years, and you're as handsome a man as you ever was, Patrick Gantly. And look at me, a worn-out old rag of a woman, not yet fifty years old."

"You've still got the heart in you, Megan. I see it."

"The heart in me is all broken up, Patrick. It's a sad woman's heart."

Patrick was about to speak, but Megan held up a hand to stop him. "... But what's with my bad manners? Let's not be talking about the likes of me when I have a guest in my house. A guest from so long ago, it seems it was a dream. And yes, Patrick, you have not aged and, as God is my witness, I don't understand it. Perhaps there is a joke in you, and you're Patrick's own son come for a bit of a laugh on an old woman?"

Patrick smiled. "No, Megan. I have no son. It's purely good living, and not so many nights in the pubs with the lads."

Patrick looked toward the kitchen. "Kathleen is quite lovely. She has your hair and your eyes."

"She is as good as gold, Patrick. A blessing to a mother. A woman couldn't ask more of a daughter, and I'm afraid I ask too much of her."

"Does she live with you?"

"No, she recently up and got herself married to a good man. He works at a shoe factory on Day Street, and he's a good worker. Never late on the job. He wants to open his own pub someday, when he has enough money saved for it."

Patrick leaned forward, lowering his voice. "Megan... I'm sorry to hear about Colin. What happened to him, if you've got the strength to tell me?"

"The strength I have, Patrick, but the heart in me is weak with sorrow and grief."

Patrick waited while Megan gathered herself. She reached into her gray day dress pocket and removed an embroidered handkerchief. Balling it up in her hand, she blotted her misty eyes.

"It was a year ago Friday next, Patrick. Colin got up from the supper table and he dropped his pipe from his mouth. I asked him if he was all right, but he didn't answer me. He went staggering down from the kitchen to the parlor, right where you sit now, and he sat. Being worried and feeling the fear rise in me, I asked him what the matter was. But then he seemed unable to answer. I saw a strange wildness in his eyes, so I hurried next door, where they have a telephone, and they called a doctor. But before the doctor arrived, Colin was gone... Just like that, he was gone. I was with him, holding his hand, and he tried to talk, to say something, but nothing came out. But he died easy, Patrick, without a move or a struggle, and the two of us were together, and I did not leave him until they came and took him away."

"You have my deepest condolences, Megan. Colin was a fine man. A good man."

"That he was, Patrick. That he was. I shall never find another as kind and as good. A man who never struck me once; a man who had only pleasant things to say about people. A man who read his Bible every night and quoted verse on Sunday before our supper."

Patrick eased back in the chair. "Are you being provided for, Megan?"

"I get by. I take in some seamstress work... enough to keep the roof over my head and some food on the table. And then Kathleen is always coming over with food for her mom, being the angel she is."

Megan reminisced about her life with Colin, pausing often to blot her tears and glance up at the ceiling, as if summoning his spirit. Patrick listened patiently until Kathleen returned, carrying a tray with a teapot and cozy, a plate of cookies and three cups and saucers. She set the tray on the coffee table near her mother and began preparing the tea.

Megan clasped her hands together. "Patrick, Kathleen bakes the best Scottish oak cakes. She got the recipe from a neighbor, and I've gone around the moon on them. You must try one."

After the tea was poured and Kathleen joined her mother on the sofa, Patrick nibbled on one of the oak cakes and delighted in the flavor. He complimented Kathleen, both on her cookies and on her thick, lustrous red hair. That softened the girl, and that's what Patrick had intended. He'd sensed Kathleen didn't trust him.

While Megan sipped her tea and Kathleen kept her sharp eyes on him, Patrick's mind filled with questions, but he didn't know where to begin or how to ask them.

"Where do you live, Mr. Gantly?" Kathleen asked.

"I'm staying at the Knickerbocker Hotel."

"And how is your daughter, Patrick?" Megan asked. "She must be about Kathleen's age now."

The question jarred him. He straightened up, lost for words.

Megan lowered the cup from her lips and turned to Kathleen. "Her name was Colleen, and she was the sweetest little child you ever did see. And she was no trouble and barely cried at all. So how is she, Patrick? Why didn't you bring your daughter with you for me to see?"

Kathleen saw Patrick was shaken and searching for words.

Megan narrowed her worried eyes on him. "Is Colleen all right, Patrick?"

Patrick placed his cup on the saucer, rattling it as he did so, his brain flaming with confusion. Suddenly, in his head, the burst of a flashbulb lit up the dark corners of his mind and, for seconds, he saw photographs—a half-remembered face, a busy street, a flying machine roaring overhead. He heard fragments of conversations.

Kathleen and Megan exchanged concerned glances.

Megan said, "Patrick... Are you feeling yourself?"

Patrick rose, his eyes moving, his mind pitching about like a ship on a stormy sea. He forced his gaze on Megan. "Megan... Did Colleen survive Emma's death?"

Megan tried to understand. "Yes, Patrick. Colleen survived, and she was a good and strong baby. What has happened to you? Don't you remember the last time I saw you?"

"No, Megan, I don't. Tell me."

"You were standing right here in the parlor, Patrick. Don't you remember? You said you had to go away, and you were taking Colleen with you. You asked me to wrap her in warm blankets and prepare her for travel. I did so, and you left with the little child, flagging down a cab in the falling snow. Forgive me, Patrick, but I cursed you for taking the little girl out into the cold winter night like that. I did curse you for it. Now, I could bite my wicked tongue, I could. But then, I was angry at you and scared to death of losing Colleen. You must remember…"

While the two women looked on, perplexed and uneasy, Patrick stared in desperate reflection, fighting to tear down the cobwebs that covered his disorganized mind.

When he softly repeated the name "Colleen," the rigid shadows that had held his mind captive dissolved into a glow of dawn. And then a powerful wave of recollection broke over him, and he swayed like a palm, engulfed by spinning shards of past memory, present urgency and a daring future. He shut his eyes, struggling to mix and match and knit the fragments together.

And then, like a boastful song, a woman's voice sang in his ears, calling out to him. "Patrick, where are you? Come to me."

In his mind, he saw the woman. He knew the woman. This lovely woman, her face eager, her blue eyes beseeching. Her arms were outstretched, her hands reaching for him.

"Remember, Patrick. If we're separated, we'll meet at Joni's! Remember, Patrick. Colleen!"

CHAPTER 27

The next morning, Sunday, November 12, Eve awoke and sat up, her eyes wide open and staring. Where was she? She glanced around the bedroom, pulling her mind from a dream and reorienting herself to the time and place. No, she was not in her bedroom in 2021; she was in one of Joni's guest bedrooms in November 1905. Patrick wasn't beside her, and dear little Colleen had vanished with Annabelle Palmer.

Dread and urgency constricted her chest. What time was it? What should she do? What could she do on a Sunday? She blinked the sleep from her eyes and began to make alternate plans, ticking off items in her head. First, find a jeweler and get cash for the bracelet and diamond ring. Both items had time traveled without any damage. They would bring a good price, enough to live on for years in this time.

Second, she'd have to find a place to live. Last night, after she and Joni had entered the house, Darius had been waiting in the living room. He had left the fireplace and met the ladies in the foyer.

Eve had been genuinely delighted to see him again, and she'd offered him a warm smile. He'd aged well, having an erect posture, no paunch, and a full head of salt and pepper hair that added distinction. It was Dr. Darius Foster who had helped save her life in 1884, after Edwin Bennett had shot her. And, working together, they had struggled to save Patrick's wife, Emma, during a difficult childbirth. They couldn't save Emma, but they had brought Colleen into the world.

"Hello again, Dr. Foster," Eve had said nervously. "I know this must be a surprise… I mean, seeing me again."

He'd stared at her for a long moment, and then lowered his eyes, not speaking. Eve saw his jaw tighten.

"I won't stay long, and I'll try not to be a bother," Eve said.

"You won't be a bother," Joni said, giving her husband a frosty glance. "Where are your manners, Darius? Can't you at least say hello?"

Darius hooded his eyes. "You're looking well, Mrs. Gantly… quite youthful."

Eve saw irritation roll off Joni in waves, and Eve didn't want to be the cause of another argument.

"You look well, Dr. Foster," Eve said pleasantly.

Darius squared his shoulders and forced a formal tone. "Thank you, Mrs. Gantly. I trust you and your husb…" He stopped. "I trust you are well. I understand Mr. Gantly is not with you?"

"No… I hope he'll arrive soon."

"Yes, well, in the meantime, you must be weary from your…" He sought the right word. "… from your travel. Please, stay as long as is necessary."

"Thank you, Dr. Foster."

"You appear unchanged from the last time I saw you, although your attire is somewhat questionable."

That had set Joni off. "Stop it, Darius! What an asinine and rude thing to say. You know where she came from and what's going on. I have clothes that will fit her. Don't worry, she won't be meeting any of your patients until she's properly dressed."

Eve shuddered. Joni's sharp words had both embarrassed and angered Darius.

"Just so," he'd concluded, his face flushing red. He'd bowed to Eve, ignored his wife, and returned to the living room and his chair by the fire.

Eve had not met either of the children. Lavinia had already gone to bed, and William, a freshman at Harvard, wouldn't return home until a week before Christmas.

Although Eve had never met Joni's kids, Patrick had, when he'd time traveled to 1925. By then, both were in their thirties and married. Patrick had told Eve about his impressions. William was austere and snobbish, Lavinia warm and generous.

In the early morning light, Eve struggled to quiet her mind and still her emotions. She dropped back down on the bed, sinking her head into the deep feather pillow, tugging the royal blue comforter up to her chin. Instinctively, her hand patted the empty space beside her, and she pretended Patrick was there, or had been there, or would be there.

She shut her eyes and imagined his warm lips kissing her nose, her cheeks, her neck, her mouth. She was hungry for his lips; hungry to feel the weight of him, the breath of him, the man of him. She was lost without him and his humor; without his magic touch and his exploring fingers. She was lost without his love.

She could almost hear him say, in his playful, exaggerated Irish accent, "Eve, my love, as my old Da used to say, 'What butter and whiskey won't cure, a good wife who can frolic through Cupid's Grove, will.'"

Eve let out a heavy sigh and whispered. "Patrick... where are you? Once again, you have to find me. I don't know how to find you."

AFTER EVE HAD ENJOYED a delicious bath the evening before, Joni had dropped by her room with a maid, carrying silk pajamas and a robe, three pairs of shoes that nearly fit, as well as two dresses, one a mauve-colored, afternoon tea party gown, and the other a white linen pleated dress, with puffed sleeves.

At a little after eight o'clock in the morning, Eve left the comfortable bed, managed an updo twist hairstyle, and applied light makeup, also from Joni. She finished with a few squirts of French perfume she found on the bureau. Then she slipped into the white linen dress, pushed her feet into low-heeled shoes, and went gliding off to breakfast.

A maid directed her to the lovely dining room, which was charmingly decorated with tasteful, bucolic landscape paintings and cherry wood cabinets and dining room set. It had a black marble mantel and fireplace, and bright natural light streaming in from tall, lace-curtained windows.

Joni and Lavinia were sitting at the dining room table, which was covered with white linen and decorated with fresh flowers. It held an elegant silver coffee pot and a rose-themed tea set. The two were speaking in whispers when Eve entered the room, feeling like an intruder.

The evening before, Joni had mentioned that Darius usually left for the hospital before eight and didn't return until dinnertime. Eve was relieved. She didn't want to feel responsible for creating a further rift in the Fosters' marriage.

Joni and Lavinia lit up when they saw Eve, and they rose together in a smiling welcome. Joni enthusiastically introduced her daughter, and Eve thought Lavinia had all the grace, polish and manners of a mature woman. Her lush, auburn hair was artfully arranged in a Gibson Girl style, a kind of fluffy bouffant; her refined features, high cheekbones and generous mouth all suggested that one was in the presence of a royal princess.

Lavinia wore a blue, patterned ankle-length dress that revealed a slim, but shapely figure; the dress was enhanced by a choker of pink pearls and matching dangling earrings. It was an ensemble designed to impress, especially since it was morning, when women usually dressed more casually, but Joni's expression of pride said it all. She wanted Eve to see her daughter as a work of art that she adored, and it was easy to see the glow of love in Joni's eyes.

While they talked and nibbled on scrambled eggs and ham, Joni showed none of her informal twenty-first century personality. Her posture was ruler straight and her words carefully chosen, with no slang peppering her conversation.

"Of course, you'll stay here," Joni said. "I won't, for a minute, let you go off alone to some hotel."

"Joni... I don't want to be in the way."

"How are you going to get in the way? It's a big house. And anyway, I want you in the way. I can't tell you how happy I am to see you again."

Lavinia's enchanting brown eyes lingered softly on Eve. "Mrs. Gantly, my mother tells me that you two met quite by accident."

Eve shot Joni a look and Joni, nearly imperceptibly, shook her head.

Eve thought, *So, what does that mean, Joni?*

Joni jumped in. "Yes... Eve and I met at a charity ball, didn't we, Eve?"

Eve's eyes shifted as she searched for the right words. "Yes... Yes, that's right. Yes, it was quite by accident."

The true story of how they'd met would not have been appropriate for Lavinia's ears. It wouldn't be appropriate for many people's ears.

Eve and Joni had first met at a Manhattan bar, a nightclub called Static. Eve had met a guy at the bar. She didn't remember his name, but his head was shaved, so she called him Baldie. They were dancing. While they were dancing, Eve had accidently bumped into Joni, who was dancing with a big, tattooed guy from Chicago, where Joni was originally from.

Irritated, Joni shouted at Eve. "Hey, look out. You stepped on my foot!"

Eve yelled back over the loud music, "Your foot's taking up half the floor. Move it outside!"

Joni, feeling a little high from her two vodka tonics, pushed her threatening face into Eve's. "Do you think that's funny?"

Eve, feeling a little high from her two vodka sodas, grinned darkly and said, "Yeah. I do. I think it's hilarious. Don't you see me laughing?"

Their eyes had locked in a challenge while their two dance partners stood by, neither knowing what they should do. Tattoo Guy was broader than Baldie, but Baldie was taller than Tattoo Guy. They both took a step back, allowing the girls to fight it out.

Eve's and Joni's hard stares held, and held, and held. Finally, Eve's mouth twitched. Joni's mouth twisted. Still, their eyes held.

The ends of Joni's mouth lifted in a slight grin. Eve's eyes widened into a mischievous grin.

Joni said, "Do you like the guy you're with?"

Eve said, "Not much."

Joni said, "Do you like this place?"

Eve said, "Not much."

"I know a bar where cops and firemen go after work."

Eve's eyes grew round with interest. "Really? Cops, huh?"

"Yeah… and firemen."

"I've never dated a fireman," Eve said.

"Me either," Joni said.

"I'd like to meet one, or a cop," Eve said. "Maybe a detective."

"Me too."

"What's your name?" Eve asked.

"Joni. Yours?"

"Eve."

"Let's go, Eve. Let's go find us a cop or a fireman." And that was it. A friendship was born.

The story ended with Eve and Joni never arriving at the cop/fireman bar. They were hungry, so they ducked into a pizza place, ate, talked and became the best of friends.

Eve was brought back to the present when Lavinia asked, "What kind of charity ball was it?"

Eve nearly spit out her coffee. She reached for her napkin and blotted her mouth. "I don't remember," Eve said. "Do you, Joni?"

Joni offered a small, cheeky grin. "I believe it was the policemen's/firemen's ball, wasn't it, Eve?"

Eve forced back laughter, squeezing her fingers into fists. Then she said, sweetly, "Yes, Joni, I believe that was it. Yes… you are so right."

Lavinia studied both women, amused, knowing full well that her mother was lying. When she was a girl, she had been thrilled by her mother's secret bedtime stories about time travel and her life in the twenty-first century, including tales about Eve and Patrick Gantly. Of course, Joni had stressed that she could never tell her father, or anyone else about them.

"These stories are just between the two of us, Lavinia," she'd said, as she'd kissed her goodnight. "Don't ever, ever repeat these stories to anyone, all right?"

That morning, Joni had entered Lavinia's room and she'd strongly reiterated to her that she was to pretend ignorance about time travel and about Eve and Patrick Gantly, emphasizing that Darius knew nothing about

Joni's and Lavinia's secret, and he'd hit the roof if he ever found out.

But seeing Eve in the flesh and knowing that she'd time traveled from the twenty-first century electrified Lavinia. It was as if she had lightning in her veins, and it took all her willpower not to fire questions at Eve.

Lavinia considered the story while she sipped her cup of tea. "How nice," she finally said, with a small smile. "Yes, what a pleasant story."

Joni frowned, seeing the eager expression on her daughter's face, and reading it. Lavinia was struggling not to reveal all that she knew about Eve and Patrick and time travel.

Joni cleared her throat. "Yes, a pleasant story it is."

As tacit humor circled the table, and the atmosphere was lightened by the glistening vase of fresh flowers and the silver trays holding a variety of foods, Eve looked at Lavinia and she suddenly felt a pang of sadness, dismay and fear.

Where was her darling baby girl, Colleen? Would she be able to find her? Would Eve have the pleasure, joy, and pride of watching Colleen grow to be as beautiful and poised as Lavinia?

Joni sensed Eve's sudden change of mood. She laid her fork aside and gazed sympathetically at her friend, her voice soft with confidence. "Eve… Don't worry. We'll find Colleen. We'll find Patrick. I know it."

Eve's smile didn't reach her eyes. "Let's start tomorrow morning. I can't wait any longer. I have to find Colleen, and I have to hope and pray that Patrick will find me."

Lavinia's curious eyes rested on Eve, keenly aware that secrets were hovering about her. Lavinia knew there was an adventure to come, and she hoped she could be a part of it.

CHAPTER 28

Eve and Joni spent Monday morning selling Eve's jewelry for cash, then browsing various women's shops to find clothes for Eve. They'd returned to the house with their purchases, and after a quick lunch, they'd climbed aboard Joni's carriage and set off for lower Manhattan, eager and determined to find Annabelle Palmer.

Eve's persistent worry over Patrick's whereabouts weighed heavily on her, but she was grateful for Joni's humor, goal-driven energy, and unfailing optimism that he would show up.

They left the carriage on Orchard Street and started off, gingerly stepping around patches of melting snow, dog poop and trash, as they entered a world quite different from the modern one.

They wandered through crowded neighborhoods with tenements designed in ornate Queen Anne and Romanesque Revival styles, housed by Greeks, Hungarians, Poles, Irish, Italians, Russians, Slovaks and Ukrainians. It was a community of pushcarts and

The Christmas Eve Journey

bustling shops, of customers and merchants shouting in foreign tongues, bartering over food, jewelry and clothes.

Eve was fully dressed in the period, complete with a broad-brimmed feather hat and high laced boots for the cold and snow. Tucked inside her coat pocket was the black-and-white photograph of Annabelle Palmer.

Although Annabelle hadn't given her exact address on Orchard Street, she'd revealed enough information so that Eve and Patrick had surmised her apartment would have been in the area. They'd agreed that their first plan of action would be to go there and try their luck, showing her photograph to merchants where she might have shopped, asking if they recognized her.

After an hour of presenting Annabelle's photo to shop owners and street vendors, and having no luck, Eve's foot was sore and swelling. They decided to find a café and warm themselves.

It was called King's Coffee and Teas, a long, narrow space with six round tables and chairs and a white marble counter. There was a display case with shelves of tarts and creamy pastry, and wooden shelves above, filled with cannisters of teas and coffee.

Eve and Joni sat near a window that had a view of a carriage house, a barbershop and a beer hall, where a steady stream of men in mustaches and bowlers came and went. They puffed pipes, chatted, nibbled street food, and picked their way through the street crowds.

"Busy place," Joni said. "Hundreds, if not thousands, must live around here. It's wild. I never knew so many immigrants were packed in like this."

Eve sighed out discouragement as she gently flexed her left foot, hoping to loosen the tightness. "I wonder if Annabelle even lives around here."

Joni flexed her feet as well. "My feet are killing me. Your ankle must be swollen. I hate to say it, Eve, but I don't think we're going to find anyone around here who knows Annabelle. Like you said, we may not even be in the right neighborhood. It's a shot in the dark."

"It's the only shot we have, Joni, so let's not give up yet. We might get lucky."

After they'd been served coffee, as well as a large, hot apple strudel with real whipped cream that they shared, Eve took a chance, pulled the photo of Annabelle from her pocket and held it up to the waiter. He was stocky and balding, with a thick, white mustache and slow, hound dog eyes.

"Have you ever seen this woman?" Eve asked.

In some thick accent that neither Eve nor Joni recognized, he said, "Vhat is dis vit dat voman? Vhy her?"

Eve said, "We're trying to find her. Has she ever come in here? Do you recognize her? Do you understand what I'm saying?"

"Ya, me understand. You lookin' for dis voman, am I right about it?"

"Yes… Yes. Have you ever seen her?" Eve pressed.

He reached into his white apron pocket for a pair of wire-rimmed spectacles and slipped them on, peering at Eve, carefully, as if he were seeing her for the first time. He took the photograph from her, sniffed, and cleared his throat. His gaze stalled on the photo, his dark eyes looming large through the glasses.

Eve glanced at Joni, hopeful. They waited.

The waiter turned the photo this way and that, considering.

"Do you recognize her?" Eve asked, sitting on the edge of her seat.

He stuck his nose into the air, as if in deep thought. He shut his eyes. He opened them, nodded, and handed the photo back to Eve.

"Ya, I know dis voman. She here, back some months ago."

Eve came to life. "You know her? You recognize her?" Eve said, making sure she'd heard him correctly.

He nodded. "Ya. A time back ago."

"How long ago?" Eve said, her pulse jumping. "How long back?"

He removed his spectacles and dropped them into the apron pocket. "Months... many months now. Not seen her for dah months. Just before dah spring she come here. She come here... two time in dah week, sometime. Ya, maybe one or two times in dah week, she come here."

Eve was vibrating with tension and hope. "Do you know her name? Did she tell you her name?"

He pursed his fat lips. "Name? No name she gives. She don't talk to me, or nobody."

"Was she alone?" Eve asked.

"Not alone. With... how do you say... little one. Girl," he said, breaking into a grandfatherly smile. "Yes, little girl, about dis high," he said, using his hand, holding it out three feet from the floor. "Ya, about dat high was dah little one."

Eve thought she could feel the floor shifting, moving. Her heart was kicking, face hot. "Do you know where she lives? She must live around here some place."

He shook his head. "No... Not dat. She come with little girl, have coffee, girl with dah milk and cookies. Then leave. No talk to me, but I wave to little girl, and she smile at me and say, 'Goodbye...'" He leaned back, proudly. "She have dah good manners, dah pretty one. Ya."

Joni said, "What did the little girl look like? Do you understand what I'm saying?"

"Ya, I know. Girl have face like little angel in dah paintings in church. You know? Ya, little angel girl."

"What color hair?" Eve asked. "Her eyes? What color were her eyes?"

He pointed to Eve's hair. "Color like yours hair, but... how do you say dis in dah English? Bright, with curls dat bounce up and down. Ya. Eyes? No... I don't see so much in the eyes of dah little girl. Busy here. Got to go now."

Reflexively, Eve seized his arm. "Please sir... I have to find this woman. Which way did she go when she left the café? Left? Right?"

He yanked his arm from Eve's tight grasp and snorted, eyes narrowing. "Left. She always go left out dat door. I go now. Busy."

They paid the bill and pushed out of the café door onto the sidewalk, turned left, and walked aggressively to a shoe repair shop. They spent the next two hours showing the photo to vendors and dray drivers, who were waiting for their flatbeds to be loaded. Eve and Joni pushed into a crowded women's shop, a bakery, and a flower shop, but no one else recognized Annabelle.

Dispirited and worn out, they clambered back into Joni's carriage and returned to Joni's house in Gramercy Park, neither saying much as they traveled.

In the late afternoon, Eve sat by the fire, staring sadly into the flames. Joni came over, stood behind her, and placed her hands on her shoulders.

"I'm sorry, Eve. We came so close."

Eve reached for Joni's left hand. "I keep thinking that our waiter could have easily been mistaken. Did you see the thick lenses in those glasses?"

"I don't think he was mistaken," Joni said. "He described Colleen, didn't he? I mean, what are the odds of a woman, who looks like Annabelle, walking into his restaurant with a child who looks like Colleen?"

Eve dropped her chin. "I suppose you're right."

"And the waiter did say it had been months ago. We should go back tomorrow and try again. If the waiter remembered her, surely somebody else will, too."

"Yeah, you're right, Joni. And, anyway, it's all we have to go on, so I have to keep trying."

Joni rounded the chair and sat near Eve in a burgundy tufted chair.

"Joni... Why was Annabelle living in that neighborhood? It was so ethnic and working class. She wasn't."

"She told you she was the best jewel thief 1904 had ever seen, right? And she had enough money to live like a queen for the rest of her life?"

"Yeah, so why live in that neighborhood, of all neighborhoods?"

Joni lifted her head. "Eve, why don't we go to the police? If she's a jewel thief, they'll know about her."

"Yes, but, as Patrick said, if Annabelle is the best at what she does, the police would have no idea where she is, and she probably uses many aliases. And maybe I've answered my own question about why Annabelle lived in that neighborhood. It was probably a good place to hide."

Joni drummed her fingers on the chair arm. "So, where did she go?"

Eve shook her head. "The only other possibility of finding Annabelle is finding her mother. Annabelle said that her mother told fortunes in a traveling circus. But where that traveling circus is…?" Eve left the thought hanging in the air.

And then, just like that, all her thoughts rearranged into an obvious fact. Eve sat up carefully. "Joni… what a stupid woman I am. I just realized that if that waiter was telling the truth, then it's fairly certain that Annabelle and, more importantly, Colleen, survived their time travel ordeal and arrived here in 1904 or early 1905. That's a relief, a big relief. That means Colleen is alive, and she's well."

AT DINNER THAT NIGHT, Darius and Joni sat at opposite ends of the table, and Eve sat across from Lavinia. The conversation was polite, dull and careful, with no one wanting an argument or a challenging word.

Darius discussed the weather, "cold and snowy and not fit for a human." Lavinia said she hoped it would snow for Christmas, and Joni said, "Christmas is still over a month away."

Eve nodded, for her dark mood was a weight that couldn't be moved. Lavinia had filled the awkward silence, stating, "The baked chicken is quite delectable, isn't it? I think it might be the most flavorful I have ever enjoyed."

Banks, the white-haired, solemn butler, topped the glasses off with a bottle of white wine.

To be polite, Eve felt she should say something. "Yes, you're right, Lavinia. Please give my compliments to your cook, Darius. And the white wine complements the dinner perfectly. It is a good choice."

"I'm delighted you're enjoying it, Mrs. Gantly. It is a favorite of mine, a fine Burgundy from my cellar downstairs."

When they heard the demur chime of the doorbell, Darius exhaled impatiently. "Now, who is that disturbing our supper?"

"We'll soon know," Joni said.

Eve's eyes strayed toward the sound as the chime faded.

A moment later, the night maid, Maude, wearing a black-and-white uniform with a white cap, entered the dining room. She was a middle-aged, thin woman with a heavy face, filled with prim purpose. She rested her sincere eyes on Darius and then bobbed a bow.

"Mr. Foster, there is a Mr. Patrick Gantly at the front door. He's asking if you will invite him in."

CHAPTER 29

Eve went rushing into Patrick's outstretched arms, and he caught her, embraced her, swung her about, and pulled her close into a welcoming bearhug.

Joni looked on wistfully, relieved, lost in delightful old memories.

Darius held himself stiffly erect in subdued awkwardness, while Lavinia was swept up in romance.

When Eve and Patrick drew back, Patrick saw Joni standing by with misty eyes. He left Eve and went to her. Being aware of Darius and his jealous ways, instead of a hearty embrace, Patrick took Joni's hands into his, squeezed them and smiled warmly.

"Hello, Joni. You're a grand sight for these tired eyes. How are you, you lovely lass?"

Joni pulled herself into him and planted a big kiss on his startled lips. Stepping back, she said, "Patrick Gantly, you haven't aged a day, and you're still one hot-looking dude."

Darius flushed with embarrassment and turned aside. Lavinia's eyes sharpened on her mother, her mind working to decipher her strange words.

"I'm so glad you're here," Joni said, again squeezing his hands. She glanced at Eve with gushing love. "I'm crazy, out of my mind, to see you both again. We've got to celebrate. Got to! We have to have a party. Now! Right now!"

Darius cleared his throat. "Mr. Gantly," he said in a low, formal voice, "Would you like some refreshment? Perhaps supper? We were about to conclude ours."

"No, Mr. Foster," Patrick said, returning the formal tone. "Thank you, but I had supper earlier."

"Well, then," Darius said, reading Joni's sudden stern gaze. "Please come in and make yourself comfortable in the parlor, and warm yourself by the fire. It is a cold night. If you need anything whatsoever, please ask Maud here, and she'll be more than happy to bring it to you."

"Thank you, Darius. I'm quite comfortable," Patrick said.

Joni released his hands and nodded to Eve, who was anxious to be alone with her husband and find out what had happened to him. She was ready to start off that instant to go looking for Colleen.

"I still say we have to celebrate," Joni said, turning to her husband with a frank stare. "Darius, we need a bottle of your best champagne."

Eve and Patrick tried to protest, but Joni wouldn't hear of it. "I insist. Darius has several bottles in his wine cellar, and if this isn't something worth celebrating, then I don't know what is."

Joni looked at Darius, and he gave her a side-long glance of hovering doubt. But the longer he and his wife held each other's gaze, the more he saw it was futile. He nodded, the decision made.

"Very well, Mrs. Foster. I will attend to it."

After Darius walked away, Joni introduced Lavinia to Patrick, telling her daughter that she and Patrick were "good, old friends," who hadn't seen each other for years.

THE GROUP RETIRED to the living room and fell into easy conversation. Since Lavinia was present, soaking up sight and sound, her pretty face aglow in the firelight, Patrick did not feel comfortable explaining to Eve or Joni what had happened to him. Whenever Eve looked at him, he saw her eager expression.

Of course, they wanted to be alone, but they didn't want to disappoint Joni. And Patrick was delighted to see her again, and to be in familiar company. But he found it disconcerting to see Lavinia as a fourteen-year-old, since the last time he'd seen her was in 1925, and she'd been a mature, married and wealthy woman in her thirties.

When Darius returned, he'd fallen into a festive mood, despite himself. He arrived bearing a silver wine bucket filled with ice, with the champagne inside. When all was quiet and all eyes were on him, Darius was ready for his performance. With a white serviette draped over his forearm, he removed the bottle, then ceremoniously presented the champagne.

"This is Veuve Clicquot, a champagne that is dominated by the structure, aromas and body of pinot noir," Darius said, as if he were lecturing students in medical school. "It is a French champagne house-based in Reims, founded in 1772 by Philippe Clicquot."

They waited eagerly as Darius expertly removed the foil and the wire cage, then gave the cork a gentle twist. It made a sigh of gas, then popped. While Banks held a tray of etched crystal, long stem wine glasses, Darius poured. The bubbles exploded and danced, and white foam rose. When they all had a glass, Joni raised hers in a toast.

"Here's to my best and oldest friends. May they have success in their journey, and the sooner the better."

Darius cast his eyes about, worried, wondering what dramatic incident had brought them back in time to 1905. Joni hadn't told him.

"Hear! Hear!" Eve said, as they all touched glasses and sipped.

WHEN THEY'D FINISHED THE BOTTLE and were feeling the gentle buzz of the champagne, Joni linked an arm through Eve's and reached for Patrick's hand. "All right, enough introductions, champagne and reunions. You two have a lot of catching up to do," Joni said, her face shining with happiness. "Go to your room and get reacquainted. Darius, Lavinia and I will retire to the library and leave you two in peace."

"I have a hotel room," Patrick said. "We'll go there but thank you for the offer."

"No way," Joni protested. "You have to stay at least one night. I can't let go of you just like that. We'll have breakfast together... Please."

Darius cleared his throat, his expression softened by the champagne. "Yes, please stay. You're as welcome as the month of May. We're delighted to have you as our guests."

Eve and Patrick traded glances and then nods.

After the Foster family had left the room and Maud had taken the tray of glasses to the kitchen, Patrick took Eve's hand and pulled her into another warm kiss. When they pulled back, he gazed into her damp, happy eyes.

"Those are tears of joy, I hope, and not tears of, 'I thought I'd finally lost that no-good rascal forever, and now here he is back again' tears."

Eve playfully nibbled on the end of his nose and stepped back, studying him. "With that scratchy beard, your hair all wind-blown and scattered about, and those bloodshot eyes, I'd say you're rough-around-the-edges handsome."

"And I'd say that you are the best thing I've seen since the last time I saw you."

She shook her head, smiling, relieved and in love. "Ahh... aren't you still the old-school romantic man I met way back in 1885."

"Well, as my old Da used to say, 'If you love a woman right, she won't kick you out of bed when you come a knocking twice.'"

Eve's grin was mischievous. She snatched Patrick's hand, did an about-face, and yanked him off upstairs to the bedroom.

DEEP INTO THE NIGHT, Eve sensed Patrick was awake. She heard his uneven breathing, and she could almost hear the motors of his brain working.

"You awake?" Eve whispered into the darkness.
"Yes..."
"Colleen?"

"Yes... Colleen."

"At least we're ninety-five percent positive Annabelle returned with Colleen to 1904, thanks to that waiter."

"You did well, my love. I'm proud of you. No good detective could have done any better, and many not as well."

"It was luck, Patrick. Pure and simple luck."

"Was it luck that you showed the waiter Annabelle's photo?"

"No, that was an impulse."

"All right, then. Call it impulse or instinct or whatever, but you got results."

Eve rolled left to see him in silhouette, lying on his back. "Patrick... Did you have your head injury examined?"

"No, of course not. I have my memory back now. There's no need."

"Is it still sore?"

"On the right side, where I must have landed on it, yes, but it's better. Don't worry about it, Eve."

"Did you have headaches?"

"Only for a few hours. Stop being a nurse. I'm fine."

"I wish I could take you somewhere and get an MRI. Maybe we should ask Darius to have a look at you?"

"No... Definitely not."

"If the soreness doesn't go away soon, I'm taking you to a doctor. You could have a concussion."

"I don't. I'm fine. How are your left leg and foot?"

"Better, but still a little sore and stiff. The *Advil* and high-laced shoes help. Thank God we landed only a few hours from each other and not a few years."

"Yes, we were lucky. It was a rocky trip from start to finish," Patrick said. "It worries me, if, and when, we return home with Colleen."

"We'll find Colleen and we'll get back. We have to."

After a few silent moments, Patrick said, "Eve… when my foggy brain cleared… I mean, when my memory returned at Megan's house, I recalled something else that Annabelle said. She said she'd learned how to shoot a revolver when she was twelve years old, from a woman who worked in a traveling circus with her mother. Annabelle said the woman fired guns at spinning, moving human targets, and she never missed."

Eve lifted on an elbow. "Yeah, so?"

"How many circuses have a woman firing at moving targets? There can't be that many. If the woman shoots that well, then she must have been advertised as another Annie Oakley."

"But Annabelle said she was twelve years old when the woman taught her how to shoot, so a lot of time has passed since then. Annabelle's in her twenties now."

"It doesn't matter. That woman would have been a rarity, and there should be somebody around who remembers her: other circus members, or theater goers. There must be old broadsides advertising the woman or, who knows, she might still be performing somewhere close by. My point is, if we find the woman, or the circus she works or worked for, we might be able to find Annabelle's mother. Theoretically, she'll know where her daughter is. So, tomorrow, I suggest that you and Joni go to the theatre district and look for any billboards or flyers advertising this expert woman marksman. Look at kiosks and marquees; ask around; search for any information you can find on her. I'll return to that East Side neighborhood and canvass the area with Annabelle's photo. If we split up, it will save time."

"Why shouldn't Joni and I return to Annabelle's neighborhood?"

"Because it might get dangerous. Thieves know thieves. They may not fancy two unknown women poking their pretty noses about. Word might get around and, in my experience, word among those types always gets around."

The silence grew in Eve's ears as she thought about it. "You're brilliant, Patrick. I would have never thought of the woman shootist."

"It's my devious, nineteenth-century detective mind, Eve. I still have a gift for remembering details of conversations. For instance, I recall something you said to me when we first met in 1885 on Twentieth Street, and I have never asked you about it."

"So, ask already."

"You said, and I quote, 'As a girlfriend of mine used to say, a woman is not what she says she is, she is what she hides.'"

Eve chuckled. "Yeah, I remember that. Do you know who that woman is?"

"I have a pretty good idea. Joni?"

"Oh, yes. Joni, it is."

Patrick cleared his throat. "So, Mrs. Gantly, what are you hiding?"

Eve leaned a hand and touched his lips with a finger. "You're the detective. Hold me…"

"Hold you?"

"Duh… Yeah, Patrick. Hold me… for questioning, of course. Get it?"

He grinned. "Come here…"

CHAPTER 30

The following morning, after a late breakfast, Patrick, Eve and Joni left the house together, taking Joni's sleek carriage to the massive Hippodrome Theater on Sixth Avenue between West 43rd and West 44th Streets.

Joni thought they might have luck there. It was called the world's largest theater by its builders; it had hundreds of employees, and its seating capacity was over five thousand.

Patrick helped Eve and Joni step down from the carriage, and they all took in the impressive, massive structure, a Beaux-Arts masterpiece with elements of Moorish Revival.

"What a place," Eve said, in awe, staring up at one of the two elaborate corner towers, which was topped by a globe and covered in electric lights.

"I know this wasn't here in the twenty-first century, but I have no idea when they knocked it down. Do either of you?" Joni asked.

Neither did.

Joni turned her back to the gathering wind. "Surely somebody in this place will have heard of the fortune-telling circus woman, or the Annie-Oakley-imitation shooter," Joni said.

"Have you ever been to a performance here?" Eve asked.

"Darius and I attended the gala opening last April and watched a four-hour extravaganza. It was wild. There's nothing like it in the twenty-first century. The first act was called *A Yankee Circus on Mars*, and it featured spaceships, horses, elephants, acrobats, clowns, a huge orchestra, hundreds of singers, and dancers leaping all over the stage. I never saw anything like it, and I can tell you, I wanted to be right up there with them. It looked like so much fun. And, like I said over breakfast, the cast rehearses every day, so I'm sure there will be somebody around here who knows about those two performers."

Eve pressed her hat down to keep it from sailing off in the wind. "Okay, Joni, let's get to it."

Patrick left them, wishing them luck, and caught a hansom cab. He headed downtown to the Lower East Side, curious to see how it had changed since he was last there in 1884.

He left the cab on Orchard Street and began his search for Annabelle. Crowds streamed around him, ditch diggers swung picks near mounds of snow and earth, and a pack of street urchins, looking for mischief, darted in and out of pushcarts and parked wagons, a street dog snapping at their heels.

As he approached a small, gated, neighborhood park, there was a scatter of birds from a tree, a baby's cry from a wicker baby carriage, and the ever-present shouts of merchants out on the streets, hawking their wares, clouds of vapor puffing from their mouths.

Patrick entered a tobacconist shop, purchased a pipe, some matches and a pouch of tobacco. He returned to the street, puffing the pipe, watchful, searching and plotting, feeling the rise of pleasure at being at work, the old detective in him awakened. He was back on the New York City streets, doing the work he'd felt was a comfortable fit, despite the lowlifes, the corrupt politicians, and the few bad cops on the take. He missed the camaraderie of cops; the stories; the dark humor. He missed the adventure. There was nothing like it in the twenty-first century.

An automobile approached the curb near where he was standing. It came to a noisy, smokey stop and, to Patrick's surprise, a woman climbed out just as the auto finally rattled into silence.

Surely, in 1905, this was highly unusual, both because she was driving an odd-looking auto, a rarity in this time, but also because she was a young female, probably no more than thirty years old. Were women even allowed to drive in 1905?

She peeled off a leather cap and goggles and shook out her hair. Hers was a delicate, pampered face; the face of privilege; the haughty expression of a queen who expected fawning attention.

To his further surprise, she strolled up to him. "Sir... Do you happen to know where Eisenberg's Deli is?"

Before Patrick could answer, she looked past him, searching the streets. "I am told they have the best pickles, and I just love pickles," she said. "You might say I'm a pickle craver. A pickle connoisseur. I'm having a private affair tomorrow and I simply must have, not just any pickles, but Eisenberg's pickles. Do you know where that deli is?"

Patrick puffed his pipe, amazed by this woman's expensive outfit: a tailored coat with mink collar, dainty shoes, and suede gloves. Hers was a standout amongst the homemade clothes of the streets—in this bustling, immigrant neighborhood of working-class men and women. And she was being watched, with low, curious eyes, but she didn't seem to notice or care.

"No, ma'am, I don't know where it is."

And then she looked him over with quick, appraising eyes. "Can you fight? You certainly look like you can, and you have the size for it."

Again, Patrick was bemused by her candid question. "Not if I can avoid it. Why do you ask? Are you feeling angry?"

She wasn't amused. "Don't be impertinent. I need a good fighting man for my party. Some of my husband's friends are hoodlums. Simply hoodlums. Well, no bother…"

And then she was off, the scent of sweet perfume briefly lingering in the still air. For an instant, he thought she might have been Annabelle in disguise, and he pivoted toward her retreating figure. But no… It wasn't Annabelle. The body type was different. The voice, the eyes. Several times that day, he'd jerked a glance at a passing woman, thinking it was Annabelle. He had Annabelle on the brain. She'd become an obsession.

Annabelle Palmer was an attractive woman, one who could turn heads, if she so desired. She was a thief, albeit a high-class one, but it didn't matter. Thieves hung around thieves, and knew thieves, and talked to thieves, and acquired tricks from other thieves. Patrick had learned that back in the 1880s, when he was a detective.

He decided to visit some saloons, find a dapper gambler or two, and pass around Annabelle's photo. In his day, gamblers moved around, and they knew people; they knew women of a certain kind, and they would rat on anyone if offered enough money. Patrick had money. He and Eve had made sure that, between them, they had enough money to last several years.

As Patrick explored the area, he was surprised by the number of taverns and saloons in a three-block radius, an increase, no doubt, to accommodate a burgeoning population. And, as far as that went, not much had changed since his time. Now, like then, the saloons were a space where men, often with little means, obtained sorely needed escapism. It was a kind of second home in a world that was tough and uncaring.

On the dark side, the saloon gave alcoholics the opportunity to indulge their addictions, ruining their health with a variety of gut-rot spirits. The criminal element could also be found on the fringes of saloon culture. These were the men that interested Patrick right now.

If anyone had known Annabelle before her time travel adventure, then they certainly would have noticed if she suddenly appeared with a pretty, little girl in tow. For the right price, they might even tell him where Annabelle and his little Colleen lived.

Patrick wandered in and out of five saloons, all of them in various states of spirit-killing gloom and degradation, most flavored by sweat and cigar smoke in stale air. The crowded rooms held dock workers and workmen who were digging the inter-borough subway tunnels, laying cables for Broadway streetlights, or laboring on East River bridges.

Patrick's trained detective's eyes didn't spot the type of man he was looking for until he entered the dimly lighted Shanty's Saloon. The tables were round, made of cheap wood, and occupied. The chairs rocked and leaned. The bar was stuffed with rowdy men and flashy women. Working girls, looking for a fast trick, leaned into men's shoulders, hoping for a free drink and an escorted trip up the stairs to a dingy room at the top of the winding staircase.

Despite the boisterous laughter, the place was cheerless, built on the shaky foundation of inebriation, false revelry, and the hope of winning a card game by any means necessary.

Patrick spotted four men in the rear of the room in the midst of such a game. Three men were dressed reasonably well, one very well. He was the one Patrick was interested in. Patrick went to the bloated bar and ordered a pint of porter. A heavy woman, with rouge-colored cheeks, thick red lips and a calculating eye, approached him. Patrick estimated her age at about forty, but her lifestyle had aged her to at least fifty.

"Hey, there, tall man with a face I could like. How about you buy a girl a drink?"

Patrick saw a weary desperation in her eyes and, despite himself, he had compassion for the woman. How many more years could she survive, living on the fringe of darkness? She was overweight, with a sagging face, held together by heavy makeup and a forced smile that held fading hopelessness.

"Yes, I'll buy you a drink. What will you have?"

She brightened a little. "Well, that's real nice of you. You're a gentleman, aren't you? Betsy, at the end of the bar, said you wouldn't give me the time of day. Well, that tells her something, don't it? She's a little bit younger than me, but not much, and she ain't got even half the experience I have, tall man. I'll have a rye. Straight."

The bartender was a stubby man, like a human fireplug, with stubby arms, thinning black hair, a pinched, oval face and the flat black eyes of a coroner Patrick had once known.

Patrick ordered, paid for the drink, and handed it to the woman.

"What's your name?" Patrick asked.

Her smile widened. "Well, ain't that just sweet of you to ask me my name. Most of the dopes who come to this place never ask a girl her name. They don't care nothing about a name. You know what I mean? Anyway, my name's Rose, just like the flower."

"Rose is a nice name. Nice to meet you, Rose."

She stared at him, growing suspicious. She tossed back the whiskey in a gulp, wiped her mouth with the back of her hand, and sat the shot glass down on the bar. A boozy man at the bar pushed up and bumped into her. Indignant, she shoved him.

"Hey, watch where you're walkin', you clumsy mudhead."

The slight man, wheezy and glassy-eyed, staggered backwards. "No need to get all mucky with me, Rose. No need for that. I didn't mean nothing. A man just needs a pee, you know. Ain't nothing wrong with that, is there?"

"Ah, shut up and go pee," Rose snapped.

The man shrugged off to the door that led to the privy out back.

Rose returned her attention to Patrick, her expression having lost some of its sweetness. "Are you a copper or something? Your type don't come in here, being nice and polite, unless you're playing pretend, like you're some shoe-shined millionaire."

Patrick kept his expression affable, impressed that she'd pegged him right off. He was out of practice and he'd been too nice. Anybody nice wanted something, and she was smart enough and experienced to know that Patrick wasn't interested in her.

He decided to be bold. "No, Rose, I'm not a copper. I'm a man looking for his baby daughter."

Her suspicion changed to worried confusion. "Baby daughter? What the hell are you selling, mister?"

Patrick reached into his inside coat pocket, removed Annabelle's photo, stepped under the glow of a hanging gaslight, and held it up to her. "Have you ever seen this woman?"

It seemed to take effort for Rose to pull her nervous eyes from Patrick to focus on the photo. When she did, Patrick watched her closely, waiting.

Rose's mouth tightened, and she blinked five times. Despite the noise and bawdy laughter around him, Patrick's one-pointed attention heard nothing, and saw nothing, except Rose.

Rose snapped her gaze from the photo to the back of the room, to the four men playing cards at a round table, lighted by a hanging brass lantern.

"I've seen her come in all right," Rose said. "She's a floosy, if you ask me, and since you asked me, I'm telling you. She's a floosy all right, but she puts on airs like she's better than me and everybody else."

Patrick's interest grew. "Then you know her?"

"Did I say I know her, tall man?" She scowled and threw fists to her broad hips, her dress tight at the bosom, revealing cleavage and abundant breasts. "You ain't looking for Rose, are you? You don't even like Rose, or give a damn about Rose, do you? No, you're too good for Rose. The likes of you are always too good for Rose. You want the girl in the photo, don't you, tall man? That's who you want, ain't it?"

Patrick had seen this before—an intoxicated prostitute rebuffed, but he didn't care. He'd seen that she recognized Annabelle.

"Do you know her, Rose? Tell me. It's important. I have to find her."

Her brassy laugh sounded like a low, rusty hinge. "You'll have to fight for her, tall man." She jerked her chin toward the gambling table. "You'll have to fight it out with that no-good louse of a man over there. The man in the silver vest and sharky smile. That's Farley Carp."

Rose pivoted, staggered and wobbled off, looking for another mark, while her younger friend at the other end of the bar slapped her knee, laughed and taunted her.

While the two women threw insults and fists at each other, Patrick started toward the table of gamblers to meet Farley Carp.

CHAPTER 31

Patrick nursed his beer and waited a fair distance away from the table where Farley Carp and three other men puffed cigars, blew smoke, and fanned and shifted through cards, their eyes sharp, attitudes wary.

Twenty minutes passed. Finally, two men folded and left the table, their faces expressing the low spirits of losers. Both shuffled off to the bar, mumbling curses, glancing back over their shoulders as if already plotting vengeance.

When Patrick observed that the two remaining men had concluded play and raked in their cash, he ventured over. He overheard one man boasting that it was "... so satisfying to fleece the ignorant suckers of the world."

The man in the silver vest, whom Rose had called Farley Carp, answered in a southern accent. "Yes, my good friend, and let us pray to heaven above, and give a hail and hardy nod to Generals Lee and Jackson, that there will never be an end to this lucrative ignorance."

Patrick moved toward the table. "Good afternoon, gentlemen," he said cordially.

Neither man looked up.

Patrick continued, addressing himself to Carp. "Mr. Carp, Rose at the bar suggested that you might be able to help me."

He barked out a harsh laugh. "Rose? You must be joking, good sir," he said caustically, still not meeting Patrick's eyes. "I do not acquaint myself with the likes of the repulsive and the never-demure Madam Rose. To be tactfully honest, sir, I don't like Rose, and I certainly will have nothing to do with her, or with anyone, be it man or woman, who deigns to mention her name in my company."

Farley slowly lifted his dark, sinister eyes. "Madam Rose is a filthy harlot of the first water and, if *she* is a despicable human being, and I can assure you, sir, that she is, then you must be equally despicable and low, if you have had any dealings with her. I bid you a good afternoon, sir."

Undeterred, Patrick took a drink of his beer while he sized Farley Carp up. His raven black hair gleamed and was meticulously combed; his white teeth were perfection, especially for 1905, and his handsome black suit, black string bow tie, and silver vest fit him to gentlemanly perfection.

Patrick turned his gaze on the second man, who had also put his dark snake eyes on Patrick, in cold disdain. He was perhaps forty, his hair retreating from his scalp to the sides of his head. The man was well built, like a wrestler, with a thick neck and a barrel chest. He presented a smirking, crooked mouth and a round and ruddy moon face that showed clear signs of combat, from a smashed, flat nose to an ugly, two-inch, red scar on his right cheek.

Carp was the kind of man who knew, or had known, Annabelle. Patrick was sure of that. He withdrew the photo of her and held it up for both men to see. "I'm looking for this woman. Have you seen her? Do you know her?"

It was instantly obvious that Farley recognized her. His forehead lifted only a fraction, and his eyes widened, just a little. Yes, Farley knew Annabelle.

"Never seen her," Farley said, looking away.

Thick-necked man looked at Patrick darkly. "I'm only going to ask you one time, friend, to step away from our table, or I, Jasper Kane, the Main Event boxer who won the blue ribbon in Brooklyn six years ago, will remove you piece by piece, and toss those pieces outside into the filthy curb snow. And, might I say, it will be a pleasure to do so."

Patrick drained the last of his beer, then stared down into his empty mug. He swallowed, considering his options. All he needed was for Carp to tell him where Annabelle was living. That was it. And he was sure Carp knew.

The drinkers at the tables behind and to Patrick's right grew nervous. Patrick set his empty beer mug down on the nearest table packed with drinking men. From their worried faces, they'd heard Jasper Kane's threats and, no doubt, they'd heard them before.

Patrick fixed his gaze on Farley. "I will leave you in peace, gentlemen. I do not want any trouble, I assure you. But, Mr. Carp, I couldn't help but notice that you recognized the woman in this photo. With respect, I'm asking for your help in finding Annabelle Palmer. It may be a matter of life and death. Please, sir, can you tell me where she is?"

A low rumble of evil laughter escaped Jasper Kane's lips as he and Carp traded a menacing glance.

Without a word, Jasper Kane shot up, his tweed suit tight against his chest, the buttons on his vest straining, just waiting to pop. He back-kicked his chair, and it jumped away and slammed against the wall.

"All right, you dumb Mick, you've got my fists to reckon with now. I warned you."

Farley rose, puffing out his chest with a steel set of his mouth, his eyes flashing malice. "You're right, big man, I do know Annabelle Palmer, and that's only one of her many names, in case you are not aware. And if I knew where she was, I'd find her and kill her. You must be her new one… one of her victims, or soon-to-be victims. She has many, you know. Well, now, my dear sir, we're going to give you a good thrashing that you will not soon forget and, when you find the bitch, you can tell her that Farley Carp was the man who sent you to hell. You should have left when you had the chance."

Patrick sensed movement out of the corner of his eye, and he knew, before he turned, that Jasper Kane was about to swing at him. Patrick danced away, keenly aware that Farley Carp rose and was coming at him from around the table, to his right. Patrick ducked and just missed the heavy fist and forearm of the attacking Kane.

But Carp had Patrick in his sights. He dropped away and kicked Patrick on the point of his left elbow, sending him reeling to his left, the pain shooting up his arm like red hot wires, burning his shoulder, numbing his left hand. Dazed and in pain, Patrick cursed, feeling a surge of rage.

Kane came for Patrick, ready to pounce, uttering threatening sounds without words, bounding around like a prize fighter, his ugly face large, his fat fists up and ready. Patrick staggered, off-balance, so he went with the motion, spinning around left, grabbing the top rail of a chair, recently vacated by one of the scattering men. With his right hand, he gripped it, preparing for battle.

As Kane attacked, Patrick flexed his right arm and swung the chair like a batter swinging at a fast ball. Kane saw it coming and threw up his hands to protect himself, but it was too late. The chair slammed into Kane's shoulder and head with a crack.

Kane screamed out in surprise and pain as he went hurtling away, smashing into a table of sitting men, gripping mugs of beer. Kane, men, beer and table went flying, Kane crashing to the floor and sliding. His head rammed into the base of the wall with a thud, his face clenched in agony, his eyes wide with shock.

Kane opened his mouth to speak, but only a hollow wheeze left his fat lips. He moved a feeble hand as if to summon help, heaving in a painful breath, but no one near him moved. His hand dropped; his eyes fluttered. He coughed. He moaned. He expelled a breath, and he was out cold.

Wasting no time, Carp reached into his inside jacket pocket and pulled a derringer, his mouth a grim, tight line, his eyes bulging with malice. Patrick had seconds to act. Just as Carp leveled the pistol at Patrick's head, Patrick dropped the chair and darted in, back-handing Carp's gun hand with a sharp and powerful swing of his still numb left hand.

The derringer flew away and went skidding across the floor. Patrick swung at Carp, but the agile gambler jerked back, and Patrick missed. Carp side-stepped Patrick and leapt toward the derringer, skidding on his knees to swoop it up. He grabbed the gun, spun around, and fired.

Anticipating the squeeze of the trigger, Patrick had skipped left, and the bullet whispered past his right ear. Patrick took two long strides and kicked Carp's gun hand as the second shot rang out but went wild. The gun sailed away. Patrick whirled about and, with his other foot, he kicked Carp deep into the stomach. The air burst from his lungs and he bent over, hands grabbing his gut.

Pressing the attack, Patrick grabbed Carp by his coat collar and, feeling adrenalin pumping through every vein, he jerked the man to his feet, holding him upright by the collar. His chin flopped on his chest like a rag doll's.

Carp's eyes were lost, sliding around, trying to find any reality.

"Do you know where Annabelle is?" Patrick growled.

Farley struggled to shake his head. "No... Saw her... but gone."

"When?"

"Months ago... She's gone. Left town."

"Left to where?"

"Don't know."

"Did she have a little girl with her?"

He nodded. "Yes."

"How long ago?"

Carp lifted his eyes and scowled. "Go to hell."

Patrick cocked his right fist and drove it into the man's nose. Blood splattered as Carp back-pedaled, tripped over his own feet, and tumbled onto the floor, out cold.

The saloon had gathered into a startled hush, all eyes stuck to Patrick, waiting for his next move. His chest was heaving, breath puffing out anger from his nose, like an angry bull ready to charge.

He strafed the room with his burning eyes. "I'm looking for my daughter. I'm just trying to find my little girl!"

"Get out!" the bartender shouted, hoisting a shotgun. "Get out of here, or God help me, I'll shoot you!"

Patrick gathered himself, turned and blundered outside into a cold afternoon wind and a noisy, busy world: passing carriages, horses' hooves heavy on the cobbles, children playing hopscotch on the sidewalk, and a pushcart selling rolls of cloth.

He walked for a time, unsure which direction he was going, not recognizing the neighborhood. He shook out his aching fist and replayed the fight. Was there any way he could have avoided it and somehow persuaded Carp to give him Annabelle's address?

No, those men were looking for a fight. That type always looked for fights, and they always would, just as they had back in the 1880s. They were hard men. Low men. Lost men. Predators, with a love for violence. Patrick had seen it in the depths of their eyes, just as he'd seen the same restless darkness in Annabelle's eyes.

And, if he were honest—and this was a day for honesty—there were times he'd seen that same restless darkness in his own eyes. But this was his secret, a secret he'd never shown to Eve and never would. But had she seen it and known it? Did she know what was hidden in his soul?

There had been times in the twenty-first century when he'd been sitting in a psychology class at John Jay College, hearing about blatant corruption or abuse, and he'd felt the call to action. To fight, not to talk or compromise or support laws, but to fight against the glaring wrongs of the world.

Often in the future, he'd felt the call of those rough and tumble days in the nineteenth century. Didn't he come from there? Wasn't he still a part of that time and place? In the 1870s, he'd fought in a gang when he was fifteen years old, brawling in the back lots and grim alleyways of a neighborhood that was only a few blocks away. As he wandered the streets, shaking off the adrenalin rush from his fight with Carp, Patrick could smell the past, feel the sting of fists and the thud of their blows.

Is that why he hadn't left that saloon when he'd been threatened? Because he had wanted to fight? *Honesty, Patrick.*

So, was he really so noble a knight? Or were these only excuses for wanting the thrill of a good rumble? *Honesty, Patrick,*" he thought. *It's a day for honesty, isn't it? The truth is, you've always liked to fight, because there is much to fight for. You have good fists, fast feet and a fighting spirit. You have the heart of a warrior, not the soft head of a sit-down psychologist. It runs against your true nature.*

You like the masculine call of man against man. It's in your blood, isn't it? So face it and be honest about it, and never, ever let Eve suspect it. Not Eve. Not Eve, the love of your life, and the one person who pulls you out of black moods and the impulse to take on the ugly darkness of the world, a mysterious world of time travel and contradictions. A "now" world where every breath is painful, because you don't know where Colleen is.

The urgency of finding Colleen agitated him and drove him on, as he searched the streets, and the shops, and the doorways. She was already a year older, and who knows what she was learning? Who knows the kind of people she was meeting, and what plans Annabelle had for her?

In desperate steps, Patrick pulled the photo from his pocket and started for the next saloon and café, shaking the numbness and pain he still felt in his left arm. Maybe someone knew where Annabelle had gone. He'd find her if it took the rest of his life, and God help her when he did. But he'd find her and his Colleen, and he'd take his little lass back home where she belonged.

CHAPTER 32

Rufus T. Fluggs was the principal director at the Hippodrome Theatre. He was a roaring, rowdy man who marched about the vast stage, ten times larger than any Broadway theater, like a gruff bulldog protecting a junk yard. He cursed like a sailor, shouted orders into a brass megaphone and, when something went wrong, he stamped about the stage like he was squashing bugs. He was broad and tightly built, and his meaty lips were clamped down on an unlit cigar that he seldom pulled from his mouth.

His plug hat was pushed back off his forehead, his white shirtsleeves were rolled up to the elbow, and his tweed pants had long ago lost their crease.

Rufus often boasted that he'd been a Rough Rider with Teddy Roosevelt in 1898 during the Spanish-American War, saying proudly, in a booming voice for all to hear, "I charged up San Juan Hill right alongside the now President of these United States. Hundreds fell under Spanish gunfire before we reached the base of the heights," Rufus would say. "… And I was right there with them, fighting like hell next to old Teddy himself."

Joni and Eve drew up to a bored ticket clerk and explained why they were there. At first, he'd been hesitant, but Eve had flashed him a lovely smile, and he was obviously taken by her. He allowed the ladies to enter the theater and sit quietly in rear seats, to watch the ongoing rehearsal.

"When they take their break, you can approach the performers with your questions," the young ticket clerk whispered, his ready eyes locked on Eve with pleasure. "But be as quiet as you can about it," he said. "The director can get all steamed up over nothing sometimes."

Eve had been dazzled by the promenade and the lobby, both rendered in limestone and marble. Inside the enormous auditorium, the interior was decorated in Roman style, with deep reds and accents of gold, silver, and ivory.

They sat near the aisle in soft red velvet chairs, hearing Rufus Fluggs barking out orders and curses.

"What the hell's the matter with you girls? The line is off, and the choreography's all wrong. You're dancing around like a herd of elephants. Now, let's try it again and get it right this time!"

Crouching down in her seat, Joni said, "I hope we don't have to talk to *him*."

Eve nodded. "Do you know who he reminds me of? That actor in *The Mary Tyler Moore Show*. What was his name?"

"Ed Asner?" Joni said. "Yeah, you're right. He does look a lot like Ed Asner. Now that's a show I'd like to see again. I loved it. I had every episode on

DVD. That's the kind of thing I miss living in this time." Then she swiftly changed the subject. "Did you see how the ticket clerk looked at you?"

"Yes... I gave him my best pleading smile look."

"I'm feeling jealous."

"Of that guy?"

"No, not him, but no man looks at me anymore. I'm in my fifties and you're, what? Still in your thirties?"

Eve looked at her friend. "Joni... I know this whole thing is weird. But look at it this way: you have a good husband and two great kids. Look what I'm doing. Still time traveling because that damned lantern won't leave us alone."

"So, stay here in this time, Eve. Even if you find Colleen, don't go back. Stay here with me and live your life."

Eve turned away. "I don't know. I can't think about anything else until after we find Colleen."

After a time, Eve said, "Joni, have you told Lavinia and William about us and about time travel?"

Joni averted her eyes. "You know me, Eve. I'd lie about it in a letter and say I didn't tell them, but the truth is, yes, I told Lavinia about you and Patrick, about time traveling and the twenty-first century, when she was a little girl. Lavinia told William, and then, a short time ago, Darius told both kids that if an Eve and Patrick Gantly ever appeared at the front door, they were to send them away. So, anyway, yes, everyone knows, although no one, including me, is supposed to admit it."

"I thought so," Eve said, smiling. "What a crazy life, huh, Joni?"

"Yeah... It's nuts, all right."

They fell into silence as they watched the rehearsal with rapt fascination, the leaping dancers, the crooning tenors and a young woman astride a milky white horse, galloping across the stage. Her flying blonde hair was several feet long, most of it covering her naked body. Joni confirmed the actress was portraying the infamous Lady Godiva.

"This act is so popular that it's written up in all the newspapers," Joni said. "Later on, this guy named Peeping Tom—yes, good old Peeping Tom—darts out on the stage and watches in wonder as Godiva rides by. Well, get this, he's struck dead by a bolt of lightning that shoots down from the ceiling."

"Wow... That's crazy stuff, Joni."

"And that's not all. Just as Godiva disappears in the wings, a midnight black stallion comes galloping out, ridden by a loincloth'd, bare-breasted, muscular man, wearing a laurel wreath crown made of gold, the same worn by Roman emperors. He goes racing off after Godiva, shouting her name, saying, 'Lady Godiva, you are my own true love. Wait for me. Pray, wait for me!'"

Eve chuckled a little and shrank down in her seat. "Talk about cheesy."

Joni whispered. "Hey, they don't have TV or the internet in 1905, okay? Like I said, this is a very popular act. Honestly, I've grown to like this kind of thing better than television. It's just so over-the-top."

Joni made a dramatic face, pressing her hand to her heart. "It's an act that just gets you right in the old heart, doesn't it?"

They both fell into laughter, then settled back, greatly entertained.

When the cast broke for lunch, Eve led Joni down the aisle toward the stage. Rufus Fluggs saw them coming, scowled, then marched downstage to stop them.

"Who are you, and what the hell are you two women doing in my theater? This is a closed rehearsal."

Eve flashed him a dazzling smile, hoping to erase some of his hostility. It didn't work.

"Get out, both of you! Who the hell let you in here? I'll kick him in the ass all the way to the Bronx!"

Undeterred, Joni spoke up, her voice meek and mild, a small voice that Eve had never heard before. "Sir, my dear departed husband helped to build this grand theater," she said in a dramatic, emotional voice. She reached into her purse and removed a white lace hankie, gently blotting first one eye, then the other.

She continued. "I am saddened to say, sir, that he lost his life during this theater's construction, falling from a great height to the street below."

Joni looked at Rufus sorrowfully for a slow five-count, then continued. "Until today, I could not bring myself to even entertain the slightest notion of stepping foot in this place. Forgive me, dear sir, but my friend here told me I must come. She said I had to see the beauty and the wonder of what my dear husband had given his life for. Yes, I had to see it just once, in my dear husband's memory. Surely, you can understand that?"

Rufus's hard, exterior shell melted some, if not in compassion, then in grudging respect for a man who had helped to build the theater he loved.

He pulled his cigar from his mouth, thought about Joni's sad words, then replaced the cigar. "Pardon me, madam. Of course, I did not, and could not, understand your motive for coming. Now that I do, please accept my condolences and honored thanks for your husband, and for his sacrifice. You may stroll at will during our lunch break and take your time about it. If anyone tries to stop you, tell them Rufus Fluggs has given you both unlimited access to the theater. Go wherever you wish and explore whatever suits your fancy. Now, if you'll excuse me, I have a show to put on."

He turned on his heel and went striding away, his boots loud on the wooden stage.

Eve turned to Joni, her blinking eyes filled with humor, her mouth a twitching smile. "Joni… You still have it, just like in the old days."

Joni lifted her chin proudly and sighed out longing. "How I miss the stage, Eve. I haven't given a performance like that since the last time you were here in 1884, at Dr. Eckland's house. Remember?"

Eve looked at her doubtfully. "Of course, I remember. But when you're with Darius, don't tell me you don't perform to… let's say… get your way with him?"

Joni grinned. "Oh, that. Well, yeah, but he's on to me now. I have to use other methods… like fainting or—and this always works—I mention the time lantern."

"Which you have, right?"

"Oh, yes. I have it all right, and only I know where it is. It will be ready for you, Patrick, and little Colleen when you're ready."

Eve's face clouded over. "Yes… Colleen. Come on, let's find some people and start asking questions."

When a trio of leggy showgirls appeared on stage, Eve led the way toward them. She asked if they'd ever worked for a circus or knew anyone who had. All three shook their heads. One said, in a breathy, girlish voice, "I wouldn't work in one of them circuses. Too many grubby men with too many grubby fingers, trying to do grubby things with a girl, you know? All them men who work in circuses are animals… And the circus animals don't smell so good either."

In the hour that Eve and Joni had before the rehearsals resumed, they'd gone backstage and spoken to stage crew and performers, but none had heard of a woman who worked for a circus and shot guns at a spinning, live human target.

One tall, gaunt stagehand pulled on a cigarette and said, "Who in Hades would let himself be tied to a spinning target, and then allow some crazy female to shoot at him? That don't make no sense, no way and no how. No, ma'am. That man would be a fool for sure."

Eve and Joni were leaving the stage when Rufus returned. He spotted them descending the stairs from the stage to the auditorium, and he called out.

"Ladies… Ladies!"

Eve and Joni stopped and turned as he approached, chewing on his cigar.

"How do you like the Hippodrome? It's a beauty, ain't it? Your husband did a good thing, madam. You can be proud of him when you gaze at an edifice as wondrous as this."

Eve felt another of her intuitive nudges. "Mr. Fluggs, may I ask if you know of a female act where a woman fires guns at a human, spinning target?"

With surprise, Fluggs jerked the cigar from his mouth. "What did you say?"

Eve repeated it.

His eyes narrowed. "Say, what's this about?"

Eve had seen Joni do it. Lie through her teeth. Why couldn't she? "My husband ran off with such a woman. I'm looking for him."

Fluggs' eyebrows shot up. "You two women have the mean, bad luck with the jokers, don't you? Maybe you should let the men alone. Maybe men ain't so good for you, or maybe you should go to church more often and meet a parson."

Eve lowered her gaze, seeking sympathy, and Joni glanced away, rolling her eyes.

Rufus thought about it for a moment. "Do you know what? As a matter of fact, I did see a shooting act with a whirling human target."

Eve and Joni snapped him a look.

He stuffed the cigar back into his mouth and stared out into the vast auditorium. "Now, let me see, as best I recall, the act was called Fanny Winkler and the Whirling Death Wheel. I even remember the banner above her act."

He grinned proudly. "I never, not ever, forget banners, ladies. It's what sells the tickets. Anyway, the banner read, **Fanny Winkler, A Sure-Shot, More Accurate Than Annie Oakley. The Best Shootist in the World**!"

"Fanny Winkler?" Eve asked, taking a step forward, excited.

"Yup, that was her name. And if I recall, I read in a paper, must be a couple of years ago now, that old sure-shot Fanny shot a guy… that is, she missed, and shot the stupid son-of-a-bitch in the head, excuse my language. Yup, she shot him right on that damned spinning wheel. Now, you've got to be polecat stupid to get yourself tied to a wheel to be shot at by some gun-toting female. Yup, and that was the end of her act. I think she went to jail for it, but I don't recall none of the details."

"She went to jail?" Joni asked, her eyes wide and round.

"Yup…"

Eve said, "Where did you see this act?"

"That's going on four or five years ago, but I'm pretty sure it was at some circus in Brooklyn."

"Do you know the name of the circus?" Eve asked.

He looked Eve over. "This husband of yours… If you ask me, he's a blind bastard if he ran off and left you. If he can't see the girlie girl you are, maybe somebody ought to track him down and shoot him, too."

Eve feigned shy flattery. "Thank you, kind sir. Do you remember the name of the circus, sir?"

"Yeah, I do, because a former girlfriend of mine lived in that neighborhood. It was called the Ballyhoo Circus. It wasn't so bad as circuses go. It had a good lion tamer, a fair high-wire act, and a big fat woman, twice my size, with the long black beard of a lumber jack. She could wrestle any size of man, and she could pin him. Big or small. Didn't matter. Yeah, that was one hell of an act. It was something to behold."

"Did you or your lady friend get your fortune told?" Eve asked.

"Of course, she got her fortune told. Tell me what woman would go to a circus and not get her fortune told? I didn't go in for it, of course, because I don't like getting fleeced or shafted. But sure, Peg did… that was my lady friend's name at the time, Peg."

Eve's pulse quickened. "Do you remember who the fortune teller was? I mean, did you meet her? Did she have a name?"

He shook his head. "No… No idea. They all look alike, don't they? They wear some turban or scarf, or some damned thing, and they stare bug-eyed into a crystal ball, and do phony card tricks. They're shysters, you know. Every one of them fortune tellers is a shyster, but they make the money, I can tell you that. A newspaper friend of mine did a story on fortune tellers. He said about ten thousand bucks a day goes out to fortune tellers in this city.

"Since there are only about a thousand of them, that means they each make ten bucks a day, and the shysters only charge fifteen cents a customer. Now, ain't that something? I'm in the wrong business, ain't I?"

Eve wanted to ask more questions, but Rufus turned to the performers, who were slouching about, sitting on the stage, chatting and smoking. He clapped his hands sharply and shouted, "All right, everybody, the party's over. Let's get back to work!"

Rufus passed Eve and Joni a final glance, then he tipped his hat. "Good luck with the gents, ladies. Sounds like you need all the luck you can get."

CHAPTER 33

Eve and Joni spent the rest of the week searching the Theater District for anyone who remembered the Ballyhoo Circus fortune teller, but without success. The only information they gleaned was from a stage manager at the Lyceum Theater: the Ballyhoo Circus had gone out of business over a year before.

Meanwhile, Patrick returned again and again to the Lower East Side with the photo of Annabelle, thrusting it into the face of anyone who might have known or seen her: café waiters, managers, pushcart vendors, bartenders and patrons. He even stopped to ask two beat cops if they'd seen her. Neither was friendly, and both said they hadn't.

At the Thirteenth Police Precinct—not his old one, the Fifteenth, because he was afraid he'd be recognized—Patrick searched the walls for Annabelle's Wanted poster, and he found it.

WANTED!
PRUDENCE RILEY
ALIAS AGATHA PARKS
A REWARD OF $1,000

Has been offered for information leading to the arrest of this notorious female jewel thief and alleged murderer. Aged in her late 20s.
DESCRIPTION: Born Dublin, Ireland/or New York City. Height 5'7." Weight: 125 lbs. Hair: Brown. Eyes: Hazel/Brown. Complexion: Fair. Known to use disguises. Could be dangerous.

Though she was listed under the name *Prudence Riley,* and the accompanying sketch failed to capture her intelligent eyes and flirtatious allure, there was no mistaking that it was Annabelle.

None of the personal information and aliases had surprised Patrick. He'd assumed Annabelle had many, and her sketch, of course, was not nearly as clear and revealing as the photo Eve had taken of the woman in 2021.

But Patrick's eyes froze on the words ALLEGED MURDERER, and then he recalled that, just before she'd fled the apartment with Colleen, Annabelle admitted she'd killed before. With new concern, he moved to the sergeant's desk and asked the cop, who looked up and ran his fingers over his wide handlebar mustache, what murder she was alleged to have committed.

To Patrick's surprise, the sergeant wasn't the least bit suspicious. If anything, he seemed grateful to have someone to talk to.

Seated behind his elevated desk, which was covered with stacks of paper and an old candlestick telephone, he leaned back in his heavy wooden chair, twirled the ends of his mustache and folded his hands before him. "Well now, let me tell you about that one," he said, his bright eyes showing enjoyment of the story he was about to tell.

"Prudence Riley... is an interesting woman." His eyes settled on Patrick for the first time, sizing him up. "Have you read about the woman, then?" he said in a good Irish accent.

Patrick expanded his own Irish accent, in the spirit of solidarity, as well as to his general advantage.

"Well, now, officer, you know, I have read about the poor lass, and I have a wee fascination for the Wanted posters, you know. It's the daft writer in me."

The sergeant's eyes expanded with interest. "Oh, you're a writer, are you?"

"Yes... Mysteries, you know, and I find this Prudence Riley woman has an interesting face, and, I says to myself, maybe there's a good, old-fashioned mystery story there, with a little romance tossed in for some spice, which is what the ladies are always fond of. If you get my meaning?"

"Oh, yes, yes, I certainly do get your meaning about the ladies. My misses likes to read the pulps, she does. Yes, that is a fact. The pulps and the romances are what she's all about on a cold winter's night. It ain't about me, I can tell you that for true. But she doesn't like the modern books. No, it's got to be the books about the rascals on horseback, some count or duke riding by and stealing the full-figured lass, with her loose hair askew, and her dress a flying and flapping behind her."

It was clear this man was a talker, and Patrick wanted to steer him back to Annabelle. "So, what can you tell me about this Prudence Riley?"

The sergeant sat up and leaned forward, ignoring a cop who was holding up a piece of paper, eager for attention, the story he was about to tell being the priority.

"They say that Prudence Riley is not only a clever jewel thief but that she also poisoned a man named Wheeler Packett, about two years ago."

"What was the evidence?" Patrick asked.

"The two were seen together many times, and they were all buttered up, they was, with the hot impatient eyes and the upturned lips. At least that's what was reported by the witnesses we found. And then there was a witness by the name of Lori Hawk. She stated that Prudence told her outright that she had poisoned the man because she learned he was two-timing her."

"And where is Lori Hawk now?" Patrick asked.

"Well... who knows if you can believe the woman. About a year ago, Lori was booked after leading police on a foot chase through the city. It was one devil of a chase, from all accounts received. She was arrested on two counts of larceny. One count was for stealing a purse from one of those swell Fifth Avenue women in a department store, and the other was for shoplifting hosiery. So, I ask you. Can you trust the word of the woman? There was some speculation that she was the woman who was with Packett, two-timing Prudence. Well, these are low women that the two of us are discussing, aren't they?"

Patrick ran a hand along his jaw. "So, there's no direct proof that Prudence poisoned Wheeler Packett?"

The sergeant excused himself and finally snatched the piece of paper from the waiting cop. He then turned to answer a question from two cops who'd just hauled in a small, pouting man for a mugging, and they were ready to book and fingerprint him.

Patrick waited, impatiently. Was Colleen living with a murderer?

The sergeant lit a cigar, puffed, and blew smoke with pleasure as he gathered his thoughts. "Can you imagine the darkness of poisoning someone, sir? We booked a woman about six months ago who had slowly poisoned her own dear mother to death, over a period of some weeks. Now think about this for your mystery story, sir. This faithless daughter needed to look into her dear mother's trusting eyes day after day, as she slowly snuffed out her good mother's life. The daughter had to play the role of nurse, or kind and trusting daughter, while she sustained her murderous intent at a pitch. That would be unbearable for many of those who've shot a gun or swung a sword. It's a bad business, it is, and the good Lord in heaven will never forgive her black soul for what she did. No, he won't."

"Why did she do it?" Patrick asked. "What was the motive?"

The sergeant shook his head in sorrow. "For the worst of all motives, sir. For her mother's money, so she could run off with some scoundrel, and don't you know that he was the one who put the girl up to it in the first place. So now they'll both hang, won't they? And the old, sad world will be a better place without them, I'll be bound."

Patrick left the precinct, more disturbed and worried for his little Colleen than at any time since Annabelle had kidnapped her and fled into the past. He had to find that woman—Prudence Riley or Annabelle Palmer. Some way or the other, he had to find her. But how?

DURING THE FIRST WEEK of December, Eve and Patrick rented four rooms on the sixth floor of the Fairmount Hotel, just off Madison Square Park. Although it was not an extravagant hotel, it boasted of being fireproof and of having full electricity, as well as a modern bathroom with a bathtub.

It was Eve who was amused by a printed card posted next to the electric light switch in the living room. Patrick hadn't noticed it.

This Room is Equipped With
Edison Electric Light.
Do not attempt to light with match.
Simply turn the key on the wall
by the door.
Please note: The use of Electricity for lighting is in
no way harmful to health,
nor does it affect the soundness of sleep.

ON THURSDAY, DECEMBER 7, Eve and Patrick were at the Bullock Café, just off Sixth Avenue, having a handsome dinner of turkey, vegetables, and baked potatoes. Their moods had progressively darkened since they'd first arrived back in November. Despite their constant searching and footwork, they hadn't found Annabelle's mother, let alone Annabelle herself, and the Gantlys were feeling the force of desperation.

"Why don't we go to the police, Patrick? Maybe they can help... I mean, if we tell them that Annabelle has our child? That she took our child."

Patrick sat in a weary melancholy. "Eve, we've already discussed this. We can't go to the police. Cops ask questions. They are suspicious. Cops don't trust humans or what they say. I ought to know."

Patrick looked at Eve's worried face. "Eve, you know we can't go to the police. We can't tell them who we are or where we came from. In turn, they wouldn't trust us or believe anything we said. No, that door is closed."

Eve took a bite of the turkey and chewed, distracted. When she swallowed, she asked the question she'd been dreading. "Okay, Patrick. What do we do now? We've been here since, I don't know, November 11 or 12, and we've got nothing."

"Not nothing. We know Annabelle and Colleen are here in this time, or at least we're ninety percent sure. Your talk with the waiter and my fight with Farley Carp establishes that Annabelle is around somewhere. We also know the name of the circus her mother worked for, and thanks to you and Joni, we know it no longer exists. It's defunct."

"But none of those gets us anywhere."

"Detective work is slow work, Eve, and it takes a lot of patience. We have to keep at it. Eventually, something or someone will come forward. It has to."

Eve set her fork down and reached for Patrick's hand. "I know I shouldn't say this again, but I can't help it. I'm so sorry for what I did, Patrick. I'm so sorry I brought that woman into our home. I just can't get it out of my head... and here we are looking for little Colleen in the dark."

Patrick squeezed her hand and rested his soft eyes on her. "Eve, my love, wasn't it you who once told me that life happens, and then we get to deal with it?"

Eve looked down. "Yes... I guess I did, and sometimes I should just keep my big mouth shut."

"So, we'll continue with our search."

Eve retrieved her hand and massaged her forehead, unable to banish her inner darkness. She knew what she was about to say would be disturbing. "Patrick, we know that Annabelle wore disguises, right?"

"Yes, we know that."

"What if when Joni and I were looking for her, or when you were searching, Annabelle was wearing one of those disguises? What if she spotted us, got spooked, and ran off?"

"Eve, we can 'What if?' till the cows come home, but it's not going to get us anywhere. I thought of that too, which is why I've spent so much time standing on corners and in alleyways, observing women's faces and bodies and the way they walk. Annabelle had a distinctive walk. She gently pitched her right foot forward and made a low sway of her hips. That was natural for her, I think. Not put on."

Eve opened her eyes fully. "Really? You noticed that? The low sway of her hips?"

"Yes."

"Well... Not that this is about me, but... What about my hips? When I walk, do I have a low sway of my hips?"

"No, Eve, you don't. You have a purposeful walk, with a girlish bit of a sashay."

Eve smiled, pleased. "Really? A girlish bit of a sashay? Well, it sounds better when you say it with your accent. But... Hey. Wow... I think I like that."

Patrick grinned. "So do I."

Eve's smile was small, and then it grew. "You can always make me feel better, and that's another reason I married you."

"And you need to forgive yourself for what happened. It wasn't your fault. Don't carry that guilt around; it adds weight to the brain and prevents it from firing on all pistons. Believe me, I know. I had a bellyful of it when I lost Emma."

Eve took in a breath and blew it out. "All right, Mr. Gantly. I'll try. Now, what do we do next?"

Patrick forked a piece of white meat. "I'm going for a different approach. I'm going to search for anyone who knew Wheeler Packett. Family. Friends. An old girlfriend who might hold a grudge."

"You mean the man Annabelle was supposed to have killed? That guy?"

"Yes."

"That could be dangerous. Who knows what kind of lowlife he was and who his friends and family might be?"

"I have to try. I'm coming up empty on everything else. Meanwhile, you and Joni keep at it. I had a thought earlier today. Instead of the theaters and vaudeville spots, why don't you try the fortune tellers on the Lower East Side? I should have thought of this earlier, when you told me about what that director, Rufus somebody, said to you. Maybe Annabelle's mother set up shop somewhere in the city as a fortune teller. I would think that fortune tellers know other fortune tellers."

Eve regained her composure. "Patrick, what a great idea. Why didn't I think of that?"

"Because we're both stressed, Eve. When one is stressed, flopping about like a fish on a sailing ship in a storm, thoughts get knotted up."

Eve reached for her glass of white wine. "I love it, Patrick. It's perfect. I'll call Joni and we'll start our search first thing in the morning."

CHAPTER 34

Eve and Joni began their fortune teller search on the busy corner of Rivington and Orchard Streets and, by late morning, they'd visited four. None were helpful, two being tight-lipped and suspicious, one a little crazy, and one downright rude.

Just as they were about to break for lunch, Eve saw a sign that drew her eyes above the Eagle Shoe Company and next door to a dentist.

PROF. DORA KLINGER
World-Famous Card Reader, Palmist and Mind Reader.
She guesses the name and age of Every Person.
Open from 9 a.m. to 10 p.m.
78 Rivington Street

Eve led Joni up the narrow concrete stairs to a heavy wooden door. Inside, the hallway had a wall of wooden mailboxes and it smelled of garlic, fresh bread, and cigar smoke.

They climbed another flight of carpeted stairs to the second-floor landing and turned right, facing a long, narrow hallway. A white door on the left had a metal embossed nameplate screwed to it, announcing PROF. DORA.

Eve knocked. The door opened promptly, and a small, squat woman with a tidy mound of gray hair, a long black dress, and a gray shawl draped about her narrow shoulders, welcomed them with a sly, friendly smile. She was gnarly and worn, with a patch of hair sticking out of a chin mole. The woman reminded Joni of a root vegetable.

"Welcome, ladies," she said in a scratchy-voiced accent. "Welcome to my humble little home. I am Dora, and I am here for you, to help you any way I can."

Eve and Joni stepped into a dim, private, snug apartment, sparsely furnish with heavy furniture. A round table with a white lace doyly held a crystal ball and some playing cards. Heavy, black curtains were slightly parted, and the place smelled of rose and baked chicken.

Eve glanced around while Joni stood at Eve's elbow. When Dora shut the door, Eve started talking, not wanting to lead the woman on. "Professor Dora, we're here for some information."

Dora's eyes sparkled. "Information? Yes, of course. That's what I do. Give you information about you, or the dead, or the living."

"Yes, but what I'm trying to say is, we're looking for a woman who also tells fortunes. She used to work for the Ballyhoo Circus."

Dora processed the strange question, and then her heavy face wadded up into tight distrust. "The circus? I never told fortunes at any circus."

"No... We're looking for a fortune teller who used to work for the circus, Professor Dora."

"The circus?"

"Yes. It's important that we find her."

"I don't know no one who works for any circus. I am a professor from Europe, not some fly-by-the-night trickster. I have good clients, and they come back to me. Always they come back. No shyster I am. I am fine, and I am true."

"I'm sure you are, Professor Dora, it's just that we thought you might know the woman."

Seeing that Eve and Joni weren't interested in her services, Dora moved to the door and opened it. "I have business coming soon. Thank you and good morning," she said, in a curt, business-like voice.

Eve and Joni bowed their heads toward the door and were almost through it, when they heard a man's voice call out from inside the room. "Ballyhoo Circus?"

Eve turned and Joni followed.

"What is it, Saul? What do you know about it?" Dora asked with irritation. "Go back to your reading."

Saul came shuffling into the room, with wire-rimmed glasses perched on the end of his nose, wearing a clean white shirt, black suspenders and baggy dark pants that were too big for him. He was a bent and peering old man, with scattered white hair, thin lips and the pallid face of someone who shunned the sunlight.

"Did you say the Ballyhoo Circus?" Saul said, wheezing in a high, breathy voice.

Eve took a step forward. "Yes, sir. That's right. The woman we're looking for told fortunes at the circus."

Saul nodded, then smiled with satisfaction. He looked at his wife, who seemed to have a dark cloud over her head.

"Dora, you remember Ballyhoo?"

"I remember nothing about Ballyhoo, Saul. If I had remembered, I would have said so."

Saul held his smile while he looked at Eve. "For a time, I did the books for the Ballyhoo Circus."

"The books?" Joni asked. "Oh, you mean you were the accountant?"

"Yes, the accountant, you could say," he said, lifting a hand, ready to say more. "That's too fancy a word for what I did, but it sounds highfalutin, so, yes, I was the accountant. I tried to keep the circus from folding, because the owner, a Mr. Cahill, gambled and drank away the profits as soon as I'd get the business in the black. So, about a year ago, it went bust and closed."

Dora blinked with impatience. "All right, Saul. Let these two women go about their business so I can go about mine."

"Dora, they're looking for Hattie."

Eve felt her heart kick. "Hattie?"

"Hattie Craddick told fortunes there at the circus. I went to see her, maybe a couple of times. She went by the name Madam Carmen. She always drew a crowd, and she made money for the circus."

Dora's mouth turned down into an inverted U. "Why did you never tell me these things, Saul? Why, I ask you?"

He held up both hands, patting her words down. "I told you, Dora, plenty of times, I told you. I told you, but you don't listen to me. Always you're with the cards, or the counting, or the money, or talking to the spirits. Yes, I told you about Hattie, Madam Carmen."

Eve spoke up. "Sir, this is very important. Do you know if Hattie Craddick had a daughter?"

Saul scratched the end of his nose thoughtfully. "Well, let me see now. She may have said something about a daughter."

"Please think back and see if you can remember?" Eve said, taking a step forward.

He twisted his mouth left and right, squinting. "Well, now that I think about it, I do recall that Mr. Cahill said something about Hattie's daughter. He said she could turn a man's head and raise the pulse."

"Saul!" Dora scolded.

He shrugged. "I didn't say it, Dora. It was Mr. Cahill."

Eve cut in. "Do you know where Hattie Craddick is now?"

"Yes, of course, I know. She has a business not so far away, on Delancey Street, and she still goes by the name Madam Carmen. You'll see the sign. It's a little, narrow place, upstairs like this, next to a bakery on one side and the Downtown Saloon on the other. You can't miss it."

Eve thanked Saul, and she and Joni were out the door before Dora made a move to close it.

Hope drove Eve and Joni ahead as they picked their way through the crowds, turning off Orchard Street onto Delancey Street. It was Joni who first spotted the black sign swinging on metal hinges. "There it is, Eve!"

MADAM CARMEN!
THE MOST FAMOUS OCCULTIST IN THE WORLD!

The ladies climbed the stairs and Eve reached for a flyer that was stuffed in a black metal box hanging next to the front door. Eve took one and read it aloud.

"Madam Carmen is an unexcelled occultist. She will tell you the past, present and future. She gives the best advice about business, journeys, law, love, sickness, family affairs, etc. Is he the right man for you? Ask Madam Carmen. She knows!"

Eve handed the flyer to Joni and looked up at the three windows on the second floor, where MADAM CARMEN OCCULTIST was displayed in block letters on the middle window.

"Let's go, Joni. This is it!"

Inside, they mounted the flight of creaky stairs, holding onto the shaky banister. Pausing on the second floor, they searched the dingy hallway for the right apartment.

Joni said, "If those old stairs and that booby trap of a banister are any indication, I'd say that if Madam Carmen is the most famous occultist in the world, she ain't doing so good right now."

Eve nodded. "It's the second door to the right. Apartment 2B."

Eve steadied her breath, then knocked.

Eve cocked an ear and Joni stepped back when they heard a deep, contralto voice speaking in an exotic accent. "The door is open, and the spirits await, and

Madam Carmen awaits. Please enter with quiet reverence."

Joni whispered, "Are you shittin' me?"

Eve made a shhh sound. "Let's go in."

Joni turned the tarnished doorknob and opened the door. Unlike Dora's room, this one was shining with light, the curtains a shimmery white lace, the sofa, chair and loveseat a velvet burgundy. A thin, wrinkle-faced woman with a transcendent expression stared at them with half-hooded eyes, seemingly lost in distant worlds and foggy dimensions.

She sat behind a round mahogany card table, facing them, wearing a golden robe with impressively embroidered bright stars and colored planets, her head crowned with a shocking red scarf, wrapped like a turban.

Joni shut the door behind them, while Eve's uncomfortable gaze cast about the room, finally resting on the woman.

Madam Carmen spoke in a deep, commanding tone, with some odd, creative accent that was part Spanish, part Italian and part French. "I am Madam Carmen, yes, the one and only. Please, both of you sit before me in the two chairs I have here, and I will peer into your very souls and tell you the most amazing things. I will reveal inner secrets known only to you. I will give you the best advice in matters of love, long journeys, and family affairs. Please sit, and let Madam Carmen read your fortunes, fortunes that will change your lives in ways you cannot now imagine."

CHAPTER 35

Patrick had returned to the sergeant at the Thirteenth Precinct and learned the name of a reporter, John Cavender, who had written a story about Prudence Riley poisoning Wheeler Packett. Packett had also been a reporter.

Patrick traveled to Park Row, where most of the newspapers of the day were located. In his hansom cab he looked from left to right, viewing the transportation center of the Brooklyn Bridge Terminal, which connected the Brooklyn Bridge's trains and trolleys to the Second Avenue Elevated trains.

Next to the terminal was a building with an impressive dome. This was Joseph Pulitzer's New York World Building. Next to that was where Patrick was headed, a small building built by Tammany Hall in 1811. It was the home of *The Sun*.

The Sun was known by those in the newspaper business as being busy, tidy and efficient. On one side of the building was a quiet courtyard, and on the other an impressive view of the city. The ceilings were high, the décor brass and brown marble. Spiral staircases led up to floors of reporters, columnists, editors, and the publisher.

Inside the building, Patrick went striding across the white marble lobby to a bank of elevators. He stepped into an open car, and the smartly uniformed operator pushed the fourth-floor button.

Patrick exited onto the fourth floor, known as the City Room, *The Sun's* center of operations. It was bustling, with copyboys darting about, typewriters clacking away, and the smell of cigars and cigarettes.

Patrick stopped at a copy desk and asked where he could find John Cavender. A teenage boy with acne, restless eyes, and a high, chirping voice pointed and gave directions.

Patrick started off, passing desks with cabinets and drawers, and rows of tables with green glass lamps, where editors sat scribbling, copyboys waited, and secretaries typed. There was a frantic, impressive competence about the place.

Patrick had called ahead, so John Cavender was expecting him. "I can give you fifteen minutes and no more," Cavender had said, gruffly. "What are you, a cop?"

"No, not a cop. I'm trying to find Prudence Riley."

He'd laughed. "Fifteen minutes. Come right away."

Patrick found John at his desk, a cigarette dangling from his lips. He was two-fingering his typewriter keys, pecking away expertly as if he were playing a Bach fugue. Patrick stood by, waiting to be noticed. When John glanced up, he gave Patrick a once-over.

"You're the fellow who called?"

Patrick nodded. "Yes. Thanks for seeing me."

Cavender pushed back and stood up, offering a hand. Patrick shook it as he sized John up. He was on the short side, near forty, with small, watchful eyes and a black, trimmed mustache. His thinning, black hair showed signs of early gray and was combed straight back, giving him a severe look.

Cavender crushed his cigarette out in the ashtray and pointed to a room close by. "We can talk in there."

Patrick followed him into a side, windowless room, furnished with a dark wooden table surrounded by green leather chairs.

"Have a seat, Patrick, and tell me your story of woe."

Patrick sat, and John sat across from him. "Coffee?"

"No, thanks."

"Why are you looking for Prudence?" John said.

"Let's just say she has something I want."

"Ha! What an answer, Patrick."

From his suit jacket pocket, Cavender tugged out a pouch of tobacco and paper, then rolled a lumpy cigarette. He placed it between his lips and lit it with a match, blowing a cloud of smoke toward the ceiling.

"She's a killer, you know."

"Are you sure?"

"No doubt."

"Have you met her?" Patrick asked.

"Tried. Almost. Missed. She has more tricks than Houdini, and more disguises."

"So, based on your research, you believe Prudence killed Wheeler Packett?"

"Killed him, yes, and probably snuffed out another, Jules Jarrow."

Patrick leaned forward. "What?"

"Yes, sir. I mentioned it in the article. Did you read it?"

"No, I couldn't find a copy in the library. I was going to ask you if you had one."

"I'll tell you all the true words and skip the rest."

Patrick leaned back, waiting, while Cavender smoked and formed his thoughts. "First, Packett. Prudence and Packett met in a saloon. She was in disguise. An old woman, so he said, and at first, he didn't give her a second glance. Little by little, she peeled some of her mask away, and she didn't look so bad underneath all that makeup. She flirted. She's an expert, I'm told. Her hands got active with Packett and he didn't mind it, if you get what I'm saying. They leave and, as the song goes, they go under the bamboo tree and dance the hoochie coochie. Their romantic scene was so pure, so bright—until Prudence learns she's gettin' two-timed by Packett."

"Did you know Packett?" Patrick asked.

"Not so well. He worked for the *New York Tribune*. We met in passing, political speeches, Tammany Hall business. Things like that. So, Prudence knows this drugstore clerk who works for the People's Drug Store over on Second Avenue. She sweettalks him, and more, and he agrees to get some arsenic from the pharmacy. You know what they say about poison. It's the dose that makes the poison. In other words, every chemical can be considered a poison if you take enough of it. Anyway, Packett dies two weeks later. Postmortem found the arsenic, and the cops put two and two together, along with witnesses who came forward to say they'd seen Prudence and Packett together, making them goo-goo eyes. Guess the name of the drugstore clerk who gave Prudence the arsenic?"

Patrick sighed. "Jules Jarrow…"

"You're as smart as you look, Patrick. Prudence would consider Jarrow to be a lose-end witness, wouldn't she? He might go to the cops and tell all for a reward. He was only twenty-two years old, and he left a broken-hearted mother and a father who's now drinking himself to death. Jarrow was found in an alley near the drugstore with a .41 caliber bullet in the back of his head. His pockets were empty. Prudence obviously wanted to make it look like a robbery."

Patrick's shoulders dropped, and he ran a shaky hand through his hair. He recalled that, in 2021, Annabelle had been charged with threatening to shoot two New York City policemen with a Remington, two-shot, .41 caliber derringer.

Cavender shifted in his seat. "Patrick… why are you really here? If you bumped Prudence a couple of times in the night, then fine, but for your own sake, forget her. Let it go and consider yourself lucky you're not dead. Yes, she's a fine gal to look at, but she ain't worth it."

"No, it's nothing like that. I want to get in touch with Wheeler Packett's family, or an old girlfriend. Someone who might know something. Anything. I have to find her."

John slowly shook his head. "You won't find her, Patrick. I tried for months… over a year, in fact. Every time I almost caught up with her, she'd slip away. She's a slippery eel of a woman, Patrick, and straight from the bowels of hell. Do yourself a favor and forget about trying to find her."

"Did you ever find the woman's address? Any address at all?"

Cavender nodded. "For a short while, maybe a year or so back, Prudence lived on Orchard Street on the Lower East Side. Before that, on West 27th Street, at a Queen Anne-style, ten-story building with a tower suite occupied by the theater actress Mary Hall. It's said, by the gossiping neighbors in the building, that Prudence's gentleman friend, a wealthy banker, had lots of greenbacks and he visited her regularly. Anyway, it's a mixed residential and transient hotel, and Prudence lived in a very modest one-bedroom that looked out on a brick wall. She ain't there anymore. Long gone. Her gentleman friend dropped dead with a heart attack over a year ago, but she had nothing to do with that. At least, not that I could find."

"Did anyone know her? Say anything about her? I'm sure you followed up with her gossiping neighbors?"

"Yeah, I asked. No one remembered her... she kept to herself and, I'm guessing here, when she did leave her apartment, she was probably wearing some disguise."

In frustration, Patrick turned his head aside.

"If the cops and me haven't found her by now, then I say, give it up, Patrick. We ain't amateurs at this."

Patrick's eyes shot to John's. "I can't give it up! I have to find her. Do you have the name and address of someone in Packett's family?"

John screwed out his cigarette in the ashtray as he gave Patrick a hard, candid stare.

"What do you do, Patrick? I smell cop. You've got to be a cop. You wear it all over you, like a fierce cologne."

"I used to be."

"Here in New York?"

"It's in the past."

"Okay... I see the hurt in your eyes. I see the rage in your eyes, and I see good old back-home fear, but I don't think that fear is in you. I don't think many things scare you all that much. You're obviously not spooning for Prudence, so you're searching for her for another reason. Okay, fine, you don't want to tell me?" He shrugged. "Okay, Packett has a sister who, last I knew, lives off Eighth Avenue, somewhere in the West 40s or 50s. I have her address in the carousel file on my desk."

"Did you talk to her?" Patrick asked.

Cavender spread his hands and tilted his head as if to say, *Of course I did.* "Patrick, come on, I'm a damned good reporter. Of course I talked to her, and her grandma who lives with her, and the husband, a nice guy who's a streetcar conductor."

"Did you learn anything?"

"Nothing. The sister knew absolutely nothing. She and her brother were not close. She's religious. He wasn't. She only saw him at Christmas. None of those three knew anything—or wanted to know anything. Blank faces. Hard, shut-up, tight faces that said, 'Wheeler's dead? Well, he shouldn't have strayed from the flock, should he? Now, he's played with fire and gone to the devil.'"

"Did you follow up with Jules Jarrow's employer and family?" Patrick asked.

"Of course. Nothing. Police came up empty. No leads. Suspicion? Yes. Proof? Nothing. The file's still open, but it's as cold as a dead mackerel."

The two stared at each other. "Prudence is a cold one, Patrick, and a smart one. If you ask me, she'll never be found. She's too clever, and she's a deadly scorpion if you threaten or cross her."

After a few seconds of silence, John said, "Now, I know what you're thinking, Patrick. I hear the cop in you ask, if Prudence killed those two men, well… has she killed others?"

Patrick's worried expression said it all.

Back at Cavender's desk, Patrick took Packett's sister's address, thanked Cavender and left the building, feeling lower than he had since he and Eve had landed in 1905.

If Eve and Joni didn't have any luck finding Annabelle's mother, he had no idea what to do or where to look next.

CHAPTER 36

Eve and Joni sat in the two chairs facing Madam Carmen. Eve reached into her purse, removed a dollar from her wallet, and placed it on the table near Madam Carmen's shaky hands.

Madam Carmen's glazed and bloodshot eyes lowered on the dollar, holding it in her gaze for a long time. A woman's opulent voice in the apartment above was singing an operatic aria. Outside, there was shouting and the sound of horses' hooves clopping by. Inside, it was quiet.

With her unblinking eyes fixed on the dollar, she said, "Why this dollar? I charge fifteen cents."

Eve leaned a little forward, deciding to be abrupt. "Madam Carmen, I'm looking for your daughter, Annabelle Palmer. Do you know where she is?"

Madam Carmen remained still, her forehead sweaty, contortion twisting her mouth into suspicion. "My daughter?"

"Yes. It's very important that I find her," Eve said.

Madam Carmen removed her eyes from the dollar and waved her thin hand in the air in a vague gesture that neither Eve nor Joni understood. "No fortune, then? You're not here to receive my wisdom?"

"No... We're not. Do you know where your daughter is?" Eve pressed.

Madam Carmen raised her eyes to the ceiling, and Eve observed that the woman didn't appear well. She was rail thin, her skin pallid, and her eyes glassy and distracted. Had she been drinking? Eve thought so.

When Madam Carmen didn't speak, Joni glanced at Eve and shrugged a shoulder, her expression saying, "What now?"

Madam Carmen pushed her chair back, looked at Eve for a moment, and then shifted her gaze to Joni. This time when she spoke, she had no exotic accent. It was a British accent.

To Joni she said, "Well, dearie, are you looking for my girl as well, then?"

Joni nodded. "Yes."

"Do you know where Annabelle is, Madam Carmen?" Eve asked.

Madam Carmen struggled to her feet. She was a taller woman than Eve would have suspected, but she was shaky on her legs and, Eve thought, maybe shaky in her mind.

"Are you feeling all right?" Eve asked.

The opera singer above burst into a high note, and it was so loud and shrill that it made Joni wince.

"Wow!" Joni said, glancing up. "That high C was like a sucker punch."

Madam Carmen didn't seem to notice or care.

"I've come a long way," Eve said, standing. "Can you please help me?"

Madam Carmen's pensive mouth puckered, her expression turning irritable. "How would I know where Annie has hidden herself this time? She hangs to the shadows, doesn't she? And she don't take so kindly to her old Mum anymore, if she ever did."

Eve felt some of the life leave her, and she sat back down, hanging her head. "Then you don't know where she is?"

Madam Carmen reached up and snatched the scarf from her head and tossed it down onto the card table. Her short, gray hair was thin and askew, and without the scarf, the woman looked old and fragile. "My daughter…" she said, with acid regret, her eyes flashing about restlessly. "Do I know where she is?"

Madam Carmen turned toward the windows. "When Annie was but a girl of thirteen, she would spend her hours reading and studying adventure novels as if they was holy relics, dug up from the exotic sands of Egypt. She always was a restless one, and also a smart one. Clever as the day is long and watchful as an eagle, circling, she was, and I'd wager, she still is, by all accounts."

Joni spoke up. "Have you heard from her? Has she written to you recently, Madam Carmen?"

The woman whipped her head around. "Call me Hattie," she snapped. "Hattie Craddick, since that's my name, the name they scribbled down in that Bible in the stone church in Painswick."

Joni turned her eyes to Eve, who was staring at Hattie, hoping for some morsel of information about

Annabelle. And then Eve told Hattie the truth. Why shouldn't she? What did she have to lose?

"Hattie... your daughter, Annabelle, kidnapped my two-year-old daughter."

With a grave, hesitant face, Hattie lowered her head in degrees and finally sank into her chair with a heavy sigh.

Silence ensued. The singer had finished the aria, but a piano played a bouncy waltz. A cat meowed outside the door, and downstairs, someone was hammering.

"I want my baby back, Hattie. Please help me," Eve said. "Can you tell me anything about where your daughter might be? She may have left town."

Hattie's mouth was hard, her jaw tight. She reached for something beneath the table. When Eve saw the blue bottle, she immediately knew what it was. Laudanum, a reddish-brown and extremely bitter liquid used as pain medication. It contained opium, morphine, and codeine.

Eve watched with concern as Hattie tipped the bottle back and swallowed, her Adam's apple moving. After she'd replaced the bottle, she wiped her mouth with a hankie she pulled from a pocket.

"Annie loved the children. Since she was... oh... a young woman... she told me many times she wanted to have them—a whole slew of them. Yes, a houseful."

Hattie's faced turned apologetic and sad. "Annie was never what you'd call an easy kind of child, and, oh, was she into the mischief when she grew into her teens. And when the bloom came to her cheeks, and she changed from a backyard weed into a lovely spring flower, well, all the blokes came around, didn't they?"

Her mouth quivered, and she wiped it again with the hankie she had clutched in her fist. "The circus wasn't no place to bring up a smart and pretty doll like Annabelle. She learned all the dirty tricks from the women, and the chiseling ways of the men. Did I try to protect her? Well, I wasn't no proper Mum likes them that come from Hyde Park, was I? But Annie never did go hungry or want for the nice and pretty things. I got them for her. And she learned a thing or two about this old knock-around world that those silly, fluttering, society girls in London will never know. Annie wasn't made for that kind of life, was she? She was born for life's adventures, and to box away the dirty tricks that life likes to put you up against."

Eve listened patiently, praying that Hattie would eventually tell her where Annabelle was.

Hattie drifted into a mood. "What do the cards say about Annie? I'm sure you want to know. Because I do seek to read them; to part the dark clouds and try to peer into Annie's future. But I've found you can never read the cards for them that's close to you. The cards' meanings just swim before my eyes and don't give up any fortune at all."

Hattie pounded the table with a fist, and Eve and Joni flinched. With a grave, hesitant face, she cursed, her eyes flashing about restlessly.

"It's the devil's work anyway, ain't it, ladies? These cards and these fortunes that I've told since I first come to that ragtag circus are all blackness and lies. I was not a fit mother, and God knows it, nor did she have a fit father, thanks to his drink and his swinging the fists at me, and then at Annie. She shot at him, you know. Oh, yes, she shot the old blighter in the arm, and he went scampering off like a wounded dog. I heard he died in Alaska of the fever, panning for gold. So, I says that the good Lord above served him up the fortune he deserved, and I hope he had a good appetite for it."

Hattie looked up, her eyes moving, beads of perspiration forming above her lip. "But I've been dancing with the devil for years now, ain't I? And maybe we've become good dance mates. But then, there are times when I've had too much of the sweet gin, and I think maybe I've told the cards' truth to one or two suckers, who went off whistlin' with the good fortune. Maybe I've even put a lover or two together; maybe I saved a good girl from marrying a black-hearted man, who'd beat her till she died. So maybe I'll be forgiven, just a bit, for all my other black sins."

Hattie pounded the table again. "I should have stopped Annie from marrying him! She married the very devil of a man, who played the horses and the cards, and he almost beat the life from her, and he did kill the baby in her womb, damn him into hell."

The room gathered into a dismal hush. Eve and Joni lowered their heads, as if in prayer, and Eve fought to keep her hope alive.

CHAPTER 37

Hattie shook her old, regretful head, a tear rolling down her cheek, her voice rough and hoarse. "My Annie was never quite right after that, and, I've got to ask you, who would be, after getting kicked about in this evil world? Huh? Who? No, Lord love her."

Hattie's damp eyes were pleading as they settled on Eve, and she spoke in a voice of endless loneliness. "So maybe you'll forgive the girl her wicked ways, now that you know the ugly truth of it; now that you know the truth about her failing Mum."

Eve stiffened, her hands forming into fists. "No, Hattie, I won't forgive her for taking my baby. Never. Would you? If you know where she is, I beg you to tell me. Please."

Hattie reached for the laudanum bottle and took another generous gulp. When she pushed up, her face was ashen, her hands trembling.

Eve and Joni followed the woman as she went to a nearby chest of drawers, opened the top drawer, reached in and removed a postcard. She returned to her chair, sitting, staring at the postcard, while Eve and Joni waited in rising anticipation.

Hattie handed it to Eve. "It's from Annie."

Eve accepted it, noticing the color sketch of the Statue of Liberty on the front. There was a clear, artistic script on the other side.

March 1905
Dear Mum:
My life has changed. Be happy for me! I have a baby, at last, and I'm leaving town. Wanted to see you and say goodbye, but time presses. Goodbye. Love, A

Looking desolate, her eyes wide with shock, her mouth falling, Eve handed the postcard to Joni. After Joni read it, the two women stared in stunned silence, fighting defeat and anger.

"Has she written to you since March?" Eve asked.

Hattie shook her head sorrowfully. "No... Not a word. Not a blessed word have I received from my Annie. But that's what she does. I may not hear from the likes of her for a year or more. I may never hear from her again. And she won't know, or give a care, when these old bones are put in my grave."

Eve handed the postcard back to Hattie and rose. Joni followed.

Eve was about to turn and leave when something stopped her. At first, she resisted the compassion she felt for the lonely woman. After all, wasn't it that same compassion that had brought Annabelle into their lives? The same compassion that had allowed this woman's daughter to take Colleen away? Eve tried to push away sympathy, but she couldn't.

Hattie's gaze was turned down, her faced rumpled, projecting a defeated weariness.

Eve moved toward her. "Hattie, are you ill?"

Hattie didn't look up. "Ill? Well, the rheumatism's got me some, as it does now and then, and my heart doesn't have the pump it used to have. I get all puffed out when I climb those stairs most days. But for an old woman, I'm still grateful to the Lord to be moving about."

Hattie looked down at her leg. "And I fell on the street a few days back and cut meself. It's been paining me some."

Eve placed her purse on the table. "Hattie, can I look at it? I'm a nurse."

"A nurse? Are you telling me the truth, then?"

"Yes, can I take a look?"

"Do what suits you."

Eve moved a chair closer to Hattie, where there was plenty of natural light. Hattie drew back the robe from her leg, revealing an ugly, two-inch wound. Eve sat down and examined it, immediately seeing that it was infected. It gave off a foul odor, and there was a yellow discharge and red streaks on the skin around the wound.

Eve reached and touched Hattie's forehead with the back of her hand. "You have a fever, Hattie."

"It won't be the first, nor the last, I can assure you."

"You should have seen a doctor. Your leg is infected, and I'm going to clean it."

Hattie lifted an eyebrow. "I washed it a day ago. Doctors cost money and they don't like old women like me."

Joni came over, looked at the wound and grimaced. "Can I help?"

"Yes. Hattie, do you have a basin?"

"Under the sink there, where I'm pointing."

"Clean wash cloths? Any antiseptic ointment or cream? Rubbing alcohol?"

Hattie pointed toward the bathroom, and Joni went to work.

Later, after Eve had washed and cleaned the wound and applied a thin layer of antiseptic ointment, she allowed the skin to dry, while Joni hurried to the nearest drugstore and found gauze and tape.

Nearly thirty minutes later, Hattie's leg was bandaged, and some of her color had returned.

Eve stood up and nodded, the task completed. "Hattie, I'm coming back tomorrow to clean and dress the wound again. It's a bad infection. You've let it go too long. You could lose the leg if you don't take care of it. When I come, I'm going to bring some pills for the infection. You must take them exactly as I tell you, understand? They'll kill the infection."

Hattie eased back in her chair, taking Eve in fully. "Why? Why are you doing this for me, the wretched old mother of the woman who took your baby? This old head of mine is in a muddle."

"I don't want you to lose that leg, Hattie."

She nodded and looked away toward the windows, where sunlight streamed in. "Well... it don't matter so much. I'm a broken-down old missus, who ain't so long for this world, and I'm not fighting that hard to stay in this plot of ground. I did the cards for meself just the other day, and they told me a thing or two about these old bones. They told me I'm about to finish my business here in this world."

Eve straightened her spine. "I'm coming back tomorrow, Hattie. Is late morning all right?"

Hattie smiled warmly and met Eve's eyes. "You're a good daughter to your Mum, aren't you, young lady? You wouldn't run off without seeing the old woman now, would you? You wouldn't leave her sick and alone and a-wondering where she was and who she was with? No, I can see it in your eyes. You've got a good heart in you."

Hattie tugged the robe from her neck, revealing a gold necklace and disc pendant with her name engraved on it. She lifted the pendant into the light, and the sun caught it.

"You see this?"

Eve leaned in. "Yes. It's lovely."

"Annabelle gave this to me about two years ago for me birthday. She had me in tears, she did. She gave me a neck hug and a peck on the cheek, and she told me she loved me."

Hattie lifted her pleading eyes on Eve. "She's not all bad, is she, when she can do something nice like that for her old Mum?"

WHEN EVE AND JONI RETURNED the following morning, Hattie Craddick was gone. Her shingle had been taken down, her flyers removed, and her door locked.

The talkative woman who lived down the hallway told them, "Hattie left last night, taking only an old sack with her. And she was limping, and I saw the pain in her eyes. She gave me a wave and a smile, and she said, 'The good Lord above is waiting for me, and I don't want to keep Him waiting.' I didn't like the sound of it, of course, but…" She left the rest of the sentence hanging in the chill, morning air.

Two days later, Eve and Patrick were having breakfast at their hotel restaurant. Eve was flipping through *The Sun* newspaper, when her eyes froze on a headline in "THE CITY SECTION."

WOMAN FOUND DEAD IN EAST RIVER!

A woman was found dead in the East River, afternoon last, and hauled from the river by a police patrol boat. She was identified as Hattie Craddick, from an engraved gold necklace found about her neck. The coroner's office stated that the body had been in the river for at least a day. There was no evidence of foul play and, based on information received from neighbors where Mrs. Craddick had resided, the police have ruled her death a suicide.

CHAPTER 38

On December 22, Joni finally told Darius what had happened to Colleen, why Eve and Patrick had time traveled, and everything that had occurred afterwards. To her surprise, he was visibly upset and shaken.

He'd only been half-listening while he read the evening paper, but he'd lowered it by the time Joni finished, his eyes staring and absorbed.

They were sitting in the cozy parlor before a comfortable fire. Their Christmas tree was glowing with pear-shaped lights, decorated with glittering tinsel and glass ornaments. Lavishly wrapped presents were arranged below.

"I helped to bring that child into this world," Darius said, standing, pacing the parlor, his hands locked behind his back. "Mrs. Gantly and I nearly lost the baby. Why didn't you tell me this sooner, Joan?"

"Because you weren't ready to listen. I tried to tell you, but you said you didn't want to know anything about it, remember?"

"My God, no wonder the Gantlys are so distraught," Darius said.

Joni set aside the book she'd been reading, not able to concentrate on it. "It's so sad. They're both so lost. They've done everything they can think of to find that woman. We've spent the last two weeks walking the streets, showing her photograph to anyone who would look at it, but..." Her voice fell away. "Patrick has exhausted all his leads, but he won't give up. He keeps saying that there's got to be someone out there who knows where Annabelle went. And Eve is still upset about Hattie, Annabelle's mother. She blames herself for the woman's suicide, sure that our visit probably depressed her and that's why she took her own life."

Darius stopped pacing, standing stiff-necked and somber. "Joan, we must have the Gantlys over for Christmas dinner. We must try to cheer them as best we can."

"But you said you didn't want them here at Christmas because of William and Lavinia. You said you were afraid they'd learn about time travel and..."

Darius cut in. "... Well, I've changed my mind. We will not bring up that time travel nonsense, of course, but I say we must have them as our guests on Christmas day. Please tell them not to mention anything about the past or what is occurring now, and they are certainly not to say anything, whatsoever, about the future."

THAT EVENING, JONI sat before her vanity, with her hair pinned back, preparing to rub cold cream into her aging face. Darius had already gone to bed, as he often did. He was an early riser, even on holidays, and she a late riser, a bed languisher—all right, she was a lazy woman who loved her bed, her lovely room and the private moments just before she had to face the day.

Staring at herself in the mirror, at the late hour, she fought sadness and regret. *What ifs* stampeded into her head like a charging army and, once again, she questioned her life and the choices she'd made. How could she not? She'd been around Eve and Patrick for many days, listening to them talk about their lives, the awful and unbelievable pandemic in 2020, the crazy politics, the shifting economy, and the mounting climate crises.

In one sense, she was happy to have missed it. In another, being the extravert and adventurous woman she was, she was sorry she'd missed it or, more accurately, sorry she would miss it.

In this time, if she lived long enough, she would live through The Great War—what she knew as World War I—as well as the Great Depression. *Why were these calamities called Great?* she thought. And then there was World War II. She might even live long enough to experience that horror.

She knew the outcomes of them all, and she knew many details about coming events she could never share with anyone, including Darius, not that he wanted to know. But it isolated her and made her feel out of sync with this time. She was in this time, but she also recalled her life, a good life, in the twenty-first century.

Joni reached for a jar of cold cream and began applying it onto her face, a face much older than Eve's. She'd lost her sexy figure, but Eve hadn't. And Joni could feel herself aging: she had stomach issues and female issues, and sometimes her feet swelled. There weren't the miracle drugs, medications, specialists, plastic surgeons and physical therapists that were available in the twenty-first century.

She thought, *"I am the sum of all the choices I have made.* Isn't that what her therapist used to say to her when she lived in the future? No one in this time went to therapists, and they didn't even know what a psychotherapist was. Sigmund Freud was an unknown. And, of course, there was no social media. That was probably a good thing. Way out in the future, she'd been addicted to it, glancing at her phone every few seconds.

And how she missed performing—dancing and being on stage. She missed flirting, something she hadn't done in years. The last time she'd truly flirted was with Henry Windsor, a wealthy man from England. She'd met him at a charitable dinner, and she'd noticed his steady and fascinated eyes following her about the room. When he'd approached her at the punch bowl, he'd said, "Have we been properly introduced?"

Without missing a beat, Joni had answered, "No, my dear sir, we have not, but don't let that stop you."

He'd smiled with twinkling pleasure.

Joni presented her hand, as she'd learned to do from years of practice. He'd taken her hand gracefully and introduced himself, and then presented a gentlemanly bow. "May I say, Mrs. Foster, you are the brightest jewel in the room."

Joni knew it was BS flattery, but she'd smiled extravagantly, enjoying the game.

He was handsome and well-mannered, if a bit on the fussy side, and he seemed like good extra-marital-affair material. But in the end, she wasn't comfortable with that. She knew other women who were, but Joni hadn't allowed herself to get swept away, even though Henry Windsor had sorely tempted her. She'd even met him in Central Park one fine spring day, when Darius was out of town on business.

Back at her vanity, Joni flashed herself a jazzy, showbiz grin. "He asked you to go with him to his private residence, as he put it, but you didn't, did you, Joni? He even tried to kiss you, and you came so close to letting him. You could almost feel his lips on yours."

Joni eased back in her chair, her eyes clear, remembering. "You shouldn't have gone with him to Central Park to begin with. Confidence and trust. That's what a marriage is built on, isn't it?"

She looked down at her hands, hands that were showing age, and she whispered, longingly. "Still, it might have been fun... Just a kiss."

Back in 1884, she'd truly fallen in love with Darius and then, instead of time traveling with Eve, Patrick and Colleen back to the twenty-first century, she'd stayed behind and married Darius. She'd leapt into the void and taken a chance and committed herself to staying in the past.

The day she'd married Darius, she'd felt her life opening up with a new promise. With every step she took down that church aisle, she knew it was true love that had brought her there. For the first time in her life, she had fallen in love.

So, what if it was with a man who, in her time in the twenty-first century, had been dead for many years?

The Christmas Eve Journey

Somehow that fact made it even more exciting and intriguing.

She was soon anchored in her new life and, in a short time, she got pregnant. She'd thrilled at giving birth and watching her children grow, with their flashing and changing personalities, like prisms reflecting light.

She loved and adored her kids and, yes, she was still very much in love with Darius, even if they weren't always so suited to each other.

But now they slept in separate beds, in separate rooms. It was the social norm. It was also practical since she, not he, snored. How irritating that was. But he'd often sneak into her room in the late hours of the night, and they would love and laugh. That was her favorite time to be with him. He was relaxed and informal, and she loved him with all her heart.

As Joni slipped under the covers and switched off the light, she let out a little sigh, recalling what Eve had said earlier in the week. "Joni, your life is a wonderful adventure; a great saga, right out of a historical novel. As far as we know, no one has ever time traveled into the past and jumpstarted a brand-new life."

But Joni couldn't sleep. Some agitated thing paced within her like a caged animal. The same question kept rising to the surface. Could she have both? Two lives in two different times?

Was she bold enough—courageous and selfish enough—to light that Tesla lantern she had secretly hidden away, hoping it would hurl her back into the future; back home to her own true time, the time she was born into? Could she have a life there, and perhaps find a man to love there, and then return to this time and continue her life here? Could she enjoy a double life? Should she do it now, before she got any older? In 2021, it would be easier to join a gym and lose weight, get a boob job and some Botox, whatever it took to look ten years younger. She could take jewelry with her and hock it for good money. She was sure she'd find a man—maybe even a younger man.

Whether or not she wanted to admit it, she still had the wild and flirtatious heart of the young Joni.

She rolled over onto her back and stared up at the ceiling, darkness and temptation circling her like an airplane, waiting for the final okay from the air traffic controller to land. Could she do it? Would she do it?

Later, when Darius crept into her bed, she was aggressive, and she took possession of him, and consumed him. It was the best sex they'd had in a long time.

As he slept next to her, Joni lay still, her mind bright and alive, as she visualized her new life in the twenty-first century.

CHAPTER 39

There was plenty of food to eat and wine to drink at the Fosters' lavish and festive Christmas Day dinner. Banks and a second tuxedoed butler served, gliding about the room in a quiet dance that impressed Eve but made Patrick nervous. He wasn't used to such finery, preferring a good old Christmas goose and a pint of beer. But he fell into the spirit of the day, joining in the toasts and the talk, soon enjoying himself, thankful to be with friends and away from his worries and his failure to find Colleen.

Patrick wore a dark suit with a white shirt and red string tie, the tie purchased by Eve for the occasion, while she wore a stunning, claret-red crepe dress with ruby earrings that Joni had lent her.

Darius and Joni were formally dressed, she in an opulent purple gown and he in his finest broadcloth dark suit. It was Darius who made sure that the day was filled with laughter and cheer, never allowing the conversation to venture onto any serious subjects.

Lavinia dazzled in her red and bottle-green gown, an elegant diamond drop necklace and matching petite diamond earrings. Her manners were impeccable, her conversation easy, and her questions to Eve and Patrick, careful but curious.

William Foster sat stiffly in his dark suit and white tie, like a pilgrim's son, neither talkative nor smiling. Joni struggled to bring her son into the conversation, but when he did speak, it was about the City's poor management of drunken beggars, and his severe disappointment in his professors at Harvard, who were "elderly, out of touch and boring to the extreme."

A dessert of port wine, cookies and sliced cake was taken in the parlor, where the scent of the massive evergreen tree was entrancing. Afterwards, Lavinia sat at the piano and Joni led the group in singing the Christmas carols *Jingle Bells*, *Deck the Halls* and *Silent Night*.

Soon afterwards, William excused himself and retreated upstairs, to Eve's and Patrick's relief. Lavinia sat next to Patrick, her beautiful eyes taking him in, the firelight bathing her in a golden glow. Eve and Joni watched while Lavinia leaned almost imperceptibly toward Patrick, politely asking him questions, and it was obvious she was infatuated with him.

Darius noticed as well, and although he would have normally asked his daughter to leave the room, the pleasure of the wine and the spirit of the day had left him relaxing in his chair, a new glass of port poised at his lips.

Joni and Eve stood near the Christmas tree, whispering. Joni said, "She's a beauty, isn't she?"

"And then some," Eve said.

Joni sipped her demi tasse of coffee. "She has a big crush on Patrick."

"Yeah, well, I've seldom met a woman, young or old, who didn't have a crush on him. And look at him, he's so casual and detached... That's why women fall for him. He seems so unattainable and uninterested, which, of course, makes him even that much more attractive."

Joni said, "I reminded Lavinia that he used to be a New York City detective. You should have seen her eyes light up. She's never met a man like Patrick. It's good for her."

Lavinia's face projected a sweet bewilderment, and Eve was sure Patrick was telling stories about his father, no doubt including one of his "old Da's" clever sayings.

Joni tilted her head toward Eve, whispering conspiratorially. "Eve... I have to ask you something, and don't get all freaked out."

"When you put it that way, it means I'm *going* to get freaked out."

"I've been thinking about the lantern. Have you and Patrick time traveled to a different time other than 1905? I mean, have you returned to a different time, when I was older?"

Eve looked away.

"Oh, God... You have! I know that look, Eve. You *have* time traveled and seen me at some other time. When? You have to tell me. You have to."

Eve drained the last of the port and set her glass on the coffee table. Banks appeared, scooped it up, and retired to the kitchen.

Joni exhaled impatiently. "Eve... tell me. You have to tell me."

Eve crossed her arms, not something women did in 1905, but she didn't care. She didn't look at Joni when she spoke. "I didn't time travel, but Patrick did."

Joni let that sink in. "Okay... Patrick did. When? What year?"

"It was 1925."

Joni's forehead wrinkled in thought. "Holy shit! Twenty years from now? I must have been old. I mean, like wrinkled, old and gray."

Joni set her demi tasse down, deep in thought. "Eve... why didn't you travel with him?"

"Because it's a long and crazy story, and I don't want to go into it. Patrick and I have crisscrossed through time so many times that I can't even keep track of it all. We just want to find Colleen, get back home, and live our lives."

Joni felt a vague anxiety. If Eve and Patrick did find Colleen, could Joni watch them light the lantern and vanish, as she had done in 1884? Could she stay behind once again and not go with them to the twenty-first century?

Joni faced her friend. "Not to bring up a bad subject on Christmas Day, but what are you two going to do next?"

Eve lowered her arms. "I don't know. We're mostly out of ideas. Patrick says we have to keep passing Annabelle's photo around, hoping that somebody will eventually recognize her, and tell us where she went. I'm not too optimistic, and I don't think he is either. But we have to keep trying."

At that moment, Darius spoke up. "Patrick... where is the photograph you and the ladies have been showing around the City? Do you have it with you?"

Eve and Joni looked at Darius in astonishment and, with surprise, Patrick glanced over. "Yes, I have it in my overcoat pocket."

"May I have a look at it?"

"Yes... Of course."

"What photograph?" Lavinia asked.

Darius' light mood turned serious, and he cleared his throat. "Lavinia, my dear. If you would be so kind as to finish your coffee and cookies in the library, I would appreciate it."

"But, why, Father? Whose photograph is it? May I look at it as well?"

"No, no, Lavinia, that is quite impossible. This is serious business that Patrick and I must conduct together, as men. Now, please, do as your father asks and proceed to the library."

Pouting, Lavinia stood up, nodded to Patrick, offered a head bow to Eve and her mother, and withdrew, passing her father a harsh stare as she left the room.

Patrick fetched the photograph as Joni sat on the sofa with Eve, both women still flabbergasted that Darius would want to involve himself in any way.

"Mrs. Gantly, Eve," Darius said soberly, folding his hands in his lap. "It is with the saddest of news that I learned from Joan, only recently, about your and Patrick's appalling and shocking situation. As a parent, I sympathize completely, and I offer you both all my hopes and wishes that you will locate your dear child. The beautiful little child that you and I delivered together all those years ago."

When he realized the disparity of time and place, he turned his eyes away, not wanting to think about it. Not wanting to accept that they had delivered Colleen in 1884, and yet, twenty-one years later, she was only three years old.

Patrick handed the photo to Darius. After clearing his throat again, Darius removed his glasses from his inside coat pocket and put them on.

Eve, Patrick and Joni all traded puzzled glances while Darius carefully studied the photograph. Then, suddenly, Darius sat up, his face coming alive. "I know this woman."

Joni gaped at him. "Darius? How could you possibly know her? A woman like that?"

He removed his glasses, his expression firm. "I've seen her, I know her."

Eve shot to her feet, and Patrick took a startled step closer to Darius.

"But how could you?" Joni said. "You must be confused or something. There's no way you know who this woman is."

Darius slapped the photo with two fingers. "I tell you, I know this woman."

He shut his eyes. "Now, wait a minute. Let me think. I just need to think. My head's all fogged up with wine."

He pinched the bridge of his nose and lowered his head, while the room seemed to hold its breath. He lifted his head and fell into deep thought, uncharacteristically, tapping his right foot.

When Darius' eyes opened, they were clear, and his face softened into a proud recollection.

"What, Darius?" Joni asked. "What is it?"

He spoke calmly and precisely. "She was admitted to the hospital. I treated her, briefly, before Dr. Welch took over her care."

"When?" Patrick asked, tensely. "When was this?"

"Well, let me see now... Last year. Yes, it was December of last year, a week or so before Christmas."

"What was she admitted for?" Eve asked, moving forward.

"As I recall, and I'd have to consult my notes and her hospital records to be sure, but I believe she presented with contusions, a hematoma on her right leg, a head wound and two fractured ribs. She was in a lot of pain and she went into shock. I do remember that."

Patrick's head began to throb. "Where was she found?"

Darius scratched his cheeks. "Found? Let me see... Oh, yes, I recall, because it seemed rather odd. She was found in Riverside Park."

Eve and Patrick exchanged a quick glance.

"Was she with a child?" Eve asked, afraid of the answer.

Darius lifted a finger, straightening his spine, his memory opening. "Yes, she was found with a child."

Eve rushed to Darius' chair. "Was the child okay? What happened to the child?"

Darius realized the importance of his words and he paused, blinking twice. "Let us not jump to conclusions. There may be an..."

Patrick cut in. "Darius, how was the child? Was it a girl?"

Darius nodded. "I did not see the child, but, yes, it was a girl and, yes, I was told the child was unhurt, but suffered from exposure."

Joni shook her head. "Do you mean that all this time we've been out pounding the pavement, searching all over hell and half of Russia for this woman, and you knew who she was all the time? What the fu…?"

Darius jumped in before Joni could finish her profanity, his face tightly defensive. "You didn't tell me, Joan. You didn't show me this photograph."

"Because you didn't want any part of it. You didn't want any part of Eve and Patrick because they'd time traveled from 2021! That's why I didn't tell you."

When Lavinia suddenly appeared, her eyes glowing with confusion and disbelief, the room fell into silence.

"What is going on? What is all this about?" she asked, her eyes searching her parents' faces. "Mother, why are you shouting? What were you saying?"

CHAPTER 40

Joni led Lavinia upstairs to her bedroom and apologized for the outburst. With difficulty, she explained what had happened.

Lavinia brought a hand to her mouth. "Oh, Mother... How terrible for them. Why do I have to keep pretending I don't know about Eve and Patrick and time travel? Perhaps I could help?"

"You know why, Lavinia. It's your father. He'd go crazy and you know it."

"Mother, he knows. All of us know, so why don't we drop this façade, pull together and try to help Eve and Patrick?"

Joni eased down on the edge of Lavinia's bed. "We have to live with your father, Lavinia, and you know what that means."

Joni reached for her daughter's hand, but Lavinia pulled away and walked to the far side of the room.

"Lavinia, we have to keep pretending, at least for a while longer. Your father is scared to death of that lantern; he's scared the truth will come out and he'll lose his clients and become a joke in society. You can understand that, can't you?"

Lavinia didn't turn around.

Finally, Joni rose and left Lavinia pacing her room.

Downstairs, Joni found Eve, Patrick and Darius locked in urgent conversation. Darius was on his feet, straining his memory for details, while the others hung on his every word.

"Like I said, as I recall, I only saw the woman twice, maybe three times... Yes! It was three times, because I saw her once with Dr. Welch."

"What happened to the child?" Eve asked.

"The child was doing well and being cared for by a team of nurses."

"What was the patient's name?" Eve asked.

"Ah, her name..." Darius echoed, returning to deep thought. "Her name... Blast, I cannot recall the woman's name. It has been so long."

"Was it Annabelle?" Patrick asked.

Darius stopped. "Annabelle... Yes, by Gad, it was Annabelle. Yes, I recall now, but I don't recall the last name, if I ever knew it."

With hooded eyes, Patrick made a fist. "What happened to the woman?"

Darius locked his hands behind his back and lifted his chin. "She was reunited with her child..."

Eve said harshly, "It was not *her* child. That was Colleen!"

Darius nodded in recognition. "Yes, Mrs. Gantly... I understand how you must feel."

Darius returned to his chair near the fire and sat. The other three remained standing, waiting for him to continue. As he pondered, he ran a hand along his jaw and stared into the dancing flames.

"Dr. Welch... Well, how do I say it? It became a sensitive situation."

"Just say it, Darius," Joni demanded.

"Dr. Welch told me he developed tender feelings for this Annabelle."

Eve sank down onto the sofa. "Oh, God."

"He had her moved to a private room, and administered personal care, while the nurses continued to care for the child. When Annabelle had sufficiently recovered, she and the child were released to Dr. Welch's care, and I believe he began to court her, which was quite uncharacteristic of him."

"Was Dr. Welch married?" Patrick asked.

"No... He was a bachelor, in his mid-forties, who loved swimming, carnival rides and five-dessert dinners at Delmonico's. We doctors were somewhat taken aback by his behavior, although we agreed that Annabelle was a lovely and attractive woman. I was informed by one of the nurses that Annabelle's husband had been tragically killed in a carriage accident, and that she was quite alone and helpless in the world."

Eve leapt up and paced, her neck and face burning hot. "Annabelle Palmer is anything but helpless. She's a devious witch from hell!"

Patrick kept his emotions in check, but his palms were sweaty, his shoulders stiff. "Darius... Is Annabelle still with Dr. Welch and, if so, do you know where they are?"

Darius's eyes held sorrow. "In February or March of this year, he left the hospital. I was shocked, of course."

"Where did he go?" Joni asked, impatiently.

"He came to see me a day before he left town."

Eve came to an abrupt stop, all ears.

Darius stared down at the carpet. "He told me he was in love with Annabelle, and they were going to be married. I was surprised, of course… and bewildered. But then, I was even more astonished when he told me they were moving to San Francisco, and they were going to marry there. I said, by Gad, man, what has gotten into you? And why San Francisco? He said, that's where Annabelle wants to go. Then I asked him about the little girl."

Patrick's eyes flamed with anger, but he remained quiet.

Darius inhaled a deep breath and let it out slowly. "He said he would raise the child as his own."

Eve's thoughts were running wild.

Patrick said, "Did you hear from Dr. Welch after he and Annabelle moved to San Francisco?"

Darius' face drooped, his lips twisted, and his eyes filled with a new and terrible understanding. "By Gad. Oh Gad."

"What?" Joni asked, her heart fluttering.

Darius stared ahead. "Sometime in July, a nurse at the hospital came into my office and told me that Dr. Howard Welch was dead."

"How did he die?" Eve asked, holding her breath.

"According to the account in the *San Francisco Call,* Dr. Welch was the victim of a robbery. His wallet was missing, and he was shot through the heart. Since that time, I have not heard if the murderer has been apprehended."

The silence was loud with frantic thoughts. More than ever, Patrick was determined to hunt the woman down and either bring her to justice or strangle her.

Eve spun to Patrick, her resolute expression a call to action.

Joni slumped down onto the sofa, her thoughts whirling. "So, you'll both leave for San Francisco," she said, resigned, already missing her best friend. "When?"

Patrick looked at Eve. "As soon as we can pack and book a train ticket."

Darius' attention returned to Eve and Patrick. "I am so sorry to be the bearer of such depressing and terrible news."

"You have finally set us right as to where Annabelle is," Patrick said. "I'd wager she has made San Francisco her new home and base of operations."

"But how will you find her?" Darius asked.

Patrick's eyes were flat and hard. "We'll find her. Make no mistake about it. We'll find her and take Colleen back home."

Joni lifted her gaze. "You'll need the lantern, won't you? I mean, you'll need to take it with you so you can return home?"

Darius stood up abruptly, the mention of the lantern obviously upsetting him. "Please excuse me, but I am quite fatigued. And pardon me if I don't see you out. Thank you for the pleasure of your company, and, if it's not an improper thing to say, given the disagreeable circumstances, I wish you both a Merry Christmas and a Happy New Year. Goodnight, and the best of luck on your journey."

As Darius crossed the room, Patrick said, "Thank you, Darius. I am eternally grateful to you for your help."

Darius didn't turn around, keeping his back to them. At the stairs, he hesitated. "Will you write and tell us if you have been successful in finding your daughter... your Colleen?"

"Yes, Darius," Eve said.

"'Tis well then. Goodnight, and Godspeed."

They settled on the sofa, Eve, Patrick and Joni digesting all that Darius had said, Eve and Patrick already plotting their next move.

Eve could feel the silence, alive with the momentum of new possibilities, followed by the inevitable stress and fear. "This really changes things," Eve said.

Joni shook her head. "Well... what a Christmas. What a friggin' crazy Christmas. Who would have ever believed Darius would know where Annabelle is?"

"It's a marvel," Patrick said. "I never would have believed it."

"Do you really think she killed that doctor?" Joni asked.

"Yes, Joni," Patrick said. "We met her. She stayed in our apartment as our guest. To men, Annabelle projects a lonely, helpless glamor and sexuality, but she's filled with a toxic darkness I've seldom seen. I've seen men whose brutal faces would make you shiver, and women from whom every grace of womanhood has been stripped away, replaced by a savage wickedness, and Annabelle is one of them. She's a twisted, sick woman."

"I wish I could go with you," Joni said.

Eve reached for Joni's hand and held it, seeing her friend's warm eyes, lovely in the firelight. "I wish you could too, Joni. I'll miss you. I always miss you."

Joni's voice was small. "I could go, couldn't I? I mean, it's not that I do anything here. William will be going back to Harvard, Lavinia will return to her studies, and Darius will spend endless hours at the hospital. Why can't I go?"

Eve looked at Patrick. "Yeah… why can't she come with us?"

Patrick nodded toward the staircase. "Joni, Darius is already scared out of his wits that you'll take that lantern, light the thing, and leave him forever. How could he cope with you chugging off with us on a train, all the way to San Francisco?"

"If I plead with him and he agrees, would you want me to go? Be honest."

Patrick smiled. "For my part, of course."

Eve stood up, took Joni's other hand, and tugged her to her feet, staring squarely into her eyes. "You don't have to ask me, girlfriend. Just come."

PART THREE

CHAPTER 41

Two days after Christmas, Patrick left the bed gently before dawn, not wanting to wake Eve. He'd had a hundred dreams and, from what he could recall, they'd all had the same pattern: either he was being chased by big, angry men with guns raised and firing, or he was running after a woman in a cloak and hood. She was hustling off down a dark and damp city street, Colleen clasped in her arms.

In the hotel living room, Patrick found his bottle of whiskey and splashed some into a glass. He gulped it down, resisting the urge to pour another. He sat for a while on the sofa and leaned his head back, closing his eyes, willing himself to relax. Their train to Chicago was scheduled to leave at one o'clock that afternoon, and it was still uncertain if Joni would travel with them. They hadn't heard from her, and Eve had found that strange.

"I wonder what's going on with Joni," Eve had said, as they lay in bed the night before.

"Why don't you call her?" Patrick said.

"Because she said not to. She was afraid Darius would pick up."

"She must have told him by now, don't you think?"

"I have no idea. She and Darius love each other, and yet they don't really understand each other. She's always going to be a woman from the twenty-first century and he's always going to be a nineteenth-century man."

Patrick had glanced over. "You mean, like us?"

"We're different."

"How?"

"We just are."

"Well, as my old Da used to say..."

Eve had interrupted. "... Patrick, excuse me, but didn't your old Ma ever have any clever things to say?"

Patrick had peered at her. "Yes. From the time I was a child getting into mischief, she used to look at me with those piercing eyes of hers, point a sharp finger at my face and say, 'Patrick, be sure your sins will find you out.'"

A KNOCK ON THE DOOR jarred Patrick and his eyes popped open. Having fallen back to sleep on the sofa, he was disoriented and shaking off another bad dream. He glanced about, heard another firm knock, and sat up, groggy. Standing, he ran a hand through his hair and moved to the door. "Yes... One minute."

Eve entered from the bedroom, her hair tangled, her sleepy eyes small.

Patrick passed Eve a look, unlatched the lock and chain, and opened it.

Darius stood bolt erect, looking a little shell-shocked, with big eyes. He held a canvas bag in his left hand and, when he spoke, his voice was tight and shaky.

"She's gone."

Eve went to the door, belting her robe. "Who's gone?" she asked.

"Joan. Joan has gone. Left me."

Patrick stepped back. "Come in, Darius."

"I will not," he said, curtly.

Eve moved next to Patrick. "Darius, where is Joni?"

Darius held up the canvas bag. "In her letter to me, she told me to give this to you. There's a letter addressed to you both enclosed. I haven't read it."

"Darius, just tell me. Where is she?" Eve asked, her eyes filled with concern.

"She's gone, for God's sake!" he bellowed. "Gone from my life forever! She lit that damned lantern outside in the garden and she's gone, just like I knew she would, if you two... *people* ever returned." He spit out the word "people," as if it were a curse.

Tears gathered in his eyes and ran down his cheeks. He turned his proud head aside and swiped them away.

He faced the Gantlys squarely, rage building. "Now that you have destroyed my life and my family, take the damnable thing and don't let me ever see it again," he said, fighting emotion, thrusting the bag forward. Patrick accepted it.

Darius narrowed his burning eyes on them. "And don't either of you ever set foot in my house again! Never!"

Darius abruptly turned and went striding off down the hallway.

Patrick slowly closed the door and locked it, staring at the bag that held Joni's lantern. Both were momentarily paralyzed by the news. Moments later, Eve wandered to the sofa and eased down. She stared at nothing, her mind unable to process Darius' terrible words.

Patrick turned and started for the sofa. He reached inside the bag, found the letter-sized envelope addressed to them, and removed it. He set the bag down and handed Eve the letter. Reluctantly, she took it.

With her eyes shut, Eve said, "Oh, God, Patrick... what have I done? I have totally screwed up our lives, and now Darius' and Joni's lives. What an idiot I am. Just one stupid choice and look what happened."

Patrick spoke softly. "This wasn't your choice, Eve. It was Joni's."

Eve hung her head. "I just can't believe it. I can't believe she did it. Why?"

"We should read the letter."

"You read it. I can't. I'm feeling sick."

"Lie down, my love."

Eve flopped over on her side, closed her eyes, and pulled her legs up into a fetal position. Patrick went to the bedroom, grabbed a blanket and returned, covering her with it.

He took the envelope from Eve, lowered himself into a chair, and opened it. It was a two-page hand-written letter, the handwriting jerky, the T's crossed high and many I's not dotted. It was obviously written in haste and anger. Patrick began to read:

Dear Eve and Patrick,

Darius and I just had one of our terrible arguments. He's forbidden me to go with you to San Francisco! He said I was being selfish. He said I have a house and children to look after. He said I have a husband to care for. I said, "I need to get away and be with my friends. I said, no one is going to miss me for two weeks."

He said, flatly, "No, you can't go. I forbid it!"

Well, you can imagine what I told him he could do with his patriarchal bullshit, "I forbid it."

He slapped me hard across the face. Can you believe it? He's never slapped me before. Not ever. I was so stunned, I didn't move. He didn't move. We stared at each other and, in that moment, I hated him and everything the men in this time stand for. They're so puffed up and full of themselves. They're the masters of the house, they say, with their chests puffed out; so arrogant, so full of shit! They believe they own their wives, and their wives must obey them unconditionally.

So, we stood there. Enemies. My entire body was on fire. His face was red hot with anger. I thought, he'll apologize. But he didn't.

Without another word, he turned and stormed out of the room.

I'm writing this five minutes after he left. I've made up my mind. I'm leaving this time. My kids will be okay. They'll be fine now. They're nearly grown. To hell with Darius. I can't take any more of his shit! Okay! I want to go home—to my real home—while I still have time to live my life the way I was supposed to live it. The way I should have lived it. I can still sing and dance a little. I can go out by myself and pick up a man if I want to, when I lose some of this weight.

Don't hate me for doing this, Eve. Patrick, please don't get all judgy. I'm so sick in my heart right now, and after that slap in the face, I realize that I have been for a long time.

God, how I want to go home to the twenty-first century and live my life as a free woman. And guess what? I can. I have the lantern, don't I? I can escape into the future. Isn't that what you said, Eve? Back in 1884, didn't you say if things didn't work out, I could always light the lantern and return home?

I have the lantern hidden in the house. I'm going to take it, and some of my more expensive jewelry—isn't jewelry the best way to get fast money when time traveling? I'm going to step out into the garden, near that big, gaudy bird fountain, and light the lantern. Poof—away I'll go.

I'm ready. I've made up my mind. I'm going.

I know you'll find Colleen. I know it. I feel it. And who knows, when I return home, you two may already be there, with Colleen, safe and happy. We'll all be together again, and I can forget about this twenty-year nightmare.

Am I being selfish? God help me, I guess I am. Well, I don't care. I'm going. Yes, I'm going. Now! Right now, before I change my mind.

I love you both. When I saw you again, I realized I couldn't stay behind and watch you two leave me. I couldn't go through it again. No way.

Okay, I'll see you soon. Wish me luck. I hope I wind up in 2020 or 2021, and not in 1884. Wouldn't that be crazy?

Have a good journey to San Francisco, and good luck.

Wish me luck as well. I have a feeling I'm going to need it.

Much love to you both,

-Joni

CHAPTER 42

The Pacific Hotel Express Train went rumbling down the tracks, its shrill whistle blasting, echoing across the countryside, its smokestack puffing black smoke. Eve and Patrick were on their way to San Francisco.

The train would stop in Chicago just long enough to offload passengers and take new ones aboard. If everything went according to plan, with the train traveling at nearly sixty miles an hour with limited stops, the entire trip to San Francisco would take about three days and seventeen hours.

Eve and Patrick paid the first-class fare to ensure they would be alone and could get plenty of rest. If the train broke down, they'd receive priority treatment and be placed on the next train.

Patrick had learned that immigrants hoping to make a new start in the West often occupied third-class coach cars. A third-class ticket could be purchased for less than half the price of the first-class fare. But at that low rate, the traveler received no luxuries, and their cars were congested, noisy, and uncomfortable. Also, the railroad often attached those cars to freight cars, then shunted them aside to make way for express trains. As a result, the third-class traveler's journey west might take ten or more days.

Eve and Patrick had a beautifully appointed car, with plush velvet seats that converted into cozy sleeping berths. The room offered steam heat, daily fresh linen, and gracious porters who catered to their every whim. They also had access to the first-class dining car, although Patrick was more inclined to eat in the club car, dodging the formality. They ate in the first-class diner one evening, so Eve could experience it, but she found the food too rich and heavy.

During the second full day, they were in their room and Eve was sitting near a window, staring out at the blur of countryside flying by. She felt Patrick's gaze on her, and she turned to him.

"What? Why are you staring at me?"

"How do you feel? Better?"

"No, not better. I feel awful. I feel sorry for myself, for Joni, for Colleen and, last, but not least, I feel sorry for you."

Patrick sat on a seat opposite her, sipping a cup of tea. "You've been in a mood since we left New York."

"I know. I have to work my way out of it. I just wish Joni hadn't done that. I mean, I know she's impulsive and everything, but I never imagined she'd do something like that. I know her. Two days after she lands, wherever she lands, she's going to regret it. She's going to miss her kids and Darius, and she's going to hate herself and want to go back."

"There's no going back, Eve, that is, if she winds up in 2021, in New York. We don't have a lantern. We gave the last one away and left the other on that Riverside Park bench when we traveled here."

"I know, but I didn't tell her that. I was going to, but with so much other stuff going on, and because I never dreamed she'd do it, I didn't tell her. Wherever she ends up, chances are she won't have a lantern to return to 1905. But then, of course, we don't know where she went, do we?"

Patrick laid his teacup aside and glanced out the window, looking up at the heavy, gray clouds sweeping across the sky. "I wish her well, but I'm sorry she was so impulsive. Why didn't she just defy the man and come with us, anyway? Why did she take such a drastic step? I don't understand it. I thought Joni was more stable than that."

"No one really knows another human being. Who knows what has been going on inside her head? It sounds like she's been thinking about doing it for years, and this argument just set her off and… well, she did it."

After a moment's silence, Patrick said, "Eve, something has been troubling me."

"Like what hasn't? We've got nothing but trouble."

"It's about San Francisco."

"Okay. What?"

"In all my reading of history when I first started using the computer, I remember reading about the tragedy of the San Francisco earthquake."

Eve shifted uncomfortably in her seat. "When was it? I don't remember. Wasn't it in 1910 or 1915 or something?"

"No… it was 1906."

"Okay, what month?"

"I'm not sure. I've been straining my mind to recall the month and date, but so far, I'm just not certain. I believe it happens in April, but I'm not positive. It could be January or… I don't know."

Eve nodded. "Okay… so we can't do a *Google* search, and there won't be anything to look up in any library, because the earthquake hasn't happened yet."

"Right."

"Dammit! Why didn't I do better in history? I mean, I've lived in all these different times and places, but how can I remember when every major historical event happened? Are you sure it's 1906?"

"Yes, I'm positive about that."

"How can we find out?"

Patrick lifted a hand, then dropped it. "There's no way other than lighting the lantern and hoping it takes us to some forward century, so we can look it up in a book or on a computer."

Eve frowned. "Well, that's not going to work."

Patrick got up. "No, not at all."

Eve blew out a frustrated sigh. "We're lost in the dark. I feel like I have fists beating on me from inside my chest."

"Once we get to San Francisco, we'll be okay. We're both better when we're in motion and have a goal."

Eve pinched her forehead with a hand. "I feel so helpless just sitting here, stewing, waiting, wondering. And then my mind jumps around all over the place, and I think, when we get there and start our search, what if we learn that Annabelle has left, gone to some other place, like Alaska or Hawaii or... God only knows?"

Before Patrick could answer, Eve shot up and answered her own question in a firm voice. "Then we'll go there, too, dammit. We'll go wherever we have to. We'll find Colleen no matter what it takes."

Patrick reached for her and pulled her into his arms. "That's another reason I love you. You're a fighter. You'll never give up, even if it takes years."

"Let's hope it doesn't take years, Patrick. Let's hope we have a little luck and find Annabelle right away. But then, what happens when we find her? What will you do?"

"I honestly don't know. And let's hope that looming earthquake doesn't occur until after we find Colleen and get away."

They stayed in each other's arms for a time. Finally, Eve said, "Patrick... What is Darius going to do?"

"In what respect?"

Eve drew back, searching his eyes. "In every respect. What is he going to tell his kids and friends? He can't say, oh, she lit this time travel lantern that Nikola Tesla made, and she was hurled off to some place in the future or the past."

"Yes, I thought of that. There is a kind of insanity about it all. It's one of those 'I've seen it and I've experienced it, but I still don't believe it' things. And then, I think about Lavinia. She will be devastated losing her mother, won't she?"

"Yes... Yes, of course she will, and she'll probably confront her father about the time travel lantern."

"That occurred to me as well," Patrick said.

"I just wish Joni hadn't done it. I wish she'd come over last night and talked it out with us until her anger subsided. In her rational mind, she would have never done it."

Patrick kissed the tip of Eve's nose. "Let's hope she's all right wherever she ended up."

ON NEW YEAR'S EVE, they ate dinner in the cozy club car, with a crisp, white linen tablecloth, a candle and crystal glasses. Eve wore a paper hat with HAPPY NEW YEAR 1906 printed on it. Patrick had declined to wear one, saying with a grin, "It will destroy my lovely hairdo."

All about them was laughter, raised glasses and a buoyant holiday spirit, but Eve said little, her mood subdued.

Patrick had also been lost in his own thoughts. As he felt the gentle sway of the train and heard the moan of the whistle, the haunting sound seemed to say, "Colleen... Colleen..."

"What are you thinking?" Patrick asked. "Don't you like the steak?"

"The steak's good. In fact, I think it's the best steak I've had since 1884. And the skin of the baked potato is coated with olive oil and salt, and the potato is very creamy and fluffy. I've never been able to get baked potatoes to do that."

"Butter helps," Patrick said.

"Well, duh, yeah, butter always helps, and this butter is so rich. I've never had any like it."

"So why the long face tonight?" Patrick asked, taking a sip of his coffee. "Besides the obvious."

"Patrick, how are we going to find Annabelle? We know nothing about San Francisco, and we don't know for certain that she's still there. It's going to be like looking for a needle in a haystack."

"Like always, we'll take it step by step. We'll find a common area, like a square or park, and start from there. I figure she and Colleen have visited the parks or playgrounds, and somebody might recognize Annabelle from her photo. Then we'll work systematically, visiting toy shops and clothing stores, or wherever they sell lace frills and ruffles for little girls. I'll leave that to you. Then, just like in New York, you'll canvass the neighborhoods, showing the photo to shop girls and café waiters, while I take my photo of her to some of the more offbeat places. I hear there are a lot of offbeat places in San Francisco. As you know by now, it's slow and painstaking work, but if we stay at it, something will turn up. I'll also talk to a cop or two. If Annabelle has been shoplifting jewelry, we might get lucky, and they might have some useful information about her. If nothing else, we'll know for certain she's in the city."

Eve dropped another dollop of butter on the baked potato, and Patrick arched an eyebrow as if to say, "Really? Even more butter?"

"So, Eve, when we find Colleen, should we light the lantern in San Francisco, or travel back to New York and light it there?"

"I've been thinking about that. I guess it depends on how things turn out. If we're on the run with Colleen, then I'd say we light it in Golden Gate Park. That's been around for a while, hasn't it? Has the Golden Gate Bridge been built?"

"No, if memory serves, it was built sometime in the 1930s."

Eve chewed a piece of steak, reaching for her glass of red wine. "On the other hand, if we have time, I guess we should travel back to New York. It might be safer leaving from Riverside Park."

Eve looked at him, feeling an exhaustive sense of dread. "Patrick, we are the only couple on this planet who have to make these kinds of weird decisions. Have you ever thought about that?"

"Yes, Eve, it has crossed my mind, more than once, and once too many times."

Eve gave him a long, serious look. "I hope that earthquake doesn't strike anytime soon."

CHAPTER 43

A day before they were to arrive in San Francisco, Eve and Patrick talked to a friendly porter about accommodations in San Francisco. He suggested they rent rooms at the Occidental Hotel, on the corner of Montgomery and Sutter Streets.

"Since you might be staying for a while... It ain't as pricey as the Palace Hotel and the New Atlantic," he said. "I knows about that place, because we porters get our boots and shoes from T. J. Broderick Boot & Shoe Store, which is right close by."

The Gantlys rented a four-room suite: a bedroom, kitchen, and large living and dining rooms, both with royal blue carpets and a blue and gold color scheme. The rooms were spacious and clean, and they overlooked the street.

As soon as they'd unpacked and settled in, they felt the pressure of launching into their search. There was no time to waste. Colleen was already more than a year older from when she'd left in 2021, and Eve and Patrick were afraid that when they finally did catch up to her, she wouldn't recognize them.

During the next few days, they struck out to explore the city to begin their search. They found San Francisco to be an energetic town, full of motion and purpose, though its people seemed reserved. There were clanging trollies, meandering autos and carriages, and people darting across the steady stream of traffic in skipping steps, a kind of everybody-for-themselves approach, similar to what Eve had witnessed in New York City in 1885.

They strolled down Market Street with its grand hotels and expensive salons. The Lotta Fountain, a golden-brown, cast-iron structure with lions-head spigots, especially impressed them.

Eve slipped into a few shops and showed Annabelle's photo to several shop girls, but none recognized Annabelle, and most showed little interest.

From there, they ambled through neighborhoods with Victorian architecture, turrets and towers, porches and balconies. They also explored the Mission District, at the time, one of San Francisco's least densely populated areas. Most of the inhabitants were from the working and lower-middle classes, living in single-family houses and two-family flats. Although it seemed a waste of time, Patrick entered two saloons, and when he showed Annabelle's photo, he got the wary eye and the firm shake of the head.

When Eve and Patrick moved through the bustling and densely populated Chinatown, holding up the photo and pointing at it, they were ignored.

One afternoon, Patrick hurried through a foul part of the city, moving through a webwork of pinched and broken streets, some muddy, some unpaved, many with leaky sewage pipes. Desperate-looking prostitutes eyed him, and rough men with hunched shoulders lowered bowlers and, projecting a dangerous energy, they watched him with dark, wolfish eyes. Patrick didn't bother to stop.

Close by was the famous Barbary Coast, the home to a diverse assortment of sordid entertainment, all crammed together along a three-block stretch of Pacific Street. Patrick strolled by dance halls, concert saloons, seedy bars, brothels, and drug stores, where morphine and cocaine were sold to addicts at all hours of the day.

Patrick reasoned that to show Annabelle's photo to anyone in this part of town was too dangerous and not worth the risk. And, anyway, he was certain she hadn't frequented the place. If he'd read her correctly, she was after the ambitious, the connected and the wealthy, and she had the intelligence, the skill and the pretty face for success.

Days later, on a breezy afternoon, Eve and Patrick climbed a steep street, paused to catch their breaths, and then found a picturesque park. While Patrick sat on a bench, Eve presented Annabelle's photo to three women whose children played close by. None knew the woman in the photo, although one younger woman, with a smart, blue feathered hat and ruby red lips said, "She looks familiar to me, somehow, but I'm afraid I can't recall a name."

Feeling low and fatigued, Eve joined Patrick on the bench that overlooked the expansive bay where, in the future, the Golden Gate Bridge would span almost two miles across the Golden Gate, the narrow strait where San Francisco Bay opens to meet the Pacific Ocean.

"It's been almost a week," Eve said. "We're getting nowhere."

Patrick smiled encouragement, but he was fighting depression as well, feeling the entire trip to San Francisco was probably for nothing. It was possible that Annabelle had already left, settling in some other city or town. Her trail was growing colder by the day.

The sky darkened, and fog and clouds swept in, bringing a cool mist, and shrouding the city and the bay. When a sudden, chilly rain blew in, they dashed off for the refuge of a gazebo and slumped down on a bench, watching the rain bounce off the wooden sidewalks and form puddles on a worn, dirt path.

"Why don't either of you have an umbrella?" a woman said, firmly. "Obviously, you're not from around here."

She was middle-aged, wearing an elaborate, deep purple hat, a long, black dress with a matching coat, and black button shoes, and sitting sheltered under a black lace parasol. The line of her mouth was stern, her scolding eyes narrowed, her face all sharp lines, finishing at her long, pointed nose.

Eve brushed raindrops from her coat. "No, ma'am, we're not from here."

"From back East, I suspect," the woman added, holding her challenging expression.

"You would be an observing woman," Patrick said, touching his bowler hat with two fingers. "We are from New York City."

"New York City, you say? So, you've come to seek your fortune out West?"

There was something about the woman's spunk that Patrick liked. Her manner reminded him of his mother's, a woman who had been known for her rough edges and honest mouth.

"It is indeed for fortune that we have come, madam, but not for gold," Patrick said. "To be honest, and you seem to be a woman who prefers direct words, we've come to find our little daughter, who was taken from us."

The woman's expression didn't change. "Well, who took her? A relative? A friend?"

"No, a very low and conniving woman. We believe she fled New York with our little girl and traveled here. That is as straightforward as I can put it."

"Then go to the police, sir. What are you waiting for?"

"A good suggestion, but because of rather complicated circumstances, we cannot," Patrick concluded.

Her suspicious eyes glided over Eve's and Patrick's faces. "Are you yourselves in some kind of trouble with the police?"

Eve said, "No, we're not."

"Then I don't understand. How do you know the woman is here? What reliable information do you have to go on? I hope it was honest information if it brought you here all the way from New York."

Patrick spoke up. "A reliable source said she came here, with a man friend."

The woman's eyebrows shot up. "A man friend? Well, I doubt that. From what you have told me, I doubt whether he was a friend at all. He was, no doubt, a scoundrel and a rogue who, when he is found, should be horsewhipped."

Eve reached into her pocket and removed the photograph of Annabelle. What did she have to lose? Eve rose and stepped toward the woman, who stiffened. "What is that?"

"It's a photograph of the woman. May I ask you to look at it to see if, by any chance, you recognize her? My husband and I have been walking the city, showing it around with no success."

The woman murmured something under her breath, reached into her purse and retrieved a pair of spectacles. "All right, young woman, hand it over and let me see it."

Eve gave it to her. The formidable-looking woman held it up, then held it back, then peered and mumbled, then brought it forward, squinting her eyes into slits. Finally, she held it out at arm's length.

When she raised her eyes to Eve, they were steady with confidence. "Yes, I recognize her."

Patrick snapped to attention. Eve blinked.

"You recognize her?" Eve asked, unconvinced.

"Yes, yes, I do."

"Are you sure?" Patrick asked.

"Well, of course, I'm sure. I said so, didn't I? Her name is Annabelle Styles."

Rain drummed on the roof of the gazebo, streamed down the tiled roof and gushed in waterfalls to the ground.

Eve and Patrick traded dubious glances.

The woman handed the photo back to Eve, who accepted it with reluctance. "How do you know this woman, Annabelle?" Eve asked. "I mean, we've shown this photo to so many other people and they didn't know her."

"Well, maybe they don't read the society section in the *San Francisco Call.* Personally, I never miss it. Annabelle married Leland Styles, twenty-five years her senior, on Christmas Eve last. It was a lavish affair, attended by everyone who is anyone in this town. Mr. Styles is the president of the Southern Pacific Railroad, as well as a partner in the Occidental and Oriental Steamship Company, and he is one of the wealthiest men in San Francisco."

Patrick stood up, convinced by the woman's confidence, impatience flashing in his eyes. "Where do they live?"

"Live? Well, they don't live like the rest of us, do they? They dwell in Mr. Leland Style's fifty-room mansion on Knob Hill, on the corner of Powell and California Streets, along with other millionaires in this growing city. But you won't find them there."

Eve's eyes drilled into her. "Why not? Where are they?"

The woman drew herself up, proud to impart the information. "Because Leland and Annabelle Styles, along with her little daughter, Colleen, have left for their honeymoon in Europe, where they're to visit London, Paris and Italy, especially Italy. Mr. Styles loves the music and the architecture, so the newspapers say. According to yesterday's paper, they'll return home around the first of April."

A raw anguish struck Eve in the gut and she stepped back, dropping hard onto the bench. She sat with the woman's words until they assembled into a movie; a movie with images of some strange, wealthy man, Annabelle and Colleen strolling leisurely through the streets of Paris, the Eiffel Tower in the background.

Patrick stood still, the bitter truth burning in his chest.

The woman continued. "I think it's safe to say that you are mistaken about the woman and her character. And, according to the newspaper story about Annabelle Burke, her parents live in a small town in Missouri and her first husband, and the father of her child, Colleen, was tragically killed when his horse threw him, and he broke his neck."

The red returned to Eve's face. "She's lying. Her name is not Annabelle Burke, and she doesn't come from Missouri."

The woman got her back up. "And I say, young woman, that you and your husband are most assuredly mistaken. By all accounts, Mrs. Styles is a fine, upstanding woman and her daughter is a little beauty."

Eve shot up in defiance, and she was about to launch into a vicious attack to challenge the woman's facts, when Patrick broke in, his voice soothing.

"Thank you for putting us straight, madam. Obviously, Annabelle Styles is not the woman we are searching for, and you have been most helpful."

Eve's hot eyes widened on him, but she held her tongue. She knew him well enough to know that he was already forming a plan.

And then, as if on cue, the rain dwindled to mist, and the rolling fog began to dissolve, letting in the sun. The woman sighed. "Well, there you have it. It rains like the dickens for a time, and then, just like that, as fast as you can say dithering Dottie, it stops."

Eve and Patrick thanked her again, exited the gazebo and descended the hill, heading back to their hotel.

Eve looked at him. "What are we going to do?"

His face was hard with angry determination. "I know you, my love, and I know what you're thinking, just as you know what I'm thinking."

Eve linked her arm in his, her face upturned into the moving, gray sky. "I'm going to get a job at the Styles mansion, working at whatever they'll offer me. I'm going to explore and get to know every foot of that place, so when the time comes and Annabelle returns with Colleen, we'll know the best escape route."

Patrick's grin held cunning. "I knew that's what you were thinking. But, Eve, what kind of work can you do in this time? You don't have the hands of a working woman, so any head housekeeper or butler will spot you right away. And your deportment is too fine. And, finally, you can't cook for a house that size, you can't sew or clean the coal cinders from the fireplaces, and you don't know the right and proper manners that are required by the butler, the head housekeeper or the family."

"Well, don't be so negative, Patrick. I can be a... I don't know, a governess or a tutor."

"Then you'll need the best of references to work in a fine house like that."

Frustrated, Eve threw up her hands. "Okay, so what will you do?"

"I will hire on as a joiner or a carpenter. There'll be much work in a house for that."

"Now that's something I've never heard you say. Pray tell, what is a joiner?"

"Joiners make doors, windows, staircases, and all manner of furniture. I believe you know what a carpenter does."

"Yes... they do woodwork, and they hammer and saw things, and build things."

"Yes, and they assemble roof trusses, do stud work, and build staircases and floors. You also have to be skilled in cutting and fitting timber structures together."

Eve pulled him to a stop. "Now, wait a minute. You have never, not ever, not once, in all our time together, talked about this... being a joiner/carpenter. Can you actually do carpentry work?"

Patrick adjusted his hat. "Before I became a cop, my dear Eve, I was a carpenter and a joiner. I apprenticed when I was thirteen years old."

"Why didn't you ever tell me?"

"Because it never came up, and you never asked."

"Won't you need to polish up your skills? I mean, it's been a long time, hasn't it?"

Patrick took her arm, and they walked on. "Yes, but it won't take me long. I had a hard teacher, a rough and fierce man, who often used his good fists to help me correct my errors. I learned fast, and it's not something I will ever forget."

Eve kept her eyes of wonder on him. "There are still so many things about you I don't know, aren't there?"

He grinned and nodded firmly. "Yes, Eve, there are."

Eve said, "Well, in the meantime, let's hope and pray that if that earthquake strikes, it doesn't kill us."

CHAPTER 44

Leland Styles' forty-two-room mansion was as impressive as the Vanderbilt Mansion in New York City, where Patrick had visited the adult Lavinia Vanderbilt during his previous time travel adventure in 1925. Patrick had also been inside the glorious Harringshaw Mansion in New York, where he had worked as an undercover cop for Alfred Harringshaw in 1885, during his famous costume ball.

The Styles mansion occupied an entire city block on Nob Hill, its large masonry structure being three stories high and finished in brownstone. The main entrance faced California Street and was sheltered by a deep, three-bay portico, supported by clustered square columns.

Inside, there was a rotunda of sixteen soaring Corinthian columns that lent the impression of an ancient Greek temple. The many stained-glass windows let in muted, liturgical light, and the polished white and gray marble floors featured luxurious red runner area rugs and blooming floor plants.

Many of the downstairs rooms had ornamental artwork decorating the walls and ceilings, while the French Renaissance and the style of Louis XV, with the graceful curves of Louis XV furniture, inspired the second-floor design scheme. The third floor featured teak wood carvings made in India, as well as extraordinary antique embroideries covering luxurious divans, walls, and door windows.

Days before Patrick's carpentry interview, he'd purchased a used, brown leather work apron and a set of tools. He'd also cut his hair short and started a beard and mustache. In case he was hired, his full beard and practiced stooping posture would help to disguise him.

On the day of his interview, Patrick wore the work apron under his coat and carried a bag of tools, hoping to impress his interviewer, the foreman Cole Kirkland.

Kirkland was a big-boned man in his middle forties, with curly auburn hair and a heavy red mustache. His weathered, florid face and deep-set, gray/green eyes were busy, missing nothing. He had the robust body of a workman: long arms, strong bowlegs, muscled shoulders and large, rough hands.

Patrick's interview was held outside, in a low hanging shed near stacks of newly piled lumber that smelled freshly cut. Kirkland sat Patrick down on a makeshift bench and puffed a pipe as he paced the space, firing questions.

Patrick had used an alias, changing his name to Liam Morgan, the name of a friend he'd grown up with on the Lower East Side.

"Where do you hail from, Liam?"

"New York."

"Irish, are you?"

"My parents. I was born in New York."

"What does your Pa do?"

"A policeman."

"Where were you apprenticed?"

"On the Lower East Side of New York. I left school at thirteen to help my family when my father took ill."

Patrick didn't tell Kirkland that his father had serious drinking and brawling issues, and that he'd been fired more than once.

"So, you were the breadwinner then?"

"Yes."

"At what place of business were you apprenticed?"

"At the Haines Piano Shop."

"And then?"

"Construction sites in the city. Rowhouses. Brownstones. There was lots of work, and that's where I got much of my experience. Then, I became a journeyman."

"Are you union?"

"I was…"

"Was?"

"I've been away from it for a time."

And then Patrick lied. "As I said, there was illness in the family. I took the jobs I could get that didn't pull me away from my home."

"Are you married, Liam?"

"Yes."

"Little ones?"

Patrick had his story ready. "We did…" he said, leaving it hanging in the air so Kirkland could draw his own conclusions and, hopefully, feel sympathetic and offer him a job.

Kirkland puffed his pipe thoughtfully, understanding the implication. The child mortality rate was high in 1906.

"You know we're not union here, don't you, Liam?"

"I heard. Yes."

"That won't last long. I'm sure you know about the nationwide, open-shop attack. Employers have locked out union carpenters in Chicago, New York, Pittsburgh, Louisville, and other cities."

Patrick hadn't heard, since he didn't live in 1906, but he nodded, playing along. "Yes…"

Kirkland pulled the pipe from his mouth and looked toward the great house. "Mr. Styles don't like the unions, Liam, so we've got to brave it out here. I'll wager that in a few years' time, a union card will be as crucial a thing to a good working carpenter as a complete set of tools. And then it will be said that the craftsman without a card is a man without a trade."

Patrick liked Kirkland. He seemed a fair, no-nonsense man. A man Patrick wouldn't mind working for.

Immediately after the interview, Kirkland offered him a job.

"Your first week is unpaid, Liam, and I trust you're agreeable with that. Since you have no references, I'll evaluate your work and get my measure of you. If you have the skills I'm looking for, you'll stay on, work six days a week from 7 a.m. to 6 p.m., and receive weekly wages as we discussed. Is it a bargain, then?"

"Yes…"

They shook on it, and Patrick recalled with pride and longing how, in the 1880s and in this year of 1906, a man's word was his bond. Patrick didn't think it held as true in the twenty-first century, with all the lawyers, bureaucracies and contracts.

PATRICK'S FIRST DAY OF WORK was Monday, February 19. Kirkland put him to work, building a back staircase that would be concealed from public view. It would be used only for the staff, traveling between floors, to serve the master and mistress of the house. It was a wise choice by Kirkland. If Patrick wasn't up to the task, Kirkland would know soon enough, and Patrick would be dismissed with no loss or complications.

What Patrick didn't know, until he went to work, was that Kirkland had buddied him up with another man, who was also testing for the job—for the only job being offered. It was a competition; both men competing for the same job.

Patrick's co-worker was the hulking, brooding Angus Hammonds. At forty, his unruly hair was chestnut brown; his eyes a dull, sinister almond; his features crudely chiseled by misfortune, booze and regret.

That first morning when Kirkland had the two men shake hands, Angus' hand clutched and squeezed Patrick's hand in a challenging vice grip. Patrick took the pain stoically, noting there was an edge about the man that was threatening, and Patrick had no time for it. He needed the job for Colleen. He had to be in the house when Annabelle and Colleen returned.

When Kirkland had left them to their work, Angus glared at Patrick with hatred and, in a cold, scratchy voice, he said, "This job is mine, so don't get in my way, you boot-licking Irish."

It was Patrick who measured the total rise, the distance from the floor to the top of the new staircase, calculating the best slope for the staircase design. Angus looked on, a smirk curling the corners of his mouth.

"You do the easy work, Irish. When the real work begins, step aside and let the better man show you a thing or two."

Patrick ignored him, puzzling over why Kirkland had given the odious man a chance. Perhaps Angus had stellar skills and good references. Perhaps Angus knew the right people, which is how it usually was.

Over the next three days, Patrick spent much of his time in the shed, measuring and cutting the risers to the length of each tread and then securing them to the stringers with wood screws.

Patrick took to the work with enthusiasm and flair, easily recalling his old skills. He enjoyed working with his hands, something he hadn't done in a long time. It was difficult work but, as long as he stayed away from Angus, all was well.

Angus had been busy constructing the staircase handrail, and Patrick noticed that the man worked quietly, methodically, and with impressive skill.

Kirkland drifted by at least twice a day, evaluated the work of both men, said little, and then wandered away.

On Saturday morning, the last day of Patrick's free labor and the day he'd learn whether he was to be hired,

The Christmas Eve Journey

Patrick was hard at work installing the stairs. He was about six feet up, ten stairs already having been cut and installed. He was kneeling on a lower tread, or step, fitting and adjusting the stair tread on the next level, when he heard the back door open and the sound of heavy footsteps.

Angus came blundering in. He was late, and he was drunk, his breath foul, his clothes rumpled, his mood dark. When he saw Patrick, he cursed him and pointed a shaky finger at him.

"You damned Irish clod. Your stair treads are too shallow. There's not enough room to plant your foot while you go up and down. One of them maids, carrying a heavy tray, will slip or miss a stair and break her fool neck."

Patrick kept his voice mild. "There's plenty of room, Angus. Even enough room for your two great boats for feet."

Angus' glassy eyes became a stormy ocean. "I'll kill you," he shouted.

"Shut up, Angus, and get to work, before Kirkland comes by and sees you in your drunken state."

Angus yanked a hammer from his work apron and staggered back, his face contorted in fury. He cocked his meaty arm and flung the hammer at Patrick's head. As it whistled in the air toward him, tumbling end on end, Patrick ducked, and the hammer slammed into the wall behind him.

"I'll kill you," Angus yelled. "Come down here and I'll kill you."

Patrick did not want to fight. Even though he was drunk, Angus was a big man, with big clubs for fists that could do a lot of damage.

"Go get your handrail, Angus. Let's see how it's going to fit."

"Go to hell, you Irish coward. Come down here and fight me or, so help me God, I'll go up there and beat the devil out of you."

Just then Kirkland appeared, his fists on his hips, his face inflamed. "What the hell's going on here?"

Angus regained his balance and stood remarkably still as his anger melted into innocence. He turned, pointing at Patrick. "He don't know what he's doin', that's all. I told him the stair treads ain't deep enough, and he threatened me. That's the truth of it, and I ain't lyin' none. He threatened my very life. Said he'd bash me with the hammer he's holding in his hand."

Kirkland looked at Angus doubtfully, and then his stare slowly traveled up to Patrick.

"Is that true, Liam?"

"No, sir, it's not true."

As Kirkland approached Angus, the man stepped back, turning his face away.

Kirkland stopped and sniffed, and his face tightened in accusation. "Angus, you promised me. You gave me your word."

"Yeah, well, I ain't done nothing. Irish there said he'd kill me. I got a right to defend myself, don't I?"

"You're drunk, Angus. Slack-eyed, piss-eyed and sailor drunk."

Angus' hands went to fists. Patrick saw a new rage rise in him. Did Kirkland see it?

"Get out, Angus! Go on home and sleep it off."

Despite being drunk, Angus's swing was a blur as his right fist went for Kirkland's head.

Patrick tensed, ready to leap down the stairs to help Kirkland.

Kirkland was cat-quick. He blocked Angus' attack with one hand and threw a hard punch with the other, which caught Angus solidly on the right jaw. Angus jerked left, spun away, slammed into the wall, and dropped with a thud to the floor. He didn't move.

Kirkland stepped toward him, placed his fists on his hips and looked down, shaking his head. He didn't look at Patrick as he spoke. "I gave him a chance, Liam. He's a damned good carpenter when he's sober, but he can't stay away from the grog. He's my wife's sister's husband, and I promised I'd give him a chance."

Kirkland turned to Patrick. "You do good work, Liam Morgan. You've got the job, but don't ever come to my place of work all grogged up. I won't stand for it."

"No, sir."

"Stay at the job now. I'll have a couple of lads come and haul Angus away."

He turned and started off, then stopped, tossing a final disgusted look at Angus. "Dammit, I'll have hell to pay at home tonight. My wife insists I'm too hard on him."

Kirkland glanced up at Patrick. "You said you have a wife, didn't you, Liam?"

"Yes, sir."

"Do you get along with the woman?"

"Yes, we get along well."

He nodded, thoughtfully. "You seem like a smart man, and your work is fine. I see you have pride in it. That's rare. It just strikes me... Well, I have a thought that just came to me, and I'll just toss it out. Is your wife good with her numbers?"

"Yes, very."

"You said you don't have any little ones at home for your wife to fuss over? Is that right?"

"Yes. My wife, Eve, is looking for work."

"So, are you reading me and my thoughts, Liam?"

"We're new to the city, Mr. Kirkland. Work has been scarce for us."

"I don't go in much for having women around the workplace, Liam. I'm not much for having women out of the home, if the truth be told, but I'm just tossing up thoughts and seeing where they land. Can I trust her to keep my accounts? Can she do that? Is she that good with her numbers so she can do that?"

"Yes, Mr. Kirkland, she can. She's as sharp as the day is long."

Kirkland thought about it, his black boot toeing at the floor. "She won't make any trouble for us, will she, Liam?"

"No, sir. She's steady and she's true."

Liam wiped a hand across his mouth, his eyes moving, his mind considering. "All right. Talk to her. If she's agreeable, bring her by. I'll test her out and, if she can do the work, I'll hire her, and we might be the better for it, or the worse for it. Ain't that the way of most things, Liam?"

"As I said, sir, she has a good head and she can do the work."

Kirkland nodded. "All right, then. And there'll be no funny business with the men stepping in to have a gander. I'll promise you that. She'll be working with me in that back shed, so she'll be safe. I have to get my books in order, Liam, before Mr. Styles returns. He's a stickler for the accounts. Right now, they're a mess. The man I hired stole from me, and I fired him yesterday. He was putting his free hand into the petty cash, of all things. Petty cash, petty man, is what I say. It's getting so I don't trust men as much as I do women. Now, ain't that something for me to say? Anyway, it's that kind of week, where the good Lord seems to want to pick a fight with me. So, bring her by, Liam. Bring her by and let's see if I can put her to work."

CHAPTER 45

Eve began her bookkeeping job for Cole Kirkland the following Wednesday, using the name Evelyn Morgan. She'd cut her hair, dyed it black and combed it tight to her head, adding a pair of glasses she'd found in a secondhand shop. Patrick told her she scared him.

"You look like Mrs. Schally, a teacher I had in the third grade. More than once she snatched a ruler from her desktop and whacked me on my hands and head. She was the terror of the school."

Eve grinned, pleased. "Good. Then I don't think Annabelle will recognize me, do you?"

"Only if she stares into your eyes. Your eyes are distinctive and quite lovely, you know."

Eve batted them, then narrowed them into a threat. "I'm warning you, Mr. Gantly," she said, pointing a sharp finger at him. "If you don't do everything I ask you to do, when I ask you to do it, I'm going to find a ruler and whack you over the head with it."

Patrick stepped back, throwing up his hands for protection.

EVE HAD LEARNED bookkeeping during her college years, while working part-time at a family-owned sporting goods store. The owner had gone to high school with her father, and Eve was hired to help wherever she was needed. Some days it was on the sales floor; some days it was in the office, typing letters or assisting the bookkeeper, who taught her the basics.

As soon as she'd opened and examined Kirkland's books, Eve realized that the previous bookkeeper had been sloppy in his record-keeping. There were errors in his calculations, as well as discrepancies between the invoices and what was recorded as expenditures in the ledger. The previous employee wasn't just stealing from petty cash; he was also padding the payments he sent out to suppliers, plumbers and electricians, probably in order to get a kickback.

It delighted Eve to have a job at the mansion where she'd soon be near Colleen, and she found Kirkland to be polite—direct and demanding, but always respectful. He never raised his voice or flirted with her, and the work distracted and galvanized her, pulling her obsessive mind away from anticipating the day when Annabelle and Colleen would return from Europe.

By the middle of March, Eve had the past and present construction and maintenance accounts in order and, when Kirkland asked, she agreed to take on the landscaping accounts as well.

Kirkland dropped by as Patrick was putting the finishing touches on the staircase, expressing how pleased he was with Eve's work.

"Your wife, Eve, is efficiency in motion, Liam. I declare the woman doesn't waste a breath while she works; head down, pencil at the ready, eyes sharp, like a hunter searching for tracks. When the master of the house returns, I'll put in a good word and see if I can convince the man to give your wife a raise."

After the staircase was completed, Kirkland put Patrick to work on a gazebo, ordered to be built by the mistress of the house, Annabelle Styles, for her daughter, Colleen.

While Kirkland was explaining the design and emphasizing that its completion was a top priority, Patrick had taken comfort knowing that, even if Colleen never played in it, the project would be a labor of love for his little girl.

His imagination immediately went to work. He would build it in a classic style with eight sides, spindle railings, a two-tier roof, a crowning cupola, and flower boxes. It would be pleasant to imagine Colleen tottering across the lawn, climbing up into the thing and twirling about as she used to do; a free dancer, all hands and wagging head with a big smile.

Kirkland snapped Patrick back to the present. "The mistress is a particular lady, Liam, so I'm trusting you to build it just so. She wants things as she wants them, and that could change day by day. At least that's been my experience with her. Between you and me, she's got a terrible eye, if you know what I'm saying." They exchanged knowing looks. What Kirkland meant was "an evil eye," and Patrick understood that.

Kirkland continued. "And she's as changeable as the weather—one day she can be pleasant with a smile; the next day the devil is making the anger boil up in her. You'll have to watch her, Liam, and don't make an enemy of the woman. I've seen her walk up to a good working man, point at him and order me, in no uncertain terms, to get him out of her sight. Like I said, Liam, she's got some prettiness about her, but she's got a terrible eye. Watch her."

ON A SOFT, PALE SUNDAY in April, their one day off together, Eve and Patrick sat on a bench in Union Square, brainstorming the best strategies for retrieving Colleen and then making a run for it, the lantern at the ready.

Patrick leaned back and crossed his arms across his chest, shaking off the cool, humid wind. "Since I have access to the house through that back staircase I built, I think I have the better chance of slipping into Colleen's room and carrying her off. And, like I've said, while I was building the thing, I could creep about and explore parts of the house. Yesterday, I talked to one of the maids who told me where Annabelle's and Colleen's rooms are. Unfortunately, they're next door to each other on the second floor toward the middle of the house, a bit of a distance from my rear staircase."

"Colleen will have a nannie looking after her, won't she?" Eve asked.

"Yes, when Annabelle is not with her, Colleen's day nannie is either Miss Emily Gorshin or Miss Rose Dolan."

"What about at night?"

"No one. Colleen sleeps alone, although I was told that Annabelle often leaves her room to check on her. As you know, Colleen always slept soundly."

Eve looked at him. "And Miss Dolan is the nannie you spoke to, am I right? And, with a name like Dolan, I'm betting she's Irish?"

"You guess correctly, my wise and observant Eve. She's a smart and clever girl, who has a crush on one of the stable grooms. I thickened my accent a wee bit and told her I was from Dingle, the same town as she. We hit it off."

"Not too well, I hope."

"Well, enough for her to give me the information we need. She's been with the Styles family for over a year."

"What did she say about Annabelle?" Eve asked.

"Like everyone else who works at that house, she's careful with her words, especially with me, since I'm still the new man about. The most revealing thing she said was, and I quote, 'She's not the kindest of women, is she? I fear her bark is as wicked as her bite. God forgive me for judging one of my fellow creatures.'"

"And a creature Annabelle is," Eve said.

Patrick took in a horizon that was pale and glassy. "Another cloudy, misty day, and it's turned chilly again. I feel sun-deprived."

Eve turned to Patrick. "I've kept a secret from you."

Patrick looked at her, his head cocked to the right. "Have you now? Don't tell me, you've found yourself a San Francisco rascal and you're two-timing me," he said with a grin.

Eve ignored his little joke. "I wrote a letter to Darius."

Patrick narrowed his eyes. "Darius? Why?"

"I had to know, for sure, if Joni really did light that lantern."

"Darius told us she was gone."

"I know, I know, but something in my gut said otherwise."

Patrick sat up. "All right. I assume you wrote this letter some time ago?"

"Yes, a few days after we arrived."

"And? Has Darius written back?"

Eve shook her head. "No..."

Eve reached into her black beaded purse, drew out an envelope and handed it to Patrick. He took it and studied its face, noting the handwriting and the return address.

"Go ahead... Read it," Eve said.

He ran a hand through his hair and down his face, before he removed the letter, smoothed it out and began to read.

Dear Eve and Patrick,

I can't tell you how happy I was to get your letter, Eve, even though it was addressed to Darius. I hope you receive this letter, knowing that you may have to run for it at any minute. Anyway, I'm sending it express to the address you included. Of course, if you don't receive it, I'll never know, will I? So, I'm hoping you'll get it. Even better, I'm pretending you're both sitting next to me in the library of our home, where I'm writing this.

I have hoped and prayed for you two, and for Colleen. You didn't say much in your letter about what's going on, so I assume you still haven't been able to get Colleen and "lantern" off to the twenty-first century. Please be careful and know that I'm praying like crazy for you.

Well, as you may have figured out by now, I never did light that lantern. I never time traveled anywhere. When I wrote those letters to Darius and you, I did intend to light the lantern and fly off somewhere, hopefully back home to the twenty-first century. But, in the end, I didn't light it. I couldn't light it. Just as I brought that lighted match to the wick of that lantern, I stopped. I said to myself, "Can you really leave your kids, you stupid woman?"

No, I couldn't. I love Lavinia too much. I love William, even though he can be a shit sometimes. Still, he's my only son and I love him. Guess what? I love Darius, too, and he's an even bigger shit than William is.

So, I decided to teach Darius a lesson for slapping me like that. And what did I do? I did something that women do in novels and movies; something that most women dream about doing, but most never do. I vanished into the night.

Where did I go? Only uptown to visit my good friend, Clara Townsend. We've spent a lot of time together arranging various charitable balls and dinners. She'll talk your ear off, but she's got a good heart. She was delighted to have me for the week I hid away from Darius.

When I returned, Darius nearly fainted. At first, he was angry, then he was confused, then he was sorry and then... well, he got angry again, and we had yet another big blowout fight. So, yadah, yadah, yadah. That's the way our marriage is, and always will be, I guess. We did finally make up, and he has promised me a trip to Chicago for a kind of second honeymoon, and I'm going to hold him to that.

Forgive me for not saying goodbye to you. The truth is: I couldn't do it. I couldn't watch you both leave, knowing I'd never see you again, and that you were taking my lantern. That meant I could never light the thing and go home, even if things went to hell with Darius and me.

Yes, it is changing our relationship... I think for the better. I no longer have the possibility of leaving him—at least not in the time travel way, and he's not so threatened by the lantern, because it's gone.

And so now, I'm writing this and missing you both. What a great time we had, Eve. We had more and better adventures than any other two girls ever had or ever will have. God, what a great time it was! I'll never forget, Eve. I'll never forget those wild days; those impossible days, and I'll never forget you and our friendship.

Eve, I'm not going to say goodbye—I mean, like really goodbye. As long as Tesla's lanterns exist, there is still a remote possibility that you will end up on my doorstep again. So, girlfriend, I'll be looking for you.

Give Patrick a kiss for me, and tell him I love him for loving you so much, and for always being there for you.

I know things might get hectic for you when you make your move to get Colleen, but if you can, please dash off a note and let me know how you are before you return home.

All right, this crazy woman is going to sign off now and go to bed. Darius just came in and saw that I was writing this to you. Guess what he said? "Tell them, I enjoyed their company, and I hope they find Colleen, that precious little girl."

Isn't he a nice guy after all? I think I'm going to live happily ever after, just like the heroines do in the fairytales.

All my love to you both, always,
Joni

Patrick lifted his eyes from the page and looked skyward. "That's good news, Eve. I'm glad you wrote. This is very good news."

After Eve replaced the letter in her purse, she took Patrick's arm and pulled him close. "I feel so much better. It's such a relief to know she didn't do it and she's back home."

"Yes," Patrick agreed. "Now we can focus all our mental energies on getting Colleen and escaping. Let's go get some breakfast. I'm hungry."

THE CLIFF HOUSE was a massive Victorian structure nestled high on the cliffs overlooking Ocean Beach and the wide spread of sea. Eve and Patrick were seated at a table next to one of the western windows. They ordered from the breakfast menu. Eve decided on fried eggs, ham, fresh baked bread and coffee, and Patrick, broiled breast of young turkey, served with ham, corn fritters and a pot of hot tea.

Eve watched Patrick eat with keen interest. "Do you know… you're always a little different when we travel back in time."

"And how is that?"

"Well, maybe it's the beard. Sometimes I like it, and sometimes I don't. You either look like a lumberjack or a pirate."

"Which do you like best?"

She grinned. "The pirate, of course. And I've noticed that your accent has thickened, and you really go for the food. I mean, look at what you're eating, not that I'm criticizing you or anything. It's just that you're eating turkey *and* ham, with corn fritters, for breakfast. Ever since we've landed in this time, you've been eating more meat and fat, and you haven't gained a pound. In fact, you look very sexy in your undershorts, with your flat stomach and those muscled-up arms."

He grinned with a little head bow. "Thank you, ma'am. I'm a working man now. I need the calories. And, I might add, I'm more comfortable eating this sort of food. It's more like what I was raised on. Your modern food doesn't taste as good, and it's often too spiced up for my taste. And you people in the twenty-first century eat too many vegetables, and you don't cook them enough. Anyway, how are your eggs?"

"Good… Very good, and the bread is heaven."

Eve glanced out the windows and down to the beach. "So down there will be our jumping-off spot?"

"Yes, don't you think? I doubt whether the beach will have gone anywhere in over a hundred years. It's safer than Golden Gate Park."

Eve took a sip of her coffee, admiring the lovely, gold-rimmed cup. "I'm getting the jillies again."

"Are the jillies related to the willies? First cousins or something?"

"Yes. I got the word from my mother. It means the shakes, the shudders."

"About what?"

"About everything. And every time I think about lighting that lantern, I wonder if, this time, our luck will run out and we'll wind up even further back in time, or somewhere way off into the future. I mean, we just don't know, and we never know."

"We don't have a choice. The lantern is our only way out of here. With Annabelle's husband's money and connections, if they catch us and we can't get to that lantern, they'll throw us in jail for the rest of our lives."

Eve set her cup down. Resting her chin on a pyramid of fingers, she stared out into the infinite, rolling sea. "I'm tired of waiting. I want to move, grab Colleen and get out of here."

"It won't be long now. Kirkland told me yesterday that the Styleses are scheduled to be back in the house on Sunday, April fifteenth."

She looked at him. "And you didn't tell me?"

"You haven't been sleeping so well, Eve. I thought I'd wait… but there it is. Knowing the date will add to your jillies, I think."

"Thanks for telling me, but I read all about it in the paper—in the society section. I've been following their trip for about a week."

"You didn't tell me?"

"You haven't been sleeping so well, either."

They smiled at each other.

Eve said, "At least now we know for sure when they're returning. This is one of those times I wish we had cell phones, so when we do make our move, we could text in real time."

"That's why we're going to keep the plan as simple as possible, with just a few moving parts."

"Have you changed anything since our last strategy session?" Eve asked.

"Not much, but things can always go wrong. They often do, so we need to prepare for that. But I still think moving in at night is best. I know where Colleen sleeps now, so it should be easier, as long as she doesn't scream, and I can get to that staircase before someone sees me."

Eve closed her eyes, sucked in a breath to brace herself, then let it out all at once, opening her eyes. "Okay… I'm really nervous. And we still haven't been able to answer the big question about the lantern. Assuming everything goes right—that we get Colleen and escape the house, jump into the waiting taxi and make it to the beach—after we light the lantern, what will happen to it?"

"That was a long question."

"What if Annabelle somehow finds it and gets her hands on it? What if by some stroke of twisted luck, she returns to 2021?"

Patrick swallowed the last of his corn fritter and wiped his mouth with his napkin.

"I thought about that, but I think it's highly unlikely she'll have any idea where we've gone. Also, I found a tide chart for the outer coast. Assuming we can snatch Colleen and get to the beach before dawn, high tide will be at 8:45 a.m. If we light the lantern near the tideline, then it might be swept out to sea or buried in the sand soon after. So, let's hope that when we arrive wherever it is the lantern takes us, that we won't be so far out at sea that we'll have to swim for it. Anyway, it's the best I can come up with."

Eve shifted nervously in her chair. "There's one more thing we haven't discussed. I didn't even think about it until a day or so ago."

Patrick waited in uneasy anticipation.

"What if Annabelle already has a lantern? The same lantern she used to time travel to 2021? What if, when she time travel back to 1904, she retrieved her lantern and brought it with her to San Francisco?"

Patrick nodded reflectively. "Good one, Eve. I hadn't considered that."

"Is there any way one or both of us could, I don't know, search the house and see if we can find it?"

"If Annabelle has it, she's too smart to leave it out in plain sight. And, anyway, there are too many servants in that house. We'd be caught and then…" He left the words hanging in the air.

They sat pondering, their eyes shifting, their shoulders tense.

Patrick slid his empty plate aside and hailed the waiter. "Would you bring me a whiskey, please?"

"Make that two," Eve said.

As the waiter walked away, Patrick pursed his lips, studying his wife. "Since when do you drink whiskey in the middle of the day? I've never seen it. Pardon my manners, but it didn't occur to me to ask if you wanted one."

"Patrick, there's an unstoppable, unbreakable aspect to Annabelle that scares the hell out of me. I need a whiskey."

CHAPTER 46

On Tuesday morning, Eve was at her desk by 8 a.m., feeling jittery, aware that the Styleses had arrived home the night before, a day later than had been expected.

Cole Kirkland entered the office shed a little after nine o'clock, looking troubled and distracted. He went to his desk and remained standing while he sifted through a stack of papers, not finding what he was looking for.

"Mrs. Morgan, I seem to have misplaced a lumber order. It contained materials for the gazebo your husband is working on. Mr. Styles and his wife want to see the gazebo this morning, and Mr. Styles will want to examine the accounts afterwards."

Eve looked at him, worried. Would Annabelle recognize Patrick? This would be the first test. He'd recently told Eve that he was going to make himself scarce when he got word she was coming to inspect the gazebo.

Eve turned to Kirkland. "I believe you handed me the invoice, and I have it here in my folder. I'll take a look."

While Eve thumbed through the stack of invoices, Kirkland stepped over, nervously fidgeting with the ends of his mustache. "I've got the nerves about me this morning, Mrs. Morgan. I'll not hide the fact that the lady of the house has an edge about her, and she'll stir up the waters we've managed to calm all these weeks. I also heard from the head housekeeper that Mr. Styles is not in a pleasant mood. Not to be a gossiper, but the good woman told me the couple had a fiery argument early this morning. You'd think they'd still have the wedding glow about them, wouldn't you? It being so soon after their honeymoon."

"Here it is," Eve said, avoiding the question, aware he was speaking more to himself than to her.

Kirkland took the invoice from her and studied it. "Yes, this is it. Is it in the books, Mrs. Morgan?"

"Yes."

"Very well, then. Mr. Styles will drop by later. He'll want to inspect your work, Mrs. Morgan. He can be a stern man, but he's a fair man."

Eve gently cleared her throat. "What time do you think they'll be inspecting the gazebo?"

Kirkland handed the invoice back to Eve with a brief smile. "Concerned about Liam's work, are you? Well, don't you worry about it. It's a fine bit of work, so I say. But what Mrs. Styles will say is quite another thing, isn't it? She'll speak her mind, that's for certain, and she'll express her firm opinion to Liam, like she's known to do. But he's a good man and a fine workman, so let us hope that the woman finds the work and the man to be agreeable and up to her particular standards."

Eve lowered her eyes. "Will she have her daughter with her, do you think?"

"There's no doubt about that. She'll bring the girl, a little angel of a girl she is, full of smiles and play. The little darling makes the woman better, if you ask me. I've observed that Mrs. Styles always has rosy cheeks and a pleasing smile whenever the little one is with her."

Eve glanced away, not wanting Kirkland to see her expression—her feral hatred of Annabelle and her restless concern over Patrick's plan to take Colleen. Eve didn't have Patrick's poker face. Her expression was honest and revealing, or so Patrick had said many times.

Their plan was set. Everything was ready. They would strike early the next morning, while there was still some darkness, Wednesday, April 18. From a backdoor to the mansion that opened near the staircase he'd built, Patrick would slip inside, steal up the stairs to the second floor, open the door that led into the hallway, then wait and watch. When all was clear, he'd make his move toward Colleen's bedroom. He would have shaved his mustache and beard, hoping that Colleen would recognize him and not scream in terror. He did not want to press his hand over her mouth.

Meanwhile, Eve would be inside a horse-drawn taxi on California Street, having climbed the steep eastern face of Knob Hill, waiting at the crest, close to the mansion. Her large tip to the driver would keep him quiet, just in case Colleen was noisy and struggling.

Once Patrick and Colleen were inside the taxi, it would rush them the six miles to Ocean Beach, where they'd light the lantern near the tideline and, with any luck, vanish, reappearing somewhere in 2021.

It was a simple plan, but would it work?

A LITTLE AFTER TEN THAT MORNING, Patrick spotted Kirkland and Mrs. and Mr. Styles leave the side door of the mansion and start walking toward the gazebo. He also saw Colleen, her little hand enclosed in Annabelle's.

Patrick's heart jumped at the sight of her. It was a confused and brittle moment. He felt a frantic love for Colleen and a murderous hatred for Annabelle. To stop his battering emotions from engulfing him, he gritted his teeth and forced himself to look away.

Earlier that morning, Patrick had been limping, and he'd told Kirkland that he'd sprained an ankle that morning as he stepped down from the gazebo. It was a lie, of course, but he thought he might need the lie if things went badly.

"I'll just go off and wrap the thing," Patrick had said.

Kirkland nodded his approval.

As Kirkland and the Styleses approached, with Colleen at Annabelle's side, Patrick ducked away and slinked off toward a back storage shed where he could wait out the visit. He did not want to face Annabelle. His goal was to get Colleen and Eve away from the place early the next morning and make a run for Ocean Beach. He'd have to stay disciplined and not seek immediate revenge, leaving Annabelle behind, instead, to face her miserable destiny.

He wasn't about to take any chances with Annabelle. Despite his beard, mustache, stoop and limp, Annabelle was a shrewd operator and perceptive observer. It wouldn't be wise to underestimate her. Patrick learned early on as a detective that it wasn't prudent to underestimate your adversary. It could get you killed.

As Kirkland nervously presented the gazebo to Mr. and Mrs. Styles, it was Annabelle who led Colleen forward, pointing at the structure, her face filled with enthusiasm.

That morning, Patrick had placed colored balloon clusters, along with hanging red and yellow ribbons, above the entrance.

"See, Colleen? See the balloons?" Annabelle said. "See the gazebo? It's all yours. It's my coming home present to you."

Colleen stared, lost in dreamy wonder, not speaking. Dressed in a creamy ruffled dress and a blue tailored coat, with a matching blue ribbon in her hair, she held up a finger and pointed at the gazebo.

"Do you like it? Isn't it pretty?" Annabelle asked.

Colleen's sparkling eyes took in the balloons and the fluttering ribbons.

"Do you like it, Colleen?" Leland Styles asked, drifting over. He was a broad, short man in his early fifties, with thinning salt and pepper hair, a stern, heavy face and perceptive dark eyes that held little humor.

Colleen was lost in a make-believe world of pixies and fairies, invisible playmates and colored balloons. She removed her hand from Annabelle's and moved toward the front step.

Annabelle spoke with encouragement. "Go on, Colleen. You can climb up and go in. It's all yours."

Colleen placed a hand on the wood railing and pulled herself up to the first step and then up onto the floor of the gazebo. She turned back to Annabelle with a sunny face and wide, cheery eyes. "Mine? Is it mine?"

"Yes, darling," Annabelle said. "It's my very own present to you."

Kirkland locked his hands behind his back, his eyes searching for Patrick. Leland Styles, dressed in a dark suit and tie, waited patiently, his restless eyes checking his pocket watch.

To Kirkland he said, "Tonight, Mrs. Styles and I are going to the opera to hear Enrico Caruso singing in *Carmen*."

Kirkland pretended to be impressed. He'd heard of Caruso, but he didn't especially like opera. "I hear the man can sing a good high note," Kirkland said, not knowing what else to say.

"That he can, Kirkland. That he can, and it is said you can hear him singing all the way to the back of the house, just as if he were standing only a few feet away from you. But, of course, Mrs. Styles and I will have a grand view from our box seats. I'm excited about the performance, Kirkland, even if Mrs. Styles doesn't share my enthusiasm for the opera. But she will," he said with smug confidence. "Yes, indeed, in time, she will."

Colleen twirled about like a little dancer, swaying gently to imagined music and rhythms.

Annabelle approached Kirkland. "Mr. Kirkland, who placed those balloons and ribbons?"

"That would be Liam Morgan, Mrs. Styles, the man I told you about. He blew them up and hung them this morning. He said, 'I'm sure the little girl will take to balloons, don't you think?' Well, of course, I agreed. Liam built the gazebo, based on what you had written in your letter. I hope you find it to your satisfaction."

Annabelle looked about. "Where is the man?"

"He turned his ankle this morning. He said it was a bit tender, and he was going to find something to wrap it, so he could continue with his work. I have found him to be a good man and a good worker," Kirkland said, offering a positive opinion, hoping it would sway her impression of the man when she met him.

"I wish to see him," Annabelle said.

Mr. Styles made of face of impatience. "My dear, I have much to do today. Is it really necessary that we see this carpenter?" He glanced skyward and held out a hand as if to catch a raindrop. "It's clouding up and will soon rain."

Annabelle stood firmly. "You go on to your business, Leland. I'll wait for the man. Will you find him for me, Mr. Kirkland?"

"Yes, Mrs. Styles," Kirkland said, offering an obedient bow. He went striding off toward the shed where Patrick was hiding, hearing the start of an argument between Mr. and Mrs. Styles as he retreated.

Patrick saw Kirkland coming, and he knew what he was in for. He rose from a wooden bench, squared his shoulders, and prepared to play the role of Liam Morgan for Annabelle, hoping she wouldn't recognize him. When Kirkland told him the Mrs. wanted to see him, Patrick nodded, dreading the grim business to come.

Patrick limped ahead, closing the distance between the Styleses and himself, with Kirkland at his left, offering words of encouragement.

Annabelle wore a royal blue dress with a tightly fitted jacket, button-up boots and a smart, ivory hat with flowers and feathers. She kept a shrewd eye on Liam as he limped toward her, his head down, his bushy black beard adding mystery.

Patrick stopped a good ten feet away, his eyes staring down at the grass.

"This is Liam Morgan," Kirkland said, then stepped back.

In the background they could hear Colleen half-singing, half-talking to a make-believe friend.

Annabelle inspected Patrick's brown leather work apron, his scuffed black boots, his short hair, and the beard and mustache. There was a vague familiarity about him that rang a tiny bell in her head; that lent additional interest to the moment.

"Your name is Liam?"

Patrick nodded, his gaze directed down. He spoke softly. "Yes, ma'am."

"The gazebo is your work?"

"Yes, ma'am."

"Where are you from?"

Patrick didn't want to be specific. "Back East."

"Where back East?"

"New York."

"How long have you been in San Francisco?"

"Only months."

"Are you married?"

"Yes, ma'am."

Kirkland spoke up. "His wife is the woman I told you about, Mr. Styles. She's a wizard at the books."

"Good man," Mr. Styles said, fighting boredom. "But you know, I'm not so inclined to have a woman working about the place. They can stir up things… trouble among men."

Kirkland lowered his head and nodded. "Yes, sir."

"What's her name?" Annabelle asked.

Kirkland spoke up, but he was interrupted by Annabelle.

"Let Liam speak. What is your wife's name?"

"Evelyn, ma'am," Patrick said, softly.

Annabelle heard that tiny ringing bell again; a sound of distant warning.

"Look at me, Liam. Lift your head and look at me."

Leland Styles said, "My dear, can we please conclude this business? The hour is waning."

Annabelle ignored her husband, her full attention on Patrick as he slowly lifted his head, his eyes fixed in a squint.

Patrick felt her icy glare on him, while his gaze was directed to a point beyond, to a beautiful blue gum eucalyptus tree.

Annabelle's face filled with dark suspicion as her mind flew back in time, and then ahead in time.

When Patrick faced her fully, his worst fears were realized. He saw recognition flare in her eyes.

"I know you," she said, in a low, alarmed voice. "I know you. You're not Liam Morgan. You are Patrick Gantly."

She whirled to her husband. "Call the police. Now!"

Leland stiffened, confused. "What?"

Kirkland jerked his hands from his pockets, bewildered.

Patrick's eyes leapt left and right. The game was up. He'd have to run for it.

"Call the police, Leland. This man has come to take Colleen!"

Patrick pivoted, glancing at the gazebo and Colleen, cursing under his breath that he was so close to his little girl, and yet so far. He broke into a gallop, heading for a patch of trees, keeping his limp, knowing that when the police went searching for him, the description would include a limp.

"Stop him!" Annabelle shouted. "Stop him, Kirkland!"

Cole Kirkland stood flat-footed, glancing around at Patrick's retreating figure, completely at a loss. "But Mrs. Styles... I..."

Leland cut in. "Annabelle, come to your senses!" he demanded. "What madness has taken hold of you?"

Annabelle turned to her husband with hostility. "Call the police right now, you stupid man, or so help me God, I'll kill you!"

Leland staggered back, stricken.

Annabelle swung her fiery gaze to Kirkland. "And get me that wife of his. Go get her and bring her to me. Now!"

CHAPTER 47

By late afternoon, Patrick stood anxiously before the bathroom mirror in a furnished house in the Mission District. He and Eve had rented it the week before, in case they needed a safe place to hide. He stared hard at his worried face, having just shaved off his beard and mustache.

Following his escape from the Styleses' mansion, he'd made a dash back to the apartment, praying that Eve had fled before Annabelle trapped her. He was feeling miserably sorry that he hadn't been able to help.

Now, he had two big problems instead of one and, with both, time was of the essence. By now, the police had surely burst down his and Eve's apartment door and were searching for him.

Earlier, at the apartment, Patrick had grabbed their leather suitcase and packed all the important items they'd need in the short term. Under his shirt, he'd strapped on Eve's money belt that contained two credit cards, their 2021 IDs, some antibiotics, and keys to their West 105th Street apartment. Before he'd bolted from the apartment, he'd grabbed the canvas bag holding the lantern and pushed his Smith & Wesson .38 revolver into his coat pocket, ensuring it was fully loaded.

Outside, Patrick had walked steadily, without a limp, flagged a horse-drawn cab and instructed the driver to take him to the Mission District. Upon arrival, he had walked casually to the furnished, single-family house and waited for Eve, praying she'd appear soon.

Everything had gone wrong. Eve was missing, and Annabelle would have ordered twenty-four-hour police protection for Colleen. His simple, intrepid plan—sneaking into the house in early morning and carrying Colleen off—was now worthless. And worse, where was Eve? If she'd been trapped and jailed, he'd have to find a way to get her out.

Patrick dried his clean-shaven face with a towel, left the bathroom, and settled onto the sagging sofa. He placed the revolver next to him and glanced at his watch. It was after four. If Eve had escaped from the mansion, she should have arrived by now.

He lowered his face in his hands and forced his mind to come up with another plan. Any plan. If Eve had been jailed, the police could only hold her on suspicion. There was no real proof that she had tried to kidnap Colleen. But then, on the other hand, Annabelle's husband was a multimillionaire. His bribes could keep Eve in jail for as long as Annabelle wished.

Patrick stood and began to pace, feeling the tension in the roots of his hair. His priority was to find out what had happened to Eve. If she were in jail, he'd have to find a good lawyer and, in the short term, get her released on bail. And then they'd have to fight fire with fire. They'd have to find a lawyer who could do battle against any lawyer Annabelle produced. But then there were the judges. Leland Styles would readily pay them off at the direction of his wife, so Patrick had to find a practical or a devious solution.

When he heard the doorknob jiggle, he moved to the sofa, snatched up his revolver and whirled toward the front door, raising it, his finger on the trigger.

A light knock made his eye twitch. Three firm knocks and one soft knock brought a crashing relief. That was their code—three firm knocks, followed by a soft one. It was Eve!

He pocketed the revolver, and in a rush, he unbolted the door and jerked it open. Eve, faint and weary, nearly fell into his arms. He seized her hand and pulled her inside, closing and locking the door, then pulling down the shade.

They stood in a tight embrace, neither speaking, their breath loud and deep.

"Thank God, Eve. Thank God, you made it."

He led her to the sofa, and she eased down, leaning her head back and closing her eyes.

"I'm so tired and stressed out."

Patrick sat next to her, placing the revolver on a side table. He kissed her forehead and stroked her hair. "I was worried sick. There was no time for me to warn you. What happened?"

"Thank God you made a friend."

"What friend?"

"The nannie from Ireland. Rose Dolan. When you were speaking with Annabelle, she came out and joined Colleen in the gazebo. Did you notice her?"

"No, I had my eyes down most of the time, for all the good it did me. And then I had to run for it."

"Rose overheard what was going on, and she took a big chance. She grabbed Colleen up in her arms, pretending to protect her, and came running into the shed to warn me that Annabelle was demanding to see me. She saved me."

"God love the girl for her good heart."

"She may have saved my life, Patrick."

"Indeed, she did. There's no telling what Annabelle would have done had she gotten her dirty hands on you. Was Colleen with Rose?"

Eve opened her eyes and turned her head to him. "Yes."

Patrick sat up. "Did she recognize you?"

Eve sighed, dropping her head. "No… I'm sure it was because of my disguise, the dark short hair and glasses."

Patrick watched her eyes spill tears, and he gently wiped them.

"She's grown so much, Patrick, and we were so close to her."

"Yes, she has," Patrick said, darkly. "I'll never forgive that woman for taking Colleen away from us. Never."

Eve placed a forearm over her eyes. "What are we going to do, Patrick?"

Patrick rose. "As I see it, there's only one thing we can do."

"What?"

"We attack."

Eve lowered her arm and sat up. "Attack? What? When? How?"

Patrick's jaw firmed up. "We can't wait, Eve. The longer we wait, the easier it will be for the police to find us. And they will find us, eventually, no matter how we try to hide. And I'm not leaving until we have Colleen."

"Okay... I'm lost, Patrick, and I'm out of ideas. What can we do? You know they'll have police stationed at all the doors. They'll have police in the house. You know Annabelle isn't going to take any chances now that she knows we're here."

"They'll be expecting me at night. It's logical. It makes sense."

Eve waited for more.

"I'm going into the house early in the morning, a little before five. Sunrise is about five-thirty, so they won't be expecting that."

Eve shook her head. "They'll catch you, Patrick."

"I'll have a hat pulled low over my forehead, and I'll be beardless, with no mustache, and I won't be limping. I'll creep in and hang out by the tool shed for a time, wearing my work clothes. The police will get a good look at me and think I'm just another workman."

"What if one of the other men sees you? Or Cole Kirkland?"

"I know his schedule. He doesn't arrive at work until just before seven o'clock. We'll be long gone by then."

Eve scratched her head, her eyes moving, her brain working. "Patrick, there'll be policemen in the house. What are you going to do, go in blasting away?"

He nodded, grimly. "Yes, if I have to."

Eve leapt up. "That's not a good plan, Patrick. If you're shot and killed, where will that leave me?"

He swallowed a heaviness. "Then you'll have to light the lantern and go home."

"No! No way, Patrick! I'm not letting you do this, and I'm not leaving Colleen. We have to come up with something else. Something better."

Patrick stepped to her. "There is nothing else, Eve. I've been grinding through plan after plan, and this one is best. It's bold. It's quick. And it will be a surprise, and that's what we need. And there's one more part to my plan. On my way over from the apartment, I stopped in Chinatown and bought some fireworks. Something told me I might need them during our escape. I'll set them off as a distraction, just before I make my move into the house. That will buy me some time."

Eve wasn't sold on the idea, but her mind had locked up. "Patrick, you won't even know for sure where Colleen will be. She'll probably be with Annabelle in her room, which will be guarded."

"I'll find Colleen. If I can get inside that house, which I will, I'll find her, and Annabelle won't stop me. Not anymore. We've come too far. I'll find Colleen and I'll take Colleen, and Annabelle better not try to stop me."

Eve's pulse soared. "Patrick, that is a massive house with over forty rooms. Use your head. Annabelle and Colleen could be in any of those rooms, hiding, or maybe Annabelle has taken Colleen and left town. There are just too many unknowns."

His voice was soft, controlled, and weary. "My love... I have to do this. We've come too far. Waiting is not an option. Bold action is needed now. Trust me. I know that Annabelle holds most of the cards, but I have to play the only card I have. Bold surprise and speed. I will be careful, for sure, and I will be deadly, if I must. And once I have Colleen safely in my arms, I will be fleet of foot. You will be in that cab, waiting for us on California Street, and we will make our escape. If we can't get to the beach, we'll light the lantern wherever we are and hope for the best."

Eve turned aside, her shoulders sagging, her voice rusty and resigned. "All right, Patrick… All right. I'll be there in that cab, praying like I've never prayed before."

CHAPTER 48

It was still dark when Patrick and Eve awoke, each lying still, staring up at the ceiling.

"Are you hungry?" Eve asked.

"No... I won't be eating until this is over. My stomach is not in the best shape."

"I have a headache," Eve said. "And a soul ache."

"It will be over soon, my love."

At three-thirty, Patrick left the double bed, took a bath, dressed, checked the revolver and slipped it into his right coat pocket.

Eve had bathed and dressed and was at the front door when Patrick put on his work apron and shrugged into his thin overcoat.

"It looks chilly out there today," he said.

Eve was silent and sullen, standing still, waiting.

Patrick stepped over to her. "As I said, I'll make my move into the house a bit before five. From Rose Dolan, I learned that Annabelle sleeps soundly until eight-thirty or nine. With only a small amount of luck,

I'll have Colleen by five-fifteen, run out of the house and meet you at the waiting cab."

Patrick kissed her tenderly. "See you soon, Mrs. Eve Sharland Gantly."

BY FOUR-FIFTEEN, PATRICK had climbed the steep hill on the west side of the mansion and was hiding in the shadows of a tree line, watchful. With several lawn lights illuminating the area, he was close enough to see the shadows of policemen patrolling the grounds. He drew closer, waited, and observed.

One cop was stationed near the gazebo, one was making a slow circle of the mansion grounds, and another policeman was positioned at the back door, the one Patrick would enter.

Long ago, Patrick had learned to use fear to his advantage. He'd mentally flip a switch, and the fear would transform into alert determination. At ten minutes to five, as soft gray and peach light tinted the horizon, Patrick sauntered onto the grounds, his gait easy, his head down. When the cop circumnavigating the mansion saw him, Patrick lifted his hand and waved, and then he made his way to the shed.

The policeman waved back and kept on going. Patrick relaxed a little. The cop by the gazebo, who was about twenty yards away, eyed Patrick carefully. Patrick nodded at the cop and whistled a tuneless song, then tugged the bill of his cap down further over his forehead.

Patrick knew that, at this time of day, there might be two handymen around. They often arrived early, but they would be inside a shed on the other side of the house, drinking coffee and bantering.

The Christmas Eve Journey

Patrick entered the empty shed and removed the three rows of firecrackers, two with short fuses and one with a long fuse. He would hide that one in the back of the shed where it wouldn't be easily found, hoping it would create a further distraction after the cops found the first two and walked away.

He glanced at his pocket watch. It was nearly five a.m. Time to act. He pulled a small box of matches from his apron, removed one, struck it and touched the flame to the long fuse of firecrackers hidden behind a stack of lumber. The fuse caught, flared, and sizzled.

With quick steps, he hurried over to the two short fuses near the front door and lit them. They crackled to life. He had only about three minutes before those firecrackers would go off. The long fuse would take several more minutes.

Patrick left the shed, stretching his arms toward the dawning sky, then he put a hand to a yawn, walking easily. The cop at the gazebo saw him, then glanced away with indifference. The policeman at the back door was smoking a cigarette, looking fatally bored. The cop circling the mansion was nowhere in sight.

At the first exploding POP-POP-POP, the cop at the gazebo jerked toward the noise. The rapid, machine-gun-like sound went bang-bang-bang-bang. BOOM. The cop at the back door threw himself forward, flipping away his cigarette.

Both cops tore off toward the shed as Patrick went striding aggressively toward the now unguarded back door that led to his staircase. Inside, he closed and locked the door, then moved toward the stairs. He glanced about and, not seeing anyone, he started up the stairs, his hand on the cool, walnut grip of his revolver.

On the second floor, he edged toward the door that led out into the grandeur of the second-floor hallway. He strained his ears but heard nothing except the exploding firecrackers. When the door was yanked open, Patrick stood, startled, facing a flat-nosed cop with narrowed eyes and an ugly, pockmarked face.

"Who are you?" he barked. "What are you doing up here!?"

Patrick didn't hesitate. He slammed his right fist into the cop's face. The cop staggered back, blood flowing from his nose. Patrick lunged forward and drove a hard fist into the man's stomach that bent him at the waist, and air exploded from his mouth. Patrick finished him with a sure blow to the right jaw.

The cop stumbled left, crashing into a priceless Louis XV table, toppling an antique vase that shattered on the floor. The cop spilled onto the floor, not moving.

His body taut, eyes watchful, his legs springy, Patrick crept down the dimly lighted hallway toward Colleen's room. The fireworks outside were whistling and exploding, sounding like battle.

When a door opened and Annabelle Styles burst out, Patrick stopped cold. She was about thirty feet away, wearing a belted ivory silk robe and elegant red slippers.

There was a partially lit, two-tiered chandelier above her, illuminating her luscious hair, which was arranged casually on top of her head and pinned, strands of it loose around her face. Her expression was not pretty. It was defiant and frigid, her stance erect, feet planted firmly, ready for a fight.

The Christmas Eve Journey

Low in her throat, she said, "I knew you'd come, you bastard."

"I'm here to take my daughter home... And I came to break your neck, just as I promised I would, way out there in the future when you took Colleen."

Her laugh was hoarse and mirthless. Patrick saw no fear in her.

"Patrick... Patrick Gantly... I thought you were smarter than the other men out there. I really thought you were special. And there are so many stupid men in the world. You have no idea. Yes, but I thought you were different. But, as handsome as you are, it turns out that you're just as stupid as all the others."

She swiftly reached into her robe pocket and whipped out a derringer, pointing it at Patrick's chest. "Congratulations on finding me, Patrick, but then, I knew you and your little, faithful wife would. But what suckers you are. You truly do deserve each other. Why do you think I married Leland Styles, Patrick? Because I knew you'd come. Yes, I did. But now, you're going to be caught or killed, because Leland is rich, and he is connected to all the politicians and judges. There's no one in this time who will help you."

Patrick's grin was a threat.

"Still not frightened by me, Patrick?"

"No, Annabelle. You may get one shot off before I get to you, but before you squeeze off the second, I'll have my hands around your throat. You'll be dead before you hit the floor."

Annabelle's expression changed to bleak amusement. She glared at him, aiming the pistol. "Goodbye, Patrick."

Patrick was ready to leap forward when a door opened behind Annabelle. For a second, she lost her focus.

The fireworks stopped. Dead quiet.

Annabelle whipped her head around to see her husband, Leland, standing there, fully dressed, his face filled with stunned confusion.

"Annabelle? What are you doing out here in your robe? Who is this man? And what in the hell are you doing with a gun? Put that thing away. Now! You must stop disrupting my home. I won't have it, I tell you. I won't have it!"

To Patrick's utter astonishment, Annabelle turned, aimed, and fired at her husband. Leland's eyes bulged in shock, the bullet slamming into his heart. Before he dropped to the floor, Annabelle whirled back to Patrick, her gun poised and ready. But Patrick had pulled his own revolver, and it was pointed at her head.

They stared, and their eyes held in a deadly challenge.

"You might hit me, Annabelle, but that's only a two-shot derringer, with one shot left. This is a .38, and it holds six rounds. I won't miss. I'm a good shot, too."

Some of the confidence left her face. "I will shoot you, Patrick."

"And I will certainly shoot you, you vile, twisted woman."

Patrick saw Annabelle's cold eyes. Saw her finger touch the trigger. In that instant, his third set of fireworks shattered the quiet, sounding like the rapid fire of combat.

For one distracted second, Annabelle flinched as she squeezed the trigger. Her hand jerked, her aim wide.

The bullet bit into the shoulder of Patrick's coat, missing flesh.

Annabelle froze, the empty derringer still pointed at Patrick, her confidence melting away, her eyes swelling with fear. Patrick started toward her, the barrel of the gun aimed at her head.

She swallowed and stepped back, lowering her gun. When she spoke, her voice quivered with fear. "You won't kill me in cold blood, Patrick. You're not the type. I know men. All kinds of men, and you're not the type."

Patrick caught the note of hysteria in her voice, as more of her courage was draining away. He advanced to her, stopping only a few feet away, his face granite hard, his eyes burning. "Where is Colleen? Where is my daughter?" he asked, in a deadly calm.

Annabelle suppressed panic. "Inside my room. She's sleeping inside. She's safe. I love her, Patrick. I love her more than I love my life. I love her more than I have ever loved anything."

Patrick's voice held barely contained fury. "Colleen is not your daughter, Annabelle. She never has been, and she never will be."

Annabelle worked to build back courage. She dropped her gun and placed fists on her hips, presenting a little sneer. "You're not going to kill me, Patrick. You don't have the guts."

Patrick's finger was itching to pull the trigger, and he truly believed that the world would be a better place if Annabelle Palmer were dead. He didn't care that she'd been damaged in childhood. He didn't care that she'd been abused. She could have made other, better choices. She could have built a better life for herself in

1906 or received mental health assistance in the twenty-first century. He didn't give a damn about this sick, evil woman. In that moment, he was more nineteenth-century man than twenty-first-century psychologist.

In a swift, sure motion, Patrick moved in, swinging a fist that was packed with revenge and rage. It slammed into her right jaw, hurling her hard into the wall, her eyes stunned and glassy. She tottered, faltered, then dropped in a heap, her hair falling loose, spilling over her unconscious face.

Wasting no time, Patrick dropped the revolver back into his coat pocket, ducked into Annabelle's vast, dimly lighted bedroom, and hurried to the bed, where Colleen sat up, blinking sleepy eyes.

"Colleen… It's Daddy."

She awoke slowly, confused, squinting. "Daddy?"

"Yes, my little lass. It's Daddy, come to take you home to see Colin."

Her cloudy eyes suddenly cleared, and her face lit up. "Daddy!" she said, reaching for him. "It's Daddy!"

He gathered her warm body up into his arms and pressed her close, his grateful eyes closed and leaking tears.

"Daddy! Where were you? Why didn't you come?"

"I'm here now, my precious girl. I'm here," he said, holding her up before him, his smile wide. "Daddy's here and we're going home. It's time to go home now."

He hugged her again. "Home we go, little girl."

Patrick knew he had but little time before the police arrived. "Do you have a coat?"

She pointed. "Yes, Daddy. My coat is in there."

"The closet?"

"Annabelle put my clothes in there last night."

Cradling her in an arm, Patrick hurried to a window, yanked the cord, and parted a curtain to let natural light in. He moved swiftly to the closet, opened the door, and slid back Colleen's dresses until he found her coat. He grabbed it and a dress, found some lace-up shoes, and stuffed the shoes and the dress in the pockets of his work apron.

He sat Colleen down and adroitly helped her into the coat.

"I need my dress, Daddy."

"Yes, I know. We'll put it on later. Right now, we're going to meet Mommy, then we'll put on the dress and the shoes. Now it's time to dash away."

"Mommy!" Colleen cried, glancing about. "Where's Mommy?"

"She's waiting for us. Let's go."

With Colleen clutched in his arm, Patrick moved toward the door. He ventured a look up and down the hallway. He saw Leland, dead. Annabelle was still unconscious, her breathing soft.

"Why is Annabelle down on the ground, Daddy? Is she sleeping?"

"Yes, she is."

Patrick exited the room, turning left, heading off toward the back staircase. When he heard a loud voice calling from behind, he glanced back. It was a cop, his revolver raised, and he was about seventy feet away.

"Hey, you! Stop! What's all this? Stop! Stop, I say, or I'll shoot."

Patrick did not pull his gun. He didn't want to shoot a cop. On impulse, he waved and smiled. "Hello." Then he broke for the hall door that led to his staircase.

The cop stood next to Leland's dead body, his startled eyes finding Annabelle's prone figure. "Stop! You! Stop!"

He leveled his gun and fired at Patrick.

CHAPTER 49

Patrick hunched his body, protecting Colleen as a bullet whizzed over his head. The next shot wouldn't miss, so Patrick took evasive action, darting away, weaving left and right. Another shot rang out—but missed. Patrick was close to the stairs. He was so close. He had to make it.

Suddenly, beneath his feet, the floor shifted. Above, a chandelier swayed. He stopped, feeling dizzy and disoriented. Something was wrong. Had a bullet struck him? He struggled ahead, but faltered when the floor wobbled, and the building groaned as if it had taken a blow. He took quick steps and fought for balance.

As Colleen cried out in fear, he glanced back at the cop and saw the ceiling plaster fall in a great shower, striking the policeman, covering him and Leland. The lights went out, the world trembled, and Patrick watched in disbelief as large chunks of plaster cascaded down, burying Annabelle's body.

"It's the earthquake!" Patrick shouted, and a great animal panic rose in him.

Colleen's eyes were spooked. "Daddy, we're shaking."

Patrick had to get outside, and fast. The entire building creaked and shuddered; windows shattered; a chandelier swung like a pendulum. Outside, he heard screams and cries for help.

Holding Colleen fast, Patrick struggled to the hall door as ceiling plaster rained down and wall mirrors fell, smashing.

He yanked the door open, and what he saw stopped him. The entire staircase was swaying. As he stood there, the handrail snapped like a pretzel stick and crashed to the floor below. Could he chance the stairs? Would they hold him? He had no choice.

Colleen started to cry. "Daddy… I'm scared. Daddy. It's shaking, Daddy. Shaking."

"It's okay, Colleen. Hang onto me, lass. We'll be all right."

Patrick paused at the top stair, praying he built the thing solid enough to hold them. He smelled smoke and was certain the house had caught on fire. He had to go, and now. Pulling a breath, he ventured a foot forward and started down, feeling the sway of the thing as if he were on a ship in a storm.

"Daddy… things are falling down!"

"Hang on, Colleen. Hang on to me!"

With her arms wrapped tightly around his neck, she shut her eyes, tears streaming down her cheeks. Each step jerked and shifted as Patrick eased his way down. As he neared the bottom, a great swell shook the entire staircase and Patrick was pitched to the right and nearly fell. He was just able to keep his balance amid flying glass, timber, and plaster.

The back door was open and swinging on its hinges, slamming against the outer wall. Patrick burst through it into the brand-new light of day, chaos all around him, servants and policemen scurrying about. No one noticed him. He looked left and glimpsed the City, witnessing a historical tragedy—flashes of orange flames and great clouds of rising smoke. He had to keep moving.

Seconds later, the shaking stopped, and the ring and clang of racing fire engines filled the air with a terrible sense of doom and destruction. Patrick glanced up at the house and saw black, acrid smoke billowing from the third-floor windows and a burst of fire shooting from the roof. The house had been built in the 1870s, and not completely wired for electricity. Patrick was sure the broken gas lines and shattered lamps had ignited, turning the interior into a raging inferno.

Colleen's eyes were wild. He stroked her hair and kissed her cheek. "It's all right, my little one. The shaking has stopped, and we're on our way home."

Patrick made a break for the far street, striding fast across the lawn, his legs strong and sure. Then he saw her. Eve was running toward him, wildly waving with one hand, the other gripping the canvas bag holding the lantern. When they'd closed the distance, Eve spotted Colleen and her face opened in joy. Eve dropped the bag and reached for her with both hands.

"Colleen!"

Eve had ditched her glasses, and her short, dark hair was free in the smoky morning wind. Patrick handed

Colleen over, and Eve swung her about, planting kisses on her cheeks and wet eyes. "Hello, baby!"

Colleen wiped tears and pointed. "Look, Mommy... it was shaking. That house. Look at that fire. Let's go, Mommy. I'm scared!"

Eve hugged her close. "Yes, darling. Yes, we're going."

"Eve, where's the cab?" Patrick asked. "We have to get out of here. There will be aftershocks."

Eve cradled Colleen, feeling the new, heavy weight of her. "The cab's gone. When the earthquake struck, the horse went crazy. I just managed to get out before the carriage bolted away."

Grimacing in frustration, Patrick looked around. "All right, we have to find something else. Let's get out on the street. Maybe something will come by."

As they started off, with Colleen tucked into Eve's arm, an aftershock shook the ground. They paused briefly, looking down, their feet feeling the unsteady vibration. When it stopped, Eve handed Colleen back to Patrick. "My legs feel like rubber, and you're stronger than I am."

On California Street, there were frantic screams and children crying, as horses whinnied and galloped, and dogs barked. Servants and masters alike watched flames shoot out from windows. Walls collapsed, and the glass roof of a conservatory splintered and came crashing down, littering the street.

Eve and Patrick frantically searched for a cab, but there were none. Returning to the center of the city wasn't an option. It was engulfed in flames and smoke.

"Should we light the lantern here, Patrick?" Eve asked, searching around.

"No, we can't take the chance. Let's go up the street. Sometimes there are delivery wagons parked up there."

Ten minutes later, they came upon a grizzled, bearded man with stooped shoulders, shabby clothes, and a dusty bowler shoved back on his head. He stood next to a battered, four-sided wooden cart, casually taking in the disaster while smoking his clay pipe. His swayback horse stood by, equally unimpressed.

Patrick handed Colleen off to Eve and approached the man. "Sir, I can make it worth your while if you'll give us a ride in your cart."

The man pulled the pipe from his mouth and took Patrick in, his two wary eyes peering out from a stale and shriveled face. "Where will you be goin' then, pilgrim?"

"To Ocean Beach, just below the Cliff House."

The man scratched his beard with the stem of his pipe while he thought about it. He pointed toward the smoking city. "It's lookin' like the end of the world, I think. My old, dear mother, rest her soul in the bosom of peace, said the end would be coming and, by God, here it be. All these mansions will be rubble and smoke by nightfall… And so goes the way of the rich, who are taking a mighty fall, pilgrim. Make no mistake about that."

"We're in a bit of a hurry," Patrick said. "I'll give you twenty-five dollars."

The man thought it over, looked at Colleen, and grinned at her. "Now there's a pretty little Miss, ain't she?"

Eve smiled at the man. "Thank you, sir. We need to take her home."

He gave Colleen a quick, good-humored smile. "Of course you do, little Miss."

Colleen embraced Eve's neck, glancing away, shyly. "Home. I want to go home."

"Well, all right then, little Miss, old Tack Hardy here, yep, that's my name, will take you where you want to go, and he'll do it for the good price you quoted. I figure with that kind of money, I'll be the lucky one to go on a bender before the devil comes along and snatches me up. All right, climb up. I've been a haulin' gravel and coal cinders, so it's going to be a might dusty back there, if you please."

They piled in with the canvas bag, Patrick sitting with his back to the side and Eve sitting opposite him, with Colleen resting on her lap. Just as they were about to get underway, Tack Hardy turned to them, pointing with the stem of his pipe to a house nearby, engulfed in flames.

"I used to haul gravel, lumber and brick to that house. Yep, I did. I just left Mr. Conners, the owner of that grand house. He says to me, 'Yesterday morning, I was worth six hundred thousand dollars. Now, this house is all I have left. It will all be gone in fifteen minutes.'"

Eve and Patrick looked on sadly.

"All right, folks," Tack said. "We'll be off, and in no hurry to get there, with old Betsy doing the work."

Tack Hardy pulled a half-drunk pint of whiskey from his coat pocket, pulled the cork and tipped it back, taking a refreshing drink. After replacing the bottle and expressing a satisfied burp, he cracked his whip, and Betsy clambered off, head down, plodding off for the steep hill as the cart rattled along.

En route to Ocean Beach, Eve and Patrick stared sorrowfully as they passed terrible scenes: debris heaped onto the sidewalks; water bursting from split mains; buildings in ruins; families weeping in the streets; smoke and fallen brick everywhere. The streets were humped into ridges and depressions, piled with the wreckage of fallen walls, and the smoke from the burning City was a frightening spectacle, and visible for many miles.

Eve and Patrick gazed at each other, their eyes tired, their faces weary. The hanging, stringy smoke was pervasive, the lowering gray sky gloomy. But as Colleen leaned back against Eve, their moods lifted a little, and they became hopeful. They'd soon light the lantern and go home.

"Can I ask?" Eve said, just above a whisper.

"What?"

Eve mouthed the words so Colleen couldn't hear. "Annabelle?"

Patrick kept his voice low. "Do you mean, is she alive? Is that what you want to know?"

"You don't have to tell me. I don't need to know what happened."

"That's one of your clever manipulations, Eve Aleta Sharland Gantly. You say you don't need to know, when what you truly mean is, tell me, or I'll never stop asking."

Her blue eyes were intensely serious, inspecting him. She gently covered Colleen's ears. "Okay... Tell me."

"I don't know if she's dead. She was inside the house when I left it. I struck her... I struck her rather hard, but she was breathing. She wasn't dead. When the earthquake struck, everything seemed to fall, the ceiling, mirrors, glass. She may have been killed then or when the house caught fire. She'd just shot and killed her husband."

Eve's eyes grew large. "What?"

"She's lost, Eve… She's a lost soul."

"Did you find out if she had a lantern?"

"No."

"Did you tell her that her mother is dead?"

"I was a little busy, and there wasn't time for a long conversation. She shot at me, but fortunately, some firecrackers came to my aid and she just missed."

Relieved and exhausted, Eve removed her hands from Colleen's ears and kissed her hair. It was a desperate kiss. A kiss that realized how fragile life truly is, and how death is always lurking. As she took in a breath, her lungs filled with smoke and she coughed.

"We'll soon be by the sea, Eve," Patrick said. "… And the air will be clean."

IT SEEMED AN ETERNITY before they arrived at Ocean Beach. Patrick left the cart first, accepted Colleen, then took Eve's hand as she jumped down. Patrick paid Tack Hardy and then watched the horse trot off as Tack took another generous pull on his whiskey bottle.

The broad beach was more crowded than they had imagined it would be, but then, they hadn't anticipated an earthquake. They looked up, surprised to see that the Cliff House Restaurant still stood. It had not collapsed, caught on fire, or fallen from the cliffs into the sea.

All around them were grieving and haunted faces, and everyone had a terrifying story to tell. Eve and Patrick moved away from the crowds as quickly as they could. They wanted to light the lantern and go home, even if there were no guarantees the lantern would do what they wished.

At a few minutes before eight a.m., they found a secluded, quiet place near a cluster of tall, craggy rocks, and decided to leave from there. The tide would rush in at 8:45, seize the lantern and, they hoped, carry it out to sea.

Patrick checked the money belt that was fastened around his waist to ensure it was snug. Then he looked at Eve and nodded. "Let's go."

They stood close, drained by the tragic events and by the entire arduous journey. Eve kneeled by the lantern, struck a match, and guided the flame into the lantern door to the wick. When the buttery flame caught and flared, Eve got to her feet.

Patrick held Colleen snugly in his left arm and gripped Eve's hand firmly in the other. When they saw the light explode up and engulf them, Eve and Patrick locked eyes and smiled.

Patrick kissed Colleen's cheek. "Ready for your journey, Colleen?"

She pouted and shook her head, her wide eyes taking in the glorious light all around her. "No…"

Eve and Patrick laughed.

Eve said, "We'll be okay, wherever we go, as long as we're together."

Twenty minutes later, a surging wave rushed in and crawled up the sand, toppling the lantern. A second rolling wave thundered in. It wrapped the lantern in a foamy embrace and swept it out to sea. As a needle-fine rain fell, two gulls wheeled and cried and sailed over the distant high cliffs, vanishing into a smoky fog.

CHAPTER 50

A weak sun rose, struggling to break through feathery clouds. It flattened out on an ocean that rolled into white crests and went roaring to shore, curling, thudding, sliding up the beach in foaming waves. There was fog and a chilly wind, and there were surfers riding waves and fishermen wading into the surf.

Seagulls flapped, wheeled and settled on jagged rocks, and a flock of pigeons surged over the broad beach, fighting a head wind.

Eve's eyes struggled open, her vision a blur, seeing the world as a kind of shining blue mirage. She was cold; she was confused; she was lying on her back. Where was she?

With a complaining effort, she pushed up on elbows, studying everything, every possible stray detail. She felt hung over, her mouth dry. She examined her dress, a deep blue color, long, heavy and damp with sand.

Nineteenth century style? Her leather boots had a slight heel, and they were tight to her feet, and they were wet.

She stretched out her stiff legs and, as the morning light caught her face, she squinted out toward the glassy horizon, where fog hovered. Sitting up, she felt her damp hair matted with sand, and she raked a hand through it, confused that it was so short. Her face broke into a worried grimace, her brain stalled, her senses dulled.

As the sun warmed her, breaking through rolling fog, Eve's mind began to clear. Suddenly, there was a dawning, as her clogged thoughts released waterfalls of memory. She sat up. Where were Patrick and Colleen?

Eve climbed to her feet, slapping sand from her dress, and saw fishermen near the tideline, casting out to sea. She saw surfers dancing across surfboards, challenging surging waves. She saw people roaming the beach.

Her brain lit up, banishing the shadows, and she recalled that she'd lighted the lantern, and Patrick and Colleen had been beside her. What had happened to them?

In an agony of despair, she pulled herself together and searched up and down the beach. She saw the jagged rocks, looming in a patch of lingering fog, about eighty feet away. Yes! That's where they were when she'd lit the lantern in 1906.

Eve hurried off, her boots stabbing at the wet sand, her heart thrumming. She looked up and saw the Cliff House, but it wasn't the Cliff House from 1906. It was a more modern building, looking ghostly in the thick fog curling around it, and the fog shrouded the cliffs beyond as the wind wheezed in her ears.

She was holding her breath when she approached a rocky bluff near a cluster of craggy rocks. Turning right into a little cove, she saw them, Patrick and Colleen, sprawled on the sand, Colleen's body tucked in close to her father. Of course, they were asleep. They had to be asleep!

Eve hurried over, dropped to her knees, and sighed out relief when she saw Patrick and Colleen were breathing. But it was cold and, like her, they were damp. They had to get out of there and find a place to warm up before they caught pneumonia.

Eve touched Patrick's shoulder and gently shook him. The ocean surf was loud and close; the wind gasped and circled.

"Patrick... Patrick, wake up... Wake up, Patrick."

A hand jumped, and his fingers wiggled, but his eyes stayed closed.

"Patrick! Wake up."

One eye opened. "Whhhaat? Go away."

Eve reached for Colleen. She was freezing, her lips blue. Eve didn't panic; she let the professional in her take over. Lifting the child, she embraced her and vigorously rubbed her back, her arms and her legs, hoping to build warmth.

Patrick stirred, groaned, sat up and winced, looking about, dazed. Seconds later, his eyes cleared, and he focused on Eve and Colleen. He tried to speak, failed, swallowed twice, and tried again.

"Where are we? What year is it?"

"I don't know, but we have to find someplace warm. Colleen is freezing."

On wobbly legs, Eve started off, Patrick clutching Colleen close to his chest. They staggered out onto the beach and saw a man wearing a ball cap, shorts, a windbreaker and sneakers, staring out to sea. Eve approached him, steadying herself with an effort, knowing she must look half crazy.

"Sir, how do we get off this beach?"

He was a heavy man with a face of pouchy discontent. He gave her a few seconds of appraisal, then pointed. "See that pier? That's the nearest way out."

Eve didn't hesitate to ask him the next question. "Sir, what's the date?"

His expression held a stern pity. "Why don't you lay off the booze, lady? It's going to destroy your pretty looks."

"Please… tell me, what is the date?"

"It's Thursday, December 2, 2021."

Eve wanted to leap for joy, but she contained herself. She thanked him, joined Patrick and Colleen, and led them off the beach.

AFTER THEY'D LEFT THE BEACH, Colleen awakened in her father's arms, complaining that she was cold. They found a taxi and a hotel, and Eve immediately gave Colleen a hot bath, while Patrick ordered food from a local pizzeria.

While Colleen splashed in the tub, Eve monitored her physical and mental health. The warm water helped to revive her, and the pizza that came later brought a squealing happiness. To Eve's and Patrick's relief, the color had returned to Colleen's cheeks; she was animated and talkative, and she was hungry.

"I didn't eat pizza with Annabelle," Colleen said while she stuffed a bite into her mouth. "I like pizza so much."

Eve and Patrick said nothing, hoping Colleen would forget about Annabelle in a year or so. They hoped she'd forget the entire encounter, though Eve realized the chances were slim, given the trip to Europe and Annabelle's obvious care and affection.

"She'll remember parts of it," Eve said to Patrick later. "But I'm hoping that by the time she's seven, she will have forgotten most of it, and it will seem like a dream."

After Eve and Patrick showered, Eve put Colleen to bed for a nap. Then, she went to the front desk and borrowed a coat from the lost and found rack. Following the desk clerk's instructions to the nearest drugstore and used clothing store, she set off.

In a local thrift shop, Eve found cheap underwear and second-hand clothing for herself and Patrick, but there wasn't much to choose from for a three-year-old. Eve returned to the hotel with a flannel shirt, a blue cardigan and a pair of jeans for Colleen, and casual travel clothes for Patrick and herself.

At ten o'clock that night, Eve and Patrick were snuggled under the thick comforter, with Colleen asleep and warm between them. They listened as her breathing slowed and deepened, and then settled.

"Patrick?" Eve asked.

"Yes…"

"As I was shopping today, I had a thought."

"I've had many. What's yours?"

"It's December second. On December fifth, Sunday, if history repeats itself, Annabelle will have time traveled to New York, and I'll read about it on my phone on that website called *Neighborhood Shout Out*... And Annabelle will be alive."

Patrick was silent.

"Do you think history will repeat itself?" Eve asked.

"I don't know. I suppose we could ask to borrow someone's phone and *Google* Annabelle Palmer and see what comes up."

"Do you want to do that?" Eve asked.

"No. And I also don't want to click on the *Neighborhood Shout Out* website on December fifth to see if some strange woman from 1904, or whatever, has been found roaming around, lost and confused."

"And another thing," Eve said.

Patrick nestled his head close to hers. "Yes, my love. Let's hear it so we can be even more baffled and confused together. On second thought, don't say it."

"Say what?" Eve asked.

"So, therefore, we will never have to time travel again, because we don't have a lantern with which to travel. All the Tesla lanterns, as far as we are concerned, are gone."

Patrick heard Eve sigh. "What's that sigh for?"

"You're right. Every time we say we'll never have to time travel again, we end up being shot off to some distant past."

"Well, it's better than being sent to the future."

"Oh, Lord, don't even think of such a thing."

"But you're right, Patrick. We are lanternless... and I know that's not a word."

There was such a long silence that Patrick thought Eve had fallen asleep.

"Patrick?"

"Yes…"

"Maybe we're just shadows… made-up dreams, and we're doomed just to search and grope and try to find some kind of truth."

"What truth?" Patrick asked. "We have to define what truth is, don't we?"

"I don't know. But look at all the times and places we've been to, and all the people we've met, and the things that have happened to us. If I close my eyes and think back on it all, it seems like a collection of weird and scary dreams."

"Thank you very much," Patrick answered lightly.

"Except you, of course. You're not a dream, and Colleen isn't a dream."

"Are you so sure?"

More silence.

"Eve?"

"Yes..."

"It's all a great big mystery, isn't it?"

Eve dropped her voice. "Yeah… for sure. The older I get, the more I realize I don't know anything for sure. Except that I love you and Colleen."

"Before I met you, Eve… Before 1885, I thought life was straightforward, practical, and defined. Now?" He let the words drop.

"And now? Go ahead and finish your thought."

"Now… We have each other again. We're a family again. Now, I want to go home and live a simple life. That's all the truth I want or need."

A long moment later, Eve spoke up again. "Patrick?"

"I'm here…"

"What will we find when we get home? I wonder if things will have changed."

"I've been thinking about that, too."

"You're okay with flying home, right? I mean, in one of those flying machines that you despise?"

He sighed. "I'd rather take the train, but I know you haven't the patience for it, and Colleen would undoubtedly fuss and fidget the entire time. So, to answer your question, I'm not okay with it, but… as my old Ma used to say, "If it's drowning you're after, don't torment yourself with shallow water.""

Eve rolled her head to him. "I don't know what that means, and I don't want you to explain it to me."

EPILOGUE

On Christmas Eve morning, the stove was on and the kitchen was hot. Colin was pacing, hoping for a doggie snack, and Colleen sat at her kiddy table, tapping a computer game. When Eve and Patrick had finally made it home, they were relieved to find that, unlike after some of their time travel journeys, nothing in the condo or in their lives had apparently been altered.

Eve and Patrick were bent over their laptop, studying a recipe, humming along with the Christmas carols that floated in softly from the living room smart speaker. Snow flurries were drifting outside the window, just as the weather folk had promised.

Eve wore her Christmas apron, a pattern of evergreen and holly, and Patrick's denim shirt was open at the neck and rolled up at the sleeves. He leaned forward so that their heads were close.

"I forgot that we have to steam this for six to seven hours," Eve said, her face hot. "Whose idea was this, anyway?"

Patrick looked at her and pointed. "Yours. You hatched this project on the plane on our way home from San Francisco. You said, and I quote, 'Let's make an old-fashioned plum pudding for Christmas Eve. Won't that be fun?'"

"Yes, yes, I remember. It was a rhetorical question, Patrick. So, where are we, here? I'm just not good at following recipes. I get nervous and flummoxed."

"Okay… We've blended the fruits, the citron, the peel, the spices and the suet, and we've placed them in a bowl," Patrick said, pointing at the bowl to their left. "I added the one-quarter cup of cognac, and we covered it tightly and refrigerated it for four days. My job was to add one-quarter cup of cognac each following day. As the prep chef, I can confidently say that I succeeded."

Eve looked at him, flashing a vast, substantial smile. "Yes, and I'm sure that while you added cognac to the pudding, you also added some to your own person, didn't you?"

Patrick grinned, showing teeth. "That goes without saying, Eve, since we are celebrating the Christmas season."

Colleen looked up, her face pinched in irritation. "Mommy, I don't like this game. I'm losing."

Eve glanced over. "Choose another one, honey. There are three or four on your computer that you like."

"I don't like them. I want another one."

"Okay, hang on."

Eve wiped her hands on a towel and went to help. While she downloaded two additional games, she looked at Patrick. "We still have to soak the breadcrumbs in milk, sherry or port."

"I'm on it, as your modern expression goes. The recipe also says we need to combine the crumbs with well-beaten eggs and sugar."

"You're the man for that, Mr. Gantly."

Patrick mumbled something under his breath.

"What was that?" Eve asked. "What were you mumbling?"

"I said, leave it to me, and I will do it right," he said, in half-teasing superiority.

Eve stuck her tongue out at him.

"That's a lovely tongue you have there, Mrs. Gantly."

Imitating her mother, Colleen jutted out her own tongue and then giggled.

"And now the ladies are ganging up on me," Patrick said.

After they'd combined the fruit mixture with the rest, Eve placed the pudding in a buttered pot, and Patrick happily added a dash of cognac before she covered the pot with foil.

Eve blew out a weary breath, flashing a confidence-inspiring grin. "Okay, we did it. Now, we'll steam it on that rack above hot water for six hours. Then, tonight, for our Christmas Eve dinner, we'll sprinkle the pudding with sugar, add the heated cognac sauce, turn off the lights, ignite the thing and bring it to the table."

Patrick added, "And Colleen has agreed to sing *Jingle Bells*."

"Yeah, *Jingle Bells*," she repeated, clapping, launching into a verse, with Patrick conducting.

AFTER EVE HAD WRAPPED PRESENTS and arranged them under the tree, she stepped over to Patrick, who was camped sleepily in the leather recliner.

"You look relaxed," Eve said.

Patrick reached for her hand and kissed it. "Is Colleen still napping?"

"Yes... When she wakes up, she's going to be hyper, especially when she sees all the wrapped presents under the tree."

"Did you check on the pudding? It smells good."

"Yes, and it's doing just fine and dandy."

He tugged her down to the arm of the chair. "While you wrapped presents, I did something I shouldn't have done."

Eve lifted an eyebrow. "Did you now? What?"

"I did an internet search on Leland and Annabelle Styles."

Eve drew her head back. "We agreed we wouldn't."

"I know... I suppose, since it's the end of the year, I wanted to finish things; close off the past and never look back again."

Eve rose and moved toward the fireplace, staring into the flames. "Okay, since you looked, what did you find?"

"The entire Knob Hill neighborhood was destroyed by the earthquake and fire, except for the granite walls surrounding the Styleses' mansion. You remember that wall?"

"Yes, of course. What about Annabelle Styles?"

Patrick hesitated.

Eve crossed her arms, keeping her head down. "Okay... go ahead."

"Two days after the fire, Leland's and his wife's bodies were found, both burned badly. Because the mansion had stone exteriors, the building itself survived the fires, and later it was cleaned and refurbished. Some silent screen movie star bought it in the 1920s."

"Was Leland Styles' wife named Annabelle?"

"No... Her name was Theodora Welford Styles, and she was from a wealthy family in Boston."

Eve lifted her head and looked at Patrick, her mind alive with thoughts. "What? If that's the case, then it means Annabelle never married Leland Styles. Does that mean we never met Annabelle Palmer, and she didn't take Colleen and move to San Francisco?"

"We met Annabelle for sure. I didn't want to tell you, but Colleen asked about her this morning."

"Oh God... this is really weird. Just another big scoop of weird on top of all the other weird things that have happened to us since I first found that lantern."

Eve lifted her shoulders and let them settle. "Patrick, what happened to us was real. It did happen. It wasn't a dream or hallucination."

Patrick stared at her. "Yes... I know."

"So, what is all this? I mean..." Eve shook her head in a slow wonder. "All these crazy things have happened to us because Nikola Tesla created a time travel Christmas toy that even *he* didn't completely understand."

Patrick clasped his hands together and placed them in his lap. "It was an experiment; something to distract him while he worked on other inventions. I wonder what he'd think about all this now. What would he think about what has happened to us? Would he even care?"

Eve shrugged. "I guess we'll never know, will we?"

After a moment of silence, Eve gave Patrick a strange, fixed grimace. "I hate to ask this. I mean, I really don't want to know... but, I have to know."

"What?"

"I'm sure you checked online looking for Annabelle. I know you pulled up the *Neighborhood Shout Out* website and checked December 5 to see if a woman was found rambling along Orchard Street, retro-dressed in nineteenth century style clothes. Did she pull a derringer on two cops and was she taken to the 7th Precinct?"

Patrick stood, deep in thought, circling the space. "Yes, I did check... And, no, there was nothing about any woman rambling about, retro-dressed and mumbling about time travel. There was no mention of any woman pulling a derringer and pointing it at two cops. The article we read describing Annabelle before we time traveled back to 1905 is not there."

Eve lowered her head and massaged her forehead. "Okay, I'm confused and lost."

Patrick blew out a sigh. "It's beyond my powers of understanding. All I know is that we time traveled, found Colleen, and brought her back home. That was true, and that happened."

Eve turned toward the bedroom. "But we still have Joni's lantern in the safe, which suggests we didn't time travel at all. The lantern we used to return from 1906 should be in the Pacific Ocean and not in our bedroom safe."

Her words robbed them both of speech. Finally, Eve went to Patrick and eased into his waiting arms. They remained close for long minutes, not speaking.

BEFORE DINNER, Eve, Colleen and Patrick bundled up, put Colin on a leash, and started off for Riverside Park. Snowflakes danced in the park lights and two inches of snow lay on the ground, smooth and glistening. Colin strained on his lead, barking his head off at dogs as they passed, and Patrick reigned him in, rewarding him with dog biscuits.

"That's it, Colin, my boy. Let them know who's boss."

Colleen wanted to build a snowman, so Eve and Patrick did the best they could with the snow available. While Colin romped, they went to work. The snowman they built was small, about two feet, but in three oval sections. When it was completed, Patrick placed his blue ski cap on the snowman's head, punched holes for eyes and a mouth, and used a stick for a nose.

"I like it, Daddy," Colleen said, jumping, cheering and clapping.

"Does he have a name?" Eve asked.

Colleen struggled to think of one. "I don't know…"

Patrick said, "Hey, how about Patrick?"

Colleen shook her head. "No, that's silly, Daddy. That's your name."

"So? It's a grand name, Colleen. A good name for an Irish snowman."

Her face brightened. "I want his name to be Ice Bear."

"Ice Bear?" Patrick asked, looking to Eve for an answer.

"From that show she watches, *We Bare Bears*."

As they were leaving the park to return home, a frenzy of snow swirled around them, and Colleen and Patrick opened their mouths and licked at the snowflakes. Colin barked, not understanding the game.

Eve watched them, hanging back, smiling lovingly, swelling with happiness. And then she felt something shifting and flowing inside her, and she knew what it was.

It was the beginning of another kind of journey. The journey of a new life. The adventure of being pregnant and of giving birth; the start of another journey that would last a lifetime.

But she'd wait until after dinner to tell Patrick; until after they'd put Colleen to bed; until she and the love of her life were alone together, sitting by the fire, relaxed and peaceful, sharing another portion of plum pudding. Then she'd tell him.

She'd look straight at him and say, "Hey, Detective Sergeant Patrick Gantly… Guess what? You're going to be a father again. Merry Christmas!"

Thank You!

Thank you for taking the time to read *The Christmas Eve Journey*. If you enjoyed it, please consider telling your friends or posting a short review. Word of mouth is an author's best friend, and it is much appreciated.

Thank you,
Elyse Douglas

The Christmas Diary – Book One
The Christmas Diary – Book Two Lost and Found
Christmas for Juliet
The Christmas Bridge
The Date Before Christmas
The Christmas Women
Christmas Ever After
The Summer Diary
The Summer Letters
The Other Side of Summer
Wanting Rita

Time Travel Novels

The Christmas Eve Letter (A Time Travel Novel) Book 1
The Christmas Eve Daughter (A Time Travel Novel) Book 2

The Christmas Eve Secret (A Time Travel Novel) Book 3
The Christmas Eve Promise (A Time Travel Novel) Book 4
The Lost Mata Hari Ring (A Time Travel Novel)
The Christmas Town (A Time Travel Novel)
Time Stranger
Time Visitor
Time Change (A Time Travel Novel)
Time Sensitive (A Time Travel Novel)
Time Shutter (A Time Travel Novel)

Romantic Suspense Novels
Daring Summer
Frantic
Betrayed

www.elysedouglas.com

Editorial Reviews

THE LOST MATA HARI RING – A Time Travel Novel by Elyse Douglas

"This book is hard to put down! It is pitch-perfect and hits all the right notes. It is the best book I have read in a while! 5 Stars!"

--Bound4Escape Blog and Reviews

"The characters are well defined, and the scenes easily visualized. It is a poignant, bitter-sweet emotionally charged read. 5-Stars!"
--Rockin' Book Reviews

"*The Lost Mata Hari Ring* captivated me to the end!"
--StoryBook Reviews

"A captivating adventure..."
--Community Bookstop

"...Putting *The Lost Mata Hari Ring* down for any length of time proved to be impossible."
--Lisa's Writopia

"I found myself drawn into the story and holding my breath to see what would happen next..."
--Blog: A Room Without Books is Empty

THE CHRISTMAS TOWN – A Time Travel Novel by Elyse Douglas

"The Christmas Town is a beautifully written story. It draws you in from the first page, and fully engages you up until the very last. The story is funny, happy, and magical. The characters are likable and well-rounded. This is a great book to read during the holiday season, and a delightful read any time of the year."
--Bauman Book Reviews

"I would love to see this book become another one of those beloved Christmas film traditions. Don't miss this novel!"
--A Night's Dream of Books

THE SUMMER LETTERS – A Novel
by Elyse Douglas

"A perfect summer read!"

--Fiction Addiction

"In Elyse Douglas' novel *The Summer Letters*, the characters' emotions, their drives, passions and memories are all so expertly woven; we get a taste of what life was like for veterans, women, small town folk, and all those people we think have lived too long to remember (but they never really forget, do they?).

I couldn't stop reading, not for a moment. Such an amazing read. Flawless."

5 Stars! -

--Anteria Writes Blog - To Dream, To Write, To Live

"A wonderful, beautiful love story that I absolutely enjoyed reading."

5 Stars!

--Books, Dreams, Life - Blog

"*The Summer Letters* is a fabulous choice for the beach or this year, so you can live and breathe the same feelings and smells as the characters in this wonderful story."

--Reads & Reels Blog

Printed in Great Britain
by Amazon